WERNER

The Jan trilogy: Book Three

Peter Haden

© Copyright 2025 – Peter Haden

All rights reserved.

This book shall not, by way of trade or otherwise, be lent, re-sold, hired out, or otherwise circulated without the prior consent of the copyright holder or the publisher in any form of binding or cover other than that in which it is published and without a similar condition including this condition being imposed on the subsequent purchaser. The use of its contents in any other media is also subject to the same conditions.

ISBN: 978-1-917525-05-3

MMXXV

A CIP catalogue record for this book
is available from the British Library.

Published by
ShieldCrest Publishing,
Boston, Lincolnshire,
PE20 3BT England
Tel: +44 (0) 333 8000 890
www.shieldcrest.co.uk

To my Partner
Brenda Roberts

By Peter Haden

The Angry Island
The Silent War

The Jan Trilogy:
Book One: Jan
Book Two: Hedda
Book Three: Werner

Prelude

Book One – *Jan*. Based on a real journey made by the author's uncle. After the severe 1920's Depression, Jan, a young Pole, is forced to seek work across the border in Hitler's Germany. His father and sister are brutally killed during the German invasion of Poland, but his brother Tadzio remains on the family farm. As Nazi persecution and blackmail increase, Jan is asked to make a desperate flight to safety with Renate, his employer's German-Jewish daughter, who has been offered safe refuge near the Belgian border. After a frightening drive across wartime Germany, Renate is delivered safely. Jan eventually reaches England. Following specialist military training he returns to Poland. With Tadzio and his partner Hedda he supports local partisans in their fight against the German invaders. But when their cover is blown, all three must eventually escape to Britain. Jan subsequently rejoins Renate to report on the build-up of German forces behind the Western front. In a dramatic climax, Jan and Renate are captured by the Gestapo and must escape to be smuggled from Germany to Belgium and finally back to England.

* * * *

Book Two – *Hedda*. France, 1940, and bilingual Polish-German Hedda is recruited by British intelligence. She volunteers for a top-secret mission: to replace an appointee to the German embassy in occupied Paris. Her partner, Tadzio, now with the British Army, survives an air attack on his tank near Dunkirk and goes underground to form a resistance cell, planning and leading major operations. With no news of Tadzio, in Paris Hedda becomes emotionally involved with Werner, an aristocratic *SS-Sturbannführer* whose family oppose Hitler. Her breathtaking espionage provides highly classified intelligence to London on Operation Sea Lion, the invasion of Britain; proof of atrocities in Dachau, enabling US President Roosevelt to enact Lend-Lease; and warning of Operation Barbarossa, the forthcoming invasion of Russia. *Hedda* is an authentic and intense account of espionage and resistance sabotage in wartime France, blending with lives and love affairs in the darkest of times.

* * * *

Book Three – *Werner*. England, Autumn 1941. English cryptographers have broken the German *Abwehr* overseas espionage codes. Werner is working with British intelligence to meet, capture and interrogate German agents parachuted into England. Waiting in Norfolk on a cold, wet night for the drone of a Heinkel aero-engine, his career with the Special Operations Executive continues...

Chapter 1

Late Autumn 1941

They lifted off from *Fliegerhorst* Venlo, on the Dutch-German border, and set course for the Norfolk coast. *It took courage*, reflected the pilot as he throttled back to safely above stalling speed, *to jump into the pitch black above England from a modified Heinkel He 111*. Modified because the bombing mechanism had been removed, allowing access to the doors in the aircraft's underbelly. Encumbered with an R-Z 20 parachute and a chest-mounted suitcase radio, the sole passenger was far from sanguine.

For a start, a central spar divided the opening into two fore and aft rectangular spaces, each barely wide enough for a clean jump. Second, the R-Z 20 demanded the confidence to make a heart-stopping, head-first exit. A standard upright departure, as enjoyed when parachuting from an Allied aircraft, would flip the user into an inverted position from which the feet would invariably tangle in the rigging. And finally, once settled into a stable, forward-leaning position with arms outstretched, there were no risers. The canopy could not be steered. The landing was entirely at the mercy of the prevailing wind.

True, the R-Z 20 offered one advantage. The German parachute allowed for a much lower exit height – less time as a helpless, dangling target for ground fire. But this sortie, for operational reasons, had to take place at the unusual height of fifteen hundred metres.

Werner

On the ground, Werner Scholtz, accompanied by three fellow British security agents, all four of them armed with a Browning nine-millimetre HP automatic, picked up the distant growl of the Heinkel's engines. They had long since cracked the *Abwehr* intelligence communication codes. He glanced at his watch, murmured, 'On time' to his companions, and gave the order for the recognition signal. The aircraft responded with a single flash of its landing lights.

It seemed to pass right over them before a splash of camouflage-coloured silk burst underneath. But something was wrong... it was far too high. With a sinking feeling, Werner realised the agent would not land on the DZ, the dropping zone – more probably almost a quarter of a mile away. He was careful to mark the precise direction. 'Come on, chaps,' he offered in barely accented English, 'we are going to have to find the blighter.' They set off at a jog across the fields.

He gave another short blast on his whistle, but there was no response. 'Has to be somewhere round here,' he exclaimed, exasperated. They all knew the recognition sentence the agent would use and the correct reply. 'We'll split up,' he ordered, 'fan out, go in four different directions. Meet back in this field in about half an hour. Hopefully, one of us will have made contact.'

But of their agent, there was no sign. Eventually, they conceded that the operation had been a failure. 'Must have gone to ground,' Werner admitted. 'But there's still the fallback plan. We'll just have to hope we can meet up later in London.' A light but steady drizzle of rain added to their discomfort. Disappointed and despondent, they set off back to where they had left their transport.

* * * *

Liam McGrath had taken his family off the land during the Depression of the early 1930s to seek a better life in the city. They settled in the predominantly Catholic area of West Belfast, and he counted himself fortunate to have found work in the shipyards. When his wife, Brigid, died of septicaemia after her fourth miscarriage, it fell to their only surviving offspring, scrawny teenage Máiréad, with her mother's red hair, green eyes and fiery temperament, to be mistress of their rented two-up, two-down terraced house, with its shared communal privy across the yard.

There had always been occasional riots between Protestant Loyalists and Catholic Republicans. That year, the majority of those killed during the Orange parades of July 12th 1935, were Protestants, but in revenge, the mobs forced hundreds of Catholics from their work and homes. Sectarian attacks were rife, and a number of Catholics died, with many more seriously injured.

Liam McGrath and neighbouring Catholic men barricaded both ends of their street. But Máiréad would never forget the night a kindly neighbour had to tell her that her father had died during the fighting from a massive blow to the head. She spent the night hiding in the privy, terrified of what might happen if she were discovered. Next morning, she found the front door battered from its hinges, shards of glass everywhere and their meagre items of furniture smashed to pieces.

Her parish priest, Father Coyle, offered a lifeline. The Republican movement had begun to make contact with German nationals in the hope of seeking support for their cause. The clergyman was acquainted with an engineer, Ernst Wagner, sent to study Naval architecture and shipbuilding at Queen's University Belfast, which had been chartered originally to counter the almost exclusively Anglican Trinity College Dublin. *Herr* Wagner had accepted a post-graduate teaching position, which also gave him excellent access to senior personnel throughout the local chamber of commerce. His technical reports were of great value to Hitler's engineers hastening to rebuild the German Navy.

Although they were not wealthy enough to employ a substantial household, *Frau* Wagner was looking for a live-in domestic assistant – a mixture of housework and help with the cooking – now she also had to cope with caring for their firstborn, a son. However, whereas Ernst Wagner's English was reasonably fluent, Hanna had only a basic knowledge. Hence, they spoke German at home. But, Father Coyle assured Máiréad, she was an intelligent young woman. She would soon adapt.

So Máiréad, who had adopted the use of Margaret, the English version of her name, began to learn German. When, in 1938, Ernst's tenure came to an end, the family returned to Hamburg. With nothing to tie her to her homeland, Margaret McGrath went with them. Now twenty, after three years in the more prosperous Wagner household, she had blossomed into a fine-looking, handsome young woman. And her German was almost perfect, with hardly a trace of an accent.

Hanna Wagner gave birth to a second child, a daughter, in the spring of 1938. Her husband, she told Margaret, had been promoted by "The Party" and now held an important administrative position within the *Kriegsmarine*, Hitler's Navy. The family circumstances had certainly changed since their days in Ireland. They now lived in a large, terraced house in the fashionable "village" area of Hamburg's Altona district. *Herr* Wagner was now the proud owner of a small Mercedes-Benz, a 1936 170H two-door, four-seater saloon. *Frau* Wagner had engaged a live-in cook as well as a housemaid, and Margaret's duties evolved into being more of a nanny for the children, as well as an occasional companion for their mother. However, she was surprised early one evening, after having just put the children to bed, when *Herr* Wagner asked her to join him in his study.

'You have been with us for quite some time now,' he began, indicating that she should be seated in one of two armchairs by the fireside. 'Almost one of the family,' he added with a smile.

'Yes, *Herr* Wagner,' she replied hesitantly, not sure where this was leading, for this was the first time she had been alone, let alone seated, with the master of the house. He was a tall, rather handsome man, although clearly a few years older than his wife, as evidenced by his combed-back dark, wavy hair, which was beginning to silver above his ears. Until now, he had uttered only the occasional polite greeting. She still felt his presence intimidating.

'And how do you find life here in Germany,' he continued, removing and polishing round, metal-framed spectacles, 'compared with how things were in your own country?'

Concerned that she might be sent back home, she rushed to reassure him. 'I like it fine, sir,' she said quickly. Then, '*Frau* Wagner has always been very kind to me, and I love looking after Gerhard and little Gerda,' she added.

'My wife has always spoken well of you,' he said to reassure her, sensing her concern. 'But tell me,' he went on more slowly, 'how do you feel now about Northern Ireland, and the United Kingdom in particular?

'I think what I am really asking,' he went on when she did not reply immediately, 'is whether you feel your loyalties might have changed? Do they still lie with the country of your birth, or have you developed a view, perhaps an affinity, even, for where you have been living and working here in Germany?'

There was a moment of silence. Clearly, Margaret was collecting her thoughts. 'We were persecuted back home, us Catholics, I mean,' she said slowly. 'Most of us don't see any great difference between the Protestants and the rest of England. After all, that's where they came from in the first place. In Northern Ireland, they control the politics, the police, all the best jobs, everything. And they even killed my poor da...' her voice tailed off.

'I have no love for the English,' she said eventually, 'quite the opposite. I like it better here. You and *Frau* Wagner, and now Germany, have been good to me. Does that answer your question, sir?' she asked.

'I think it does,' he said thoughtfully. 'So, tell me, Margaret,' he continued, deliberately using her first name, 'if you have no great love for the English, would you be prepared to help me, and by definition, also to help Germany, if we asked you to undertake a few harmless tasks on our behalf?'

The following morning, at the request of her husband, *Frau* Wagner took Margaret in hand. 'You are to travel as an upper-class young lady,' she told her. 'Fortunately, you have learned German in our household, so already you speak only *Hochdeutsch*. You are always very respectably turned out,' she went on, 'but now you will need outfits to match a new persona.'

They visited several of Hamburg's best emporia, even buying several items imported from France that would also have been available in London.

Her fur-trimmed coat alone cost more than half a year's wages. Attention to detail extended even to satin undergarments. When *Frau* Wagner selected a suit and a day dress, Margaret's head was spinning at the expense. 'Relax,' she was instructed. 'You are working for the Party now, and they are not short of funds.' Finally, there was a pale tan-leather suitcase and matching bandbox. 'Very smart,' commented her mentor. 'You won't have any trouble with officialdom. In fact, with your looks, they will bend over backwards to be helpful.'

'She did well,' Ernst Wagner reported to his superior two weeks later. 'Our man in Barrow-in-Furness indicated – in so many words – that he had absolutely top-class material, but it was too sensitive to take a chance with the usual post. Would have led straight back. We know that the British are watching our embassy people,' he went on, 'and our man is too valuable to risk a compromise, so he needed a courier. Turns out he had managed to photograph a set of drawings for HMS *Greyhound*, the latest G-class destroyer launched by the British in 1935. More importantly, the civilians in Vickers-Armstrong's design office were careless. Included were documents on the ASDIC system, their sonar, and useful information on British minesweeping gear.'

Wagner inverted his hands. 'She travelled on her British passport, picked up the film, return ferry via France as an extra precaution, and then back in Hamburg a day later. Went like clockwork. We had her under surveillance for part of the time. She seemed to relish the experience. Cool as you like! I gather that Dönitz, among others, is absolutely delighted. The information is enormously important to his U-boat commanders.'

Wagner was both surprised and flattered two weeks later when he was invited to take lunch with the *Kapitän zur See*. 'Ingeborg and I,' Dönitz opened, once drinks had been served, 'have just spent a weekend as guests of Wilhelm and Erika.'

He knew that the reference was to *Admiral* Wilhelm Canaris, head of the German military intelligence organisation, the *Abwehr*. 'Where was that, sir?' he asked politely.

'At his parents' place – Aplerbeck, Dortmund,' came the reply. 'Carl and Auguste were really the hosts.' Wagner was aware that the head of the Canaris family was a wealthy industrialist. His interest quickened. This was an insight into the heady heights of Hitler's intelligence power base.

'The *Admiral* confided,' Dönitz continued, 'that he thinks hostilities will break out against the British, probably within the next twelve months. He is anxious to recruit agents that can pass easily as British nationals. We could always send in people with false Dutch or Scandinavian passports to cover an accent. But this is never ideal. I confess,' he added almost apologetically, 'that I mentioned your Irish girl and the one mission she has already undertaken. Canaris was most impressed. She would be an invaluable asset to the *Abwehr*.'

'My dear,' Ernst said to Hanna one evening after dinner a few days later, 'there is no reason why Margaret should not remain with us when she is not required for other duties. I have yet to talk with her in greater detail, but she has indicated that she would welcome further opportunities to serve the Fatherland. Both of our children are old enough to enrol for *Kindergarten*. Or, if we prefer, we may employ a governess and educate them privately. The Party wishes to show its appreciation for all that we have done, and they are particularly interested in developing the potential offered by Margaret. So, either way, they will meet all of our expenses. I might add,' he concluded, 'that my – our – cooperation can only reflect well upon my career.'

Margaret, now recruited into the *Abwehr*, found the training exhausting and brutal at times, but mindful of her intense dislike of the English, she resolved to succeed. And now, she received a generous *Abwehr* salary. At home, for this is how Margaret now thought of Hamburg, her status changed. With a governess engaged, she became more of a house guest. Margaret now took her meals with Ernst and Hanna. Ernst remained a member of German Naval Intelligence whilst she continued to work as a courier, undertaking only their highest priority and most sensitive assignments, where it was important to use a British national.

When not staying with the Wagners, she also had the use of an *Abwehr* apartment in Berlin, with no shortage of officers, both military and civilian, attempting to engage her affections. Margarete Wagner, as her German *Ausweiß* now evidenced, was enjoying family life in Hamburg, the vibrant social scene of Berlin, and the heady excitement of her occasional mission. For a young woman barely in her twenties, this was a far cry from what she could have expected in a lower working-class district of Catholic Belfast.

It came as no surprise to be summoned again to 76/78 Tirpitzufer, the headquarters of the *Abwehr* in Berlin, next door to the *OKW* building, which housed the Armed Forces High Command. She was shown to the office of *Gerneralmajor* Hans Oster, a courteous and rather distinguished-looking officer, and the head of the Central Division, or *Abteiling Z*, of the *Abwehr*. This was senior company. *Generalmajor* Oster reported directly to *Admiral* Canaris.

'We have a problem,' he began once coffee had been served. 'You will recall that *Unternehmen Seelöwe* was cancelled; Operation Sealion, the invasion of Britain.' he repeated in English. Quite unnecessary, she thought, having understood perfectly the first time.

He reverted to German. 'But by way of preparation, we had already inserted a number of agents into the United Kingdom. Unfortunately,' he told her, 'it was all something of a rush. They had only limited training, and we believe many of them were captured by the British. We have every reason to believe that some of them have been turned. Now, when we do receive messages, we suspect that the intelligence is either at best very low level or at worst, deliberately false.'

Margaret was aware of this but chose to keep silent, suspecting where he might be leading. 'More recently,' he went on, 'we have been able to deploy better-trained people. But again, the pattern has continued. Only rarely have we achieved the required result. All of which,' his head lifted so that he was looking at her directly, 'makes us think that not only have many of these agents also been captured and turned, but even worse, we suspect that our codes have been broken.' He paused to let this information sink in. His hand slapped the desk in frustration. 'Because the British seem to know when we are coming, and they are waiting for us on arrival,' he concluded harshly.

'What are we going to do about it?' she asked quietly.

'Your code name will be "Shamrock",' he told her. And she would have papers in the name of Margaret Minogue – an Irishwoman of the right age who had died in Germany just before the war but whose death had not been reported to the United Kingdom. 'Always best to keep the same Christian name, where you can,' he added, 'less risk of ignoring someone if they use a different one. And we'll change your appearance as much as we can for your Margaret Minogue photograph. I'm afraid you will have to lose your lovely long, red hair. You can dye it light brown or become a dark honey blonde, whatever you think is best. So long as you make yourself look as different as possible...'

* * * *

It was a good landing into lightly wooded farmland. The pilot had judged it well – safely over the recognition signal, but not so far that the error looked deliberate. The wind direction had helped, carrying her even further away from the reception party. Margaret knew that they would be looking for her. Her parachute she bundled into a culvert where a small stream passed under a country lane. It probably wouldn't be found, but even so, by then, she would be long gone.

Now came the dangerous part. She had to stay put whilst someone tried to make contact. She did not have long to wait. Lying under a hedge, she watched a male in civilian clothes, blowing a whistle and holding an automatic, advance towards her. It was all she needed to know. Margaret wriggled back, then set off at right angles to his line of advance, crouching at first, using the hedge as a shield.

Ten minutes later, faintly, on the wind, she again heard the sound of whistles, but they were way in the distance. Even so, she carried the radio for another half an hour as an extra precaution. Finally, carefully noting her precise location, she left it under a dense patch of bushes just inside a field bordering a minor road. The suitcase would be all right, wrapped in its oilskin cover, for the short time until she could retrieve it.

In the east, a faint lightening of the sky told her that dawn could not be far off. It was an unseasonably mild night, and to her relief, the drizzle had stopped. She walked for another hour, then settled in a copse on the edge of a good-sized village. She looked at her watch. Probably another three hours to wait before there would be enough people around to mask her presence. She breakfasted on a bar of English chocolate taken from a British Red Cross parcel.

When, at half past nine, she walked into the village, it was coming to life. She settled on a bench opposite a post office and store. A man, a stranger, might have been noticed, which was one of the reasons why they had been keen to send a woman. And particularly one who spoke English fluently, even if with a genuine Belfast accent. But there was still a risk: sitting on a bench with no apparent purpose. Surely the village would have a policeman…

Her luck held. She was not challenged. A few customers entered and left the shop. To her relief, after about twenty minutes, a young woman of about her age rode up on a bicycle, leaning it against a wall alongside the shop's front door. It could not be observed through the window. The rather smartly dressed woman took a string bag from the handlebar basket, which suggested to Margaret that she would be buying more than one item of shopping. Hopefully, in an empty shop, she would pause briefly to pass the time of day. Margaret crossed the road, glanced in both directions, seized the handlebars and stepped through the frame. Seconds later, she was pedalling strongly along the road, exhaling with relief when she rounded a bend and was no longer in sight. There had been no hue and cry, and the owner would have no idea in which direction to look for her bicycle.

She made good progress, thanks to the flat, fenland landscape and the three-speed Sturmey-Archer gears. Her destination, which she reached at lunchtime, was the city of Norwich. She had memorised the directions and the address.

The owner of No. 43 Keswick Gardens, a small, detached house, taught languages – French and German – at the local grammar school. His colleagues and pupils, however, were unaware that he had been a member of the former British Union of Fascists, subsequently the British Union, now a proscribed organisation and with its leader, Oswald Mosley, imprisoned.

'Mr Barr?' she asked politely as he opened the door. 'I'm Margaret Minogue. I hope you are expecting me? Oh, and I am supposed to say, "The sky is blue",' she added, feeling slightly self-conscious.

'And I should reply that it will rain later,' he said with a half-smile. 'But leave your bike there, Margaret, and come inside. Gertrude,' he called into the house, 'she's here.'

Malcolm Barr was a fairly short man with Brylcreemed black hair, combed sideways in a vain attempt to cover a bald patch. Probably in his thirties, thought Margaret. He was thin to the point of looking under-nourished, and a beaky nose and thick spectacles certainly gave him a bookish, altogether unprepossessing appearance. Perhaps, she thought, the sort of man who, through fascism, found something that eluded him in an otherwise humdrum existence.

'I'll make us some tea,' offered his wife. Gertrude was taller than her husband and clearly a few years younger. A chubby, wavy-haired blonde, she was quite pretty in a rather blousy sort of way. 'Please sit down, make yourself at home,' she invited. There was a pronounced "Narfolk" accent. She had married up, Margaret decided, and ideologically, would probably be totally under the influence of her husband.

She was shown to a small, single bedroom furnished with only a bed, a side cupboard and a cheap, varnished plywood wardrobe. Over a meagre lunch of tinned meat and potatoes, Margaret announced that tomorrow morning, she would take a bus to the city. 'I'm well provided with funds,' she told them. 'But I jumped with just a radio, so now I need to buy some clothes.'

There was a definite look between the two of them. Was Malcolm Barr trying to signal something to his wife? 'Not sure if you can,' said Gertrude, "cos the government introduced rationing at the beginning of June.'

'That's all right,' Margaret replied. 'Don't know where they came from, or even if they're genuine, but I've been provided with a book of coupons.'

'In that case, I'll come with you,' Gertrude said quickly, 'show you the way – we can make a day out of it, an' all.'

She had not been challenged the previous day, riding her bicycle, on the assumption that there would have been a gas mask in the basket. 'Don't want to get fined for not having one,' observed Malcolm before they left. 'Take mine. The cardboard boxes ours came with were useless. Like lots of people, we have had shoulder bags made.'

Once in the city centre, it did not take long to purchase a couple of sets of underwear, a skirt, two more blouses and a few toiletries. Finally, she added a small, easily-handled suitcase. But when she was ready to return to the bus station, Gertrude tried to insist that they find a café for lunch.

She ignored the idea. On the way into the city, the woman had been noisy and chatty. Now, on the way home, she was quiet and morose. Margaret could not be absolutely sure, but her training – every instinct – told her that something was not right. It was almost as if the Barrs were playing for time. And there could be only one reason, Margaret suspected. It would give someone, or some organisation, time to organise a surveillance operation, a small team to follow her when she moved on.

Approaching the house, she looked around carefully, but there was no sign of watchers having been deployed. Everything appeared normal – for now. But *Oberst* Karl Schröder, her immediate *Abwehr* superior, had told her to ensure that a trace would be absolutely impossible. Once indoors, she retired to her room, packed her case and dropped it, together with the gas mask she had been carrying, by the front door. The Walther she had left, barely concealed, in the wardrobe. Malcolm Barr had probably searched the room but left it alone to avoid suspicion. They were both in the kitchen when they died, each from a single shot to the forehead.

Chapter 2

'What do you think happened?' asked Lieutenant Colonel Frobisher.

'Not one hundred per cent sure, Quentin,' Werner responded. Although the section head had a military rank, he made it clear from the start that as his staff were all civilians, he wished to run the unit as informally as possible. The more junior members addressed him as "Colonel" rather than "Sir".

'I think initially there was a pilot error,' he went on. 'For some reason, maybe inexperience or nerves, he was too high. So when our man jumped, the wind took him too far from the DZ. After that, he probably decided to play it safe – went to ground. After all, he has a backup plan here in London.' His right hand turned over, fingers apart. 'Obviously, we'll try again; see what happens next time.'

'We have to wait for a couple of days,' Frobisher observed. 'You have been up all night. Might as well go home and get your head down for a few hours.'

He had the use of what the military called a "Car, Light Utility 4x2", but on a fine morning like this, he preferred a drab olive-coloured Ariel W/NG 350 c.c. motorcycle. A fast, twenty-minute ride took him to a small, two-bedroom cottage in a country area not far from Richmond. Werner counted himself fortunate to live with his wife, Anneliese, and Charles Dieter, her son by her fiancé who had been killed the previous year in a London air raid. He was only too happy to raise the boy, now a toddler, as his own. However, they were on the cusp of trying for a brother or sister for Charles Dieter, a child of their own.

* * * *

Fortunately, the houses, although modest, were set reasonably well apart. Even if the inhabitants of the neighbourhood had been at home at that time of day, Margaret's execution of the Barrs did not appear to have raised an alarm. She placed her suitcase in the basket, looked around carefully, and pedalled away. It was almost impossible to tail someone on a bicycle for long without being observed, and Margaret was soon confident that she was not being followed.

Her priority was to retrieve her radio, which she secured on the bicycle's luggage pannier. Next, she had to reach London. By now, it was just possible that the bodies of Malcolm and Gertrude Barr had been discovered. Although she was confident that her identity was not known, there might well be additional police and security checks on all forms of transport leaving Norwich. She could not risk her suitcase radio being discovered. But for the moment, it was unlikely that the net had widened beyond the city.

She reached the market town of Wymondham, some twelve miles southwest of Norwich, where she abandoned her bicycle and took a bus to Thetford, from where she was able to access the British railway system. She was confident that a woman travelling alone, with only one medium and another hand-sized suitcase, would not attract attention. Even at this late hour, the trains were packed, mostly with travelling servicemen. There were frequent hold-ups, and it was not until shortly before seven the next morning when, travel-stained and weary, she stepped down onto a platform at Liverpool Street Station. In the "Ladies", she changed into the smarter clothes she had bought the previous day. After visiting the left luggage office, she took breakfast, just tea and toast, in a nearby café. But despite a sleepless night, morale was high. She had landed successfully, evaded her reception committee, disposed of two agents who had almost certainly been turned, avoided surveillance and finally, unknown to the British security services, inserted herself into the teeming anonymity of the nation's capital.

She took a bus to Hammersmith. Some houses had a vacancies sign in the window but also, underneath, "No Irish". However, at one slightly run-down terrace, the door opened, and a tired-looking, middle-aged woman in a pinafore, her hair in curlers under a cloth knotted at the front, took in her appearance.

'Can I help you?' she asked evenly. To her relief, Margaret detected a hint of her own accent. She paid cash for two weeks, in advance, for the spare room – thus far, no questions asked. She had to share the one bathroom, and Mrs Mallory would provide breakfast, an evening meal, and sandwiches for lunch. Margaret handed over her ration book, just hoping that the forgery people back in Berlin knew what they were doing.

The following day, she sought out one of the first addresses memorised back in Berlin. Here, there was also a vacancy sign in the window. If the agent – the one who had supposedly transmitted her landing instructions – had been arrested, the British authorities might have asked the landlady to report any attempted contact. It was quite a large house, probably with three or four rooms to let. She waited nearby. It was early evening, the time when "guests" would return for their evening meal. A man carrying a briefcase opened the gate to a small front garden.

'Excuse me,' she called softly, waving a prepared envelope towards him. 'I live on the next street, but this has been delivered to me by mistake. Obviously, it's for this gentleman here. Would you mind awfully giving it to him, or perhaps leaving it on the hall table, or whatever?'

17

He took in the rather pretty young woman and then the envelope. 'Wouldn't mind at all, Miss,' he replied pleasantly. 'But Jack Warnes moved out a while back. Haven't seen him for a couple of months or more.'

'Oh, thank you,' she replied, trying to sound disappointed. She turned, giving him a half-smile, then, still clutching the envelope, walked away. Over the coming days, she failed to make contact with even one of the names given to her in Germany.

* * * *

'Obviously, we followed up on the fallback arrangement,' Werner reported to his head of station. 'It was on the Embankment, near Cleopatra's needle. A man was leaning on the balustrade overlooking the Thames an hour before the time set for our meeting. It didn't seem quite right, but when he left, soon afterwards, one of our team followed him.' Werner smiled deprecatingly. 'He walked to the nearest police station. Turns out he was a detective sergeant waiting to meet a snout who failed to show up.'

'And...?' put in Frobisher.

'We carried on with the stake-out, as planned,' came the response. 'Almost an hour before, and then another one afterwards. Our man did not show, either.'

'So we are at a dead end,' observed the colonel.

'Maybe, but perhaps not quite,' Werner said slowly. His head of station raised an eyebrow.

'We know that the agent landed,' he pressed on. 'So, I got the local police to ask around in the area. See if anyone had noticed a stranger or someone who might have been injured in a drop, that sort of thing. It's a country area. People talk.

Eventually, the landlord of a nearby public house reported to his local bobby that some kids out playing pooh sticks had found a parachute stuffed into a culvert. He managed to retrieve it before their mother stitched up the silk into a pile of knickers. As you would expect, it's a German R-Z 20...'

'But how does that help us?' broke in Frobisher, impatiently.

'Of itself, it doesn't,' said Werner. 'But we got lucky. Our village bobby is a keen youngster, not an old plod. Apparently, the only reason he hasn't joined up is because of some medical condition. Anyway,' he lifted his hand to forestall any further interruptions, 'he immediately returned to the area and cordoned it off. When they were able to make a proper search, the kids' footprints were all over the place. But there were some more prints, the only ones further away in the mud leading to and from the ditch. There can be no doubt. German men don't take a ladies' size six. We have been looking for a man. But our parachutist was a woman.'

Frobisher was quiet for a moment. 'You were *SS*,' he said eventually. 'I'll give it some thought, but I'd be interested to hear your stance on this.'

'First off,' Werner replied, 'I think we've been had. All the traffic we intercepted suggested a normal insertion. But I'm beginning to suspect that the drop was deliberately high. I believe he – or rather she, as we now know – missed the DZ on purpose.'

'Why, do you suppose...?' put in Frobisher.

'Only one reason,' said Werner. 'On the ground, there should have been one of their agents to meet her. But I think they suspected there might be a hostile reception party. She probably stayed around long enough to confirm this, then bugged out. But the presence of our team gave the game away – she had her answer.'

Frobisher nodded his agreement. 'So now they know their agent has been turned,' he added slowly. 'And unfortunately, they have also confirmed that one way or another, we have access to their cyphers. But why use a woman…?' he pondered, almost as if he were asking himself the question or thinking out loud.

'Because the *Abwehr* were making use of the best person they had available,' Werner replied. 'You know, of late, we have picked up men with false Dutch and Scandinavian papers – which tells us that they don't have British male assets, at least not at the moment. That's how they were able to avoid sending someone with a foreign accent.

'I can only guess at this latest mission,' he went on, 'but she will probably try to find out how many of their previous agents, if any, are still at large. She will have to travel around. Talk to quite a lot of people. To be able to do this, I wouldn't mind betting that they wanted someone who either is or can pass for a British national. And when the public thinks of spies, they tend to assume that it'll be a man. They won't be nearly as likely to suspect a woman. Two very good reasons,' he concluded, 'why, if they were fortunate enough to have one available, they would use a female.'

'So all we have to do now is find her,' Frobisher replied. 'And I have to confess,' he added with a sigh, 'I haven't the slightest idea where to start.'

* * * *

Margaret had one more task to complete before leaving London. She knew her people back in Berlin would be anxious to receive a report, but no way would she transmit from the capital. The chances of detection were too high. Her radio remained in its locked case on top of her wardrobe. The tell-tales she had left behind told her that Mrs Mallory had not even entered her room, let alone lifted it down.

She still had most of her funds left, but having failed to make contact with any of their agents, she had drawn the obvious conclusion. It also meant that she had to proceed with her alternative orders: in the event phase one proved negative, there was no point in trying to insert further agents in the same way. Her remit, therefore, was to establish a new pipeline, one unknown to the British and which they would be unable to penetrate. That would involve a return to the east coast. However, to establish and maintain her cover, she would require a regular source of income.

The transfer had originated from Third Reich funds held in Switzerland. Routed via a neutral Dublin bank, it finally arrived at their London branch. Ostensibly, it matched invoices for vital coal shipments from the United Kingdom, although Irish food exports formed the greater part of wartime trade between the two nations. Their man in London, Devlin O'Carroll, a staunch Republican, handed her a banker's draft for the not inconsiderable sum of five hundred pounds sterling. He also undertook to set up a trust fund in Margaret's name, with members of the bank as trustees.

Pleased with her morning's transactions, Margaret returned to her lodgings and informed Mrs Mallory that she would be leaving in the morning. 'But you have paid for two more days,' came the response. Reassuring her landlady that she would not be asking for a refund, Margaret told her not to be concerned about the money. She would be leaving after breakfast, so the return of her ration book would be appreciated. And she would be grateful for a couple of sandwiches for the journey. With the money situation settled, Mrs Mallory was only too happy to oblige. 'Back to Belfast,' Margaret replied in response to a final query.

But it was to East Anglia that she returned the following day, taking a room in a pleasantly upmarket King's Lynn guest house. Whether arriving by air or sea, its proximity to the continent made this sparsely populated area of farms and fenland marshes ideal for illicit landings. The port and market town were more than large enough to accommodate yet another stranger. Her priority was a bank account.

She chose at random, telling the counter clerk that she would like to speak with the manager. A tired-looking middle-aged man, almost certainly promoted to his ceiling, asked about the nature of her business.

'I wish to open an account,' she replied.

'I can have one of our clerks attend to your details,' he suggested.

Margaret had already reasoned that junior staff were more likely to gossip. Her confidentiality, and hence her security, would be much better protected by someone more senior.

'Nevertheless, I would prefer to see the manager,' she responded politely. At the same time, she extracted the banker's draft from her handbag and placed it, face up, on the counter, although she kept her fingers on it and did not slide the draft under the glass. He had to lean forward to inspect it.

His attitude changed immediately. 'Kindly take a seat, Miss.' He gestured towards chairs and small tables set against a far wall. 'I am sure our Mr Henshaw will attend to you personally as soon as he is able.' As she turned, he left his counter and retreated into the bank.

She did not have long to wait. Minutes later, a door labelled "Manager" opened, and a well-dressed man in a rather better-quality suit emerged. She was the only person seated. He walked straight towards her and halted with just the slightest hint of a bow. His hand indicated the open door, then, 'Good morning, Miss, won't you please join me in my office?'

The introductions completed, Margaret explained that as a recently qualified botanist, she would be spending a few months in the area studying coastal and fenland management on behalf of a charitable trust established by her family. They could be contacted, should he require a reference, through her bankers in London and Dublin. As she explained, the draft would serve as an initial deposit, and further sums would follow as the trust hopefully extended its activities in this field.

'But mindful of the situation in Europe,' she added, 'Ireland needs to protect our neutrality. Therefore, if I open an account,' she placed heavy emphasis on the "if", 'it is important that it is handled with the utmost discretion. It would be most unhelpful if junior staff were to make casual mention of it to persons not employed by the bank.'

The war had not been good for business. There had been a general decline in the banking industry. And although just in middle age, Henshaw was relatively young to be the manager of a branch of this size. He was still ambitious, and this new account would reflect well on their turnover – he was in no mood to delve too deeply.

'Rest assured, Miss Minogue,' he told her. 'I will handle this personally. Our staff are trained to be discreet, but I will put a note on your account that any queries are to be referred only to me. Would that ease your concerns?'

She indicated that it did. 'Now,' he responded, 'if I may take a few details from your documents?'

Her next requirement proved rather more tedious. It involved the purchase – this time – of a bicycle and a visit to each of King's Lynn's lettings agencies. Using the same botanical and fenland cover, she explained why she wanted to rent a small property, preferably not too far from the coast. After several days of exploring the area, she chose an isolated, two-bedroom cottage not far from the village of Snettisham. It backed onto woods and, ideally, was less than a mile from the nearest beach. The cottage was well appointed and was being let on behalf of a family unable to use their holiday home because of the war. Margaret took a six-month tenancy with the option to renew. She had little to fear when using her radio in such a rural and sparsely populated area, whose only industries were agriculture and a shingle and gravel quarry works behind the main beach. She sent her first report, including her contact details, using a unique cypher in which a page, line and indent number replaced pre-written words. Unless the other person had a copy of the same book, it was unbreakable.

Margaret's next task was to integrate, gradually over a period of time, into the village community. They had agreed in Berlin that she would not become fully operational until her presence was a regular and unremarkable local occurrence. She used the village shops, chatted extensively with the local farming community, and even paid the occasional visit to The Rose and Crown, the village public house built in the fourteenth century to accommodate workmen constructing a church further along the lane. Within a month, nobody thought twice about seeing the Irish botany woman out and about her business, her acceptance frequently confirmed with a friendly wave.

* * * *

'It's been six weeks now, and we still have no idea who or where she is,' Lieutenant Colonel Frobisher complained bitterly to Werner, frustration evident in his voice. 'We set out to sweep up the old network, and all we have done is make them start a new one. By now, she could be operating from anywhere. I had a phone call from Sir Manners Fitzgibbon just now. He has set up a meeting for the three of us tomorrow morning.'

Werner was aware that Sir Manners had an overview of the SOE, or Special Operations Executive, but in precisely what capacity he was not quite sure. Rumour had it that he reported directly to Winston. But he knew that Sir Manners and his wife Madeleine, Lady Fitzgibbon, had been extremely kind, looking after his wife Anneliese when her fiancé had been killed.

They sat in comfortable armchairs around a low table, waiting until coffee had been served. Finally, Sir Manners steepled his fingers. 'We are all aware of the present impasse,' he began. 'Would you agree, Quentin,' he turned to Frobisher, 'that as things stand, we have little or no chance of finding this agent in England?' The colonel conceded the point.

'So for now,' he went on, 'the Germans, by which I mean the *Abwehr*, are once more able to communicate using codes of which we are entirely unaware, and even as we speak, they are almost certainly sending new agents into the country, agents of whom we have no knowledge, and we are therefore quite unable to apprehend.'

'Serious though it is, Sir Manners,' Frobisher admitted, 'I am afraid that is indeed the case.'

'We can't find her here because we don't know who or where she is or even what she looks like,' Sir Manners continued. 'But that information has to be available somewhere. Werner,' he went on, 'you were *SS*, albeit that you were there to operate within their organisation, as part of a wider plot to report on their activities. You mentioned you were not the only such person within their ranks. There are others. You also told me that your father is a senior member of this highly confidential, anti-Hitler movement within Germany.'

Werner dipped his head by way of agreement.

'I am embarrassed to have to ask this of you,' Sir Manners said apologetically. 'But it's a few months since you left Paris. Do you think, if you were to return to Germany, there would be any chance of using your contacts to try to find out the identity of this woman?'

'Don't answer straight away,' he added quickly, raising a hand, his palm towards Werner, 'think it over. Because we both know that if you are caught, they will be merciless: you will be tortured and shot.' Their discussion continued for some time afterwards until Sir Manners invited them to lunch at his club.

Werner and Anneliese talked long into the night. They agreed that she and Charles Dieter would return to Stonebrook Hall, Sir Manners' home. He telephoned Sir Manners the next morning. Werner would go back to Germany.

Chapter 3

Whilst she was quite prepared to meet and guide agents, whether landed by air or sea, Margaret had no intention of allowing them access to – or knowledge of – her cottage. The most vulnerable time for a newly inserted agent was immediately after landing. Having someone who had confirmed that the DZ was safe, who only then would flash the recognition signal, and who could guide the new arrival to the British public transport system would greatly reduce the risk of the insertion. There was no need for the new arrival to speak with anyone else or to risk an action that might arouse suspicion. In the past, more than one agent had attracted attention by asking for directions with a foreign accent or by making the elementary mistake of trying to buy a glass of beer before opening time.

Margaret's function would be to see her charges safely onward. She would not know the agent's name, destination or mission. By now, she felt secure within the Snettisham community; her identity and cover were accepted. She had no fear of being discovered locally. The greater danger came from the possibility of an agent being arrested. But he would know neither her name nor from where she operated. It would be impossible for her to be betrayed to the British. In the worst case, the agent might hang, but her mission would continue.

Tonight, she had pedalled to an area of open farmland adjacent to woodland on the densely fern-covered Sandringham estate. The nearest house was over half a mile away. She picked up the drone of engines and then the distinctive shape of a Heinkel He 111 silhouetted under the cloud base. The aircraft was low, ready to deploy its passenger. She flashed her recognition signal. The pilot did not respond, but seconds later came the faint but familiar 'crack' as the canopy opened. She ran towards the far end of the field. There was hardly any wind. Able to stand upright, the agent had released his belt and buckles and was beginning to gather his parachute into a bundle.

'Welcome to England,' she greeted him.

'Thank you,' he replied. 'So what do we do now?' She was pleased to hear that there was no trace of a foreign accent. This one would probably survive.

'Put your radio on the back of my bike,' she told him. She handed him a couple of straps from her basket. 'I think the drop went fine, but we'll walk for a mile or so, just in case. Then we wait till daylight. I've found somewhere safe and not far from a bus stop,' she added. 'There's one just after half past seven that will take you to King's Lynn. It stops near the station. From there, you can take a train to wherever you're going. And in case they haven't told you, I would travel second class – you're not quite dressed for first.'

Just before the bus was due, she held out her hand. 'Goodbye, and good luck,' she told him. 'We won't meet again unless there's some sort of emergency, in which case Berlin will let me know.'

'Thank you,' he said simply. His bus rounded a corner. Removing his suitcase, he stood, waiting. Margaret watched whilst he boarded the bus – what could appear more natural than being waved off by a wife or girlfriend? Finally, she lifted a pedal and scooted away for the long ride back to her cottage. After all their planning, she thought, feeling rather pleased with herself, a successful first incursion, and hopefully not the last. Ernst Gericke breathed a sigh of relief as the bus gathered speed. He had landed safely in England and was on his way to his final destination: Birmingham, in the British West Midlands, where he would identify targets for the bombers of the *Luftwaffe* and send reports afterwards on the success or otherwise of their bombing campaign.

* * * *

The one drawback to her existence was that she spent almost all her time on her own. Apart from the occasional conversation in a village shop or a rare discussion with local farmers or land agents, she hardly spoke to anyone. She had *The Times* and a local weekly newspaper delivered, and in the evenings, she listened to the wireless. But after the heady social whirl enjoyed in Berlin, or even the company of the Wagner family in Hamburg, she was, Margaret finally admitted to herself, now lonely.

She was also bored. Having established her identity, the occasional task imposed by Berlin did not much occupy her time. Margaret found that tending to the cottage and garden, whilst she did not mind doing it, also left time on her hands. Neither was it intellectually stimulating. She decided to study her purported occupation. In fact, she might even write a paper on the local agricultural scene. Not only would better knowledge be useful when talking with local landowners, but an academic document could also be produced in evidence should the local authorities ever have cause to investigate her existence. Father Coyle had attested to her intelligence, and the Wagners had always been complimentary of her ability to learn their language. Surely botany could not be all that difficult? There was an excellent public library in King's Lynn and a good bus service from Snettisham. Margaret began to develop an enjoyable enthusiasm for her project.

She was standing in the weak winter sun, a chill westerly on her back, studying the grass from the edge of a rather marshy field, when a tractor and trailer pulled up on the other side of the gate leading from the adjacent lane. The engine was switched off, and the driver jumped down from a side step. 'Can I help you?' he asked pleasantly, leaning his elbows on the gate.

'Oh, hello,' she replied. 'Is this by any chance your field?' A hand pushed aside a lock of blond hair that had stuck to his forehead. He was, she realised, a tall young man – at least six foot. A young-looking but weathered face and broad shoulders suggested a physique accustomed to heavy farm labour. *Rather nice-looking*, she thought.

A nod indicated that it was indeed his field. 'So why are you standing in it?' he responded, but it was said with a smile. He did not seem at all put out by her presence.

She gave her standard explanation of studying the management of similar land before asking if it would be all right for her to walk over a few of his fields.

'Help yourself,' he replied affably. 'I'm sure you know to shut the gates and all that. But be careful of the next field but one, over there,' his hand indicated directly away from the gate. 'Old Angus is a bit tetchy. He's the bull – not a very original name, I'm afraid. So please don't risk it.'

It came out on impulse. 'Why don't you walk with me?' Margaret suggested. 'Then you could tell me about the farm, how you cope with the conditions and all that.'

A thumb indicated over his shoulder. 'Sorry, but I need to get those sheep off the trailer.' Then, after a moment, 'Tell you what, though, when you're through here, why don't you ride on another half mile or so – the farmhouse is the next building on this side of the lane, you can't miss it. We can talk there, over a hot drink. You look as though you could do with one, and I know I could.'

'Are you sure?' she asked. 'It's a tempting thought.'

'Leave it with you,' he replied, 'the offer's open.' With that, he turned and climbed back onto the tractor. Margaret watched as he set off along the lane. She walked a little way into the field, then turned aside to an overgrown hedgerow and sat in the sunshine, her back to a small tree.

Every instinct told her that she should avoid further, unnecessary contact with locals. But, she argued with herself, he was just a farmer... there could be no harm... it might even add to her cover. And besides, he seemed a pleasant enough young man. She had not realised, back in Berlin, what it would be like to live, week in, week out, with hardly any human contact. And besides, she really would welcome something to warm her up. After a while, ample time for her to have walked over a couple of fields, she stood and brushed down her skirt. She wished now that she had taken more trouble with her appearance that morning. But there again, it would probably be just the one conversation... Her conscience appeased, Margaret climbed back over the gate.

* * * *

Sir Manners Fitzgibbon conducted the meeting. There was no need for introductions. Werner had first met the two Special Operations executives, Doreen Jackman and Bill Ives, immediately after fleeing France and landing in England. After a few polite queries about his new role, Sir Manners called them to order.

'Our purpose this morning,' he began, 'is to work out how best Werner might return to Germany and make contact with his father. I gather the general spends most of his time on the estate now that he's retired?'

Werner confirmed that he did. 'Buchbach is about sixty kilometres east and slightly north of Munich,' he informed them, 'and my home, Buchbach Manor, is some six kilometres outside the village. It's quite a large estate, well isolated. But I would have to walk from the village, and even taking a bus from Munich might be a risk.' He paused to look up at all three of them. 'My family is well known. If I were not recognised on the way there, once in the village, I would very possibly be seen by someone who could identify me. And I wouldn't put it past the Nazis to have asked around once I had gone missing from France, so it's more than likely the locals have been alerted. There could even be a substantial reward. I could make an air drop onto the estate, though...' he mused.

Bill Ives spoke for the first time, shaking his head. 'I contacted the RAF in advance of this meeting. They are only just recovering from the Battle of Britain and the Blitz, so their long-range bombing strategy is still in its infancy. Munich is plus of a fourteen-hundred-mile round trip, and it's well defended. A Halifax would have the range, but there are no mass bomber raids planned for the moment. Apparently a single aircraft would be very dicey – not a great chance of making it there and back. So,' he concluded, 'I don't think we can ask the RAF to risk an aircraft and its crew of seven just to land one man.'

Werner felt a mild sense of relief. He would have volunteered, of course, but he was an infantryman, preferring to have his feet firmly on the ground. He really did not fancy parachute training, let alone a flight to the other side of Munich and then a night drop into the German countryside.

'I think,' said Sir Manners eventually, 'that we will have to insert you from Switzerland. There's still a regular train service. Security is tight, but for a native German speaker with the right papers and a change of appearance, it's perfectly possible. It's a route we have already used from time to time. If you take the train to Munich,' he looked at Werner, 'would it be possible for you to make your way safely on to Buchbach Manor?'

He did not reply immediately. But then, '*Ja*,' the first time he had lapsed into his own language for a long time – perhaps it was the prospect of a return to his homeland and family. '*Ja, Ja*,' he repeated, 'if you can get me to *München*, I think I have a plan.'

* * * *

'I will need German clothing,' he informed Doreen Jackman and Bill Ives after Sir Manners had left. 'Everything I was wearing when I left France had been bought in Paris; the style would stand out in Germany.'

'I think we should send you in as some sort of upper-class person,' Doreen suggested. 'There will be civilian police on the train. If they are not sure who they are dealing with, they tend to be a bit more circumspect with any questions.'

They decided to make him a Swiss-German banker based in Switzerland with dual nationality. Brigadier James Summerton, the defence attaché at the Bern embassy, had developed a contact in their industry who would confirm that *Herr* Erich Richter was indeed an employee responsible for the accounts of important German clients banking in Switzerland. The surname was traditionally associated with a member of the legal profession, that of a judge. His cover persona suggested a strong association with important members of the Third Reich. His role explained clearly why he had not been required to enlist for military service.

Doreen did her best with his appearance. His blue eyes would not sit well with dark hair, so his blond curls were dyed with just a hint of ginger. As were his eyebrows, and, to his embarrassment, she told him not to neglect everything on and below his chest and stomach. A pair of steel-framed glasses with only the most minor correction – clear lenses would have been a giveaway – suggested a more clerical, less military background. His identity documents were those in the name of a German citizen who had died in London but whose death had not been reported to his country of birth. It was a good, solid cover that would withstand any initial interrogation.

Werner flew commercial via Lisbon to Madrid, from where the Americans were only too happy to offer him a lift on one of their regular flights to Geneva. He could not stay at the embassy but moved instead into an apartment rented on his behalf by the brigadier's banking friend. He spent the first day shopping in emporia established to support the well-heeled, expatriate German community in Switzerland. By the time he boarded a train in Geneva a few days later, he looked entirely the part.

His papers were checked at the border with just a cursory glance from the Swiss police. When asked for them by one of two plainclothes officials on the German side, he held them up without so much as a glance away from his newspaper. It was very much the arrogant attitude to officialdom of an entirely at ease, self-important, first-class passenger.

'*Herr* Richter?' asked the older man, presumably the senior, holding open the German passport. Werner looked up so that his face could be compared with the photograph. 'Yes, what is it?' he asked languorously, his voice courteous but suggesting a complete lack of interest.

On the right-hand side, opposite the photograph, the first entry atop the page showed his *Beruf* or occupation. A bank director – typical! The policeman hesitated, then, 'Thank you, sir,' he replied, handing back the document. Werner managed a half-smile before they departed but then a long, slow exhalation of relief. He was safely back inside Germany.

There was little sign of the war at the *Hauptbahnhof*, Munich's main railway station, except perhaps for a few more men in uniform. It was quite a walk, but he was reluctant to take a taxi or even to use public transport. Eventually, he stood opposite his apartment building, last used months ago when on Christmas leave from France.

When the property had been purchased before the war for the use of his father whilst on business in Munich, the general had simply ordered his steward to make the purchase. It was registered to the Buchbach estate, not by name to any member of the family. It was a gamble, but unless they had gone through the pre-war accounts or land archives, there was no way the Gestapo could be aware of the apartment's ownership.

Werner blessed the fact that he had thought to pocket all his keys before fleeing Paris. He pulled down his hat to hide the change of hair colouring and removed his glasses. Letting himself into the vestibule, Werner was pleased to see that the concierge from his small glass-fronted office was busy talking to another couple he did not recognise. He walked quickly to the lift dedicated to serving only the penthouse. Two minutes later, he was inside. It looked as though the apartment had not been used since he was last in residence. Werner set down his case, removed his overcoat and poured himself a stiff three fingers of cognac.

'Welcome back, *Herr* Scholtz,' the concierge greeted him the following morning. 'I saw you arrive last evening, but my apologies, I was attending to another resident.'

'Good morning to you, Heinz, and thank you,' Werner responded cheerfully as the door was opened for him. The apartment had only ever been used intermittently. Clearly, his return had been accepted without question. At least he now had access to his own wardrobe. This morning, he was dressed casually in grey flannels and a warm pullover.

He walked to a less affluent area of the city, one where there were a number of small businesses, many of them vehicle repair shops – back-street garages. It took some asking around, but eventually, he found what he wanted.

'I'm told you might have a motorcycle for sale,' he greeted a rather fat, elderly mechanic wiping his oily hands on an equally dirty piece of cloth. A stained off-white vest was visible beneath the straps of a grubby and torn boiler suit. Werner was careful not to recoil from an obnoxious whiff of grease and body odour.

'I might have, for the right price,' came the guarded reply. Werner removed a roll of high-value *Reichsmark*, then replaced it in his trouser pocket. The man shrugged, beckoning Werner to follow him to the rear of a large shed. Behind two vehicles, both with bonnets raised and obviously being worked on, stood a BMW R12.

For a used machine, it was unusually clean and looked well-maintained. 'It's the twin carb version,' the mechanic told him. 'Boxer engine, 736 c.c., so it's good for more than one hundred kilometres an hour.' He lifted a leg over the saddle and kick-started the engine, demonstrating that it revved well, then letting it tick over smoothly for a minute before shutting it down.

It would be ideal for his purpose. 'How much?' asked Werner.

'Fifteen hundred.' said the mechanic flatly.

'Fifteen hundred *Reichsmark*?' Werner exclaimed. 'That's probably twice what it cost when it was new four or five years ago.'

The mechanic shrugged his shoulders again but said nothing. 'Papers?' asked Werner.

A faint smile and just the merest shake of the head. The motorcycle had probably been stolen. On the other hand, if it did not come with papers, Werner knew the seller would not be asking for his. But clearly, the mechanic intended to stand his ground. The price was not up for negotiation. Werner unscrewed the filler cap. The tank was almost empty.

'All right,' he said eventually, 'but can you fill her up?' He counted out the asking price, then added another twenty. 'And if you can find an old leather helmet, that would be appreciated.'

The mechanic also returned with a jerry can and funnel. Finally, he explained the working of the shift lever on the right-hand side of the fuel tank that operated the four-speed gearbox. It was a few years since Werner had last ridden a motorcycle. But with only a slight wobble, he rode carefully away from the garage.

For many years, the estate had rented a lock-up garage near the apartment. It currently housed Werner's 1936 Mercedes-Benz 500K Special Roadster, but the vehicle was far too conspicuous for his purpose, hence the purchase of the motorcycle. There was room to leave it on its stand behind the car before locking up again. Back in the apartment, he reflected on his first two days back in Germany. Thus far, everything had gone well. But tomorrow, he would begin the mission proper and return to Buchbach Manor.

Chapter 4

The gate into a large farmyard had been left open. A tractor and trailer were parked on the far side in front of a long barn constructed sideways-on, parallel with the lane. A red brick farmhouse, set well back to her left, had a front door facing a broad strip of gravel separating it from the hedge and a small, separate gate, also leading into the lane. But it looked as though the only frequently used entrance to the house was a stable door facing into the cobbled but muddy yard. The top half was not quite closed. As she pushed her bicycle towards the door, she saw through a window that it led into a kitchen. Her farmer was standing at the sink. He waved and moved to unbolt and pull back the bottom half of the door.

'Just lean it against the wall; it'll be fine,' he told her. 'So glad you felt able to call. Come inside into the warm.'

It was a large kitchen with plenty of room to walk around a long table and eight spindle-backed chairs. At the far end was a dresser. Opposite the sink stood a line of three waist-high cupboards, their top surfaces cluttered with a mix of ornamental bowls, framed photographs and several piles of paperwork. The furniture had clearly been in the farmhouse for a long time. Margaret's overall impression was one of dilapidated neglect.

'I'm Robert Chapman,' he said, offering his hand, 'but everyone calls me Bob.'

'Then I shall call you Robert,' she replied, extending her own, 'and I am Margaret.' She did not offer her surname. If he noticed, he was too polite to ask.

'Tea all right?' he suggested, opening a door alongside the dresser leading into a larder. There were shelves on either side and a meat safe at the far end standing on a marble shelf. He returned with a tea caddy and rummaged in the dresser for a teapot and two cups and saucers. They did not match, Margaret noticed. Neither did they look too clean, so she was relieved when he rinsed and dried them. Perhaps, she thought, it was usually a tin mug. 'Milk and sugar?' he invited, setting a jug and a glass dish on the table. She added just a dash of milk. The hot drink was welcome after a morning standing in the cold.

'Please,' he said, his hand gesture indicating that she might like to take a chair. He sat opposite, his back to the window. 'Who else lives here?' she asked softly. 'Surely you don't farm on your own?'

'I have help,' he replied. 'Another Robert – he's "Old Bob", been with us for years, and lives in the farm's cottage. He still insists on calling me "Master Robert".'

'Do you live here with your parents?' she queried.

Robert shook his head. 'My father died a few years ago.' he told her, 'just as I was finishing at Hadlow College – it's an agricultural training institute down in Kent. Then my mother and I managed the farm between us,' he went on, 'but she died just after war broke out. I still have Bob, but other than that I'm on my own.' An inverted hand gestured over the kitchen. 'As you can see, I don't have much time to be tidy or for housework.'

'You must miss your mother,' she replied. 'I'm sorry.'

'Don't be,' he said quickly. 'I can cook a bit, and perhaps I'll get one or two of these Land Girls they are talking about. I gather they might even be conscripted any day now.'

She was not to know that this was just a light-hearted attempt to deflect from his situation. Irrationally, she almost felt a pang of jealousy at the idea. 'Thank you for the tea,' she told him, setting down her cup and standing to leave.

'Please wait,' he said, rising automatically. 'Would it be all right if I asked to see you again… perhaps we could have a drink together, or something?'

'We have just had a drink together,' she replied with a smile. 'But I don't live very far away. There's a nice pub in Snettisham,' she offered.

'I sometimes go to The Rose and Crown,' he said quickly. 'I know a few people there to talk to. Perhaps you would you let me call for you?' he asked. 'Are you free on Saturday – would that be all right?' It had all come out in a rush. *Had he made a fool of himself*, he wondered, *been too forward?*

'I would like that,' she replied without thinking. Then, after a pause, 'Tell you what, why don't you meet me there?'

He was visibly relieved. 'Saturday it is then,' he confirmed. 'I'll see you there as soon as I can after milking.'

Afterwards, pedalling home, she realised that she had no idea what time "after milking" would be.

When she arrived, he was already leaning on the bar, nursing a pint of bitter. She accepted a half of the same. They moved to a table next to the fireplace, and the saloon gradually filled up, mostly couples enjoying a Saturday night out. Talk came easily. He told her about life in the countryside as a boy, growing up on the farm.

In response to his questions, she spoke of life in Belfast in the thirties, then the death of her father and looking after children, a position found for her by the parish priest. She did not, however, reveal the nationality of her employers. Neither did she mention the fact that she had returned with them to Germany. Instead, she said that by the time her services were no longer required, she had saved enough to be able to study for a year before applying for her present position with a Dublin-based trust. Then, the conversation turned to the war and what he hoped to do afterwards.

She was surprised when, at just half past nine, he asked if he might walk her home. 'Early morning milking,' he explained, 'one of the hazards of being a farmer.' She hesitated for a moment – she had not told him where she lived. But there could be no harm… and in any case, if he wanted to find out, he would probably only have to ask the landlord at The Rose and Crown. Fortunately, her cottage lay in the same direction as his farm. They stopped by the gate.

'Thank you for a lovely evening,' she said, for she had genuinely enjoyed his company. Without thinking, she had rested her palm on the lapel of his jacket.

'I would like to see you again,' he replied quietly.

'I've had the line reconnected,' she told him, reciting her number, 'if you would like to call me.'

By way of an answer, he took her hand, gently squeezed her fingertips, and wished her good night.

Closing the door behind her, she sat with a nightcap of whiskey and thought about the evening. Robert Chapman was an attractive man – she had enjoyed talking with him, and he was a good listener. It had been an absolute pleasure not to have to spend yet another evening on her own. She knew that a relationship could easily develop. But she would not make a decision now… just wait and see what might happen.

Her radio schedule the following night brought a rude awakening. Berlin confirmed that she was to assume command of the network in Britain. She would continue to determine which existing agents – if any – were still at liberty and brief them on the revised communication arrangements. She would also retain responsibility for meeting future insertions, although the next agent to arrive would do so independently and would contact and brief her on arrival. They did not transmit details. This latter news concerned her. It meant that another person in the field would be aware of her location and identity.

* * * *

Werner dressed warmly and not just for the ride. He could not risk approaching the house. Anna, his former nanny and now their housekeeper, would never betray him, but of any other servant girls, he could not be so sure. He would have to make contact elsewhere, and that could involve hanging around on the estate for quite some time. He pushed a scarf, one given to him by his mother as a Christmas present, into the pocket of a long leather coat. Picking up his helmet and the keys to the R12, he set off for the lock-up garage.

He had made a fairly early start, but it would be much safer than a night-time run. It would take just over an hour to reach the estate. He was confident that his papers would pass any routine police inspection, and once safely outside Munich, he was pleased to see that there were no checkpoints deep inside rural Bavaria. There had been hardly any traffic, and it was unlikely that anyone would take the slightest notice of a solo motorcyclist. It was mid-morning when he arrived and cold even in the winter sunshine. He rode past the open gates to the manor until he came to a densely wooded area that opened, unfenced, onto the country road. As a boy, he had played over every last inch of this landscape.

He turned onto a forest track that he knew emerged from the trees only a hundred metres or so from the manor house. More to the point, it was where his mother took her morning ride. He pushed the BMW into the undergrowth, placed the scarf on the edge of the dirt track as though it had been dropped accidentally, and then retreated to sit alongside the motorcycle. He could just make out the track through the bushes. He was confident his mother would recognise the scarf instantly and dismount.

The morning passed, but she had not appeared. Werner retrieved a piece of sausage and some cheese from his coat pocket. Perhaps his mother had not wished to ride, or Beatrix, her mare, had gone lame. Werner began to wonder whether he would have to devise some other method of making contact. It was mid-afternoon before a figure stooped to examine and then pick up the scarf. But it was not his mother. It was the general, his father, standing supported by his cane in one hand, the scarf now in the other.

Werner stepped through the undergrowth. 'Hello, Father,' he said quietly. The general's head jerked upwards towards the source of the voice. He stared intently for a full two seconds. As Werner took another pace forward, the old man rushed to embrace his son. '*Mein Gott*, Werner,' he whispered, drawing back to hold his son at arm's length, 'it really is you.' Werner felt a lump in his throat. There were tears in his father's eyes.

'I have come from the apartment,' he said quietly, pointing to the motorcycle. 'I was waiting to meet Mama.' The general looked at him. It was only last Christmas when they had been together, but his father had aged visibly. The retired *Herr General* with the stiff, military bearing had become a nervous old man, fearful even. Tears were running down his cheeks. Werner sensed that something was terribly wrong. 'What is it, Father?' he asked gently. 'What has happened?'

The old general produced a handkerchief, wiped his face and blew his nose. Only when he had regained his composure could he look again at his son.

'They came to the house...' he began, speaking almost in a whisper, 'said that you had deserted, a traitor. We were taken to *München* for questioning – separate rooms,' he broke off. His father struggled to continue. It was difficult to make out the words as they were uttered, staccato, between heaving sobs and frantic intakes of breath. 'I told them we knew nothing... begged them... I never saw my Johanna again.'

Werner's own tears were welling. He pulled his father into his arms. Eventually, the old general seemed to recover. He walked away, just a few steps, and again wiped his eyes. Turning back, he addressed his son, the words a desperately controlled monotone. 'A heart attack, they said, before I was eventually released. I was not permitted to see her. Told me I was allowed to arrange a private burial only because of my rank and previous service to the Fatherland. They gave orders to the funeral directors and our parish priest... no lying in, only a closed coffin. She's at peace now in our village churchyard. Your dear mother is interred in our family vault.'

It was Werner's turn to struggle for composure. 'You had better come to the house,' said his father.

'What about the staff?' he queried.

'There's only Anna,' his father replied, 'and she will have gone back to her cottage. Things are not the same anymore, my boy. I have let the others go and closed off the wings and most of the rooms in the main house. Anna looks after me – cooks, and so forth. All I do these days is a bit of farming and collecting rent from our tenants, and that's not worth much, thanks to the war. Don't worry,' he added, anticipating Werner's question, 'the horses are out to livery. Still, at least we do not want for food. I suppose we must count our blessings.'

It was a strange homecoming. Inside, the closed-off manor house seemed a small shell of its former self. He was even more surprised when his father led the way into the kitchen, where an open-fired wood-burning range warmed the room. Someone had stacked a small pile of cut logs, enough for the evening, on the slate surrounding the fireplace. His father produced a bottle of Armagnac and two glasses. From the depth in the tumbler set before him, Werner wondered how much his father was drinking these days.

'You'll stay the night?' his father asked. 'Your old bed's made up, and you only need to put a match to the fireplace. I'd trust Anna with my life, but even so, I'll sort out the room myself afterwards.'

The idea of his father doing even the slightest domestic work was a complete anathema to Werner. Yet more evidence of how times had changed. He confirmed that he would stay overnight. 'I'll go and fetch the 'bike,' he replied. 'I can make an early start tomorrow, and it will be safer to go back to the apartment in the daylight.'

When he returned, his father had placed cutlery, glasses and two opened bottles of wine on the bare wooden table. 'We'll talk after we have eaten,' the general said, setting down a casserole dish that had been left to finish off in one of the range ovens. He poured two large glasses of red. 'Not quite like the old days,' he said with a faint smile, the first Werner had seen since that afternoon. 'But I don't mind telling you, I thought I had lost everything. It does my heart good to see you, dear boy.'

Over the remains of the bottle and then into the second, Werner brought his father up to date. When he asked if the general knew of any contacts that might be able to help with his mission, his father was quiet for a moment.

'*Ja, Ja,*' he said slowly. 'We are still active. I am glad to be able to help. Before, I was afraid. Maybe for myself, but more for my Johanna. Now, there is nothing more those Nazi bastards can do to me. You will have to go to Berlin, but I will give you the names of two senior officers with whom I have served and also those of their sons – members of our organisation in the Party, who are tasked as were you.'

'Just two things, then,' said Werner, 'before we raise a glass to the memory of my mother and finish off that bottle. I need the name and a good description of whoever heads up the Gestapo in Munich. And do you mind parting with that Walther you used to show me – the one you neglected to return, as you used to say, when you finally retired?'

Chapter 5

It had been easy enough, dressed in civilian clothes, to follow at a safe distance on the BMW when the staff car left the Gestapo headquarters.

The tree-lined Isar *Allee* opened at its far end onto the bank of the river from which it took its name. *SS-Sturmbannführer* Kurt Roth lived in a detached house overlooking the water. A former schoolteacher from a modest, middle-class family, but for the Party, he could never have imagined living in one of eastern Munich's most fashionable and expensive districts. Its previous occupants had been a wealthy Jewish family. *Herr* Goldschmidt owned a small but prosperous jewellery store in the *Altstadt*, the old part of the city, but he had been forced to sell his business at a knockdown price to an Aryan, a Party member. The Goldschmidts counted themselves fortunate. Before their property had been commandeered, they had the funds to secure documents allowing them to escape from Germany, initially to Sweden and then to America: choice gemstones, hidden in body orifices, provided the means for a fresh start in their new land.

The Roth dwelling in Bogenhausen was several kilometres from Werner's more central apartment: too far to walk, and he was reluctant to make regular use of public transport. His Richter papers would withstand scrutiny, but this was his home city. It was perhaps unlikely, but he could not afford even the slightest chance that he might be recognised. He dressed in the long raincoat and hat adopted by so many members of the *Gestapo*. When, next morning, he flashed his original *SS* identity document, the owner of a small hotel barely looked at it, much less registering the officer's name. His front desk was questioned daily by the authorities. His livelihood survived only with their goodwill. If the officer wished to place his motorcycle in their secure courtyard for a few hours, he would be only too happy to oblige.

Unfortunately, there was no obvious place in the *Allee* from which to watch the house. This was not the sort of area to offer a convenient bar or coffee shop. Neither, in houses surrounded by generous grounds and high walls, were there rooms to rent. But three along, on the other side of the road, a property bore a sign advertising it for sale. Solid double gates were closed and locked. Alongside, a much smaller wrought iron pedestrian gate offered a partial view of the drive and an overgrown front lawn, but it was secured with a padlock. That evening, he returned after dark on the BMW. There were lights on in adjacent properties, but satisfied that he was not being observed, it was the work of seconds to force the padlock with a tyre wrench.

He pushed the motorcycle inside and left it by the wall, replacing the padlock with one taken from his pocket before approaching the house. It was in darkness, curtains drawn, and almost certainly uninhabited. Sliding a knife under the frame, Werner slipped the catch on a kitchen window at the rear of the property. Holding his fingers over the head of a torch, he explored the ground floor. He found a set of keys, including one labelled "main gate", hanging on a hook in the kitchen. Sheet-covered drawing room furniture and a faint musty smell suggested that the house had been empty for some time. Back in the kitchen, he flicked a light switch on and off, but nothing happened. The electricity supply had probably been disconnected at the main fuse box. But he could not risk turning it back on: if lights had not been turned off in other rooms, the house would suddenly light up like a Christmas tree. A quick tour upstairs revealed a small menorah on the mantel shelf in a child's bedroom. It would not be long before this Jewish family's former home was also re-allocated by the Party.

Werner had seen enough. He had no intention of spending the night in an unheated house, even if he could find blankets for the bare and undoubtedly damp mattresses. Back in the garden, he wedged the window shut with a short length of twig. It would not swing open and would pass all but the closest inspection. He pushed the BMW away from the gates before riding away. It was time to return to his apartment for dinner, a bottle of wine and a few hours rest. He would return before first light.

Shortly before nine the following morning, the gates of the Roth property were opened from inside. Minutes later, from an upstairs window, Werner watched as a black, four-door Opel *Kapitän* turned into the *Allee*, slowing as it passed before turning into the drive. On its way back to the main road, he noted that both the driver and his passenger in the rear seat were in uniform. He had to assume that they would each be carrying a side arm. Almost certainly the guard or guards inside the grounds would also be armed, probably with a Schmeisser submachine gun. He was absolutely determined that, for the sake of his mother's memory and his father's sanity, in his last seconds on earth, Roth would know the reason why he was about to die. But any action in the immediate vicinity of the Roth property would be suicide. For the next two days, Werner confirmed the *SS-Sturmbannführer's* routine.

He also explored the road onto which the Opel made a right turn as it left the *Allee*. Running parallel with the river, it was a mix of detached dwellings and low-rise apartment blocks, with the occasional upmarket restaurant or small commercial enterprise in between. More importantly, at that time of the morning it was fairly busy – some horse-drawn but mostly vehicle traffic. Even when the exit from the *Allee* was clear,

Roth's driver paused to look carefully before accelerating away. That brief pause was all he needed.

Werner opened the main gates, left the BMW behind the wall, and at ten minutes to nine, walked the fifty metres or so to the end of the *Allee*. By the time the Opel arrived at the junction, the gates to the Roth property would be closed. But even if not, it was extreme range for a Schmeisser. Werner watched as the car approached and slowed to a crawl; he stepped off the kerb as if about to cross, then paused to wait politely for the officer's vehicle to halt before stepping behind it.

Roth was on the far side of the rear seat. In one swift movement, Werner opened the door behind the driver and slipped alongside the *Sturmbannführer*, the Walther raised to his brow so that it was clearly visible to the driver in his rearview mirror.

'Keep going!' he barked.

Neither Roth nor his driver had the slightest opportunity to draw their weapon. To reinforce his threat, Werner pushed the end of the Walther's barrel hard into the skin just behind the *Sturmbannführer's* left eye.

'Do as he says,' Roth shouted urgently. Then, 'Who the hell are you, and what do you want?' He had obviously not recognised Werner's somewhat changed appearance.

'*Halt die Fresse!*' he snapped back. It had the desired effect. Clearly, the *Sturmbannführer* was not accustomed to being told, in the coarsest language, to shut his gob. Taken aback, the driver waited for a safe gap in the traffic, then made a right turn onto the main road.

After about a kilometre, they crossed a bridge over the river into an area of parkland. 'Pull over now and stop here,' Werner commanded. Then, 'Put your sidearm on the dashboard, just a thumb and finger on the trigger guard, leave the engine running, get out of the car and keep walking. You will not be harmed.'

Werner shifted slightly on his seat so that his back was in the corner, half against the door. It placed him a little further away from his target. He waited until the driver was a good fifty metres ahead. 'You know my name,' he said quietly. 'You went to Buchbach Manor, looking for me, then arrested my parents. My mother, a healthy woman in the prime of her life, died under questioning in your custody.'

'I... I assure you,' stammered the *Sturmbannführer*, 'it had n-nothing to do with me. It was an accident...'

'You were in charge of the interrogation,' Werner broke in. 'My father told me. He was not even allowed to pay his last respects. I will grant you a courtesy you did not extend to my mother. If you are a religious man, you have thirty seconds to make your peace. You may pray.'

The Walther had not wavered, but his eyes were on the *Sturmbannführer's* hands. Even as a fist clenched and an arm began to lift in a desperate attempt to sweep the barrel aside, Werner fired. Most of the blood and grey gore hit the cloth-covered panelling between the side and the rear windows, then dribbled slowly down. He opened the door and stepped out before leaning back inside, cupping the dead man's neck and pulling him down so that his torso lay across the seat.

Werner closed the door. Hearing the shot, the driver had stopped and turned around. Werner pointed the Walther at him, indicated a circular motion with his other hand, then waved the back of his fingers at him and along the road, indicating that the other man should keep walking. As he did so, Werner settled behind the wheel and executed a rapid three-point turn. He would be back at the *Allee* long before the driver could have any means of raising the alarm.

No vehicles or pedestrians – the *Allee* was deserted. Werner parked the Opel in the drive, but where it could not be seen from the pedestrian gate. He wheeled out the BMW and locked the double gates behind him. The Opel and Roth's body would not be found until someone had cause to visit the property – could be days or weeks. He set off for the estate. His father needed to know what had happened. Then, he would return the BMW to his lock-up garage and take the train for Berlin.

* * * *

'We now know that the British have broken our codes,' said *Generalmajor* Hans Paul Oster, seated in a comfortable chair in his *Abwehr* office at 76-78 Tirpitzufer. His assistant, *Oberst* Karl Schröder, inclined his head in agreement. 'Fortunately,' Oster continued, 'a few agents have been in place since well before the war, so unlike those inserted more recently, the British may still be unaware of their existence.'

'*Natürlich*,' concurred Schröder, 'but as you know, I have new transmission arrangements in place with *Fraulein* Wagner. I have already sent a warning order confirming her new responsibilities. We now have a book-to-book code, and the British do not know which one we are using. As an additional precaution, many standard phrases are substituted with a single numeral. Margaret will pass on the new instructions. And unlike the old *Abwehr* codes, I believe this new system is unbreakable.'

From her base in Norfolk, Margaret had managed to trace and brief only three pre-war agents still at liberty. She also carried on with her cover project, cycling out occasionally. And, as required by Berlin, she spent hours observing various sections of the coastline. Much of the sea and beaches had been mined, but there were gaps so that fishing fleets could sail and return. In the wash, horse-drawn cockle carts left at low tide, driving out over the mud as far as the eye could see, in a race to dig until wicker baskets in the small carts were piled high before the tide turned. Margaret made careful charts, adding prominent features on land so that at high tide, two- or three-point compass fixes would guide a small craft, launched from a vessel further offshore, along a safe channel. But despite all this work, there were no messages ordering her to assist with an extraction. She began to feel more relaxed.

On Saturday evenings, Margaret enjoyed a drink at The Rose and Crown with Robert, and on one occasion, they caught the bus to watch *Gone With The Wind*, starring Vivien Leigh and Clark Gable, at the cinema in King's Lynn. But much as she enjoyed his company, and she sensed the feeling was mutual, he made no move to develop their relationship, which seemed to have stalled at the point of occasionally touching or holding hands or a kiss on the cheek. In a way, Margaret was relieved. But, during mellow late evening moments, with nothing more than yet another glass of Bushmills for company, if she were brutally honest with herself, she was disappointed.

So she was pleasantly surprised when one Saturday evening, Robert suddenly announced that it would be nice if they didn't always have to meet in the local public house.

'If I made lunch tomorrow,' he said, 'would you join me – at the farm, I mean?' It had come out so suddenly and in such a rush that she was quite taken aback.

He mistook her hesitation for refusal. 'I'm sorry,' he added more slowly, 'if I have embarrassed you – I'm not much good at this sort of thing. Running the farm, it's a solitary sort of life. I haven't made friends with any girls. I mean young ladies,' he corrected hastily. 'Not, that is, until you came along, and I found you standing in my field…' he tailed off. 'Sorry,' he said finally. 'Please forget what I said.'

Margaret reached out to touch his fingertips. 'Don't be silly,' she chided softly. 'Thank you for asking me. And yes, I would love to come.'

She took extra care with her appearance on Sunday morning. Cycling for miles around the coast of Norfolk had trimmed her figure and added a healthy, outdoor complexion. He had offered to collect her, so fortunately, she did not have to dress to withstand a squally, inclement morning, what she had heard the locals refer to as "Irish weather". A soft lamb's wool jumper made little secret of the shape of her breasts. A wartime pattern skirt, bought in Norwich and cut to fall barely below her knees, offered a fair glimpse of shapely legs.

She was waiting by a window when he arrived, in what she later learned was a ten-horsepower Austin. Margaret saw a rather boxy-looking four-door saloon, beige with contrasting dark brown wings. He opened the front passenger door and looked away politely as she settled herself into the seat.

'This is rather nice,' she offered as he turned the key in the ignition and reached to pull a starter knob at the far end of the dashboard.

He turned and smiled. 'Middle-class motoring,' he said lightly. 'Father bought it not long before he died so that I could take him to hospital appointments in King's Lynn. Fortunately, I got my licence before they brought in the driving test in 1934. It's a great little motor, but you need quite a long piece of road if you want to push her much over fifty miles an hour. This is the luxury model, though – leather seats and a sunshine roof.'

She could see that he was rather proud of his transport. 'But I thought petrol was rationed?' she queried.

'It is,' came the response, 'but that's one of the few advantages of being a farmer. I'm allowed a tank on the farm for the tractor. A few drops to collect you on a wet morning won't go amiss, and the car's hardly used anyway, so she needs a run from time to time.'

'Something smells good,' she said as they walked into a kitchen warmed by a range with an oven alongside the open fireplace. She noticed that a considerable effort had been made to clean and tidy the kitchen. 'I hope you don't mind eating in here,' Robert said, pulling a chair for her from under the kitchen table, 'but I'm afraid there was only time for a bit of rather frantic last-minute housework.'

A bottle of red wine, cork removed, stood on a side cupboard alongside two polished glasses. 'I'm usually a pint of bitter man,' he said as he poured for them both, 'but Father had quite a good stock from before the war.'

He produced a large, lidded pot from the oven and set it on the table. Next, he extracted a joint of beef which he placed on a wooden carving board, and from which he carved meltingly tender slices. 'Slow-cooked brisket, my mother's recipe. Would you like to help yourself?' he invited, indicating a ladle. 'There's vegetables and loads of gravy in the pot.' But he had forgotten to warm the plates. Somehow, she found this rather endearing.

'This is absolutely delicious,' Margaret complimented him as she tried first the beef and then everything else. She had found potatoes, carrots, parsnips and quartered chunks of still crispy cabbage – which he had obviously added just before setting out to collect her. 'This must have cost you a whole month's ration,' she said with some concern.

'Second advantage of being a farmer,' he replied. 'Everything here came off my land.' He lifted his shoulders. 'Usually, I stick to the rules, but I wanted to give you a nice lunch.' He had briefly set down his knife and fork. She reached across and squeezed his hand. 'And you have,' she said simply. 'Thank you.'

'Advantage number three,' he said, placing a bowl of blackberries on the table and then a jug of fresh cream.

Margaret insisted that they washed up. After which, they finished the wine and listened to the wireless. Robert made no move to suggest that they leave the kitchen. Perhaps, she thought, he was embarrassed because his lounge was still in need of emergency housework.

'Would you like to drive me home?' she asked. 'Presumably, it will soon be time for milking?'

'No need to rush off,' he countered. 'Old Bob has agreed to do it for me. When I went round to ask him and told him why, his wife insisted on it.'

An idea formed in her mind. Her cottage was much more comfortable. 'Tell you what, then,' she began. 'This lunch has been lovely, but you have to be up in the morning. Take me back. I'll light the fire, and we'll have a cosy drink, then you can still have your early night.'

The cottage lounge was cold, especially after the warmth of his farmhouse kitchen. Margaret put a match to paper and sticks and added some of the smaller logs stacked on the hearth. In minutes, there was a roaring fire. 'Keep building it up,' she instructed, 'and I'll get us something to drink. Would whiskey be all right?'

She did not tell him that her source was an Irish banker in London. Hearing a clink of glasses from the kitchen, he wandered idly over to a bookcase. It was almost empty. But one of the few volumes on the top shelf drew his attention. It was lying flat, separate from the others, and had a grey spine with a contrasting red front cover. On it, in black foreign lettering, was the title and name of the author: *Hauptmann Ladurner,* by Luis Trenker. He had opened it at random and was gazing at the German text when she returned with their drinks.

Her heart almost stopped. The radio was well hidden, but she had completely forgotten that her code book was still there, ready for the next schedule. Silently cursing her stupidity, she forced a smile and handed him two fingers of Black Bush Irish malt.

Chapter 6

The infant Henry Merceret's name was put down for Harrow. When his father was killed in The Great War, there had to be a family conference. Financially, the situation was not disastrous. His widowed mother, Dorothy, owned property and had limited private means, but without her husband's earnings from the family's successful London law firm, adjustments would have to be made. She agreed to sell their elegant London home and move into an adequately spacious Hampshire cottage inherited from a spinster aunt.

Dorothy Merceret had the funds for a modest lifestyle, and Edmund Merceret, Henry's uncle and the senior partner in the firm agreed to cover his nephew's school fees. But the war had seriously reduced his practice income. Finances were stretched, and his own sons' education would have to take priority. After prep school, for Henry, Harrow would be out of the question. Fortunately, Edmund Merceret had been at school with the head of Parkbury, a minor public school in The West Country.

Henry's early years in the Hampshire countryside were happy. As an economy measure, he attended the village school until, at the age of eight, he boarded. Henry was not in any way reluctant when it was time to leave home for Parkbury's prep school – he had become increasingly aware of his mother's dependence on alcohol. But exeats and holidays became more and more difficult. He was eleven when the village lady who cooked for them handed in her notice, which left only their cleaning "daily". By now, it was not unusual for him to have a supper of bread and cheese after helping his mother to bed quite early in the evening. But that did nothing to lessen his grief and devastation when, almost at the end of his final year, he was summoned to the head's study. A grim-faced uncle Edmund told him that he was so terribly sorry, but his mother had taken her own life.

Tears blurred Henry's vision. He felt his uncle's hands on his shoulders, and then he was drawn forward into an embrace. Edmund Merceret nodded at the headmaster, who quietly left the room to offer them privacy. He handed his nephew a handkerchief before taking a half step back.

'Don't worry, my boy,' he said softly, blinking back a tear of his own, 'you are not on your own. I'm going to take you home with me now, back to London. Your aunt Edith and I will look after you, and Conrad and Joseph break up next week. We will take care of everything. There will be a suitable ceremony, and we will all pay our respects to your dearest Mama.'

Matron had already packed a few things into a small suitcase, now on the back seat of Edmund's Armstrong Siddely. Henry's trunk would follow. The headmaster waited just inside the front entrance to wish them farewell. Matron gave him a hug and a kiss on the cheek. Henry Merceret left his prep school for the last time. Next term, he would begin at Parkbury.

Everyone was very kind. His cousins, already at Harrow and briefed carefully by their parents, included the younger Henry in their activities through the summer of 1929. Nothing was said, but Henry was painfully aware that whilst his cousins were at Harrow, his alma mater would be the less prestigious Parkbury. His mother had been unable to cope after the death of her husband and had committed suicide. But in Henry's mind, there was only one reason for the loss of both parents, his intense, if suppressed distress, and a reduced station in life: The Great War. Within his psyche fermented a hatred of Germany and all things German.

Werner

* * * *

In 1932 Leopold von Hoesch assumed in London the appointment of chargé d'affaires for the Weimar Republic. An old-fashioned diplomat, his move to England followed highly successful tours in China and Madrid. He was accompanied by his principal secretary, Wilhelm Naumann, an ambitious protégé within the German diplomatic service. Hoesch, a bachelor, enjoyed life at number nine Carlton Terrace, formerly known as Prussia House, which had been the ambassador's home before The Great War. Occupied by the Americans and Swiss for the duration, it had finally been handed back to its German owners in nineteen twenty.

Naumann, who, like the ambassador, also came from an established and wealthy background, enjoyed life in London. He spoke English well, although not as fluently as his superior, and his wife Ellen revelled in her role as society hostess for the bachelor Hoesch. This also meant that Wilhelm and Ellen were well acquainted within the highest stratum of British politics — including John Simon, the Foreign Secretary.

Both Ellen and Wilhelm were concerned, however, for their son Max, an only child. Much against her husband's better judgement, his mother had persuaded Wilhelm that their son should accompany them to China and Spain. But time in these foreign parts, despite a number of private tutors, had not given fourteen-year-old Max the formal education with his peers that his father considered essential for a future career. The boy had an ear for languages, but Wilhelm Naumann did not consider a working knowledge of Mandarin or Spanish to be a particular asset. And Max had only a poor command of English.

On being asked how he was enjoying life in London, Wilhelm mentioned the problem of Max's education to one of John Simon's aides, with whom he had struck up a friendship.

'My alma mater's jolly good,' Mathew Stead confided. 'Parkbury's not absolutely top-hole, like Eton or Harrow, but it's a lot less expensive. Might suit the lad better, seeing as he'll have to blend in despite not being English. And, of course, he hasn't taken Common Entrance,' he added, 'which could pose a problem. Would you like me to have a word with my old headmaster? He's still there; hasn't changed since my time.'

The head was only too pleased to mention Stead minor's success – scholarship from School to Oxford and a meteoric rise in the Civil Service – to the parents of prospective pupils. The son of an important foreign diplomat, notwithstanding The Great War, now some time past, could only enhance the school's reputation. Over sherry in his study, he explained to Wilhelm and Ellen Naumann that although their son was a year older than the usual age for entrance, he could offer a place with the first years in September. In the meantime, his parents were encouraged to engage a private language tutor as soon as possible. This could be continued at school for as long as necessary, although, of course, it would have to be billed as an "extra". His mother was less keen, but his father accepted gratefully. The die was cast for Max Neumann's future Nazi career.

By September, his English was much improved. On a sunny morning, his trunk was loaded onto the luggage rack of his father's Opel Ultra, and the family set off for The West Country. Max was introduced to Matron, a rather young, plump lady with a jolly smile and bubbles of light brown hair. Also, Mr Sykes, his housemaster, a rather tall, thin individual who, in response to a question from Max's father, admitted that he had only recently joined the school from university. He also reminded both parents that Max would spend his first year in Admissions House, after which his form would be assimilated into the main school building. Once Max's trunk had been deposited in his dorm, they were encouraged to make their farewells so Matron could show him how to unpack.

There were thirty beds in the dorm, some surrounded by other parents and boys, but Max suddenly found his world reduced to his own bed with a small cupboard on one side and a narrow, single-door wardrobe on the other. Once his parents had departed, Matron simply gave him a drawing showing where everything should go inside his wardrobe and left him to get on with it. She would, she told him, come back later and make sure that all his things were in the right place. His tuck box was to be handed in unopened.

Max sat on his bed and watched as the afternoon wore on. He discovered an Alan on one side and a Rupert on the other. One of the boys looked as though he might be Chinese, although his bed was at the far end of the dorm. At half past five, their housemaster showed them to a small dining room where they were given tea, after which they were shepherded into a common room where they could talk, play board games or listen to the wireless. A much older boy, who announced himself as Hawkins, told them that he was there to supervise and keep order before settling in the best chair by the fire to read a book.

It would not do for Hawkins to acknowledge his younger brother, James, also one of the first years, although they had been together briefly when their mother took her leave, kissing them both and urging Frederick to look after his brother. Bursting with pride at – in his eyes – his new and important public school status and anxious to seek Frederick's approval as a source of information, James had blurted out the news that his year boasted both a Chinese and a German new boy. Frederick left the room when Matron arrived to supervise the bedtime routine, and Mr Sykes gave them a behaviour lecture before lights out.

It was unfortunate that Frederick Hawkins roomed with Henry Merceret. And doubly so that Hawkins casually passed on the news – there were two foreign boys in his brother's dorm. One was Chinese, the other German – the first of that hated nation to whom Merceret would soon have access.

* * * *

Rodney Sykes had a suite of rooms adjacent to the boys' dormitory. Normally, he would be seated for dinner at high table in the main school dining hall, but attendance on admissions day was not compulsory. Indeed, as Headmaster had advised, it would be wise to be on hand for their first night at school, in case there were any problems with boys settling in. So Molly Manders, the matron, had invited him down for supper in her flat on the ground floor and diagonally distanced from the dorm.

He had accepted for two reasons. First, it avoided having to make a meal in his own small kitchen – his culinary skills were limited to a boiled egg or something on toast. And second, Molly, in her late twenties or early thirties, had already insisted that he use her first name when they were alone together. Perhaps a little on the plump side, but her flirting and body language had already hinted that she might provide personal comforts for their mutual satisfaction – an overwhelming temptation for the sexually innocent Sykes. Instead of listening out for his charges, he was enjoying a glass of beer and admiring the shape of his hostess's breasts as she prepared supper: he would probably not be the first to enjoy her body, but there was every hope and expectation that he would soon lose his virginity.

The dorm settled for the night till one of the boys drew back a curtain. It was still light outside. They formed small groups, sitting on adjacent beds and chatting quietly, mostly swapping information. Suddenly, the door opened, and a crowd of older boys rushed into the dormitory, their faces covered with a scarf.

'All right,' said one of them, 'which one's the Kraut, and where's the Chink?'

'There he is,' another shouted, pointing a finger to the far end of the dorm. The one who had asked the question grabbed the nearest boy by his pyjama jacket and pulled him to his feet. 'Tell me, the Kraut?' he demanded, his other hand raised, palm open, to slap the boy across his face. His lower lip began to quiver. He did not know Max.

A year older than the other boys, Max was also taller and more heavily built. He was no match for the senior boys, but he could not let the smaller boy take a beating on his behalf. Besides, someone would give in eventually, and he would be pointed out. He stood.

'You are looking for me,' he said quietly.

His tormentor let go of the younger boy, and four of them approached Max's bed. The older boy reached out to grip Max's pyjamas, but he brushed the hand aside. 'Why you...' his assailant uttered, lifting a hand to throw a punch. Max saw it coming and closed the gap between them before sinking his fist as hard as he could into the older boy's stomach. It was all over in seconds. Someone else's fist smashed into his nose, two more grabbed his arms, and he was thrown, face down, onto his bed. Dazed, his legs were seized, and he was lifted and carried horizontally. As his head was turned towards the centre of the dorm, he saw a small patch of blood on the coverlet. He could also see that the Chinese boy was receiving similar treatment. He began to struggle, but a fifth assailant slapped his head hard and told him to shut up.

They were carried into the washroom, and a cubicle door was opened. The Chinese boy's head was shoved right into the lavatory bowl, and a hand went up to pull the chain. Water cascaded over him. The others were laughing as he was pulled from the cubicle. He stood, still held by the arms, tears and water running down his face, his shoulders shaking as he sobbed in silence.

'Now it's your turn,' said the boy holding an arm, the one he had punched. 'Take my place,' he ordered to no one in particular before going first into the cubicle. Max now knew what would happen. It would be unpleasant. There was no point in struggling, but he would not give them the satisfaction of tears.

His head was pushed into the bowl, and then the hand holding it down was withdrawn. He turned his head sideways, trying to see what was happening, when he was struck on one side of his face by a stream of warm liquid. He turned his face down in horror as urine showered down on the back of his head. Then, the aim shifted back and forth from his crown to his neck.

Finally, mercifully, it stopped. 'Right, wash him down,' said a voice from behind. He did his best to let the flushed water wash off the piss, but when they lifted him out, he could feel and smell it running down his back and chest. Then, suddenly, they were both released, and their assailants were gone. The two boys removed their pyjama tops and dried themselves as best they could.

They staggered into the corridor, where they met a boy coming from their dorm. 'I'm going to fetch Mr Sykes,' he rushed to tell them. 'They left someone in the dorm guarding the door. We didn't know what was happening on the other side, so we stayed put, but now they've all gone.'

Downstairs, their housemaster, replete with supper, was seated in an armchair, Molly Manders sideways on his lap. So far, he had unbuttoned her blouse, and she made no objection as he fondled her breasts. She cupped his chin for a kiss. His hand moved to her thigh and slipped to bare flesh above her stockings. Their pleasure was interrupted by a sound from above of someone banging on a door and a voice, as yet unbroken, shouting his name.

'Damn,' he said, struggling to ease her away and stand at the same time. 'Sounds like trouble upstairs. Best if I go. Be back later as soon as I can.' She was buttoning her blouse as he left the room.

Having calmed the boys, he sat on a bed and gathered them around. They were content for the German boy, Max, to speak for all of them. Although interrupted by the others from time to time and still with traces of blood on his face, he gave an account of what had happened. Sykes knew that he was in a difficult position. He should have been next door, where he would have heard the commotion and put a stop to what had obviously been some sort of sixth-form induction prank that had seemingly got out of hand. The proper course would be to settle the boys now, then report to Headmaster in the morning. It would be up to him to discover the culprits, which, with his authority backed up by threats of expulsion, would not be difficult.

But that would invite too many awkward and embarrassing questions. At best, it would be a reprimand. He could even be dismissed with no chance of a reference. Times were hard, and he had been lucky to secure this teaching post. Financially, he could ill afford to lose it.

'Max,' he instructed, 'go downstairs, knock on Matron's door, call out who you are, and ask her to join us up here.'

When they were all assembled, he said, 'Right, boys, this is what we are going to do. It's not unusual to have some sort of initiation ceremony, a bit of a lark, but those boys who came here tonight went a bit too far. On the other hand, if I report it,

I have a concern that they will try to make your lives a misery until they leave school at the end of the year. If I don't, they will think that you have not sneaked on them. You will have earned their respect, and they will leave you alone. If they don't, just tell them that I already know what has happened, and if they touch you again, Headmaster will find out, and they will be expelled. What do you think?'

There was silence for a moment, then a nodding of heads and a general murmur of agreement. 'Good fellows,' he said. 'I'm going to ask Matron to run a bath for Max and then sort out dry pyjamas for Max and Zheng. Then we'll all have some hot cocoa in the common room, and you can each have a treat from your tuck box.' He grinned at them. 'It'll be a not-quite-midnight feast, so don't tell anyone.'

Eventually, he settled the dorm again, telling them that he would leave his door open so he would immediately hear anything untoward. As he was about to enter his rooms, Molly placed a hand on his chest. 'You're going to have to wait, darling,' she said quietly.

Alone with his thoughts, Rodney Sykes felt confident that he had diffused the situation and protected his career. A pity about Molly, he reflected, but there would be another night. Perhaps she should come upstairs rather than the other way round. But now that tonight's nonsense was over, at least the upper sixth would leave the first years alone.

He could not have been more mistaken.

Chapter 7

Traditionally, they would have lined up the first years in their dorm, debagged them one by one, made them bend over, and given each boy an initiation slap with a slipper. Not too hard, nothing too unpleasant. Not enough noise to alert the housemaster.

But as Merceret argued, this was the first time the school had admitted foreign boys. And if the school could change, so should they. His hidden agenda was to get the Kraut.

'We need to put the two foreign boys in their place,' he had insisted. 'Let's leave the English boys alone but show the foreigners they are not the equal of us British fellows. If we take them down a peg or two, as it were, they'll know not to try and lord it just because they come from another country. One up for the British Empire and all that. What do you say, chaps…?'

'So what shall we do with them,' he was asked. After that, the toilet bowl idea was easy to sell. The Chink would go first, just a harmless flush. Then, although he had not told the others, just for starters, he would piss all over that bloody German's head. And his evening had gone according to plan. Merceret shared two illicit bottles of beer with his roommate. The problem, he mused to himself, was where to go from here.

* * * *

As the only other foreign boy in their year, it was not surprising that Zheng was drawn to a friendship with Max. It was cemented when, to Zheng's surprise, the German boy correctly pronounced his name in Mandarin, the "Z" something of a "Ch" sound. He was even more impressed to learn that Max had a basic competence in the language.

Both boys were under instruction from parents to become fluent in English, if possible with no hint of a foreign accent. But Zheng, as with almost all in his year, was at first homesick. Both he and Max were separated not just from their parents but also from using their own language. Zheng enjoyed explaining to Max, in Mandarin, that his father was a senior official at the Chinese Legation in Portland Place, London. The friendship of the older and rather bigger German boy also spared him from at least some of the taunts that his nationality and appearance might otherwise have attracted. Max, for his part, enjoyed teaching Zheng a few phrases in German. 'You can impress my people at half term,' he told him.

Their friendship was not lost on Merceret, who saw a way of getting at Max through the Chinese boy. His cronies in the upper sixth were encouraged to bully the pair of them. Shoulder barging in the corridor was an everyday occurrence. Out of class, the two boys did their best to make themselves scarce. A clearing in the woods at the bottom of the playing fields was a favourite place to share a bar of Cadbury's Dairy Milk. Inevitably, their walks to and from this refuge did not go unnoticed. Suddenly, they were surrounded. At first, they thought that they would just have to surrender the chocolate. But it did not stop there.

'We want to know what's best,' Merceret told them. 'German size or Chinese speed. Take off your blazers. You have to box.'

'We are not fighting,' said Max nervously.

'Either you do it, or you take on one of us,' came the reply. 'Hawkins is pretty good in the gym, so he'll have a go with Chinky here. And I'm not so dusty if I say so myself. So I'll give you a boxing lesson, Kraut boy.' Seeing that they had little choice if they were to avoid what would probably be a nasty beating, reluctantly, the two boys began to take off their blazers.

They were saved by two Springer Spaniels bounding into the clearing, followed by a master's wife. Clearly, something untoward was afoot. 'What's going on?' she shouted, striding towards them. 'Stay where you are!'

Max grabbed Zheng's arm. 'Run,' he shouted, and they bolted between the older boys and ran for the playing field. Those left behind tried to look sheepish as she gave them a piece of her mind and warned them of the punishment for bullying before storming off deeper into the woods.

'Nothing happened,' Merceret insisted afterwards. 'She probably thinks she's dealt with it. Won't report us. And even if she does, we were only joking, just fooling around. Got it?' he demanded, to murmurs of assent. 'But we'll have to lay off for a bit,' he conceded.

Max and Zheng thought at first that everything would be all right. But Merceret and his cronies now had a taste for tormenting the two foreign boys. The shoulder barging started again. Satchels were pulled from their shoulders. One ankle was hooked behind the other, and a push sent the victim sprawling, often grazing hands and knees. The older boys were careful to take turns. No individual could be held responsible for repeated torment. Although slowly, the attacks became fewer and less frequent, nevertheless, despite their best efforts to be careful, for Max and Zheng, life was not very pleasant.

'I think we are going to have to do something,' Zheng said to Max one evening in the common room.

'We could ask to have a talk with Matron, or perhaps Housemaster would be better,' Max suggested.

'He didn't even do anything after what happened on the first night,' Zheng pointed out. 'He'll just tell us what's going on now is something that happens to new boys, and they'll soon give up.' He raised his hand, forestalling a reply. 'I don't think he wants to admit there's anything wrong with the way he's looking after the first years,' he added. 'And anyway, he and Matron are as thick as thieves. I've seen her going into his rooms lots of times.'

'Chinese way better,' added Zheng. He looked around to check that they were still alone in the room. From his blazer's inside pocket, he produced a knife, the blade sharpened on both sides and the tip shaped to a point. String had been wound tightly around the handle, thickening towards the blade into a makeshift hilt so that it gave a better grip and more resistance.

'Where on earth did you get that?' Max demanded.

'I made it,' said Zheng simply. 'It was easy enough to take a knife from the dining hall. But it took me ages to grind it down on a stone slab. Then I stole the string from Matron's laundry room – there's loads of it there. Do you want me to make one for you?'

Max was tempted. Two of them, each armed with a knife, should be able to threaten off the older boys. But he wasn't sure. 'Come on,' he said without answering the question, 'or we'll be late for supper.'

He was still undecided a week later when Zheng announced that he had acquired another knife, and he was going to start filing it. Apparently, the concrete blocks cast as a base for the walls of the senior boys' bike shed were ideal for the purpose, and with its open side facing away from the school buildings, the shed also had the advantage of shielding him from view. Max still had some prep to finish and promised to join him later.

Almost there, he recognised the voices of Merceret and Hawkins. Then a 'You little shit' was followed by a hollow thump and a gasp of pain. Hawkins said something that Max did not quite catch, but the response was a piteous 'no, please…' from Zheng. Max wanted to turn and run, but he was even more frightened by what they might do to his friend. If they did something really bad to Zheng, Max would feel responsible. His heart was thumping in his chest, but he walked round the edge of the wriggly tin wall and stood in the entrance. Hawkins was behind Zheng, holding back his upper arms. Merceret was poised to punch him again.

'Leave him alone, or I'll tell,' shouted Max. 'Mr Sykes knows what you did on our first night. He'll report you to the head.'

'All right,' Merceret sneered at Max but then turned back as if poised to land a final farewell punch. The distraction gave Zheng his chance. He wrenched his left arm free from Hawkin's grasp, and his hand disappeared into his blazer. It emerged clutching the knife. He struck at his opponent.

Merceret saw it coming and, in desperation, slashed the side of his right hand at Zheng's wrist. It broke his grip, and the knife flew through the air to land on the concrete floor, only a couple of paces in front of Max. Merceret followed through with a vicious low blow to Zheng's stomach.

Max knew there was no going back. He and Zheng were in for a very serious and possibly dangerous beating. He had to stop them. Picking up the knife, he ran towards Merceret and pushed the blade hard against the older boy's side. Zheng's makeshift design proved highly efficient. With his fingers gripping the string as tightly as he could, he was able to drive the stiletto blade through the older boy's blazer and into his flesh.

He pulled out the knife, but at a different angle, which widened the wound, then stepped back. Merceret's hand disappeared inside his blazer. When he lifted it aside, his hand and shirt were covered in blood. He staggered, and Hawkins let go of Zheng to support his friend, who was slowly sinking to his knees.

'You stupid little sod,' called out Hawkins, 'run and get help. Tell them to ring for a doctor…'

Afterwards, Max and Zheng had only a vague memory of running back to the house and banging on Mr Sykes' door, Max still with the knife in his hand. Fortunately, Matron had also been there. She rushed out to the bike shed whilst the housemaster telephoned for help. Remembering her first aid training, she used Hawkins' shirt to make a pad and stem the bleeding. Merceret was placed on a stretcher and carried to the sanatorium, where the local doctor reported that Merceret had been extremely fortunate. The blade had not penetrated deeply enough to damage a vital organ. But it would have to be stitched. Mercifully, the boy fainted.

The school's retainer made a substantial contribution to his practice income. Merceret recovered, and the doctor acquiesced to the headmaster's plea for discretion. However, four sets of parents had to be notified and summoned to the school. There were several meetings – without sherry – in the headmaster's study. Edmund Merceret demanded that the German boy be expelled.

'Not going to happen, I'm afraid,' came the unexpected response. 'I have conducted a very thorough investigation. Both Housemaster and Matron have given evidence, and I have also spoken privately with all four boys, although as things stand, I do not intend to make my findings public.

'That said, I can tell you that your nephew has been conducting a nasty bullying campaign against the two foreign pupils,' he continued, 'which has been going on since the beginning of term. And much as I deplore the use of a knife, it was very much a desperate act to save a friend.'

What the headmaster did not say was that mention of the presence of two sons of senior foreign diplomats had not only been most favourably received by visiting parents of prospective British pupils but there had also been enquiries from other embassies. Parkbury's future depended upon his ability to attract income. And he had been surprised by the potential generated by the arrival of Max and Zheng.

So, the two foreign boys had to remain at school. Any expulsion, not that he felt it to be justified, would risk bringing the whole affair into the open. Both Housemaster and Matron had been negligent, but in exchange for their discretion, they would be reprimanded but not dismissed. The problem of the doctor had already been addressed, which left only one possible outcome.

'I'm afraid,' he told Merceret's and Hawkins' parents, 'that their conduct has gone well beyond what could be excused as a schoolboy prank. On occasion, they have been guilty of serious assault. Therefore, I must ask you to make alternative arrangements for the final year of their education. You may wish to choose another school or perhaps employ private tutelage. If the former, it will be up to you to offer a reason for the change of establishment. For my part, if I am contacted, I shall be prepared to give a good reference and make no mention of this lamentable affair. If the latter, then I will allow the boys to return, but only to take their end-of-year examinations. I will also provide advice to any tutors you may engage on how best to complete the Parkbury syllabus.'

The news was met with stunned silence. 'And the term's fees?' asked Hawkins' father eventually.

'I believe, Gentlemen, that we have nothing further to discuss,' replied the headmaster. 'I have already given instructions for both boys to be ready to leave today. Please take them with you now as you depart.'

Left alone in his study, despite the early hour, he poured a generous glass of sherry.

* * * *

Max and Zheng continued their education, no longer troubled by boys from the upper sixth. But Max continued to feel not fully accepted at Parkbury. Merceret and Hawkins had been popular. He knew other boys viewed him as being responsible for their departure. Over time, he developed a growing awareness that he was addressed less warmly by some of the masters. Although he enjoyed team games, he was not selected to represent the school. When it came to casting for school plays, not once was he chosen for a lead part. But academically, he was gifted. And he took pride in rubbing his examination results into the noses of his English classmates. His only real friend was Zheng. As for the other boys, if they found him arrogant, he did not care. He despised them.

In 1933, a year after Leopold von Hoesch assumed his post for the Weimar Republic, it ceased to exist. Instead, he found himself the representative in London of the Third Reich. On 10th April 1936, his tenure ended abruptly when he suffered a fatal stroke whilst in his bedroom at Prussia House. In his obituary, *The Times* paid warm tribute to the charming, old-school diplomat who had worked assiduously to redevelop and improve Anglo-German relations.

His successor was a politician and diplomat already well known to – and a supporter of – Adolf Hitler. Ulrich Friedrich

Wilhelm Joachim von Ribbentrop, appointed ambassador to the Court of St James in 1936, served for barely a year before returning to Germany. During that time, he worked closely with Wilhelm Naumann. But it was the boy, Max, in whom he was most interested.

During off-duty evenings with the family, he listened avidly to the boy's experience of an English public school and to the views Max had formed of his host nation. Most importantly, the young man spoke the language fluently, with no trace of an accent. During lengthy discussions about the future with von Ribbentrop, Max expressed a keen interest in politics and a wish eventually to become a Party member.

In 1937, Hitler recalled von Ribbentrop to Berlin with the intention of appointing him Foreign Secretary the following year. When Max Naumann left school in 1938, his results would have earned him a place at either of England's finest universities. Instead, he accepted a position within von Ribbentrop's entourage.

Chapter 8

'I want you to continue your education,' announced von Ribbentrop.

'But I'm almost nineteen,' Max objected. They were in the study of a chalet on the banks of the *Großer Wannsee*. Covering almost three-square kilometres and the largest of Germany's inland lakes, the location in southwest Berlin housed a number of luxury homes popular with the highest ranks of the Nazi Party.

'It's not a school,' countered von Ribbentrop. 'Think of it more as a university for the elite of the Third Reich. *Ordensburg Vogelsang* is one of three such institutions built on the express orders of the Führer. It opened in 1936 and is designed to produce the future senior leaders of the Party. You will be one of only the third year to enter, and most of your fellow students – who are called *Junker* Cadets – will be a little older than you, although still in their twenties. The entry requirements, apart from the usual Aryan rules, include former military service. But you have a different diplomatic and language background. I have made enquiries. Because of my Party influence, I can tell you now that there will be no difficulty in securing your place.'

'But what would I study, and how long would I have to be there?' Max persisted.

'Perhaps one year, maybe two,' came the reply. 'As for your studies, emphasis is placed on geopolitics, with particular reference to the policies of the Fatherland, together with a total understanding of Nazi racial theories and their practical implementation. There is a strict regime of sport and physical fitness,' he added, 'which should not present any problems.

Equestrian activities are popular, and *Vogelsang* has its own airfield where you will be taught to fly.' Von Ribbentrop could see from the expression on Max's face that he was now interested.

'Eventually,' he continued, 'I want you to join the *Abwehr*, our military intelligence service. Your father may have told you that I am not liked by many of our Party's hierarchy. It's pure jealousy. I come from a distinguished military family. Most of my peers are common upstarts. I speak French and English; I have lived abroad. And the Führer has always valued my understanding of foreign affairs. Perhaps above all,' he informed Max with a hint of pride, 'in 1933, I was instrumental in helping him become Chancellor. You may not be aware that, to this day, I am the only person able to meet with *Herr* Hitler without a prior appointment.

'But there are many who would rejoice at my downfall,' he went on. 'So I have cultivated a number of assets in other departments of state, men loyal to me, who are senior enough to be able to keep me informed of their masters' intentions.

'As a graduate of *Vogelsang*,' von Ribbentrop explained, 'together with your knowledge of English life and fluency in their language, you would be an attractive prospect for the *Abwehr*. And an invaluable source of information for me. I am now the Reich's Foreign Secretary. With my patronage, your future would be assured. So do we have an understanding?' von Ribbentrop asked. There was no warmth in his smile.

Max did not need time to consider. He would have to make his way in the world. Increasingly, there was talk of a possible war with England. The *Abwehr* would be heavily involved with espionage against a country and people for whom he had retained a dislike bordering on hatred. And an education at *Vogelsang*, plus service with the *Abwehr* and the patronage of a Secretary of State who enjoyed the Führer's friendship and confidence… his future within the Party would be assured. Dazzled by the prospect that one day he, too, might aspire to high office, he did not hesitate to agree.

Located in the rolling uplands of the vast *Eifel* National Park, *Ordensburg Vogelsang* was constructed on a wooded mountain spur above the *Urfttal* dam. Its barrack-like buildings, made of concrete but faced with dark stone, looked brutalistic and forbidding. The accommodation was in *Kameradschaftshäuser*, comrade dormitories, each housing fifty *Junker* Cadets. The sports and recreational facilities, however, were superb.

Early morning physical training, mostly running, was at first exhausting, but Max had little difficulty keeping up with his fellow students. They were soon at their peak of physical fitness. Mornings and evenings were allocated to academic studies, but afternoons and weekends were devoted to sports. He soon became a confident equestrian, which he quite enjoyed, but it was the Bücker Bü 131B that captured his affection. The latest biplane to be built in Germany had two open tandem cockpits and fixed landing gear. Max trained on the version with the 105-horsepower Hirth engine. Fast and agile, he loved it. By the end of the first term, he had soloed. He was soon a competent aerobatic pilot. His instructor assumed that Max would progress to the *Luftwaffe*. He could not have been more wrong.

A small group of Max's intake had an additional element within their syllabus. Twice a week, they were separated from their fellow students. Under strict orders to reveal nothing, they were trained in the skills needed in a future role for which they had been provisionally selected.

Unarmed combat training was brutal. But Max, knowing that his future depended upon proving himself and that there was no alternative, no way back, applied himself with the grit and fortitude nurtured all those years ago in an unpleasant British boarding school.

Weapon and explosives training he quite enjoyed. Tradecraft he found fascinating. Especially when, at the end of this section, they were driven to Bonn and had to put their instruction to practical tests during a week in the city. He excelled at losing his pursuers, following unseen, covert surveillance, and achieving undetected hand passes and dead letter drops. His code work and radio transmission speeds were amongst the fastest of his group.

When, after two years, he was recalled to Berlin and ordered by von Ribbentrop to apply formally to join the *Abwehr*, the former boy from an English public school was now a trained agent. Moreover, he was a committed Nazi and almost entirely without conscience. His first appointment was as a junior intelligence officer on the staff of *Abwehr* headquarters Berlin. Von Ribbentrop's plan began to bear fruit.

* * * *

Werner's journey, travelling first class by train from Munich to Berlin, was uneventful. The *Anhalter Bahnhof* terminus station, known as "The Gateway to the South", took its name because it passed through the historic state of Anhalt. He checked his case into the left luggage office and made his way into the *Askanischer Platz*. His priority was to establish a base before embarking upon his mission to identify the agent now running the *Abwehr's* operation in Great Britain.

He purchased a street map of the greater Berlin area, several local newspapers, and settled himself inside a *Kaffeehaus*. If possible, he did not want to book into a hotel where he knew the documents of new arrivals would be examined by the state security services. There was also the possibility that a former *SS* colleague might recognise him. As he read through a list of accommodation offers, one advert caught his eye: a guest house not too far from the city centre, towards the Potsdam area, offered "superior rooms and cuisine for discerning ladies and gentlemen". It was a fair walk, but after all those hours on the train, he did not mind.

It was a large, terraced building, probably dating from the last century when it would have been the home of a well-off senior official or perhaps a minor industrialist. Unfortunately, there was no sign in the window indicating vacancies. Nevertheless, there was no harm in asking. A well-built, red-haired woman of indeterminate middle age answered the door. She was handsome rather than attractive, but she would have been a beauty not too many years ago. He removed his hat.

In response to his query, *Frau* Hartmann invited him inside. She had a room available on the first floor, whilst the attic, once the servants' quarters, had been converted into a small suite with its own bathroom. Meals were taken in the dining room. The suite was considerably more expensive, so she was delighted when Werner indicated that he would take it. Perhaps an indefinite stay, but he was content to pay for a week in advance, with thereafter a week's notice on either side. And no, she confirmed, she did not need his documents. As this was a small, private business establishment, she was not under the thumb of the authorities. Werner suspected that the lack of a window sign had more to do with trying to avoid tax, but the arrangement was ideal for his purpose. He informed her that he would eat out, collect his suitcase, and return later that evening. His *Reichsmark* secured keys to the suite and the front door.

Entering the dining room for breakfast, he was pleased to see that it offered individual tables. He helped himself to *Brötchen*, a selection of cold meats and a hard-boiled egg. As he was buttering one of the rolls, a waitress – black dress and white lace headband – entered with a pot of coffee. It was indeed, he reflected, superior accommodation and cuisine.

Werner's next problem was making contact with one of the recently retired *Abwehr* officers named by his father. The trouble was, their meetings had been arranged through *Herr* Kühn's office when he had still been in post. The general did not have a home address, although he recalled Conrad Kühn once mentioning that he and his wife lived in Spandau, not far from the *Spandauer* forest, where they enjoyed walking their dog. But once retired and no longer active within their like-minded group, and as opposition to Hitler's ever more powerful régime was ruthlessly exterminated, the general had judged it safer to allow contact to lapse. For Werner, marching into the headquarters of German military intelligence and asking for a forwarding address was not an option.

His problem was solved by a visit to Potsdam's main *Reichspost* office. Conrad Kühn had been a senior *Abwehr* officer. There was every possibility his position would have entitled him to a telephone at his residence. Perhaps, on retirement, he had been allowed to keep it. If so, he would be listed simply as a private subscriber, together with his address. Werner was jubilant! There it was: Kühn, Conrad, *27 Gartenstraße,* Spandau.

He took the *S-Bahn*. *Gartenstraße*, as its name implied, lay alongside a beautiful municipal park not far from the forest. Number 27 was a detached villa in its own grounds. Not surprisingly, as the home of a former intelligence service officer, it was surrounded by a two-metre-high wall. But *Herr* Kühn was now retired. One of the double gates to the driveway stood open.

An elderly gentleman, roughly his father's age, answered the door. '*Herr* Kühn?' Werner enquired politely. 'And who are you?' came the cautious response.

'Sir, my name is Werner Scholtz. You are acquainted with General Scholz, my father. He gave me your name.'

'Hans Scholtz is your father?' came the reply.

'No, sir,' answered Werner. 'My father is General Gustav Scholz, and I am – or was – *Sturmbannführer* Werner Scholtz.

'You had better come in,' said Conrad Kühn, stepping back to hold open the door. The quick, initial identity check was not lost on Werner. Clearly, the retired intelligencer's mind was as sharp as ever.

He followed the older man into a combined study and snug. *Herr* Kühn waved him to an armchair on one side of a fireplace, then seated himself. Werner had already decided that there was no point in being other than absolutely honest. He offered a precise but accurate account of recent events, including his role inside the organisation working within Hitler's régime, although he was now working for the British.

'I still have my contacts,' said Kühn when he had finished. 'Some of us retired, others still serving. We meet occasionally, mostly for a good lunch. Or as good as you can get, now that Hitler has started this *verdammter* war. The talk was that you had deserted. Knew no son of Gustav's would ever have done that. Pleased to hear the truth.'

Werner explained how the original *Abwehr* network had been broken by the British but that now, a new operation had been set up in Great Britain. It was running *Abwehr* agents again, but headed up, they believed, by a woman. 'If you agree with my father that Hitler will ruin Germany unless he is stopped,' Werner concluded, 'then we have to identify this woman. That's why I am seeking your help.'

Herr Kühn was silent for a moment. 'There was office gossip at the time,' he said eventually. 'It was highly unusual, a woman in the building who wasn't a secretary or a typist. I saw her several times. Pretty little thing. Lovely red hair. But my speciality was Naval intelligence, not the section handling our operations in Britain. We only spoke once, briefly, when she was on her way out after a meeting. Tapped on my door and said she had been asked to pass on regards from a former colleague, Ernst Wagner. Apparently, when she wasn't in Berlin, she lived with Ernst and Hanna in Hamburg. Had done for years.

'I'm afraid that's all I can tell you,' he said after a brief pause. 'But you are welcome to stay for a coffee, or perhaps something stronger if you prefer.'

This last remark sounded rather hopeful, as if the old intelligence officer would welcome the excuse, but Werner sensed that, at last, he might be getting somewhere. 'This *Herr* Wagner in Hamburg, what can you tell me about him?' he persisted.

'Good man,' Kühn offered. 'Spent some time in Northern Ireland before the war. Did a lot of work for us. In fact, I remember now, rumour had it that it was Wagner who introduced the girl to us in the first place because she was also fluent in English. That help you?'

His mind was spinning. There could well be a trail. Ireland... Wagner... Germany... intelligence... fluent in English... unknown to MI6... an ideal candidate to rebuild their operation in England. She could be the one.

'Tell me,' he asked, trying to keep any hint of excitement from his voice, 'do you by any chance have an address for this *Herr* Wagner?'

Herr Kühn extracted a Rolodex from a desk drawer, flipped open a card, and handed the open index to Werner. 'I can't go making enquiries in my old building,' he stated flatly, 'far too suspicious. But if you want to trace the girl, you might find out who she is at the Wagners' place in Hamburg. But mind how you go. I happen to know Ernst's a Party member.'

Werner thought for a few seconds. Then, 'If it's still on offer,' he said to *Herr* Kühn, 'I would welcome something a little stronger.'

Chapter 9

Werner's train journey to Hamburg passed without incident. Unlike Berlin, he was a stranger to the city. There was no chance of meeting someone who might recognise him, so he had no concerns about booking into a hotel. He did not expect to be there for more than a few days, and his Swiss-German papers identifying him as *Herr* Erich Richter were in order. Moreover, a banker would have every reason to visit the city. He suspected that the police would check on new arrivals at city centre hotels every day, but probably not those in the suburbs. He found a small, rather expensive but very comfortable guest house adjacent to the Altona district, but just a little further away from the city centre. A well-dressed, middle-aged lady behind the reception counter looked at his passport and then set it aside, telling him that if he wrote down his address, she would make an entry in the register as soon as she had a moment.

There was no question of being able to search Ernst Wagner's office. The Naval intelligence building would be far too well protected. If there were any clue to the identity of the red-haired girl identified by Conrad Kühn, he would have to look for it at the house she had shared with the family.

The Wagner residence was a large, terraced affair on a tree-lined *Allee*. Its three floors and basement suggested generous accommodation for a family and perhaps one or two live-in servants. The front door opened to steps leading directly onto the pavement. Alongside, a second set descended to the basement. Looking over the railing, he saw that the top half of a door at the bottom had two good-sized vertical glass panels separated by a narrow pillar of wood. A walk around the block revealed a walled garden to the rear. A set of double gates gave access from a smaller, less imposing street, presumably used for tradesmen's deliveries.

Had he been able to watch the routine of the house for a few days, he would have preferred a daytime visit when the house might have been empty. Unfortunately, there was nowhere offering a suitable vantage point – not a single café, beer hall or even an empty building. And he could hardly loiter there, in the street, hour after hour, in broad daylight. So it would have to be a night entry. In some ways, more risk, but there was no alternative.

He used the rest of the day to purchase the tools he needed: a diamond-tipped glass cutter, some putty, and a torch and batteries. He also bought a heavy black polo neck pullover. This and a pair of dark flannels would not look out of place on the streets during the evening. He would not attempt an entry until the early hours, well past midnight, when the family would be sound asleep. But he would be conspicuous walking the streets at that time in the morning. Fortunately, many of the more desirable suburbs boasted a small park, with benches for the elderly to sit and admire the flower beds or perhaps to watch a children's play area. There was one not too far from the Wagner house. Werner made himself as comfortable as possible within a thicket of bushes.

At half past two, he walked to the house. Opening the iron gate, which squeaked only quietly, he descended to the basement door. It was the work of minutes to putty the bottom left-hand corner of the pane, cut and lift away a piece of glass, and feel carefully through the hole. His luck was in. The key had been left in the lock. It turned almost soundlessly – the soft click could not have been heard from two floors above.

He switched on the torch and found himself in a laundry room – double sinks and draining boards, a boiler, a mangle, and overhead, pulley-operated drying racks. There were two doors. One led to a boiler room at the rear of the property, the other to a staircase.

The ground floor was tiled; the wooden staircase carpeted. Werner had to find the room used by the young woman when she was in Hamburg. Slowly, treading on the side of each stair to reduce the chance of a board creaking, he made his way to the upstairs corridor. The master bedroom would almost certainly be at the front. The door to the one next to it was ajar. With his fingers over most of the lens, he shone the torch onto the foot of one of two children's beds. Quickly, he moved the light away and pulled the door almost shut. The next room contained two full-sized single beds but was unoccupied – presumably a guest bedroom.

Finally, at the rear of the house, he found a room also empty but littered with telltale personal possessions. There was a pink dressing robe on the bed, slippers underneath, and a tennis racquet leaning against the wall in one corner. A wardrobe contained a woman's clothing. He moved to a small writing desk set against the window and looked through both drawers. There were several documents and letters, all addressed to a *Fraulein* Margarete Wagner, but nothing bearing a photograph. And even if she were the woman they were looking for, she would not be using her German name in the United Kingdom. He searched the rest of the room, including the bedside cabinet, but it looked as if his journey had been for nothing.

Werner made his way back down the stairs and turned towards the basement staircase when he noticed that the door to the drawing room was ajar. On impulse, he walked in and shut it behind him. The room was expensively furnished with heavy, damask chairs, as well as a baby grand piano. Perhaps it was not often played because the lid was down and almost covered with framed photographs. He passed his light over them. They were nearly all of the Wagner family. At first, it was a young couple, then a mother and father with first one and then two children, from babes in arms to the present: a family history taken at one-year intervals.

But one small, horizontal picture gripped his attention. It was an informal family group, *Herr* Wagner and his wife, a glass of wine in hand, seated on cane chairs in a garden. Standing behind them was a young woman holding a small child, probably less than a year old. The photograph was black and white. *Herr* Wagner had fair hair, Hanna's was dark. The other young woman's was somewhere in between. And she was pretty. Could this be the visitor to the *Abwehr* headquarters described by *Herr* Kühn? Werner was fairly confident that it was. Only a close family friend or associate would have merited a place in the collection on the piano. He slipped the photograph, still in its silver frame, into his pocket, then rearranged those around the gap to cover its removal.

As he closed the basement door behind him, he knew there was nothing he could do to conceal the forced entry. Hopefully, it would remain a mystery to the family. Someone had broken into the house, but it would appear that nothing had been stolen. With any luck, they would never notice – or at least not for a long time – that one small photograph was missing.

Werner did not return to his guest house until just before breakfast. Approaching the lady proprietor, now standing behind the reception counter, he remarked that it was cold for an early morning walk. She smiled politely – assuming he must have left when she was attending to the dining room. He informed her that he would be leaving in half an hour and would take breakfast on the train. Adding a generous tip to his bill, as she returned his passport, he asked casually whether the police had commented upon a visitor from Switzerland.

'Oh no, sir,' came the response, 'I'm not expecting them till tomorrow or the next day.' He couldn't help smiling as he returned to his room. If he knew how these establishments operated, almost certainly, a register entry for an overnight visitor had not yet been made. Nor would it be, not now. His *Reichsmark* would pass directly to her pocket and not through the books. *Sometimes*, he thought, *human nature could be a wonderful thing.*

Werner allowed himself an extra day back in Munich, spending it with his father at Buchbach. At the news of the assassination, the old general merely lowered his head in sadness at the memory of his late wife. 'You do not bear any responsibility for this, *Vati*,' he told him, anxious to spare his father any further pain. 'Remember, it was my decision to ask for his name and to borrow your Walther. I won't go into detail, but when he died, *SS-Sturmbannführer* Roth knew who I was. And what's more, I would do the same again.'

Their evening was tinged with sadness, not least because neither of them knew when – or even if – they would see each other again. But the old man was cheered a little by Werner's account of his time in Berlin and Hamburg and particularly by the news that his old friend Conrad Kühn was alive and well in retirement.

'He was a great help,' Werner recalled, telling his father how there was now at least a possibility of finding the head of the *Abwehr's* operation in Great Britain. The thought of another blow to Hitler's régime lifted the old man's spirits, as did the bottle of decent brandy they finished between them. All he needed now, thought Werner as he took himself to bed, was a safe journey back to Switzerland.

Before taking his leave, Werner returned his father's Walther, together with the caution that Roth's body would be found eventually, and his father might be a suspect. Fortunately, he had an alibi. Anna could confirm that on the day in question, her employer had been at Buchbach. And, the General recalled, that was also the day he had discussed selling his late wife's mare with the farmer providing livery.

'Even so,' Werner warned, 'forensic ballistics could link the weapon to the remains of the bullet that had killed the *SS* man. So whatever you do, make sure it can never be found.'

'Still got my 12 bores,' the old man replied with just the hint of a smile. 'But you never know when this might come in handy again, so the Walther will be well wrapped in oiled cloth, inside a waterproof container, and finish up half a metre or so under the surface, somewhere on the estate.'

Werner quite enjoyed his morning ride back to Munich but felt sad to garage the bike for what could be the last time. Taking a last fond look at the machine and then his Mercedes, he locked the doors and returned to the apartment. With his hat firmly pulled down to hide the slight change of hair colour, he was relieved to learn from the concierge that there were no messages and that no one had been asking for him. Stepping away from the building, he paused to don his spectacles, then set out for the *Hauptbahnhof*.

As before, his papers were scrutinised on the German side of the border. But again, the arrogant indifference of a well-dressed Swiss-German banker travelling first class did the trick. Although he could not help a feeling of relief when, after a cursory check by the Swiss border police, the train set off for the capital.

* * * *

Back in London, after an exhausting return journey, again flying via Madrid and Lisbon, he was met at Croydon airport and driven directly to the office of Sir Manners Fitzgibbon.

Doreen Jackman and Bill Ives were summoned to join them. 'We'll get this photograph enlarged and run off a few copies,' announced Sir Manners after Werner had given them a verbal account of his time in Germany. 'And jolly well done, by the way. But if this Margarete Wagner is our woman, she won't be using that name over here. She could be on a fake passport using a completely different identity.'

'On the other hand,' offered Doreen Jackman, 'if she speaks English fluently, as this retired German intelligence man told Werner, and if the Wagners lived in Belfast before the war, there might be a connection there. Perhaps she's a native of the city and went back to Germany with them. If so, she would have needed a passport. It's a hell of a long job, but we could check the photograph against those on the passport applications of all young Belfast women issued in the years before the war.'

'There's another avenue,' put in Bill Ives. 'We know this Wagner fellow was Naval intelligence and that he was in Belfast. He would have to have had contact with our shipping industry. We could make enquiries within the business community over there and see what comes up. It's not that long ago. Someone might remember the family and whether this girl had any association with them.'

Sir Manners thought for a few seconds. 'Tell you what,' he turned to Werner, 'I'll have you driven home. Take a long weekend; you more than deserve it. But I would like you to travel to Belfast on Monday.'

* * * *

'*Herr Generalmajor*,' he replied, 'if you had been sent to an English boarding school, you would dislike them as much as do I.' But Max knew that he had not been summoned to discuss British public schools. Hans Paul Oster, Deputy Chief under *Admiral* Canaris, slid a photograph across his desk. 'Recognise this man?' he asked.

Max glanced at the image of a fit, good-looking man in civilian clothes, probably in his early forties, although it was difficult to tell. He was a snappy dresser. 'American?' he guessed. 'Where was this taken?'

'Right first time,' said Oster. 'Yes, he's an American. General Ira C Eaker is second in command of the United States Eighth Army Air Force. However, the important point is that this photograph was taken very recently, outside the American Embassy and Consulate in Grosvenor Square, London. It confirms what we have long suspected would be the case. The Americans have decided to give priority to the war in Europe. They are about to station a significant portion of their Army Air Force in Britain.'

'Which, presumably, *Herr Generalmajor*, is why I am here today,' observed Max.

'*Jawohl*,' came the curt confirmation. 'Once we knew for sure that the British had broken our codes, we had to rebuild our network in the United Kingdom. It is now headed by a very capable young woman operating under the name of Margaret Minogue. But neither she nor her operatives are particularly attuned to aviation. Nor does she have any particular affiliation with the Americans. However, she will be your initial contact and will help you to establish a base somewhere in the area.

'I have new transmission arrangements in place with *Fraulein* Minogue,' he went on, 'and she has been sent a warning order confirming your arrival. We now have a book-to-book code, and the British do not know which one we are using. As an additional precaution, many standard phrases are substituted with a single numeral. And unlike the old *Abwehr* codes, I believe this new system is unbreakable.

'Now, to return to your mission. We believe,' the *Generalmajor* explained, 'that the Americans will either take over existing Royal Air Force bases or build new ones – probably both. We need to know as much as possible about their deployment, now and when they become operational. Where they are, types of aircraft and defences. Anything that might help us to disrupt and degrade this new threat to the *Reich*.'

He steepled his fingers. 'You are to become a new, parallel organisation in England, designed specifically to operate against the American Air Army. A unique asset, Max,' he added by way of encouragement, mistaking the younger man's surprised expression for one of concern. 'You are able to blend seamlessly into what the English call their upper class. Your cover will also give you the ability to appeal to and integrate with all ranks of Americans.' He lifted his shoulders. 'I wish I could give you more detailed guidance, but I can't. I can tell you only that this is your mission: to penetrate and operate effectively against Britain's new and powerful ally.'

Max was quiet for several seconds. 'That's a very broad and rather vague remit,' he said at last, 'although the aim is clear enough. Resources?' he queried.

'Almost limitless, within reason,' came the reply. 'Money, certainly. We envisage that you will recruit and develop your own local sources. If you need specialist help from Germany, we can, of course, fly people in. But they won't have your fluency or background. Although, unlike your good self, they will be expendable.

'We can continue this conversation over lunch,' he said, rising to his feet. 'Afterwards, think it over, and we'll talk again. But I want to fly you in sometime next week. It'll be a night drop from a Heinkel HE 111, but you've done that before.' Max knew that lunch in the General's private dining room would be excellent. But right now, his mind was in turmoil.

* * * *

Conditions were not perfect. Sea fog, which had not been predicted, had forced the pilot to fly higher than he would have wished. He just had to hope that he would still be under the English radar. 'Better get ready; we'll be over the coast in a few minutes,' he warned his passenger. Max acknowledged and handed his headset to the dispatcher, who double-checked his fixed line before patting him on the back. Max readied himself for the dreaded head-first exit.

Seconds later, the fuselage shuddered, and the man next to him was almost cut in half as a Hawker Hurricane night fighter raked the fuselage with its four, twenty-millimetre wing-mounted Hispano cannons. It had attacked from above and behind. The dorsal gunner, distracted by headphone traffic, had been caught napping and had not fired a shot. The Heinkel's side, ventral and nose guns had been blind-sided. It looked as if the co-pilot was also dead, and from the ominous glow on the canopy, Max realised that the port engine was on fire.

'Jump!' screamed the pilot. Max didn't hesitate. As soon as he was stable, he watched the stricken aircraft, blazing now, as it went down in an ever-steepening dive. The Hurricane pilot did not follow it down, but neither, thankfully, did he turn back towards Max.

At first, knowing that the prevailing wind was from the south and west, he was concerned that he might land in the surf. But a high somewhere over Scotland had produced a gentle north-easterly. Max reckoned that he had jumped from somewhere around four hundred metres. He was drifting gently towards farmland. Smoke from a nearby cottage confirmed that there was only a light breeze. But the landing did not go according to plan. The deeply ploughed field was frosted hard, its ridges like concrete. A decent pair of boots would have helped, but he had jumped only with stout shoes. An ankle went sideways. Had Max not been badly winded, he would have gasped with pain.

Fortunately, he was able to gather in his 'chute, awkward though it was on one knee. The nearest hedge was not too far away. Max prised himself upright, his weight on his good leg. But as soon as he tried to balance on two feet, the stabbing pain returned. It was bad but just about bearable, which told him that the ankle was sprained, perhaps badly, but not broken. Luckily for him, the nearest hedge was only about twenty metres away. Carrying his 'chute, he half hopped, half hobbled to shelter beneath its overhanging branches. At least he would be able to ball up and shove his parachute well into the undergrowth. But first, he took a knife from his belt and cut one long strip of camouflage-patterned silk.

Removing his right shoe, he bound the ankle and foot as tightly as he dared. It was difficult to put the shoe back on; it would lace only loosely across the top two eyes, but at least now, walking slowly and with care, he could just about support his weight.

His 'chute hidden, he intended to be well clear by daylight, which from the gradual lightening in the eastern sky, could not be far off. But as he turned away from the hedge, something moved in his peripheral vision. About twenty-five metres away, a figure, almost certainly the farmer, was advancing towards him. Already aiming from the waist, he was holding a twelve-bore, double-barrelled shotgun. Max dropped his knife and half-turned towards the newcomer, who was now clearly visible over his right shoulder. Fortunately, his light-fawn, long riding mackintosh, with its belt and epaulettes, resembled a British military pattern.

'My dear sir,' he announced in his best English public school voice. 'I'd be obliged if you didn't point that thing at an officer. It just might go off.' The farmer continued his advance but with less certainty now. Confused by what he had heard, he lowered the weapon, the barrels now pointing halfway between them, towards the ground.

Max slowly moved his partly concealed right arm to undo a button and slide a hand under his mackintosh. Fingers found the flap of a holster, then the butt of his 9mm Walther semi-automatic pistol. You never knew, hitting the ground, who or what might be waiting. He blessed his precaution of having jumped with a round chambered, using the decocking lever to lower the hammer safely. He needed to apply only one long, double-action trigger pull for the first shot.

Still only half-turned towards his target, Max raised the weapon. They fired almost simultaneously. The farmer's discharge slammed into him, knocking Max to the ground. His head hit something hard, and everything went black.

Chapter 10

Werner took the overnight ferry from Liverpool to Belfast and checked in to the central Midland Station Hotel.

There were three facts to go on: first, Ernst Wagner had been in Naval intelligence; second, he had spent some time in Belfast before the war; and finally, he had introduced the red-haired girl who spoke fluent English to the *Abwehr*. So there was every chance that this girl had accompanied the family on their return from Belfast to Germany. But initially, she had almost certainly been a native of the city.

There was an obvious connection between Naval intelligence and shipping. He showed the photograph to several maritime companies. In two of them, Wagner was recognised as an academic associated with Queen's University Belfast. He struck gold. Enquiries there revealed that Wagner had held a post-graduate teaching post before returning to Germany in 1938. Oisin O'Kelly, a somewhat wizened senior lecturer past retirement age, had stayed on for the duration. He took the photograph, placed half-moon glasses on his nose, tapped the photo with the back of his fingers and announced, 'Delightful chap. The wife and I had dinner with the Wagners several times. Knew how to throw a good drinks party as well.'

'And the girl standing behind *Herr* Wagner and his wife, with a small child?' he asked, almost holding his breath.

'Their nanny,' came the reply. 'Lovely looking girl, but you can see that for yourself.'

'Can you give me a name?' Werner asked. Now, he *was* holding his breath.

O'Kelly thought for a moment. 'It was a few years ago,' he said slowly, 'but she was a Belfast person. Margaret something or other, but I can't remember if I was ever introduced formally. Sorry, but I don't think I ever knew her surname.'

Werner could not hide his disappointment. 'I'll give you my phone number,' he said eventually. 'If you or your wife should remember, or if you can think of someone else who might know, I would be grateful if you would give me a ring. It really is rather important…'

'Do better than that,' the old man replied. 'Tell you who would know. I remember Hanna telling my wife how pleased they were with her. She was living in, because she had nowhere else to go. Her father had been killed in the riots. Apparently, she was recommended to them by their local parish priest.' He gave Werner the name of the street in which the Wagners had rented their house. It was not difficult to ascertain the address of the nearest presbytery.

Werner knocked on the door and raised his hat to the rather squat middle-aged woman who opened it. 'Good morning,' he greeted her. 'I am hoping to have a word with Father Coyle.'

'Is he expecting you?' she asked.

'No,' he replied, 'but I have come rather a long way, and it is a matter of some official importance.'

'I'm just the housekeeper,' she replied. 'Breda Sullivan's my name. Father Coyle is out at the moment, but he said he'd be back for coffee. He won't be long, so you're welcome to come in and wait.'

He was shown into a room over-stuffed with heavy, dark brown leather furniture that obviously served as a lounge for the occupants of the presbytery. Werner settled onto a two-seater sofa. 'Can I get you a cup of tea or coffee, sir?' asked the housekeeper. 'Coffee would be most kind,' he replied. As she left, he extracted the photograph from his inside pocket and set it on a low table.

She returned a few minutes later bearing a tray on which stood a cup and saucer, a bowl of sugar lumps and a small jug of milk. 'It's only Camp, sir, I'm afraid,' she told him, 'but it's all we can get.' Setting down the tray, she glanced at the photo. Her eyebrows lifted.

'Do you recognise anyone?' asked Werner, more in hope than expectation.

'The young girl, standing at the back, holding the child,' she replied. 'To be sure, that's Máiréad McGrath,' she said, picking up the photograph and looking at it more closely.

'You know her?' asked Werner, surprised.

'Indeed I do, or I did,' came the reply. 'The poor wee girl was orphaned before the war. I knew her and her father. It was I who told the good Father of her plight, and he found her a position with one of our parish families. I remember, because it was unusual at the time. They were foreigners – German, I think the Father said. Of course, they're not here now, not with the war and everything.'

'Mrs Sullivan,' he began, his voice low and serious, 'this is a security matter.' He produced a military identity document from his inside pocket, but she barely looked at it. 'We need to trace Máiréad as quickly as possible,' he went on. 'It's for her own protection. All we needed was a positive identification, which you have kindly provided. But the fewer people who are involved in our search, the safer she will be. I shall sip my coffee quickly and then take my leave, but I would be most grateful if you did not mention my visit here this morning to anyone, not even to the good Father. May I ask that of you, for Máiréad's protection?'

Breda Sullivan, as did most of her class, held an innate respect for authority, touched with a hint of fear. Nothing like this had ever happened in her life. She simply nodded her agreement. Afterwards, as she washed up his cup and saucer, she thought about her visitor. She had absolutely no wish to be caught up in any sort of "security" business, whatever that might mean. Clearly, it was in her best interest to do as he had asked.

They reconvened in Sir Manners' office. Doreen Jackman reported that the photograph of the girl provided by Werner matched that used in a 1938 passport application by one Máiréad McGrath. Werner's investigations in Germany and Belfast confirmed her identity and linked her conclusively to the *Abwehr*.

'There's no doubt,' concluded Sir Manners, 'that this is our woman. She won't be using her own name, but Máiréad – or Margaret – McGrath is now the head of their operation in this country.' He tapped the edge of the table with his fingertips. 'It is absolutely essential,' he said softly, 'that we find her, and as quickly as possible.'

* * * *

Max opened his eyes. His head was pounding, but he forced himself to look at the farmer, who was lying motionless on his back, perhaps twenty metres away. He could barely feel his right arm, and blood was seeping through a ragged tear in his mackintosh, just above the elbow. He managed to sit up, his back to the hedge. Using his foot, he hooked the Walther from where it had fallen. The weapon was undamaged, but when he tried to pick it up, pain lanced through his arm. He used his left hand to push it, for now, under the belt of his mackintosh.

Gripping the trunk of a bush, he managed to stand. Limping and swaying, he crossed to the farmer and dropped to one knee. It had been a good shot, centre mass. The man had died instantly.

Max broke open the side-by-side 12 bore, ejected the fired cartridge and lifted the unused one from the barrel. Patting down the farmer, he removed several more from a pocket and put them into his own. Despite the waves of pain in his arm and a swimming head, he managed to drag the corpse to the hedge and roll it underneath. He had to find warmth, rest, and shelter so he could attend to his injured arm. By keeping to the edge of the field, it was easier to walk, and with his left hand holding the shotgun by the end of the barrels as a makeshift support, he set off slowly for the nearby farm cottage.

Walther in hand, he called out from the yard and then banged on the door. There was no reply. It was unlocked. A quick tour confirmed that there was no one at home, although a fire was burning in the kitchen. A framed wedding photograph in the lounge showed a young couple, with another of the same couple and two children alongside it. From the untidy and non-too-clean state of the cottage, the farmer was a widower, living alone.

Despite an overwhelming urge to sleep, he undressed to his waist and inspected the arm. It was a mess, but only within a small area. And fortunately, it had been birdshot, not a heavier small game pellet. But quite a lot of it had penetrated his skin.

A kitchen cupboard yielded half a bottle of disinfectant. From the whiff of the sink, it probably hadn't been opened in a long time. He washed the wound, still with some pellets embedded, but he would worry about that later. He tore some bandage strips from a clean but unironed shirt taken from a bedroom drawer. The bed did not smell too savoury, but he found clean blankets in an airing cupboard. Max was exhausted. He locked the back door, dragged through cushion squabs from the sofa and chairs in the lounge, and crashed out on the kitchen floor in front of the fire.

His watch said three o'clock. His arm was tender and painful. The pellets had to come out. He found a cutthroat razor in the bathroom and sterilised it in boiling water. After half an hour of cutting, squeezing, and picking with his fingernails, he had a small mound of shot and fabric on the kitchen table. When he lifted his arm to the horizontal and splashed on some more disinfectant, he almost passed out. But the swelling around his ankle had eased. The farmer's body would probably not be found for days. He would risk one more night in the cottage.

Taking advantage of the fading daylight, he inspected the only other building, a small barn. Inside, he found an old tractor, the key still in the ignition. The fuel gauge said three-quarters full, and it started easily enough. Back in the kitchen, with wood from the barn, he rescued the fire from the embers and, despite the filthy condition of the top of the stove, made himself a stew from tins in the larder. He ate from the saucepan. The leftovers would do for breakfast.

He burned his bloodstained mackintosh and took what was probably a Sunday best jacket from a wardrobe. Who would question a tractor driven along country roads? Max knew that most signposts had been removed, but he had studied a map of the area. He would head west till he came to somewhere served by public transport, confident that he would reach Snettisham by nightfall.

* * * *

Margaret and Robert were spending more and more time together. She sometimes went to the farm on a Saturday evening, when they listened to the wireless and shared a bottle of Bob's wife's homemade blackberry and apple wine. Occasionally, they returned to The Rose and Crown. They were almost, but not quite, a couple. Fortunately, Robert had accepted her story: that *Hauptmann Ladurner*, a tale of Great War veterans trying to overthrow the *Weimar* Republic, had been given to her by Hanna Wagner when she had gone to work for them in Belfast and needed to learn German.

Bob's wife, Maeve, a large, kindly lady with a weathered face and work-worn hands, dwarfed her stick-insect husband. She told Margaret privately that she was delighted Robert had found a girlfriend. Now that his parents had died and he was living alone, running the farm, she had almost given up hope. Any time they wanted to spend a Sunday together, she offered, giving Margaret a not-so-gentle elbow nudge, her Bob would always volunteer to do the evening milking. 'Her Bob', Margaret suspected, had not been given much choice in the matter. They developed a routine of Sunday lunches and lazy evenings, alternatively at the farm or her cottage.

Margaret's coastal survey was long since completed and transmitted. Her hand-drawn maps and charts were sent to Berlin via London and Dublin. Neither was there any real need to continue with her outdoor land and botanical activities, although she still cycled around the countryside to preserve her cover. Twice, she met and assisted with a parachute insertion. Other than that, Berlin made little call on her time, although during her most recent schedule, she was less than delighted to be informed that she would receive a visitor, to whom she was ordered to extend every assistance.

Her relationship with Robert had developed slowly. He was, she realised, a reserved, old-fashioned-formal individual: prep school at eight, then a minor public school. No sister with friends offering a quick feel and fumble. Not even an exploratory kiss. And agricultural college was an almost exclusively male affair. It came as no surprise that it was at least two months after their first evening together before his kiss on the cheek progressed eventually to a touching of lips, accompanied by a tentative embrace. Perhaps it was just as well, although Margaret was both puzzled and frustrated. She found it hard to be sure of her own feelings. Much as she wanted Robert and, she finally admitted to herself, she did want him, she found it difficult to reconcile a future together with the lie she was living.

It was Christmas day, with 1941 about to morph into the new year and America now at war with Germany and Japan, when she was forced to confront her situation. That morning, Robert was in the milking parlour when she leant her bicycle against the sill under the kitchen window, lifted a small parcel from the basket and let herself into the house. She put four sausages into the oven and set the frying pan and eggs next to the range, ready for his return. She had dressed for the occasion but could only hope that her soft, woollen cardigan would not finish up smelling of fried breakfast.

Afterwards, over a cup of tea in front of a lounge fire, they exchanged gifts. Margaret's London banking contact had obtained a pair of soft, fur-lined leather driving gloves from Harrods. He handed her a carefully wrapped small box. She was almost moved to tears when she opened it to reveal a beautiful and very obviously expensive antique cameo broach.

'Robert,' she said quietly, her eyes glistening, 'thank you. I have never owned anything quite so beautiful.'

They listened to the wireless whilst she prepared lunch. Robert had raided the henhouse and killed, drawn and plucked a good-sized cock bird. She blessed her time at the Wagner household, where she had learned how to roast it with potatoes and parsnips.

They opened the first bottle of this year's wine. Margaret and Maeve had developed almost a cottage industry. The farm had apples, plums and blackberry hedges in abundance. The problem was that bacon, butter and sugar had been rationed since January the previous year. Bacon and butter they could produce for themselves, but eight ounces of sugar per person per week was not going to ferment much alcohol.

So that year, Robert had planted beet. Maeve, remembering country ways taught to her by her Irish grandmother, had boiled, strained and reduced the root vegetable to produce a dark, honey-like molasses. Sprinkling all the bowls they could find with just a tiny amount of rationed white sugar, this had helped the poured liquid to crystallise. Bob unearthed an old stone hand mill from one of the outbuildings. The resultant ground sugar was almost identical to its commercial brown counterpart. What's more, it imparted a honeyed bouquet to her wine that Maeve pronounced to be her best vintage ever.

After a fine lunch, for which Robert thanked her profusely, they were back in front of the lounge fire, side by side on a two-seater sofa. 'Be nice if we had a brandy,' he remarked. 'I might have been able to buy some in King's Lynn, but there was none to be had in the village.'

She patted his knee. 'I had almost forgotten,' she said, crossing to open a tall corner cupboard, from which she extracted a bottle and two small, stemmed glasses. 'Maeve gave me this. It's not brandy, but it's just as good. It's her homemade plum liqueur.'

He laughed. 'Don't tell me,' he said good-naturedly, 'it's her variation on the theme of potcheen! Will we go blind if we drink it?'

'Don't try to be so superior,' she chided with a smile. 'Maeve's very proud of it. She explained how you have to discard the first and the last part of the distillate, and she always errs on the safe side. Her family have been doing it for generations. And I'm Irish too, let me remind you. So that's two of us you will be insulting.' She poured and handed him a glass. 'Take a sip,' she offered

It was incredibly smooth, with a heady nose of fruit. It also induced an extremely warm glow. 'Well, I'm dashed,' Robert exclaimed. 'Maeve could charge a fortune for this.' He inserted a new needle into the gramophone arm and lowered it onto a twelve-inch Bakelite record of Christmas carols. One glass became two, and then three. At some stage, his arm rested around her shoulders, and she leant contentedly into his embrace. Afterwards, she remembered how they were kissing in a haze of plum alcohol. She pushed her tongue gently between his lips, then her own were apart, and he, too, was exploring. She felt his hand on her breast.

She did not mind, but suddenly, he slipped off the sofa onto one knee. 'Margaret,' he said seriously, 'will you marry me? Will you do me the honour of becoming my wife?'

Margaret was taken completely by surprise. A hand flew to cover her mouth. Her mind was racing. Should she accept or ask for time...?

He mistook her hesitation for rejection. 'I'm sorry,' he said. 'You were not expecting...'

Instinct came to the fore. 'Robert,' she responded, taking his hand and pulling him back up to sit facing her on the sofa, 'yes, of course I'll marry you, with all my heart.' Their kiss was urgent, almost bruising, but his hand did not return to her breast.

'You must have a ring,' he said, leaning away but gently holding her shoulders. 'We'll go to Lynn on Monday. I didn't dare hope... Margaret, I can't tell you how happy you have made me.'

'For God's sake, pour me another drink, my head's spinning,' she begged him. It gave her brief moments to think. There would be an engagement, but the wedding did not have to be immediate. He had never mentioned relatives, and she did not have any. Neither had he mentioned religion, and her Catholicism had lapsed long before leaving Ireland. Almost certainly, he would agree to a registry office, which would save the publicity of having banns read in church.

She could keep the cottage, at least for a while – just tell him she had signed a long lease – even though eventually, she could probably operate just as well from the farmhouse. Might have to tell Berlin there had to be a few changes, but that was a long way off. Somehow, she would make it work.

'I love you,' he told her, handing over her drink and setting his own on the floor beside the sofa. 'I want us to be together,' she said softly, placing a hand over his and giving it a small squeeze. 'But can we wait, till after the wedding, I mean…'

By way of agreement, he pressed the back of her hand to his lips. They sat for another hour, talking quietly about the future. 'It's getting late,' he said eventually, 'perhaps I should drive you back. I have to face the morning milking, and we have Bob and Maeve for lunch tomorrow.' He stood, extending a hand to help her up. 'It's been quite a day,' he told her, 'but I can honestly say, the best of my life.'

Chapter 11

Margaret had arranged to meet him at The Rose and Crown. At least she now knew what time he would be free after Saturday evening milking. They enjoyed a couple of drinks, chatting quietly, with the pleasing prospect of Sunday lunch and an evening together tomorrow. The landlord noticed that Margaret's hand on the table was covered permanently by Robert's. He nudged his wife and inclined his head towards them. 'That's a new one,' he said quietly. 'Reckon there be something afoot there.'

As usual, Robert did not come in; he just said his goodbyes at the gate, although their kisses these days hinted at a desire that was ever harder to ignore. They broke apart. Breathing deeply, she patted his chest, then watched as he walked along the lane. She did not turn away until he had disappeared into the night.

Max moved deeper into the lounge, well back from the window, as she walked to her door. He heard the swish of a heavy blackout curtain, and a hall light was switched on. She opened the lounge door and gasped as the loom revealed the dark outline of a figure seated in a chair, one hand resting on its arm, fingers half covering a black pistol.

'Máiréad,' said a male voice softly, 'or is it Margaret now? Don't be alarmed. Did they not tell you I was coming?'

Only then did she remember Berlin's warning, although they had not specified a time or date. It had annoyed her back then that, despite her questions, no other details had been forthcoming. Afterwards, with everything else that had happened, the information had slipped her mind.

'You are...' she began, leaving the question hanging.

'My English name is Max Staunton,' he said in German. 'He died in Germany with no living relatives in this country.'

'Who briefed you for this mission?' she asked in the same language, her composure somewhat recovered.

'*Generalmajor* Hans Osker, at 76-78 Tirpitzufer,' he replied. 'They did not give your details to the other agents you have assisted. I am told you simply helped them on their way. But I am here separately to target solely the Americans in this country. Rather than risk setting up a second base, they took the view that it would be more secure to make use of what you have established already. At least initially,' he added, 'although I may have to move on, depending upon how things develop.'

The exchange of information and the switch of languages satisfied them both. 'So, Max Staunton,' she reverted to English, 'you had better tell me what you believe I am going to do for you.'

'Would it be too much of an imposition,' he began politely, 'if I were to ask whether it would be possible for you to pour me a stiff drink? I have had a difficult and somewhat wounding journey. The stronger the better, although whatever you might have would be acceptable and very welcome.'

'It's Margaret now,' she told him, 'although I still have my original passport.' She put a match to the fire laid in the grate, then poured him a quarter tumbler of Maeve's plum liqueur and a smaller measure for herself. With the fire drawing nicely, she threw on a couple of extra logs and settled into the armchair opposite. He raised his glass by way of salute and took a generous pull before raising his eyebrows, together with a smile of appreciation.

'Our 'plane was hit crossing the English coast,' he told her. 'I got out just before it went down in flames. There were no other survivors. There was an altercation with a farmer, or perhaps he was just a farm hand. Either way, I had to shoot him, but he had a shotgun, and I collected a few pellets in my right arm.

'It's all right,' he added quickly, seeing her look of concern. 'If it's my health you're worried about, I patched it up myself. Although if you have a first aid box, I would like to change the dressing.'

She confirmed that she did.

'And if it's the mission you're anxious about, don't be,' he continued. 'The farmer's dead, and I can guarantee that I was not followed when I made my way here to your cottage.' He gave her a brief outline of the rest of his journey.

'So what is it you want from me?' she asked when he had finished.

'My radio will be delivered via Dublin,' he announced, 'new idea, safer method. So, for now, I want you to let Berlin know that I have arrived. They might wonder why it has taken a couple of days, but that's all they need to know. After that, I would like to rest up until my arm heals and I have full use of it again. Hopefully, no more than a week or so,' he suggested. 'And in the meantime, if we can, I need to find out where the Americans are putting their air bases in East Anglia.'

Margaret told him about Robert and the farm and, more immediately, how they would have lunch together tomorrow. 'Afterwards,' she said, 'he usually drives me back and comes in for a nightcap. You can't be here. If you want to stay for a while, it will be all right in the week, but I have to think of how best to explain away your presence. For you to be here suddenly tomorrow evening wouldn't be plausible. And you can't just sit out of sight in the spare room. This is an old cottage. If you so much as move from a chair, it makes the boards creak.'

Even a visit to the village pub would be premature. Max would wrap up warmly and go for a walk. They agreed timings. She would turn the outside light on when Robert left.

Not for the first time that Sunday, before taking his leave, he mentioned the subject of travelling to Lynn tomorrow to look for a ring.

'Are you all right, darling?' he asked when she was quiet for a couple of seconds. 'You seem distracted. Not having second thoughts...' he tailed off.

She kissed him to cover her confusion. 'No, not at all,' she replied. 'But it's a big step for a girl. I'm all alone,' she reminded him. 'And it's not as though either of us has any family to share our happiness and gather around to support us. I'm fine,' she added, with a conviction she did not feel. 'Now kiss me again, and come and pick me up in the morning.'

Robert left, and after a few minutes, Max returned, red-nosed and obviously very cold. He kept his coat on whilst she poured him a drink. But when they finally went to bed, her mind was still in turmoil.

* * * *

It was old Bob who provided the vital clue. Midweek, Maeve and Margaret were hard at work, brewing and bottling liqueur from the last of their plum wine. They would try making Calvados next from their store of apples.

When Bob came home for lunch, he told Maeve that their son Anthony and his wife would not be over for supper that evening. 'The shingle works has a new contract,' he informed her. Margaret had visited the quarry off the road leading to Snettisham beach. The supply was almost unlimited. Already, there was one deep, water-filled gravel pit where it had been easier to leave the old excavation and move to an adjacent site. The extraction plant provided much-needed jobs and made an important contribution to the local economy. She was vaguely aware that Bob and Maeve's son, who lived in the village, drove a delivery lorry for the shingle works.

'He's got to take a load to Swanton,' he told her. 'Must be near on a hundred miles, round trip. By the time he's offloaded at the other end and driven back, it'll be well after dark. Jenny says she'll stay at home and make sure there's something hot for him when he gets back.'

'What's at Swanton?' asked Maeve. 'Never heard of it.'

'Small village not far from Peterborough,' he replied. 'There's an RAF station. Quarry gaffer told our Tony, rumour has it that it's got to be made ready for the Americans. The runway's too short. Hence the shingle – lots of heavy construction.'

Maeve turned to Margaret. 'I've made a stew, love,' she told her. 'Now there'll be far too much. Do you want to take some with you, for you and Master Robert? Save you cooking after we're finished here today.'

Brushing down her pinafore to hide her excitement, she could hardly believe such good fortune: this was a significant piece of intelligence about the American arrival. For Margaret, it was doubly good news. Not only would it help Max, but it also suggested that he would not be staying for long. Almost certainly, he would want to move from Snettisham to somewhere near the airfield.

When she finally returned to the cottage later that night and passed on the news, Max agreed. He promised to send her his contact details as soon as he had found a place to live. Margaret explained that she now spent most of her time with Robert on the farm. 'So I'll give you the address and 'phone number,' she added, 'in case you need to contact me there.'

* * * *

His passport identified him as Richard Maximilian Staunton, born in New York to a British father and an American mother – hence a middle name more popular in the United States than in his father's native Channel Islands. It was, from an *Abwehr* point of view, a perfect cover.

The real Richard Staunton, foreign correspondent for an American newspaper, had died in Germany shortly after the outbreak of war. His death had not been reported to his employers; they had simply been sent a typed and "signed" letter of resignation indicating that he wished to further his career as a freelancer. Neither were his Jersey-based parents informed. They had been safely isolated from Great Britain since the German invasion in June 1940. However, in the unlikely event of an investigation, it would reveal an authentic record of his birth and employment in the United States. He had dual nationality – an accident of circumstance that made him acceptable both to the American community and their British hosts. And it was always helpful to keep the same Christian name whilst undercover.

After an uncomfortable journey and several changes, his bus eventually deposited him in Peterborough. Carrying his suitcase in his left hand – his right arm still ached occasionally, although it was much healed after a few days' rest – he booked into a central hotel. By the time he returned for lunch the following day, Max had opened a local bank account. His funding would be provided via the same London branch of a Dublin bank that supported Margaret. That afternoon, he made arrangements to view two semi-rural properties to the east of town, about halfway to the airbase. He eventually settled on a two-storey detached thatched cottage, chosen not for its old-world charm but because it was isolated and set well back, secluded from the lane by a tall hedge. The presence of a British-sounding journalist with both British and American passports came as no great surprise to those with whom he came into contact.

* * * *

Spencer Almeter was not looking forward to being sentenced. True, his offence wasn't that serious. He had a good voice, and after a night out singing with a band in a local dance hall – unfortunately for free beer, not dollars – he'd taken a car for a joyride in Atlanta but crashed it. He was also guilty of driving under the influence. And this wasn't his first offence. White judges in Georgia were not kindly disposed to coloured folks. He reckoned this would be something of a Jim Crow sentence. His state-provided attorney reckoned he had but one chance: America had entered the war. If he offered to join up, he might avoid a custodial sentence.

After a short pre-hearing discussion in chambers, Judge Donald Geistwhite hooked two fingers of his right hand and, with an intimidating gesture, beckoned Spencer's attorney to the bar. They confirmed their previous agreement. Sentencing, the judge announced, would be suspended whilst a deputy escorted Spencer to the recruiting office. What was not said was that afterwards, once he had signed on the dotted line, somehow the paperwork would be filed, and eventually, once he had completed basic training, it would disappear.

Almeter enjoyed boot camp – decent food and the first-ever taste of order and discipline in his life. Of course, as a Negro, he could not expect to join a combat unit, but he was content to be assigned – because he could drive – to one of black construction engineers. His parents, former sharecroppers forced off the land during the Depression and mechanisation of the late 1930s, and who now subsisted on casual work, were proud of their son in his smart new uniform. And they rejoiced to see him escape from the slums and gangland culture of their Atlanta Negro ghetto. Of course, the Jim Crow laws that denied them economic and cultural rights still existed in the Armed Forces, but for the first time in his life, Spencer would have a regular fifty dollars a month in his pocket.

Which, he reflected as he spewed up his guts yet again on a slow, rolling rust bucket taking ten days to cross the Atlantic, was scant reward for being corkscrewed from side to side and up and down for days on end in a late winter gale. There were no cabins for the servicemen; they slept with their vehicles and equipment in the cargo hold, which, by the time they reached Liverpool, was swimming with a mixture of seawater and human pollution.

On dry land, they formed up and marched to a British Army holding barracks. At least they could now wash with hot water and attend to their laundry, even though they slept side by side, on crude cot beds, in Nissen huts with only one stove and an inadequate ration of coal.

They had to wait for their ship to be offloaded, but two days later, Spencer Almeter was reunited with his drab olive green Mack EH truck. The heavy-duty lorry, with its 110 horsepower, six-cylinder gasoline engine, had a top speed of barely 35 miles per hour. Allowing for occasional breaks, it would take the best part of a day to make the journey to Swanton. Unfortunately, somewhere near Nottingham, Spencer's engine began to overheat. He had no choice but to pull out of the convoy and wait for it to cool down before he could check the radiator. It was dry. And he was in the middle of nowhere. From the marks on the top hose, the problem was a Jubilee clip that must have worked loose. Easy to tighten, but he needed more water.

Spencer walked to the nearest cottage. Two young girls in the garden took one look at him, squealed, and ran indoors. As he stood at the gate, a woman, probably in her late twenties or early thirties, came to the door, wiping her hands on a pinafore.

'You'll have to excuse the children,' she explained, smiling pleasantly. 'They have never seen a black person before.'

'Dat's nah bother, ma'am,' he said politely, from force of habit taking off his headdress whilst speaking to a white lady. 'Mah truck needs sum more watah. Can you please help?'

If she was taken aback by his American Negro English, she was too polite to show it. 'How far away is your vehicle?' she asked.

''Bout five hundred yards back,' he replied, indicating along the road with his thumb.

'I can lend you a watering can,' she told him. 'We can take the rose off, and there's a tap in the back garden. Won't you please follow me?'

They walked round the side of the cottage. 'Help yourself,' she said, pointing to the tap on the wall, 'but I'm afraid you might need to make more than one trip.' It took four. He drove back to the cottage and parked by the gate. As he stood, watering can in hand, she came out to meet him.

'Thank you, ma'am,' he replied, offering it back. 'I'll be on mah way.'

'I'm so glad America has entered the war,' she told him. 'Before you go, would you like something to eat or drink? I could make you a cup of tea or perhaps a sandwich. I'm sure I can find something to put in it…' she trailed off.

They had all been given a lecture stateside. Spencer knew about the U-boat blockade and that the British had to accept food rationing. He turned, opened the driver's door and stood on the step. Reaching across his seat, he opened a paper bag. They had been well provided with rations for the journey. He took out a tin of Spam, jumped back down and handed it to her.

'Don' gots any fresh bread, ma'am, but you is welcome to this.'

She took it nervously and beckoned for him to follow her up the path. She used half of the Spam to make him a huge sandwich, although he noticed that she used only a thin scraping of margarine, not butter. But the addition of home-pickled onions added to the flavour. He did not care much for tea and declined milk and sugar, but as a hot drink, it was welcomed. The strangest thing of all was to be seated at a kitchen table with a white woman offering him food and drink. And even serving it to him herself.

The two little girls entered the kitchen, stood shyly by the door, and watched him eat. When the lady offered him another sandwich, he declined politely. Spencer had every intention of leaving her the other half of the tin of Spam. 'M'duck, I'm so grateful,' she told him quietly as he pushed his chair back under the table, 'the girls will absolutely love it for their tea.' All three of them followed him to the gate. Again, he stood on the step and leant across his seat.

He handed her a D Bar of military chocolate. 'Fo da children to share, ma'am, an' thank you fo da refreshment,' he said before turning and climbing quickly into his cab. The diesel rumbled to life, and with a wave, he drove off. His last sight of them, in the outside mirror mounted on the front of his cab, was of two excited little girls jumping up and down alongside their mother.

Spencer was so absorbed, thinking about his first experience of English people, that he forgot to drive on what, for him, was the wrong side of the road. Fortunately, he met only a cyclist, who shook his fist at him as he swerved across to the left-hand side.

The last few miles were even slower going, with only two slits of beams from his headlights. His ID was checked at the gate, and he was directed to park his truck at the motor pool. The accommodation was not in one of the brick barrack buildings. Those, he was told, were for the whites. His company was housed in an old barn on the other side of the airfield. They had military camp beds and two blankets per man but no pillows. The floor was uncovered concrete, and there was no heating. A row of field latrines had been built outside, but not far enough away to mask completely the smell of piss, shit and oily disinfectant that lay at the bottom of each trench.

A marquee had been erected to serve as a combined mess tent and recreational facility, complete with a makeshift bar. Someone had scrounged – or liberated – a motley collection of wooden topped folding tables and garden chairs. Duck boards covered some of the grass floor. In one corner was a small shop area, with only a limited range of the items he was told were available in the main PX. That, too, was for whites only.

The next day, Spencer was taught to operate a bulldozer. With only a poncho to cover his uniform, it was often a long, cold and, at times, wet day in the English weather. At least now, they could try to dry out. The Army had realised that without heating, the men would go down with pneumonia. Stoves had been installed in the barn and mess tent. Although they took the chill off the air, they were barely adequate. The company worked six days a week, with Sunday their only day of rest. Unlike his parents, Spencer had never been religious. Which was just as well: the whites attended the indoor service on base; there was a separate one, out in the open, for blacks.

By the end of the month, the first runway extension was almost complete. Even the company commander, who was white, admitted that they had done a good job. And they had been paid. Spencer and a couple of friends determined that they would forget their miserable, segregated conditions and enjoy a couple of hours in the nearest public house. They were told that spirits were not readily available, but beer was plentiful. And at least they would be warm and dry. According to their sergeant, proper Nissen huts, with decent stoves for heating, were to be constructed. But they had yet to arrive. SNAFU: situation normal, all fucked up.

Spencer and his friends took pride in their appearance. After an early evening meal – they made sure to be at the front of the queue – they washed and brushed as best they could. There was no transport. But it was not raining, and the temperature was benign for a spring evening. The landlord of The King's Head provided a log fire that contributed handsomely to the warm fug in the lounge bar. He wished them a pleasant 'Good evening' and poured their pints. The beer was warm, but as Spencer pointed out, they were probably here for the duration, so best get used to it.

As they took their seats in a corner of the bar, several of the locals nodded a greeting, some of them raising their glasses in silent salute. One of them looked directly at Spencer and growled a broad, 'Ar yer orrite bor?' He didn't understand a word but smiled back gratefully.

They chatted for half an hour. Heads turned when a young woman appeared behind the bar. The blonde had a victory roll hairstyle, which fell to her shoulders. But she had chosen a tasteful pink lipstick rather than the more popular bright red. Her face suggested a no-nonsense intelligence – she was somehow nice-looking without being beautiful. And she was quite tall. A plain, rather severe high-cut blouse made no secret of her figure. Spencer looked at his friends. 'Time fo anothah round,' he said with a grin, 'an' it's mah turn.'

His friend Joseph followed him to the bar. 'Help you carry,' he said with a sly smile. They were unaware of a white American sergeant who had arrived to stand behind them.

'Yes, gentlemen?' she asked with a smile.

There was a deliberate cough. 'Excuse me, lady,' the sergeant said politely, 'but you serve the white folks first.' His head dipped towards Spencer and Joe. 'In fact, I'm not sure they should even be here.'

The landlord had just finished serving another customer and had closed the till. He caught the conversation and moved to stand alongside his assistant. 'Everything all right, Flossie?' he asked.

Flossie Harding stood her ground. 'We don't do that here in England, sir,' she replied politely to the sergeant. 'These gentlemen were here first, so I'm serving them now. Then, I would be only too delighted to take your order.'

She poured their three pints, and Spencer paid. When he and Joe turned to carry them back to their table, the sergeant had moved to an empty space along the bar to be served by the landlord. Not long afterwards, Flossie moved through the room to wipe spillages from table tops.

'Thank you, ma'am,' he said, beginning to rise to his feet and copying the English pronunciation. Spencer was only halfway up when she settled a hand on his shoulder and pushed him back down. He was a big man, she realised. Another second or two and it would have been a stretch to reach.

'You're welcome,' she told him. 'I hope you'll feel that you can come here again.' With that, she finished wiping their table and went back behind the bar.

The irony was not lost on Spencer. Here they were, fighting for freedom from fascism, yet they were not treated as equals by their own countrymen. And yet the woman on his way here, and now the locals in their public house, did not appear to hold any such prejudice. All his life, there had been segregation. Back home, they had to accept it as just part of life. But Spencer realised that over here, he was beginning to ferment an ever-increasing resentment of the way their fellow countrymen were treating them.

They were about to leave when a well-dressed civilian, glass in hand, arrived to stand by their table. 'Good evening, gentlemen,' he began. 'Would it be all right if I joined you?' He pulled back a chair without waiting for an answer, although he did not sit down. A hand caught Flossie's eye, and raising two fingers, he made a circular motion for another round. She lifted the flap and walked over to collect their empty glasses. 'I heard what happened at the bar,' he told them, 'and I just wanted you to know that all Americans are welcome in this country. My name is Max, by the way.'

Chapter 12

Robert had agreed that they would not rush into marriage. With all the uncertainty of war, they would wait at least until autumn, when with America now over here, the outcome might be a little more certain.

Over that winter and spring, Robert taught her to drive. She loved his ten-horsepower Austin and quickly became proficient, although Margaret was spared having to take a test as they had been suspended in nineteen thirty-nine, and the examiners redeployed to traffic duties. She occasionally borrowed the car to return to the cottage, particularly if it was raining, always bringing it back the following morning.

Margaret and Robert spent most of their evenings together, as well as weekends, but she did not move out of her cottage. Very occasionally, with the excuse of a "washing my hair night", she was able to absent herself in order to meet and assist an agent. But she felt guilty about using Robert's car, and even more so when, from time to time, she took small amounts of fuel from the tank on the farm to cover her nocturnal activities, for which she could not use Robert's coupons – the authorities officially referred to petrol as "motor spirit".

Margaret was living a double life. These days, she rarely went out on her cycling expeditions. Part-time spy and her fiancé's quasi-housekeeper who often helped him on the farm, this strange existence gradually took on a normality of its own. When she did reflect on her situation, which was not often, it was to take comfort from the fact that whichever side won the war, her situation would be secure. And in the now less certain event of a German victory, her contribution would probably allow her to continue living a privileged life on the farm with her future husband.

Had she known, Margaret would have felt less secure, given the knowledge that the Special Operations Executive had asked the police to circulate her photograph to all forces in the country, with strict instructions that in the event of a sighting, no action was to be taken, other than to notify the chain of command. Thus far she had been saved by one simple accident of police organisation. Snettisham did not have its own constabulary. It was served by the station at Dersingham. And Sergeant Wilkins, now approaching retirement age, who lived there with his wife in the police house, had neither occasion nor inclination to pedal to the village just over two miles away. For Charlie Wilkins, it was exercise enough to take a short stroll to The Feathers, where he was a regular. It had to be before the war when he had last visited The Rose and Crown.

So he contented himself with pinning the photograph on his office notice board, just in case.

* * * *

Max Staunton was a regular visitor to The King's Head. He found that lunch times were best for a quiet exchange of views with the landlord, whereas in the evenings, he made friends with the enlisted airmen. Over the course of a few weeks, he got to know Spencer Almeter quite well.

But the intelligence gleaned from casual and overheard conversation was low grade. He learned, for example, that initially, the airmen would fly RAF twin-engined American Boston bombers until the arrival of the heavier, four-engined B17 Flying Fortresses. With a crew of ten, including the bombardier/nose gunner and upper fuselage, waist, belly and tail turrets, each mounting twin 0.50 calibre machine guns, flying in tight defensive box formations of 9 or 12 aircraft, the B17s were more than a challenge to enemy fighters. But Max needed greater detail: specifically, if possible, of future American plans and operations. And to have any chance of obtaining those, he somehow had to get onto the base.

'You don't see many white officers in here,' he remarked casually one Saturday evening to Spencer.

'They go to da big hotel in Peterborough,' came the reply. By now, Spencer's English was beginning to lose black American pronunciation, although his accent was still strong.

'Why so?' asked Max, leaning to one side so that Flossie Harding could remove empty glasses.

Spencer was quiet for a moment. 'I'll tell you why,' she said to spare Spencer's blushes. 'The white Americans don't like to mix with these gentlemen. A liaison officer came here and asked if we would have some nights set aside for them and others only for the whites. The landlord, and he's my Uncle William, by the way, said we don't do that sort of thing in this country. Uncle Bill told him that if these gentlemen were prepared to come over here and help England, they were more than welcome in The King's Head.'

Max was surprised that the Americans had tried to import their racial segregation to England and said so.

'The liaison officer comes in from time to time,' Flossie told him, 'usually on a Saturday night. One of the few that does – white officers, I mean,' she added. 'Maybe he's supposed to check up, see that there's no trouble. Next time he does, if you are here, I'll introduce you, if you like. You can talk to him, ask him yourself.'

Which was how, ten days later, Max made the acquaintance of First Lieutenant Chuck Hawkerson, a tall, almost cadaverous

Texan with a pronounced drawl. Hawkerson, he learned, was, like his cover persona, a newspaperman and had volunteered to serve. But because of his eyesight – he wore thick, pebble-round glasses – he had not been assigned to more active service.

'They figured as a liaison officer I could handle the British press,' he informed Max, 'and take some of the local admin heat off of the station commander. Not what I wanted to sign up for, but somebody has to do it.' As a liaison officer, Max noted, Hawkerson drove himself around in a US Army jeep.

Max extended his drinking habits to Peterborough – it did not take long to confirm that "da big hotel" was The Manor Hotel, a favourite drinking and dancing destination for American officers from the former RAF Swanton. One evening, he stood alongside a group enjoying a postprandial drink at the bar.

'How are you finding it over here in England?' he asked a young captain in the process of ordering a round of drinks for his table.

'Just fine, sir,' he replied. 'Y'all have made us very welcome.'

'Actually, Captain, technically I'm not one of the "you all", as you put it. I was born stateside.'

His reply interested the captain. 'But you sound just like a limey,' he replied. 'No offence,' he added quickly.

'None taken,' Max responded. 'British father, American mother, although I was brought up in Britain. I'm a newspaperman. Used to be a foreign correspondent for a Boston newspaper, but I'm freelance now. I work mostly in Europe. Or I did, before the war started.'

His order completed, the captain surveyed the tray before him. An officer bearing the insignia of a major came to join them. 'You need a hand?' he asked.

'Just chatting to this gentleman, sir,' the captain replied. 'He's one of us, but he sounds British. Sorry pal,' he said, turning to Max, 'but I don't know your name.'

'Max Staunton,' he replied automatically, extending his hand, which the captain accepted.

'Tony Bianchi,' the captain offered, 'and this here's my boss, Major John Strauss. He runs the base.'

'Would you like to bring your drink over and join us?' Strauss invited. 'I'm intrigued to meet a fellow American who doesn't sound like one.' A wave of his hand accompanied the invitation.

Introduced to two other officers already seated, Max repeated his cover story, which was intended principally for Major Strauss. In response to his observation that an airbase was an unusually large command for a major, he learned that Strauss's remit was to complete the runway construction. 'When the aircraft arrive, I'll be replaced, almost certainly by at least a lieutenant colonel. Don't know if he'll fly missions, but he'll be a qualified bomber pilot,' he added.

'Bostons and then B17s, I gather,' offered Max deliberately.

Strauss looked at him for a couple of seconds. 'You're well informed,' he said slowly.

Max feigned a laugh. 'I sometimes drop in at The King's Head,' he admitted. 'Your men like to chat amongst themselves. Sometimes, you can't help overhearing. And besides, I'm a newspaperman. We keep our ear to the ground.' He deliberately did not mention that he had met Chuck Hawkerson. 'But if you think there's anything I can do to help with what you're doing over here,' he added, 'just let me know.'

Strauss let that pass. Max insisted on buying another round of drinks and then excused himself. Those left at the table moved into the ballroom where a lively band – presumably from the base – was in full swing.

But an idea was now well formed in Max's mind. All that stood in his way was the existence of one American liaison officer.

* * * *

Max knew he had to position himself inside the Swanton base, and for that, he needed a lorry.

Hours spent cycling around the industrial area of Peterborough revealed the premises and yard behind a sign proclaiming "Jackson's Haulage". Parked in the yard was a single medium-sized drop-side vehicle. A wooden shed, the only building, looked to be the office. Max had no intention of making himself known to whoever ran the company. His next visit would be after dark.

He wore overalls and took with him a bag containing a selection of tools. At night, the area, mostly small factory units, was deserted. There did not appear to be any security guards. The padlock on the chain securing the double mesh gates was big, old and rusty. It jemmied open easily enough. There were now two lorries parked in the yard. Obviously, one of them had been out on task earlier in the day. Max pushed a screwdriver under a window frame to gain entry to the office.

By the light of a torch, a handbook from one of the desk draws indicated that the vehicles were four-wheeled AEC Monarchs, with a payload of seven tons and an eighty-five horsepower four-cylinder diesel engine. Two sets of keys hung from screw hooks set into the wooden shed. He took both and inspected each lorry's cab. The fuel gauge on the vehicle that had been out showed nearly empty, but the one parked up earlier had been refuelled, ready for its next load.

Max studied the inside of the cab for a few minutes, then pressed the starter button. Minutes later, he was out of the industrial area and on the road to Swanton. His cottage was set well back from the road, and he was able to park behind it, reversing the lorry into a small, semi-derelict wooden barn. The doors would not quite close, so he draped a tarpaulin over the cab. He judged it safe enough till Saturday.

Max watched Chuck Hawkerson order a beer, then slipped out of the bar without being noticed by the American. He knew that if he followed his usual routine, Hawkerson would sink a couple of pints, which gave him enough time to check that the Willys jeep was outside the public house before cycling back to the cottage to collect the lorry. He had already chosen the spot, halfway along a straight stretch of road where a gate led into a field. He opened the gate, reversed into the field till the front of his bonnet was level with the hedge, and switched off the engine. From the cab, he could see both ways along the road.

Hawkerson's jeep had to slow for a fairly sharp bend leading into the straight. Once round it, he changed down a gear and, his judgement clouded by the adrenalin from two pints of beer, floored the throttle. Changing back up to third, he watched, exhilarated, as just over two litres of engine powered a fairly lightweight vehicle of less than two-and-a-half thousand pounds almost to its top speed of sixty-five miles per hour.

The moment Max sighted the jeep, he had the engine running. He watched intently. Too soon, and the vehicle might manage to swerve safely off the road. Too late, and he would miss altogether. His timing was spot on: the front of his AEC slammed into the jeep just aft of its centre line, behind the driver's seat. Pushed sideways, it executed a slow roll in mid-air to land upside down, screeching at an angle along the tarmac.

Finally, it cannoned into a tree in the far hedge and, seconds later, burst into flames. Whatever was left inside of Hawkerson's flayed and mangled body burned with it.

If necessary, Max would have torched the lorry alongside the burning jeep. He had planned what would have been a cross-country escape route back to the cottage. But the lorry had hit the side of the other vehicle front on. Apart from a minor dent and a few scratches, it was undamaged. He would not risk driving past The King's Head. Instead, he reversed partially back into the field, executed a right and accelerated as fast as he could past the still-burning jeep.

Max had always worn gloves, both when stealing the lorry and tonight. Even so, he wiped anything he might have touched, parked the lorry in a deserted wood a couple of miles away, and set fire to it. It would, eventually, be identified as the one stolen from Jackson's yard, but there was absolutely nothing to connect the lorry with the crashed jeep, nor himself with the lorry. It was a long walk home, but he was well-satisfied with his evening's work.

* * * *

Robert decided that as it promised to be a fine day, he would repair the potholes in the yard. There was still a small pile of gravel alongside the barn. And he had a few bags of cement stored inside, in the dry, left over from before the war when he had mixed and laid a small manoeuvring area in front of the barn. Unfortunately, Margaret had parked the bonnet of the car right up against them, which made it impossible for him to load his wheelbarrow. With a sigh, he went back into the house to fetch the ignition key.

As he started the engine, he glanced at the odometer. At first he could not work out why something did not seem to be quite right. Then it came to him. Last time he had used the car, he noticed that the recorded mileage was about to pass through twenty thousand. Now it was twenty thousand and fifteen – more than he would have expected if Margaret had driven only to the cottage and back. Curious… he would ask her about it later that evening.

'You obviously did some shopping,' he said evenly, 'when you borrowed the car the other night. The extra miles are on the odometer – that's the mileage number inside the speedometer dial,' he explained, seeing her confusion.

Margaret had indeed been thrown into a panic. Having the use of a car was such a new part of her life that she had completely overlooked the fact that Robert might notice its mileage. Forcing herself to remain calm, she bought a few seconds by taking a sip from her glass of wine, setting down her glass only slowly on the kitchen table. She came up with the first rational explanation that entered her head.

'You're right, I needed some shopping,' she replied. 'Ladies' things. I don't want to embarrass you with details, but they were out of stock in the village shop. I made a quick trip to King's Lynn before parking up in the barn. I didn't think you would mind.'

'Not at all,' he replied, and the moment passed. As her panic subsided, Margaret took a longer-than-usual sip from her glass. Which Robert noticed, but his mind was elsewhere – still on the odometer reading. It showed about an extra ten miles. King's Lynn was nearly three times that distance, there and back. If the Austin had been driven to Lynn, the reading would have to have been about twenty thousand and nearly forty miles. Something did not add up. He thought about pushing the issue, but that would effectively mean calling her a liar. He knew Margaret would resent being interrogated. Their relationship was too precious to be put at risk over a minor discrepancy. Besides, there might be a perfectly rational explanation. Perhaps she had not gone all the way. There were several villages in between. She could have shopped anywhere. But try as he might to put it from his mind, there remained a nagging doubt.

What followed was a normal enough evening. They enjoyed supper. As a local farmer, Robert had an understanding with the village butcher, who had let him have a couple of excellent lamb chops. Afterwards, they listened to the wireless over another glass of wine, laughing at *ITMA – It's That Man Again*, with Colonel Chinstrap's 'I don't mind if I do' and charlady Mrs Mopp's 'Can I do you now, sir?' But when she turned to leave, his goodnight kiss did not develop into quite their usual intimate embrace. Margaret sensed that she had made a mistake… that Robert was troubled. Back at her cottage, she realised that there was only one way to repair the damage. Inexperienced as she knew Robert to be with women, it was clear that she would have to increase his dependence.

Chapter 13

Two weeks later, Max again visited the hotel in Peterborough on a Saturday evening. He recognised John Strauss standing at the bar with an officer whose oak leaves identified him as a lieutenant colonel. He ordered a beer and then stood next to them, politely waiting for a lull in their conversation.

'Major, I don't want to intrude,' he said quietly. 'I read about the accident in the local paper. Just wanted to offer my condolences on the death of Lieutenant Hawkerson. I spoke to him a few times in The King's Head. I'm very sorry. Now, I'll leave you gentlemen to your deliberations.'

He turned as if to move away, but only slowly. He was gambling on Strauss's good manners, and he was not disappointed. The American officer's hand settled on his arm.

'Colonel,' he began, 'let me introduce Max Staunton. He doesn't sound like it, but believe it or not, he's one of us, born in New York.'

Max could not have hoped for a better introduction. As he knew he would be, the colonel was also intrigued.

'Born in New York. English father, American mother,' he replied in response to the senior officer's query. 'Brought up over here but worked as a foreign correspondent for a Boston newspaper, *The Daily Record*. I'm freelance now. May I ask who you are, sir..?'

'Isaac Hofmeyer,' he introduced himself, extending a hand. 'Like you, I'm a bit of a mixture. My father immigrated from Holland before the turn of the century.'

'And what brings you over here, Colonel?' Max asked evenly. 'Apart from the war, I mean.'

'The colonel is our new base commander,' broke in Strauss.

If the colonel was irritated by Strauss's interruption, it did not show. 'The construction phase is almost completed,' he added. 'I'm here to make the base fully operational.'

'So our sleep will soon be disturbed by the arrival of aircraft,' said Max, deliberately making it come across as a lighthearted statement, not a question. The colonel did not respond. It was time to play his last card and then retreat. He deliberately aimed his final words at John Strauss.

'I was going to say, Major, that if there is anything I can do after the sad loss of your liaison officer, please don't hesitate to call me.' He handed over a business card listing his name and occupation – Freelance Journalist – together with a telephone number. 'Chuck Hawkerson and I use, or should I say used, the same local contacts. If I can help the American war effort in any way, just ask...' he let the remark drift off. 'Enjoy your evening, gentlemen,' he added finally, excusing himself with a polite nod of the head. Max had no idea if they would take the bait. If not, he would have to think up some other overture.

* * * *

American airmen, white aircrew, were now arriving on the base, together with the first of their aircraft. According to comment in the local hostelries, Colonel Hofmeyer's embryo command was now alive with test flights, aircraft maintenance, and the delivery of warlike materiel, including fuel and munitions.

The build-up of American airmen brought new prosperity to Peterborough and the hostelries surrounding the airbase. But it also brought tensions. Spencer's construction company found itself increasingly outnumbered by the latest arrivals. And The King's Head was the nearest – and possibly the most attractive – hostelry within reach of the base.

Flossie Harding was fascinated by Spencer and his group of friends. When she had a break, she usually enjoyed a drink and a cigarette in a small staff room upstairs, in the living and administrative area of the pub. But when, usually on a Saturday night, the construction boys were in, it was more fun to sit down and enjoy a chat and a laugh with them. And they certainly enjoyed the company of a pretty young English girl.

On a Saturday night, the place was heaving. The bar was packed with airmen, some of them more than a little the worse for drink. Flossie flopped down next to Spencer, a glass of lemonade in hand. She dabbed a bead of sweat from her forehead.

'Thank the Lord it'll soon be closing time,' she said. 'Uncle Bill said I can have ten minutes. But how are you all doing?' she asked to the table in general.

Before they could answer, a short, stocky white airman tapped her on the shoulder. 'Excuse me, ma'am,' he began politely, although his speech was slurred, 'Private First Class Chester Arnold,' he offered by way of introduction. 'Me an' my friends over there wondered if you would care to join our table.' His thumb indicated a group of airmen in the middle of the room.

Flossie could almost feel the sudden change in the atmosphere. Spencer and his three friends had stiffened in their seats as if expecting trouble. There were several other tables of construction company men in their corner of the room. They, too, were watching quietly, although the general hubbub in the rest of the bar continued unabated.

'Thank you,' Flossie said pleasantly. 'That's very kind, but I'm quite happy where I am. I've known these gentlemen for a little while now, but thank you all the same for the invitation.'

If she had hoped he would return to his seat, Flossie was to be disappointed. 'Fact is, ma'am,' he replied, his voice now a little less obliging, 'it don't seem right to us, a pretty little girl like you seated with these nigrahs when you should be with us good white folks over there. Please...'

His hand reached down and cupped Flossie's elbow, lifting it slightly, encouraging her to stand. Spencer half rose to his feet, leaning forward, his knuckles on the table. 'Take your hand off of her,' he said quietly.

Chester Arnold seemed oblivious to the fact that he was outnumbered. 'Ah don't take orders from no black boy,' he replied, and with his other hand went to push Spencer back down into his seat. Flossie took her chance to lift her arm free and stand to one side. Spencer used the back of his knees to push back his chair and stood, his hands now at his sides. 'We don't want no trouble,' he said, not aggressively but loud enough for the nearby tables to hear.

Arnold looked at the big, fellow American and turned away. But, misunderstanding Flossie's intention in moving out of the way, he made the mistake of gripping her arm and, with a, 'You come with me, little lady,' trying to lead her across the room. She turned to face him. 'I'm not your little lady,' she said firmly, 'and you're hurting my arm. Let go of me.'

Chester Arnold appeared not to have heard her. He took half a pace towards the middle of the room. Flossie stood there, refusing to move with him. The impasse was broken when Spencer's huge hand bunched the back of Arnold's collar and pulled hard, causing him to release her. Fuelled by a mix of alcohol, racial hate and redneck temper, he turned, lowered his chin almost to his chest and swung left and right haymakers aimed blindly at Spencer's head. Flossie screamed, and the bar was suddenly icy quiet.

Spencer had been raised in a far rougher school than his opponent. He simply stepped back, out of range, then, choosing his moment, took a half pace forward and planted a massive right jab on Arnold's nose. Old Jeb's instruction from his local gym back in Atlanta flashed through his mind. 'Don't punch at him, punch through, as if you is aimin' fo' the back of his head. And one's no good, boy, you gotta follow through. Keep a-jabbin. Jab, jab, a-jabbin!' So Spencer did.

Arnold's table dashed over to support their comrade. White airmen outnumbered the construction crew, but years of injustice boiled to the surface, and they fought hard. Flossie managed to crawl across the floor till she was under the bar flap, where she took cover as glasses and chairs flew through the air. Her uncle was nowhere to be seen. After what seemed an age, the fighting began to die down just as a police whistle, an almighty long blast, sounded from the doorway. Their village constable stood there, one man against thirty or forty, forearm extended horizontally, elbow back against his body, truncheon vertically to attention in his hand.

Slowly, the room fell quiet. Constable Hargreaves was corpulently and comfortably approaching retirement, but it was not the first time he had handled situations like this. 'All right, gentlemen,' he said firmly, taking a step forward. 'Move back, away from each other. White men, you are nearest the door. Outside, now. You black gentlemen, move away into that far corner. We don't want to have arrests and trouble with the law, now do we?'

Several men were unconscious on the floor. Others were cut and injured, faces covered in thick smears of snot and blood. But miraculously, Constable Hargreaves had the situation under control. Until a truckload of military police arrived from the base and, with a senseless shrilling of more whistles, barged past him into the room and tried to arrest the construction boys. What followed was even more vicious and bloody.

* * * *

It was their first mission with the Hudsons: a relatively straightforward daylight run across the channel to attack a major marshalling yard not far from Rhiems. Almost – but not quite – a training flight. Isaac Hofmeyer would command the bombing raid. It was not his first operational sortie, and as station commander, he was acutely aware that there were only three ways to lead: by example, by example and by example.

High-level release would mitigate – but not entirely eradicate – the flak, which could exceed the Hudson's ceiling of twenty-four-and-a-half thousand feet. As he ran up the engines, there was the usual sensation, a cocktail of concentration, adrenalin, and thoughts of what might happen, which he shoved to the back of his mind. His hand on the open throttles, as always, Hofmeyer experienced that brief moment of relief when freedom from contact with the ground told him that the two Wright Cyclone 9 cylinder radial engines, each capable of producing 1100 horsepower, had hauled his medium bomber, with its 750 pounds of bomb load, into the air. Gear up, he settled into a climbing turn, waiting for the following aircraft to formate.

Walter, his bombardier in the nose, and Al, his dorsal gunner, were both youngsters flying their first mission. In fact, he was old enough to be their father, he reflected, setting course for France. The twelve bombers flew a loose box. They would tighten up on future raids as his pilots became more accustomed to flying in formation. There was some flak crossing the coast, but radio silence – and their luck – held. They had a clear run to Rhiems.

The Hudsons released over target, but Hofmeyer was only too aware that bombing from this height, even in daylight, was notoriously inaccurate. Turning for home, he was not to know that flak had claimed one of his aircraft, which had exploded in mid-air, mercifully killing the crew instantly. Behind him, the box reformed, but the Germans had scrambled an intercept. They had barely crossed the French coast when Messerschmitt Bf 109s bounced them. Al screamed a warning that they were coming from above and behind. Isaac slammed the throttles wide open and shoved the nose down for speed. Even in level flight, the aircraft was capable of over two hundred knots.

But at this height, the Bf 109 could push well over three hundred. Isaac heard the noise of their two .303 dorsal Brownings through his headset, then felt the Hudson shudder as the German pilot's rounds struck home. He watched as it flashed past, diving away to port. Twice, he tried to raise Al, but there was no response. The Hudson flew on; it had a reputation for bringing its crews home, and mercifully, the Messerschmitt had climbed away to seek other prey. He radioed for an ambulance, but Alan Wooding was dead when they lifted him out. Of the twelve aircraft that had set out that morning, three did not return. Which meant that he had sixteen letters to write to grieving next of kin. And he still had an appointment to visit The King's Head, although he was already exhausted.

But first, he had a phone call to make. A *Peterborough Standard* reporter had phoned the base the previous day, asking for comment on what they called a riot at The King's Head the night before. His second in command had taken the call, responding that it was purely a United States matter and so reported indiscipline was being investigated internally within the base. But by Monday, the story had spread to the national *News Chronicle*, who were requesting an interview.

Not a Southerner but a native of New Jersey, Isaac had some sympathy for the way in which the coloured airmen were treated. He could deny reporters access to the base, but off-duty men would talk, and he could ill afford lurid accounts of racial fights within the US Air Army. Right now, he sensed a gathering administrative storm to which he was ill-equipped to respond. Isaac sorely missed the services of his liaison officer, who, in addition to taking a load of admin off his hands, had so skilfully handled the constant stream of local newspaper interest. And now, the UK Nationals looked likely to dump a shitload of bad press coverage on his command. He reached for the telephone.

'Max Staunton,' came the response.

'Isaac Hofmeyer,' he responded. 'Max,' he went on, 'when we met the other evening following the sad demise of Chuck Hawkerson, you offered to help Major Strauss and the American war effort in any way that you could. May I ask if that offer still stands?'

'It most certainly does, Colonel,' said Max firmly. 'How might I be of service?'

'You will be aware of events at The King's Head on Saturday evening,' Isaac went on. Max confirmed that he was. 'I find myself under increasing pressure,' the Colonel continued, 'and not just from our local newspaper. It seems the nationals are becoming involved. At all costs, I have to try to prevent bad press coverage that could sow descent amongst my men and damage our war effort. As a fellow American and an experienced newspaperman, would you be prepared to help me?'

Max was exultant, but kept his voice under control. 'That goes without saying, Colonel,' he replied evenly. 'What do you want me to do?'

'If you would come and see me in my office tomorrow morning, that would be greatly appreciated,' Isaac told him. 'I'll send transport to collect you. I hope eight o'clock will not be too early?'

Max confirmed their appointment, and the conversation ended with the usual courtesies. He replaced the receiver but could not help clenching both fists in delight. There could be absolutely no doubt that he was about to be recruited to help out at the airbase. His ruse had worked. He was in!

Isaac changed into a fresh uniform. His driver was waiting in the outer office. It was almost seven in the evening when they reached The King's Head. There were no lights on inside, and a notice pinned to the doors announced, "Closed for Refurbishment". Isaac banged with his fist. Seconds later, a light came on, and a door was opened.

'Mr Harding?' Isaac enquired politely. 'We haven't met, but I'm Isaac Hofmeyer, the base commander. Thank you for agreeing to meet with me.'

Bill Harding took in the crisply uniformed figure. Hofmeyer was an impressive sight. At least six feet, with a trim waist but the upper body of a linebacker – which he had been both at college and as a junior officer. His fair hair was cut unfashionably short, almost a stubble, but it was still all there. He just found it more comfortable that way under a headset. His face was angular, not handsome, but Bill's first impression was that the man seemed a pretty genuine sort. He opened the door wide.

'Come in, Colonel,' he invited. 'My niece Flossie is here, as your officer requested when he phoned. Between us, we can probably tell you everything you need to know.'

He closed the door behind them, turned off the light and led the way to the far end of the bar, where there was plenty of daylight from an adjacent window. On the way, they passed a pile of damaged and smashed furniture stacked against a wall. A young woman who had to be Flossie was seated at a table. Bill Harding made the introduction.

'Mr Harding,' Isaac kicked off, 'first I want to apologise on behalf of the United States Air Army for what happened here on Saturday night. It was inexcusable. I want you to know that I have the authority to cover the cost of any damage, including the replacement of your furniture. If you order whatever you need, we will either meet the bill or, if you prefer, show me an invoice, and we will reimburse you. We will also meet any clean-up costs,' he went on, 'and, perhaps most importantly, I am able to reimburse you for any loss of profits until you are able to open fully again. And that's just my initial offer, but I hope you will find it acceptable.'

Bill Harding waved an arm to encompass the ruined bar. 'That's generous of you, Colonel,' he said slowly. 'But it's no more than fair. After all, it was your boys who did the damage. But I have to ask.' he said thoughtfully, 'are there any conditions attached? What might you want from me in return?' Isaac Hofmeyer smiled. He had, thought Flossie, a rather kindly and honest face.

'Two things, Mr Harding,' he responded. 'First, I have to tell you that the incident on Saturday threatens some real bad press for my command. It won't help our war effort if, as a result, my black and white airmen are at each other's throats, so to speak. If you are questioned, would you be prepared to play down what happened: a minor brawl, nothing too serious, not the first time... it used to happen before the Americans arrived? You get my drift? And I would be particularly grateful if you could avoid mentioning any racial element. It was just a bar fight between a few drunks...' He let the statement hang.

Bill Harding thought things over. 'Happy to do that, Colonel,' he said eventually. 'Especially if it helps the war effort.

But what about the evidence of Constable Hargreaves? His police report won't back that up. And he'll likely be interviewed, too.'

'My people have already spoken to the Chief Constable,' Isaac replied. 'The officer's evidence won't contradict anything you might say.'

Bill Harding reflected on this. 'You said two things,' he said eventually. 'We seem to have covered one. What's the other?'

'Some of my men were quite badly hurt on Saturday,' the colonel told him. 'Fortunately, we have the facilities to treat them on base. But they are nearly all from the construction unit. Which is to say, they are black airmen.

'I demanded a report from the captain commanding my military police detachment,' he went on, 'but in this regard, I have two things to say, and I want you to respect my confidence.'

A pronounced nod from Bill Harding confirmed that they would.

'First,' Isaac said slowly, 'I am concerned by the way the US Air Army treats my coloured airmen. But that is my problem, not yours. And second, I detect the same degree of prejudice in the captain's report. Frankly, I think it's bullshit,' he broke off, 'sorry Miss Harding,' he said quickly, 'please excuse me.'

'It's all right, Colonel,' she said quickly. 'I'm a barmaid, not a nun.'

Isaac had to suppress a smile. 'A load of charges have been levelled as a result of Saturday,' he told her. 'But from what Constable Hargreaves has already said, the construction boys are being held unfairly to blame. And, as CO, it worries me that I am facing a serious miscarriage of justice, one that could really sour relations on the base. I need to know, in detail, exactly what happened.'

In the fifteen minutes that followed, Isaac Hofmeyer's eyes were opened. She told him how white men had demanded to be served first for drinks. Flossie's evidence regarding Saturday night was particularly damning. There had been no problem before the aircrew arrived. They had tried to move her by force away from her table. Far from starting a fight, Spencer Almeter had wanted to avoid trouble. But in the end, he had protected her before he, in turn, had been attacked. Others from the white airman's table had joined in. Constable Hargreaves arrived and had everything in hand, but then the base police turned up and just waded into the coloured boys. After that...' she tailed off. 'Well, you know the rest,' she finished quietly.

'Thank you,' he said after a long pause. 'You have told me what I needed to know. Thank you both,' he turned to Bill Harding. 'I'll leave you kind folks now.'

Chapter 14

Flossie Harding did not see Spencer until the Saturday evening following Isaac Hofmeyer's visit to The King's Head. But she had been hard at work all week helping her uncle to restore the interior of the public house. She had to admit, however, that the colonel had lived up to his word. Uncle Bill had telephoned his usual supplier and new tables and chairs arrived forty-eight hours later. The base had confirmed that the invoice could be sent to them, and, he learned later, it had been settled promptly. Friday, they spent unpacking and restoring the lounge bar to its former glory. A notice on the front door announced that they would be open for business as usual on Saturday. A contingent of the construction unit arrived soon after opening time, as did a smaller number of white airmen. She had no idea what had happened or been said on the base, but all of them, not least the whites, were subdued and respectful.

It had been a difficult conversation with her mother-in-law. They lived in a modest terraced house at the other end of the village from The King's Arms – Flossie, Gladys and young Jimmy, her daughter-in-law's son by Sergeant James Harding, 2nd Battalion, the Royal Norfolk Regiment, of whom nothing had been heard since Dunkirk.

'I want to walk out with him on Sunday afternoon,' said Flossie. 'He's away from home, they all are, and I know he would be overwhelmed to be invited into a British home, even if it's only for a cup of tea.'

'Have you asked him yet?' said Gladys, a bit sharply, Flossie thought. 'Jim might still be alive, you know. And you say this here American's black. What will the neighbours think?'

'You know what the regiment's officer said when he came to see us,' Flossie countered. 'I can remember every word. The battalion was part of the 2nd Infantry Division, covering the retreat to Dunkirk. They made a last stand until shelled and outnumbered, they were forced to surrender. Unfortunately, it was to an *SS* Division. According to accounts that reached us via the locals, the prisoners were marched away to another farm, where they were lined up against a wall and machine gunned.

'There's no doubt in my mind that Edward's dead,' she said sadly. 'If he'd survived and been taken prisoner, we would have had a Red Cross form by now.'

Although she would not admit it, Gladys agreed. She had long since ceased shedding tears for her son, although, like Flossie, she still ached at the loss. Her daughter-in-law was a good mother, a hard worker and a nice-looking young woman. They survived on her earnings as a cleaner by day and Flossie's by night when Gladys was at home to look after young Jimmy. But Gladys was realistic. Flossie was too young to be thrown onto the scrap heap by war.

'All right,' she said eventually. 'Walk out with him on Sunday afternoon, if you must. And bring him home for tea. I'll make one of those boiled-up war recipe cakes because we don't have enough fat for anything proper. It'll have to do.'

Flossie gave Gladys' arm a squeeze. 'Thanks, Mum,' she whispered.

She took her chance early on Saturday evening when one of Spencer Almeter's two companions was being served by Uncle Bill, and the other had disappeared into the gents.

'Two minutes,' she said to her uncle as he began pulling the first of three pints. Leaving the counter flap raised, to Spencer's surprise, she walked quickly to his table and sat beside him.

'This is nice, Flossie,' he said. 'Didn't expect to talk to you till latah.'

There was no time to start with a spot of gentle flirting; the others would be back any minute. 'Told our Mum about you,' she said quietly. 'If you're free tomorrow and would like to take me for a walk, you're invited to tea afterwards.'

His beaming smile was all the answer she needed. But already, his companion was bringing the first two pints to their table. Quickly, she patted the back of his hand. 'Outside the village church,' she told him. 'Three o'clock.'

'Evening Joe,' she said, taking her leave.

'Man, you look like da cat dat got da cream,' Joe said, rejoining his friend after setting down their third drink. To his irritation, Spencer said nothing, just kept on smiling as he reached for his pint.

* * * *

He telephoned to reserve a table. Max had decided to treat himself to a drink and Sunday lunch at the Peterborough hotel favoured by the Americans. On the way, he purchased a copy of *The Sunday Times*. Ordering wine at the bar, with his first glass he settled to reading the front page. The rest of the bottle he would send through before moving to his table. Recent legislation, designed to prevent wealthier diners from taking advantage of a lack of rationing in restaurants, limited the amount that could be charged for a meal to five shillings. Even so, Max was confident that this sum, which he could afford easily, would provide several generous slices for his roast platter and perhaps even some pudding.

But he could not settle to his paper. It had been, he reflected, taking a sip from his glass, a remarkable week. His thoughts went back to Tuesday morning when he had been collected by a junior officer and driven to the base…

'Mr Staunton, Colonel,' announced the senior warrant officer who ran the outer office. Isaac Hofmeyer rose to meet him and came round his desk to shake hands, indicating for Max to be seated. He settled into one of two armchairs on either side of a small round table, in front and to one side of his desk.

'Thank you for coming,' the colonel greeted him.

'My pleasure,' Max responded. 'I… er… gather from our brief conversation last evening, you feel there may be some way in which I might be of assistance? So here I am.'

'Max,' the colonel went on, 'may I use your first name, by the way?' A nod of the head indicated consent. 'As you know, the late Chuck Hawkerson was officially my press officer. But in reality, he was much more than that.' He explained how Chuck had handled much of the routine administration between the base and the local community. 'It all added up to a full-time job,' he stated. 'Chuck was forever out and about, talking to the local council as well as the one in Peterborough – not to mention sorting out any problems with the neighbourhood business community. Even down to keeping an eye on The King's Head, as well you know.

'But my biggest problem, right now, is the press wanting to report on the events of Saturday night,' he confided. 'They seem hell-bent on featuring the differences in race relations between America and the United Kingdom. Not least by comparing how our coloureds are treated back home with their experience of life in Great Britain. Stateside, we have Jim Crow laws; here, you don't. And I regret to say they seem too interested in the fact that there is also segregation within the US Army Air Force. Personally, I don't agree with it,' he added quickly, 'but it's there nonetheless.'

'All of which is the type of publicity you just don't need,' Max Staunton offered. 'So you need someone to hand off the press queries and play down the race card.'

'That's the immediate problem,' the colonel agreed. 'If it were just the locals, that wouldn't be too bad, but yesterday, we had a call from a national newspaper. I couldn't deal with it. At the time, I was leading a bombing raid over France, for God's sake. I'm beginning to realise just how much I depended on Chuck Hawkerson. But the bottom line is that all this is going to be bad for morale on the base, and that's not going to help the war effort.'

'So am I right in thinking you want me to step in and take on the job?' asked Max. It was both a question and a statement. 'And would this be a temporary or permanent arrangement?' he added.

'I'm almost begging you,' Isaac confessed. 'I'll have to clear it with command, but with your nationality and background, I don't see a problem. And in any case, I can't wait that long.'

He went on to explain the steps taken so far with the landlord of The King's Head, as well as the local constabulary. 'Just play down the story,' he concluded. 'Kill it if you can, but if not, at least try to cover up the race element.'

'When would you want me to start?' asked Max.

Rather than reply, the colonel walked to a connecting door set in the far wall and opened it. On the other side was a smaller office, but Max could see a desk, a chair and a telephone. 'We can sort out the admin – remuneration, your officer status as a civilian, and so forth – in slow time. But right now, if you can get one London newspaper off my back, you'll be doing the US Army Air Force in general, and me in particular, one hell of a service.'

Opening a hatch to the outer office, he shouted for all the files handled by Max's predecessor. Max shook hands with the colonel and walked through to his own office, closing the door behind him.

It was his English accent that did the trick, not just with the editor of the *News Chronicle* but also with a couple of Peterborough papers. Mention of security concerns, damage to the war effort and so forth, plus the promise of insider briefings to come, were enough to appeal to a mix of patriotism and self-interest. Aside from a mention of a minor disturbance in one local paper, the story was dropped.

The colonel was relieved and absolutely delighted. Max decided to settle into his role very gently. But he now had access to the headquarters building and, not least, to the colonel's office. Isaac Hofmeyer, he noticed, had a habit of leaving files and documents on his desk. Sooner or later, there would be worthwhile intelligence.

He had no need for accommodation on the base, but as his presence became a matter of routine, membership in the officer's club also began to yield useful nuggets of information. As a bonus, the colonel arranged for him to be able to purchase from the base post exchange – the PX – the same imported goods available to American servicemen. On a personal note, this was a major benefit. But despite all assurances, fearful of Britain's code breakers he decided against sending a report detailing his important new status to *Abwehr* headquarters, Berlin.

* * * *

Spencer was already waiting outside the church when Flossie arrived, even though she was five minutes early. His uniform had been pressed to perfection: olive drab four-button jacket, razor-sharp trouser creases, matching shirt and a light khaki tie. But it was his wide smile as she approached that warmed her heart. Not for the first time, she took in his height, something over six feet, broad shoulders and narrow waist. When he extended an arm to shake hands, hers was tiny by comparison. An honest and open face was marred by a nose that would have been aquiline for his race. *Perhaps*, she wondered, *white genes in his ancestral past, probably dating back to slave days*. But it had clearly been broken, maybe more than once, transforming what would have been handsome to something more akin to a kindly rogue. It was the first time she had seen him outside of The King's Head, and more and more, Flossie Harding was liking what she saw.

She took his arm as they set off down an adjacent lane. 'We live at the end, on the other side of the village,' she told him. 'It's about half an hour if we don't hurry. Just in time for tea,' she added cheerfully.

'So how are things at the base,' she queried, 'after that dreadful fight in the pub?'

'Damn Snowdrops!' he exclaimed, disgust evident in his voice. 'US military police,' he explained, seeing the puzzled look on her face. 'Comes from their white helmets. First they beats the hell out of us, then we is all on a charge.

'But old Colonel Hofmeyer, he's a good man,' he went on. 'Pays a visit to da construction company. First time that's evah happened. Tells us he knows da truth, an' all charges is dropped. What's more, da MP captains's gone an' da first lieutenant's taken ovah.

'We is gonna git our own buildings, too, same as da whites' he added. 'An' all da same PX goods. Da colonel's dun everythin' he can to git rid of Jim Crow.'

Flossie squeezed his upper arm with her free hand. She had little idea of the full extent of discrimination suffered by black G.I.s. But she was pleased for him. 'That's really good,' she offered encouragingly. They walked the rest of the way in companionable silence. She admired this big, hulking man, who seemed not to harbour an ounce of hatred despite their unfair treatment. For his part, Spencer felt proud to have a fine-looking young British woman on his arm. This would never have happened back home.

'We're almost there,' she said eventually. 'It's this end house on the right. Come and meet my mother-in-law, but don't worry – Gladys' bark is worse than her bite!'

Spencer's first impression was that the house was very small. The front door led directly off the street into a living room. It was simply furnished – a table and four chairs, two easy chairs on either side of an open fire, and a folded-down sewing machine cabinet by the window with an aspidistra on top. A tall, dark-haired Englishwoman rose to meet him. She had once been handsome, he thought, but now her face was careworn, her hair streaked with grey. 'This is Spencer Almeter,' Flossie said simply.

The woman extended her hand. 'I'm very pleased to make yo acquaintance, ma'am,' Spencer said politely, surprised that a white woman, a stranger, had offered to shake his hand. Alongside Gladys, a small boy, perhaps three or four years old, clung to her skirt with both hands, half hiding his face. Flossie had been nervous about this moment. There just hadn't been the right time to tell him.

'This is Edward James,' she said quietly. 'We call him Jimmy. His father – my husband Edward – died at Dunkirk.'

As if asking for permission, Spencer nodded to Gladys, who had yet to say a word. Taking silence for assent, he knelt in front of the boy and took a D ration from his jacket pocket. Most of the airmen carried something so they could respond to the pleas of children. 'Jimmy, this here be one of Mr Hershey's chocolate bars,' he said softly. 'You like chocolate?'

There was a barely perceptible, anxious nod of the head.

'Then I'm gonna give it to yo grandmother, an' Mrs Gladys will know best when to give it to you.' With that, he stood and proffered the bar with a simple, 'Ma'am?', at the same time giving Jimmy just the gentlest ruffle on top of his head.

Evidently, this did not meet with just Jimmy's approval. 'Thank you, Mr Almeter,' she responded, 'and you are most welcome here. Sit down, and we'll have tea.'

Flossie could have wept with relief. Not for the first time, her heart went out to Spencer.

* * * *

His golden opportunity came on Tuesday afternoon. Max was in the adjacent office when he heard an orderly rush in to tell the colonel that the flight was returning. In response to the sounds of fire engines and an ambulance, the entire orderly room rushed out behind him to watch the runway. They stood, backs to the office windows. He could have followed through his own office door, but there was also a way out through the colonel's office.

He paused to look at the solitary file, now closed, on the colonel's desk. Max lifted the front cover. He could hardly believe his luck. The most recent document, which the colonel had obviously been reading, was a warning order. It was all there. Twelve B17s would arrive at Swanton Field from Canada's St John's Field, Newfoundland. Well within ferry range. No bomb load, but gun turrets manned… date, E.T.A, key personnel – everything. Max quickly returned to his own office, closed the connecting door behind him, repeated the details to himself to lock them in his memory, particularly the Estimated Time of

Arrival, then went out to join the others. A badly damaged aircraft landed wheels up. Sparks flew, but the fire crew were on hand to douse it, and the crew evacuated safely.

That evening, Max sent a message to *Abwehr* headquarters, Berlin.

* * * *

His command did not include a military band, but Isaac Hofmeyer knew that a number of his men, black and white, were competent amateur musicians. Isaac came from a musical family. Granted, his parents preferred the classics – his mother was still a fine pianist, and his late father had played the violin. But Isaac loved jazz, and he was no mean clarinettist. He posted a notice order: anyone interested should attend a meeting in the main mess hall. Both white airmen and members of the construction company were invited.

It was well attended. He decided against auditions: you could play, you were in. The orderly room warrant officer was dispatched to Peterborough to procure sheet music, mostly but not entirely Glen Miller numbers. Together, the volunteers formed an under-rehearsed and, at times, ragged band. But there was no doubting their enthusiasm. And the sound never failed to excite an overwhelming itch to dance.

Swanton had a good-sized village hall, thanks to a generous bequest from a wealthy landowner. A teacher from the village school produced several posters, each with individual but creditable artwork. Max was asked to liaise with the W.I., the local branch of the Women's Institute, and the base supplied the rations for mid-evening refreshments. Isaac could have asked his own men to provide drinks facilities, but as Max pointed out, it might be politic to let Bill Harding set things up and make a small profit. Flossie, however, refused point blank to help behind the bar. She had one ambition for the evening of the dance: Spencer was summoned to Gladys' house, where she watched with interest and a certain amount of envy as Spencer taught her daughter-in-law the steps to the jitterbug.

They didn't have music, but he explained and demonstrated. Holding hands facing each other, Spencer took a slow step to his left and then leant back onto his right. 'That's a slow, slow,' he told her. Then he took a quick step back, putting the toe of his left foot behind his right, before transferring his weight back again onto the front foot. 'That's a quick-quick,' he explained, 'da basic rock step. An' now we're ready to start over, with anothah slow to da left, an' so on. All you gots to do,' he went on, 'is da exact opposite. A slow to yo right, then back again, an' now da rock step away from me. Da beat be slow, slow, quick-quick, and we can repeat da basic move as many times as we want.'

He called the steps as she practised. Flossie loved dancing, and this was a whole new experience. Not just the dance, but the physical contact with her partner. Suddenly, he was humming, 'Don't sit under the apple tree with anyone else but me.' She knew it was a Glen Miller and the Andrews Sisters hit from earlier that year. Now, he was singing the words, a baritone, despite his size, but his powerful frame was injecting a real rhythm into the lyrics. And they were dancing. Were they dancing!

They took a break, and Gladys produced three bottles of Franklin's Ginger Beer.

Next, he taught her a couple of turns, underarm and inside. Finally, they moved on to the cuddle step, where he turned Flossie so that she danced with her back pressed against him before spinning around again. After over an hour of this, they were both exhausted and sank gratefully to finish their drinks at the table.

'Reckon you got a grasp of da jitterbug,' he told her. 'We'll be steppin' out on Saturday night.'

The dance was almost too well attended. There were more construction boys than whites, but his orderly room had leaked that their CO would double as clarinet and dance band leader, and a good number of the less prejudiced airmen were there as well. Flossie had spread the word in the village. Every single girl over the age of sixteen was present, as well as a good number of younger married women whose husbands were far away. For many, this was their first carefree night out since the start of the war.

Flossie could not afford a new dress, but she wore her Sunday best blue floral pattern with a flared skirt. Fortunately, she still had her Yardley's Natural Rose Lipstick and English Peach Complexion Powder, both of which she applied sparingly. Gladys lent her a short, bolero style fur top. 'From back in the day when I could afford decent clothes,' she said wistfully. 'Knew it would come in handy one day... aired it as much as I could... hope it doesn't smell of mothballs.' She helped Flossie to slip it over her shoulders.

There was a knock on the door.

'Spencer's a lucky man.' Gladys told her. 'You look lovely, my dear. Enjoy yourself – you deserve a bit of happiness.'

Flossie kissed her mother-in-law on the cheek and went to open the door.

Spencer's expression said it all. 'Million dollars!' he whispered softly.

For some reason, he had insisted on being there early, before the first dance. 'Got a surprise for you,' he said as they waited whilst the musicians settled themselves on the low stage and placed the first number on their music stands. Facing the floor, Isaac Hofmeyer made no announcement. Just extended his right hand out to one side, executed a brisk, four-time, down-left-right-upbeat, and at the next down stroke, the band crashed into the Glen Miller "Apple Tree" number.

'My pal Herman, he's da lead trumpet,' he shouted in her ear. 'Asked him fo this, special. Shall we?'

Several other couples joined them, both black and white men asking the ladies to dance. All the construction boys could jitterbug, and they were busy showing their partners the first steps. Some of the airmen, too, although others preferred a more conventional style of dancing. But they were all having a great time. There was a slow realisation, however, that in the centre of the floor, a real jitterbug was taking place… a construction guy, the village girls realised, with young, widowed Flossie Harding.

Slowly, the other dancers formed a circle, to watch and clap in time to the music. Herman stood to take a solo, then to the amazement of the Americans, Isaac put in another one on clarinet, adding a high, wailing improvisation above the lines. It was classic jazz, an impressive virtuoso performance, and now feet were stamping. Although Flossie's only concern, as she came out of a cuddle step and spun back to face her partner, was that she was almost certainly flashing her knickers. When the music and then the applause finally stopped, and she realised the extent to which they had been putting on something of an exhibition, she went bright red with embarrassment. Spencer just laughed and took her elbow. 'Dat was just great, girl, just great, an' ah'm proud of you.'

The British women, particularly, were enjoying their refreshments during the break. The Americans had been generous. The W.I. had prepared sandwiches with gifted ham and pickles, chicken and mayo, flown-in avocado – which none of them had tasted before – served with prawns on crackers. Likewise, mock paté de foie gras made with liverwurst and several other treats not seen since before the war. Flossie was wiping her hands on a napkin when the colonel approached them.

Spencer tried his best to stand to attention – not easy with a plate of food in one hand – but Isaac touched him on the arm. 'Stand easy, Soldier.'

He turned to Flossie. 'Just wanted to thank you, Miss Harding,' he said with a smile. 'Your first dance really got the evening off to a fine start.'

'Flossie, Colonel Hofmeyer, please,' she invited.

'Thank you.'

He turned to look at Spencer. 'But I guess you had a good teacher.'

He had never spoken to a senior officer before, let alone a white one. But here, blacks and whites sharing a dance hall, everything seemed to be different. Spencer felt emboldened. 'Colonel, sir, if I am allowed, you is one hell of a fine clarinettist. But dat band needs vocals. Ah gots dun sum croonin' before da war. If we can git a mike, I would love to help out.'

'You got it,' he replied. 'And now, I think it's back to work… if you will excuse me?'

Isaac Hofmeyer made his way to the stage. He was looking forward to the second half of the evening. Even so, he was tired. All day, newly arrived ground crew had been unpacking a mass of ammunition, bombs, spare parts and equipment. He tried, not entirely with success, to push from his mind the fact that in less than forty-eight hours from now, the base had to be ready to receive – and send to war – a squadron of B-17s.

Chapter 15

*H*auptman Ulrich Vogel, "Uli" to his friends, raised the undercarriage of his Focke-Wulf Fw 190A-2 and set course over the North Sea. Glancing to left and right, he checked that the other five aircraft were holding station. They had taken off for the final leg from as near to the coast as possible to give them maximum time over target.

As always, once airborne, he lost the feeling of anxiety and slight nausea that preceded every mission. Uli had confidence in his aeroplane. The Fw 190 A-2 was more than a match for the Spitfire in all but turn radius. And this was not too much of a disadvantage. Many a time, he had rolled away from combat over Britain and used his superior speed to run for the coast. In a dogfight, his two fuselage-mounted 7.92 mm machine guns, plus another pair and two 20 mm cannon in the wings, which could punch through 10 to 12 millimetres of armour, were more than sufficient. They also made the 190 A-2 an excellent *Schlachtgeschwader*, or battle wings, their nickname for a ground attack aircraft.

Halfway across the North Sea, they dropped almost to wave height so that the British radar would not be able to predict their destination. Again, he checked his course and gauges, the fourteen-cylinder BMW engine singing like a fighting hornet. The aeroplane was quite rightly popular with its pilots. Uli's thoughts turned to their target. The mission planners had allowed for the B-17s to be refuelled and dispersed after landing, but he just hoped the Americans had arrived on time.

They would be unlucky to be jumped by enemy fighters but could expect intense ground machine gun defence from prepared sand-bagged emplacements. Fire from 7.62 mm weapons was bad enough, but his real fear was the 20 mm Oerlikon cannon, which could blast his aeroplane to pieces at more than 250 rounds a minute.

Max looked at his watch. The overwhelming temptation was to be off-base when the attack was due. But he couldn't do it – far too suspicious. Even so, although the B-17s were their target, he made ready for a sprint for the nearest air raid shelter, which was no more than a large slit trench, walled with sandbags and topped with wriggly tin under yet another layer of sandbags on top. Being a civilian, he didn't even have a tin hat.

The arrival time had been scheduled for 1100 hours. A tailwind had taken an hour off their crossing. The B-17s had been refuelled and taxied to dispersal positions. The crews were already enjoying a late breakfast in their mess halls,

Uli was concentrating hard on navigation. They had stayed over water for as long as possible, over the Wash before crossing the coast near King's Lynn. Now, they were fast and low, treetop height, lifting only for the occasional power line. He had spent hours memorising the landmarks – villages, rivers, contours, churches, railways… he was confident as they flashed over the final hamlet that the enemy airfield would be directly ahead.

The anti-aircraft gunners were caught by surprise. The air raid warning sirens had not even begun to wail when they heard the sound of aero-engines. Uli and his Focke-Wulf 190s roared towards the base, barely above ground level. Two of his pilots fired at the same aircraft, but after a single pass, three of the Flying Fortresses were ablaze.

'Starboard turn, one more pass and then home,' confirmed Uli calmly into his R/T. But on this run-in, the return fire was intense. He selected what appeared to be an undamaged aircraft, but tracer coming directly for his nose made him pull hard left stick and rudder, his wingtip almost touching the ground. By the time he had his aeroplane straight and level again, he was over the perimeter track, and the field was behind him. Off his port wing, there was an orange flash and a mid-air explosion. Out of anti-aircraft range, he throttled back to allow the rest of his flight to formate, but two were missing.

'Who else went down?'

'Hans, Leader,' came the reply. It was Rudi transmitting. 'He ploughed in. No chance he survived.'

'*Ja, ja*,' said Uli softly. 'Let's get home.'

For the loss of two brave pilots, Max was later able to confirm that Uli's flight had completely destroyed four B-17s, and three more would not fly again for several weeks. As a raid, it had been an outstanding success.

The only upside, if it could be described as such, remarked Isaac Hofmeyer bitterly, was that there had been no loss of American lives. One anti-aircraft gunner had been nicked by a piece of shrapnel but would survive.

Back in his office, he threw his helmet viciously into an armchair. 'The bastards knew the B-17s were coming,' he barked at the orderly room staff, Max amongst them. 'But how? There has to be a leak here on the base.'

'Perhaps,' offered Max quietly. 'But it might have come from St John's Field. I bet the Germans have people all over the bases back home.'

Hofmeyer considered this. During the years leading up to the war, Germans living abroad were encouraged to associate within groups designed to sustain German nationalism and ideals and to lend their support for the Nazi Party. Formed in 1936, the *Amerikadeutscher Volkbund* began operating youth training camps across the country, staffed by sympathetic German dual nationals or Americans of German descent. Just before the war, its membership numbered tens of thousands. In February 1939, some twenty thousand rallied in New York's Madison Square denouncing – amongst other things – President Roosevelt and Jewish plotting. It would be foolish to assume that the same sort of thing had not happened in Canada. Max, he conceded, could well be right. But a nagging doubt remained.

* * * *

Later that evening, in the bar of the officer's club, he tapped his intelligence officer on the shoulder. Major Sam Heimy was a Jew. No way would he be a Nazi sympathiser. He indicated that Sam should follow him to a quiet corner of the room, well out of earshot.

'I want you to run an investigation into the background of every man on this base,' Isaac opened, holding up a palm to forestall the obvious reaction. 'It's a big task, I know, but I'm not asking you to do it yourself. Go back to your people in the States. Tell them about today and that I want to be sure there's no collaborator on the base. Ask them to put a team on it. You can ignore the coloured men, just the whites. I want the name of every man who has a German family background. And I want it fast.'

Three days later, Sam Heimy stood in front of his desk. 'Three men, Colonel,' he announced. 'The details are there,' he nodded at a sheet of paper he had placed on his CO's desk. 'Two pilots and an air gunner.'

Hofmeyer read the report. 'I don't think so, Sam,' he said eventually. 'All born stateside. And all flying combat missions. No way any of them are going to be helping the Krauts.'

'Agreed, sir,' the IO replied. 'But I know one of the men assigned to the team back home. We trained together. He sent me a separate wire. You didn't ask about civilians, but he was the one ordered to run the check you asked for not long ago on Max Staunton. Half American, half British. It was just a fairly basic family and document search. Occupation listed as journalist. Nothing on him at the time. But when the team didn't come up with any military suspects, my contact rang Staunton's former employer. Seems that he resigned unexpectedly shortly before the war. But apparently, he had been working overseas for quite some time. In Germany.' He left the statement hanging.

* * * *

'It wasn't a bad winter, but all the same, I was grateful for a warm spring,' Robert remarked to Margaret as they finished their Sunday lunch. She had sensed a brief cooling in their relationship after the mileage incident, but life soon returned to normal – his thoughts of a few weeks ago long since forgotten. 'The Americans are here now,' he went on, 'and well and truly into the war. It's not over yet, not by a long chalk, but we did say we would take a view sometime around now.'

Margaret realised that in an oblique sort of way, *typical of a rather shy Robert*, she thought, he had returned to the subject of the two of them. They were almost – but not quite – united as a couple, although some heavy petting had brought them close at times. She knew that this was not entirely satisfactory for either of them. She was sure Robert was a virgin. Several casual relationships back in Berlin had introduced her to the pleasures of sex, but riding Robert's finger whilst she stroked him to a climax was a poor substitute. And as much as she had feelings for him, she was equally conscious of the need to bind the two of them together.

'What exactly are you saying?' she asked disingenuously.

'I suppose I'm asking if you would like to name the day,' he responded slowly. 'Perhaps early August before harvesting starts because it won't be over till the end of September?'

Margaret couldn't help it. She burst out laughing. Then stopped instantly when she saw the hurt look on his face. 'I'm sorry, Robert,' she said quickly, setting down her wine glass and placing a hand over his. 'It just struck me as funny, having to play second fiddle to fields of wheat. But I suppose I had better get used to it if I'm going to be a farmer's wife.'

'Let's choose a Saturday at the end of July.' She gave his hand an affectionate squeeze. 'Then we can book the Registry Office in Lynn. Afterwards, we can celebrate with just a few witnesses – old Bob and Maeve, obviously, and anyone else you might like to invite.'

'Richard and Susan from The Rose and Crown,' he suggested. 'I've been going there for years, and they knew my parents. But really, I can't think of anyone else,' he added wistfully.

She walked around the table and kissed him on the forehead whilst he was still seated. 'It's not the size of the wedding party that counts,' she said, her arms over his shoulders. 'It's the man I'm going to marry.'

Margaret had been wondering how and when to put her thoughts into action, and events were playing out in her favour. 'I'll do the dishes,' she told him, 'then I'm going to take a bath. I've been slaving in the kitchen all morning. You can relax in the lounge but pour us both a glass of Maeve's brandy.'

The dishes washed but left to drain, she joined him briefly for a quick drink. 'Top us up,' she offered, setting down her half-empty glass. 'I'll join you as soon as I can.'

She had long since kept a dressing gown and a change of clothing in the spare room, even though she had never spent the night there. It could be a grubby business, helping out on the farm, and she refused to have supper in a haze of pig manure. After her bath, she dressed only in her dressing gown and went back to join him downstairs. It was a cotton robe with a matching cloth belt. She did not tie it too tightly, just with a loose, single knot.

He had put on a seventy-eight of Glen Miller's "Along the Santa Fe Trail", with its languorous tempo and sensuous, romantic melody. Margaret didn't say anything, just picked up her refill and sat next to him on the sofa. His arm went around her shoulders, and she leant into him. He was trying not to make it obvious, but her robe had eased out at the top, and he could see most of her left breast. She pretended not to notice.

The record finished and he quickly put in a new needle to play it again. This time, his left arm again round her shoulders, his right hand crossed to slip inside her robe, caressing her breast, thumb and forefinger teasing her nipple. When the record came to an end, it was Margaret who stood to cross the room, lift the arm and set it back on its rest. The knot was hanging loose, barely holding closed her robe. Instead of sitting down again, she stood in front of him, took his hand and pulled him to his feet. She unbuttoned his shirt and pushed it back from his shoulders, then unfastened the belt on his trousers. The invitation was obvious. She stepped back to allow him to finish undressing. His hands went under her robe and around her waist. She could feel him, hard, against her stomach. From the right-hand pocket of her robe, she took a condom, already unwrapped. She sensed he was almost trembling as she slowly rolled it down his shaft.

Margaret shook the robe from her shoulders, let it fall to the floor and settled herself on top of it, one knee raised, just slightly apart. She widened her legs as he knelt between them. Then he was pushing inside her. He came almost instantly. She had not climaxed, but that did not matter. She caressed his back, smiling as he buried his face in her shoulder.

They made love again, this time to her complete satisfaction, then ran another bath and soaked in it together. Afterwards, both now robed and seated at the kitchen table, he covered her hand with his own. 'We were going to wait,' he said gently, 'but now I'm glad we didn't.'

'Your intention holds to make an honest woman of me, Robert Chapman,' she replied with a smile, 'so I didn't see any point in waiting. And I wouldn't have wanted it any other way.'

He was besotted. She was happy enough. Everything was back on track.

Until the gypsies arrived.

'They come every year, in fact twice,' he explained a few days later. 'Usually about now, and then again towards the end of August. I let them have a month's free parking – more if they want it. In return, they help with all the hedging and ditching, then the spring planting. Later on, it's the harvest, then they pick the apples for me and lift the potato crop. I pay them, but they don't charge anything like as much as it would cost to hire extra local labour. It works to both our advantage.'

* * * *

Their work completed, seated on the steps of his vardo, old Django told the other men he thought it was time they were moving on. 'Master Chapman been fair to us both times,' he said, knocking the dottle from his pipe. 'But this Norfolk coast bain't be the best place this late in the year.'

That evening his son, Bartley, conferred with his closest mates. It didn't happen everywhere, but occasionally, the night before leaving a site, they would commit a local robbery. Their favourite target was a public house. Cigarettes and liquor they could sell on, keeping just enough for themselves. A local bobby might have his suspicions but would have no idea where they had gone. So far it had worked every time.

'Reckon we do The Rose and Crown tonight, then,' he concluded. There were murmurs and nods of agreement.

They were skilled and experienced. Gypsies were good with natural medicines. Common *Valeriana* grassland root had been in use since Greek and Roman times. Richard and Susan Cooper didn't hear a thing. Their dog in the yard had left its kennel, eaten the heavily laced meat and fallen onto its haunches. Gloved hands quietly prized the catch on a lounge window and only one of them climbed through. For the next half-hour, he passed the contents of the shelves behind the bar to those waiting outside. When they came downstairs the next morning, the Coopers were astonished to find that they had been stripped bare.

They phoned Sergeant Wilkins at Dersingham to report the burglary. He drove over later that morning to take details, bringing with him a civilian to dust for prints. There weren't any. Wilkins was unaware even that the gypsies had been at the Chapman Farm, let alone that they had departed that same morning. The Coopers were left cursing their loss. 'I'll get this typed up,' he told them, taking his leave. 'I'll need you to stop by later today or tomorrow to sign a statement.'

They cycled over that afternoon, after lunchtime service, and were shown into Charlie Wilkins' office. Richard sat in front of the sergeant's desk. Whilst he was reading through the document, Susan idly perused a notice board on the wall. She was struck by a photograph. At first, she could not place the subject. Then it came to her. The person in the picture looked as if she just might be a younger version of the newly married Mrs Robert Chapman.

She wouldn't jump to conclusions… not in front of the sergeant and make herself look foolish. But there *was* a resemblance. Susan determined to talk to Robert once they were back home.

'Can't be!' he argued, not for the first time.

'I'm telling you again, I think it might be…' Susie Cooper was annoyed now. Richard could be irritating at times. She rubbed down hard on the zinc bar top. They had closed the doors early after the last lunchtime customer had left The Rose and Crown.

'Did you have your glasses on?' He knew she was too vain to wear them half the time. It was the wrong thing to say. Susie slapped her cloth down and turned to face him, hands on hips, arms akimbo. *Still a handsome woman*, Richard thought, *and she had always been high-spirited.*

His thoughts flashed back to when she had first come to work in their pub. His father had been the landlord back then. The daughter of a gamekeeper on the Sandringham estate, Susie had been blessed with an upturned nose, an enticing rosebud mouth and jet-black hair styled in a close, almost gamin cut. She also came with a narrow waist topped by the perfect attraction in a barmaid and one which she was happy to show off. A bit heavier now, but still able to draw the punters' eyes. Twice his mother had caught them together, back then, the second time with his hand inside her blouse.

Later that day, 'You'll either leave her alone or marry that girl,' she said harshly. Richard knew his parents wanted to retire. They had more than enough put by to purchase a small cottage in the village. Susie was happy enough to accept his proposal. After all, he was a nice-looking lad. *Not a bad deal*, she thought to herself. *A landlord's wife, helping to run the business, and a happy escape from home life under a domineering father.* Richard was over the moon. He had won the best-looking girl for miles in any direction. But his Susie stood no nonsense, neither from customers nor her husband. Richard decided quickly that the argument wasn't worth the hassle. He raised both hands, palms open towards his wife.

'All right, I still don't think it's very likely, but if it makes you happy, I'll cycle over and take a look for myself.'

Susie's knuckles came off her hips. He could see that she was at least a little bit mollified. Richard inclined his head towards the window. 'But not in this… that rain's settled in for the day. It was hardly worth opening this lunchtime for all the trade we did. I'll go as soon as the weather's halfway decent.' Susie knew her husband was too stubborn to be bullied. He would go, but in his own time. She accepted the compromise.

It was a few days before her husband announced his intention to return to Dersingham police station. He phoned Charlie Wilkins that morning and set off after lunch, leaving her to close down for the afternoon.

'Susan's got this bee in her bonnet,' he explained, walking over to the notice board. 'Thinks this girl,' the back of his fingers tapped the photograph, 'resembles Robert Chapman's wife. Load of rubbish if you ask me, but you know what women are like. Said I'd come over to take a look, if only to keep the peace.' Sergeant Wilkins grinned and nodded sympathetically.

But, Richard had to admit to himself, as he studied the print more closely, Susie had a point. There was a likeness. Hesitantly, he turned back to his policeman friend. 'Now, I'm not so sure, Charlie…' he trailed off.

The sergeant was quiet for a moment or two, fingers stroking his chin. 'Tell you what,' he said at last. 'Neither of you are certain, but there's a war on, so we have to be careful. Why don't I stop by at the farm? If I think there's a good enough likeness, I'll pass it on to the relevant authorities. How does that sound?'

Richard Cooper was only too pleased to have the responsibility lifted from his shoulders. He agreed readily enough that neither he nor Susan would say a word to anyone. Charlie Wilkins told him that if he could, he would let them know what, if anything, transpired.

Chapter 16

Spencer wanted to take Flossie out for a meal. 'Saturday night,' he'd suggested. 'No construction guys, like in The King's Head. Just da two of us, so we can sit an' talk across a table. If you agreeable, Flossie Harding.'

She knew there would come a time when she would have to confront, full-on, the fact that he was black and she was white. Flossie had felt secure enough at the dance. Both black and white airmen had been there, together with women from the village. But that was not the same as being a white woman out in the wider world, in the company of a black male – Flossie was not sure just how open-minded the broader British public would be… how they might react.

But she had an ever-deepening affection for Spencer Almeter. No, she corrected herself. Her feelings were stronger than that. Flossie set her misgivings aside. 'It's a lovely thought,' she replied, 'but what do you have in mind?'

'Just a quiet place, somewhere you would like to go – in Peterborough, ah guess, but I don't know where…' he tailed off.

Flossie thought for a minute. 'Let me talk to Uncle Bill,' she suggested. 'We weren't people that could afford to eat in a restaurant, even before Jimmy arrived. I'll have to ask.'

Bill Harding came up trumps. 'There's a sort of informal club, an association, if you like, of people who run licensed premises in this area. Mostly pubs, like The King's Head, but quite a few eating places, too. Smaller family businesses. Do you think your man has ever tried proper British fish and chips?' he asked. Flossie confessed that she had no idea. But it was unlikely.

'There's this Italian chap I know,' went on Bill. 'I helped him out with a job when he was a refugee in England, before you were born,' he added. 'We chat from time to time. 'Tonio runs a small place in Peterborough. It was a takeaway chip shop before the war, but now it also has a very nice dining room at the back where you can sit down for a meal. What with the war and everything, he has to make do with whatever he can serve, but he often dresses other things up as Italian, and I'm told it's very popular, not least with visiting G.I.s. Why don't you give him a ring?'

'Thanks for the suggestion,' she mentioned to her uncle that evening. 'I did 'phone him, told him who I was. We had quite a conversation. Said if we wanted to eat there Saturday, he'd save a nice table.'

They caught the bus and arrived in Peterborough at seven. It was a ten-minute walk to the harbour area, where, to Spencer's amusement, a sign above the establishment read "Tonio's Plaice". It was a traditional fish and chip shop, with a queue snaking out of the door and along the street. Inside, a man – Tonio, presumably – and two lady assistants were serving frantically. But there was a separate restaurant room. It was packed. There were about fifteen tables, all quite close together and each taken, save one set for two in a corner with a "Reserved" sign on it. Four tables were occupied by American servicemen: three by officers, one by senior NCOs.

Two dark-haired young ladies, female versions of Tonio, almost certainly daughters, were both busy with other tables. 'That one has to be ours, over there,' Flossie pointed out. 'Let's sit down, then we can order a drink.'

Spencer sensed that the level of conversation hushed when he drew back a chair for Flossie before seating himself. One of the waitresses, the older of the two, came to join them.

'I'm ever so sorry, sir, madam,' she said quietly, looking first at Spencer and then Flossie, 'but we are unable to serve coloured American servicemen in the restaurant. We would be happy to offer whatever you might like to order in the shop, though, for you to take away. I'm sure you would enjoy it,' she added almost desperately.

Although she had spoken softly, conversation immediately around them had ceased entirely. Other tables were looking and listening.

Flossie felt her cheeks burning with embarrassment. It had not occurred to her to mention that Spencer was not white. Next to her, Spencer had his hands on the table, making ready to rise. Something inside her snapped. She placed a hand on Spencer's forearm and pushed down hard. She rose to her feet, pushing back the chair, not caring how much of a scraping noise it made.

'I made this reservation personally with Mr Tonio, who is a family friend,' she replied firmly. 'Perhaps you had better ask him to join us.' She had spoken moderately, but even so, most of the nearby tables heard her response. She sat down again, deliberately pulling up her chair to the table, an act of defiance that said they were not going anywhere.

The girl turned away, obviously unable to cope with the situation and only too relieved at the suggestion to let her father deal with it. Spencer placed his hand over Flossie's. 'Don't want nah trouble, girl,' he said anxiously. 'We can still go through to da shop.' His accent, she noticed, was more pronounced than usual.

Flossie was saved a reply by the appearance of Tonio approaching their table, wringing his hands on his apron, and accompanied by his daughter.

'Miss Harding,' he said anxiously, 'I'm so sorry. But you did not tell me...' he paused, then found his voice again. 'It's the

Americans. They say that if I admit coloured folks – that's what they call you, sir,' he said apologetically, looking at Spencer – 'the whites will not come to my restaurant. They will place it out of bounds. I can't afford… it's nothing personal, sir,' he tailed off, still looking at Spencer, as if imploring them to leave.

An elderly gentleman, seated with his wife at an adjacent table, struggled to his feet, one hand pushing down on a walking cane. 'George darling, please,' she said nervously. His other hand now on the table, he slipped his grip a short way down the glossy black shaft and banged the cane's solid silver spaniel's head hard on their table. It commanded instant attention.

He wiped a moustache left and right with a forefinger before glaring at the restaurant. 'For those of you who don't know,' he began imperiously, 'my name is Houghton. That's Colonel Edwin Houghton.' Elderly and a little frail he might have been, but he stood to attention and his voice was vibrant.

'I was in the last lot.' he barked at the room, as if addressing a parade ground. 'Attached as a liaison officer to the French Army. Under command, we had the 369th United States Infantry Regiment. They earned the name and reputation from the Hun as "Hell Fighters". It is a matter of fact that they never lost a man through capture, and they never lost so much as an inch of ground to the enemy. They came late to the war but fought for almost six months in the trenches. Many died, but the entire regiment was awarded the Croix de Guerre for gallantry.'

He lifted his cane, pointing it in the general direction of the American tables. 'Those gallant soldiers were black to a man,' he thundered. The old colonel was a natural orator. There was a deathly silence. He turned to Flossie and Spencer. 'Sir,' he said, just a little more quietly, 'this is a large enough table. If you and your lady would care to join us, we would be honoured to have you dine with us.'

'And if there are any objections,' he turned back to the assembly, 'just bring me your number, rank and name.' This, clearly, was addressed to the remaining Americans.

A deathly quiet. Then, a first, hesitant handclap, followed by a trickle more. Soon, the entire restaurant burst into applause. Towards the end, before it died away completely, to their credit the American tables joined in, though whether it was a salutation to the old soldier, the force of his argument, or the men of the 369th, it was impossible to know.

Tonio and his daughter rushed to draw back chairs for Flossie and Spencer, who moved self-consciously to join the colonel and his lady. 'Proud to have you as my guests,' he told them, before resuming his seat. 'We have only just ordered, so if Tonio would kindly bring back the menus, we can all eat together.'

'Now then, my dears,' his hand embraced them both, 'what'll you have to drink? Then you must choose exactly what you would like.' His wife offered Flossie and Spencer a warm smile. 'Edwin, I was only worried that you might have a heart attack,' she admonished him. 'Nonsense, my dear,' he replied. 'Needed to be said. Besides,' he added, 'haven't enjoyed myself so much in damn-well ages – pardon my French, ladies.'

* * * *

By autumn 1942 the United States Army Air Force base at Swanton was fully operational, its construction almost completed. Isaac Hofmeyer had been promoted to full colonel and now had four squadrons of B17s, each commanded by a major. On a perfect day, they could put thirty-two aircraft into the sky, flying in a three-layer box formation. But casualties were heavy. Anything over twenty-four aircraft was considered a triumph of maintenance and repair. There were always losses to flak, particularly once control had been handed over to the bombardier, whilst the enemy fighters had developed the tactic of a high-speed dive through the formation, trying to pick off one or two aircraft on the way down. They were a particularly difficult and fleeting target for the B 17's dorsal, waist and lower ball turret gunners.

Hofmeyer did not fly many missions, but it was a point of honour. When one of his squadron commanders was not available, he allowed the second in command to lead the squadron, to gain experience, whilst he flew the commander's ship. Bomber crews did not usually like to fly with a replacement skipper, but Hofmeyer was both admired and respected. Rumour had it he had once been grounded for slow-rolling a B17 whilst on his conversion course. And he was a lucky pilot. Hofmeyer had already flown nearly half of the twenty-five missions that would entitle aircrew to rotate home, and after the switch from Hudsons, he had yet to bring home a Flying Fortress with a killed or injured crew member.

Today, it was an air marshalling yard at Amiens. Hofmeyer was roused from sleep at two a.m. and took breakfast in the mess hall at three. Pilots and radio operators were briefed separately before the mission, after which Hofmeyer collected his survival kit, including compass, maps and gold coin. After a walk-round with his crew chief, he signed for the aeroplane. Encumbered by his electrically heated suit, he clambered up the ladder and pulled the hatch shut behind him. Settling into Curtis James' seat, he thought briefly of the squadron commander, booked to have a painful molar extracted later that morning. Better by far to be flying a mission rather than face the dentist's chair. Curtis ran a tight ship. There was no unnecessary chatter. Gunners were checking and re-checking their weapons and belt feeds. He thumbed his throat mike button.

'Pilot to all hands.'

This was a permanent joke. Hofmeyer's father had been a Navy man. Rudy Ansbach, in the right-hand seat, gave his usual, 'Co-pilot.'

'Navigator to pilot.'

'Bombardier to pilot.'

'Engineer to pilot.' Johnny Carstairs was the dorsal gunner, but he was also the flight engineer. He thought it sounded more important.

'Radio operator to pilot.'

'Ball turret to pilot.' Isaac did not envy Brad Pierce, cramped up like a foetus in his Sperry turret, a Plexiglas ball hanging off the bottom of the B17.

And so it went on, waist gunners, tail gunner, each in turn, till all nine crew members had responded.

The intercom and pre-flight checks completed, and with all four engines ticking over at one thousand rpm, the co-pilot cleared for take-off, and Isaac's inverted right hand pushed the four throttle levers forward. *Righteous Rosie* began to gather speed. Curtis, the son of a Baptist minister, was also a religious man. His crew thought the name brought them luck – perhaps even a hint of protection from some higher authority. Isaac held *Rosie* down to gather speed. He wanted a clean take-off, not letting the wheels bounce before leaving the ground. Then they were airborne, more speed, and climbing to a holding pattern whilst the squadrons formed up.

Finally, there were three staggered layers of box formation, each one hundred and fifty feet of height apart, six aircraft to each layer. They were in the top layer. Middle was favourite, the safest, but Isaac was glad not to be on the bottom, even though the bombs had to drop about five hundred feet before they armed. And the *flak* would be bad around the marshalling yard. They closed up, crossing the French coast, wingtips only feet apart, making the machine gun fire from mutual support as dense as possible.

Rich Ruddich, the bombardier, had the con on the bombing run. This was the part Isaac liked least of all. They were committed, impossible to manoeuvre. Fortunately, the sky was empty of enemy fighters. Balls of flak smoke were creeping uncomfortably closer. *Rosie* shuddered, hard, and there was a rattle of metal somewhere against the fuselage, but she flew on, apparently no serious damage. Then they were through, and Rich had them lined up for the last few seconds. Isaac looked around. Way below and left, a B17 took a hit from the ground. Not a flamer, but two engines were smoking, and it dropped slowly from formation. Easy meat for a fighter, once out of the box. But if their luck held, they could fly home on the other two.

He felt the upward lift as Rich released their bomb load of twenty 250-pounders. That overwhelming sense of relief: he had control again as the formation turned for home. It looked as if they had been pretty much on target. Hopefully, another crew of ten would not have to risk their lives over Amiens because they had missed. Hofmeyer was grateful for the absence of Fws and Messerschmitt 109s. Over the channel, they relaxed the formation, flying a little further apart. He invited the co-pilot to land *Righteous Rosie*.

He might have been a relative rookie, but Rudi Ansbach was competent. On finals, he pointed the bomber's nose into a strong crosswind, kicking off with rudder to line her up with the runway just before the first touch. Speed was a shade high, but otherwise, the approach was perfect. *Rosie* touched smoothly, lifted, touched gently again, barely lifted a final time, then sighed quietly onto the runway. But the rush of adrenalin relief after a safe return produced exuberant cries over the intercom.

'One, two, three,' someone counted.

'Bumps a daisy,' came next.

'Upsie-downsie, just like a French tart's drawers.'

'Not so much a landing, more of an arrival,' intoned a fourth.

The props windmilled to a standstill. Had Isaac been out of action, Rudi would have brought them down safely. 'Well done,' he announced over the intercom, grinning at his co-pilot, 'and take no notice of the passengers, they're an ungrateful lot.'

Back in his office, Hofmeyer sank into his chair and reached for the bottom drawer of his desk. Extracting a glass, he poured a good three fingers of Jack Daniels. Some time later, there was a knock on the door. He left his empty glass where it was. If someone didn't approve, too bad. Especially if they didn't fly missions over France.

It was his intelligence officer, Sam Heimy. He knew the colonel would have taken a stiff drink after the mission. He also knew he would want more than one. 'Any chance you have a second glass, sir, so I can join you?' he asked tactfully.

In response to a wave of the CO's hand, he settled into a chair in front of the desk and took a sip of his whiskey. 'Had an interesting 'phone call from London this morning,' he began once the colonel had joined him. 'Been asked to go to a meeting there tomorrow. When our people told me about Max Staunton, I wired them a copy of the ID photo we took for his base pass. They showed it to his old newspaper people. Bottom line is, Staunton's a phoney. Almost certainly, he's a spy. And the source of our leak.'

'And...?' responded Isaac. He felt drained after the mission, and the whiskey wasn't helping.

'They want us to do absolutely nothing until after the meeting, Colonel. If it's OK with you, I've made arrangements to be there tomorrow.'

'Who's "they", and where's "there"?' Isaac asked, forcing himself to concentrate, knowing that this was important.

'Some outfit I've never heard of,' Heimy told him. 'They're in Grosvenor Street, Mayfair. They call themselves O.S.S. for short. Apparently, it stands for "The Office of Strategic Services".'

Late morning the following day found Sam Heimy outside 72 Grosvenor Street. There was no plate on the outside of the building, but a reception desk manned by two gentlemen in suits suggested that this might not be a traditional British corporate head office. When one of them demanded his ID with a distinct New England accent, Sam would have guessed Boston, it came as no surprise.

Suit number two consulted a list and pressed a button. Moments later, a third suit invited Sam to follow him to an elevator. A plaque on a door said William Joseph Casey. He was shown into a large office overlooking the street. A civilian gentleman, introducing himself as Bill Casey, stood from behind a desk to offer his hand. He had dark hair combed back from his brow. Casey wore spectacles and had a slightly fleshy, rather oblong face with a protruding lower lip and something of a generous chin. A totally innocuous appearance belied his appointment as the newly formed O.S.S.'s Director of European Operations.

'Please be seated, Major Heimy, the director invited with a wave of his hand – or may I call you Sam?' he asked. 'How much do you know about our organisation,' he continued without waiting for an answer.

'First I heard of it was yesterday,' Sam replied. He rather resented being summoned to London by someone outside his own service and was not yet ready to gift this civilian a "sir".

'Let me give you some background,' Casey began. 'Time was when the US military and other organisations conducted their own intelligence. Roosevelt was concerned that this approach was too fragmented – important information was slipping through the cracks. A senior British intelligence officer suggested that the president draw up a plan based on their more coordinated Secret Intelligence Service and Special Operations Executive – their S.I.S. and S.O.E. systems. One William J Donovan was given the job, and he recommended a single agency responsible for foreign intelligence and special operations.' He paused for emphasis before finally stating: 'We, the O.S.S., were established by presidential decree on 13th June this year.'

'Wild Bill Donovan?' queried Sam. It was the only name he knew. He had never heard of William Joseph Casey before meeting him today.

Casey grinned. 'His troops gave him that nickname in The Great War. It stuck.'

'So,' said Sam, then after a pause, 'Mr Casey, you didn't bring me all the way to London just for a history lesson. I presume this has everything to do with Max Staunton.'

'You presume right,' came the instant response. 'You see, the people you originally approached are now part of my organisation, and they also brought Staunton to our attention here in London. Which only goes to prove the value of this joined-up approach.

'I've also been in touch with both the British S.I.S. and our own people,' he added. 'We don't know Staunton's true identity yet. But almost certainly, he's *Abwehr*.'

'What are you going to do with him?' asked Sam.

'Nothing, for the moment,' came the reply. 'We have a great idea for using him to send disinformation back to Germany, but for that, we have to let him think that he's still in the clear. So what I want you to do, apart from briefing your CO that this information is for his and your ears only, is simply to tell me anything on Staunton that you think might be useful. What he does, where he goes, who he associates with – anything at all, no matter how trivial. Unless anything important turns up, a weekly report should be fine.'

Sam thought for a moment. 'But surely,' he said eventually, 'you can't be intending to let him carry on sending information back home. Hell, this could put us all at risk.'

'Don't worry,' the director assured him, 'we'll be carrying out our own surveillance on Staunton. Trust me, he won't be able to do anything to endanger the base. We want you and your people to keep him under a tight watch whilst he's there on duty, and obviously, you won't tell him anything he might find useful, but we will do all that it takes to monitor his off-base activities.'

Sam was not reassured, and said so, not mincing his words.

'Point taken, but there's more to this than just Staunton,' Casey responded. 'The Brits have authorised me to share their information with you. They think they may have identified a German agent – a woman – in the Norfolk village of Snettisham. Two *Abwehr* agents, just a few miles apart: there *has* to be some sort of connection. It looks as though the Krauts are setting up a new operation in the UK. If we pull in Staunton now, we risk alerting this female in Snettisham. We have been asked to stand back, at least until they have had a chance to question her, which I gather is imminent, and maybe for much longer after that. It all depends,' he said, and Sam detected a degree of concern in his voice, 'on how things pan out.'

Chapter 17

The summons came early that morning. There had been a possible sighting of the woman they were seeking. Werner was only too happy to ride his Ariel 350 c.c. military motorcycle into Town – it was much more convenient than using public transport, and, perhaps illogically, he always felt safer not being trapped in an omnibus or railway carriage. He was expected. At reception, his pass produced a young female escort, and minutes later, he was seated in Sir Manners' office.

'I think it might be more than just a possible,' said his host. 'What the RAF would term a "probable". She's been calling herself Margaret Minogue, although she recently married a local farmer, so she's Mrs Margaret Chapman now.'

'It's been quite a while since we put out the notice,' observed Werner. 'Why has it taken so long to find her, and why now, all of a sudden?'

'If it is her, she's in rural Norfolk,' Sir Manners replied. 'It only came to light when a village pub in a place called Snettisham was burgled. Apparently, the landlord and his wife went to the nearest police station, another god-forsaken place called Dersingham, to sign a statement. While he was doing that, his wife amused herself by looking at a noticeboard. Lucky for us, she made the connection. The local bobby, Sergeant Wilkins, provided a second opinion. He also thinks she's the woman in our photograph. And I'm sure you are aware,' he added ominously, 'that rural Norfolk is also airbase country, a lot of British and American bombers.'

Charlie Wilkins was surprised to receive a 'phone call from no less a personage than his Chief Constable. It had never happened before in all his years of service. Eyeing the noticeboard as he took the call, throughout their conversation he used only two words: "yes" and "sir". But when he replaced the receiver, Sergeant Wilkins had agreed to offer every assistance to an intelligence officer from London. And he had been sworn to secrecy.

It was a pleasant enough journey, although it took nearly all day, but by early evening, Werner was unpacking his suitcase in a comfortable room at The Feathers. He had been offered an evening meal of shepherd's pie in the saloon, and he was wondering whether there might be a glass or two of red wine or just beer. He was delighted to find that, apparently, there was not much call for wine in these parts. A decent French red had been sitting in the cellar since before the war.

Werner set down his knife and fork. It had been a simple but truly excellent supper. He was in the act of pouring a second glass when a rather portly figure in corduroy trousers and a sports jacket, long since leather-patched at the cuffs and elbows, approached his table.

'Landlord says you be Mister Scholtz,' he said, proffering a warrant card. 'Sergeant Charlie Wilkins, sir. I figured you would probably be staying here, so I thought I might call by and introduce myself.'

Werner invited him to sit down, at the same time producing his own identity document. 'That's good of you, Sergeant,' he replied. 'Can I offer you something to drink?'

Before he could reply, the landlord had set a pint of beer on the table – Charlie was, after all, a regular. He nodded politely to both men and retreated to behind the bar.

'You don't sound English, sir,' said Wilkins, just a hint of doubt in his voice.

'I am originally from Germany,' Werner replied. 'But as your Chief Constable told you yesterday, I was once a refugee, and now I work for British intelligence.' The insider knowledge of his phone call was more than enough to settle Charlie Wilkins' mind. The saloon was filling up with other patrons, all of whom were known to – and knew – their village sergeant, so their duty conversation was confined to confirming that Werner would be collected by car at nine the following morning. For most of the next hour, and over a second pint, Sergeant Wilkins described to Werner life in rural, wartime Norfolk. It was not so different, he reflected sadly, from that on the family estate in Buchbach. He could but hope that his father was still alive.

'Nice morning for it, sir,' Charlie Wilkins greeted him cheerfully from behind the wheel of a black Wolseley patrol car. Werner settled himself into the front seat, wriggling to adjust his mackintosh so that the service revolver in his pocket was no longer digging into his ribs. He had nowhere else to put it.

He asked to be taken first to The Rose and Crown, where Richard Cooper confirmed that Mr and Mrs Chapman would indeed be at the farm. They had not gone away for a honeymoon even though it was no longer harvest time.

'None of my business,' put in Susan Cooper, 'but I think she's been living there for a long time now, as well as helping out on the farm.' Werner, who had been introduced simply as "an officer sent from London", confirmed with them that Margaret's cottage would almost certainly be unoccupied. Having reminded the Coopers not to discuss their visit, he and Sergeant Wilkins returned to their car.

They found a forest track in the woods near the cottage and reversed until they were out of sight from the road. A short push through the undergrowth brought them, somewhat scratched and breathless, to the fence around the cottage garden.

Sergeant Wilkins watched in silence as Werner opened the blade of a penknife, forced the catch on a kitchen sash window, and lifted it to climb inside. 'Wait here,' he told him, 'and I'll let you in through the door.'

'What do we do now, sir?' he asked, once inside.

'We search,' Werner said simply. 'If she's who we think she is, she probably won't have taken anything suspicious with her to the farmhouse.'

After an hour and a half, they had found nothing. Werner began to wonder whether, after all, there was perhaps no more than a close resemblance, and he was on a wild goose chase. Back in the kitchen, he stared at the garden. Right at the bottom, up against the fence, stood a dilapidated greenhouse, its door hanging open on one hinge, many of the panes above a low wall broken or missing. 'Better make sure,' he muttered to Sergeant Wilkins.

The inside smelled of damp and rotten vegetation – long dead tomato plants lay on the benches lining both sides, some with a shrivelled fruit still attached. But the dirt floor was surprisingly clean, not as littered with dead leaves and blown-in detritus as Werner would have expected. Squatting down and starting at the door, he began poking at the earth with the blade of his penknife.

It was near the far end, under an area where the roof panes were still intact and the interior fairly well protected from the rain, that his blade penetrated for no more than an inch and a half. Brushing away the dirt with his hand revealed a panel of plywood. Werner lifted one end. Underneath, well wrapped in an oilskin cover, was a suitcase, and lifting it onto a side bench, he brushed off a few patches of dirt with the back of his hand.

Twin locks secured the lid. A spike designed to remove foreign objects from horses' hooves snapped open the locks in short order. Sergeant Wilkins let out a low whistle. Inside was a radio, a pad and pencils, and one copy of *Hauptmann Ladurner* by Luis Trenker.

Werner lowered the lid. 'Perhaps, Sergeant,' he said quietly, 'you would be so kind as to put this in the back of the Wolseley. I'll close up the cottage and meet you at the car. I think it's time we paid a call on the not-so-good former Miss Minogue.'

Werner and Sergeant Wilkins arrived at the farmhouse just after lunch. Robert was seated at the kitchen table; Margaret was drying up. He saw them pull into the yard and went to meet them at the door.

'Sergeant Wilkins,' he offered. 'Good to see you. Have you come about the reports of stock thefts? We've been lucky so far, haven't had any.' He looked at Werner. 'And who's this gentleman?' he asked. 'Don't tell me Lynn has sent plainclothes support to Snettisham over a few head of sheep? Anyway, come on in. We have just finished lunch, but I think there's still some tea in the pot.'

Werner followed them both into the kitchen. Margaret dried her hands, placed the cloth on the draining board and turned towards them.

'Darling, Sergeant Wilkins you know,' said Robert. 'And this is...?' he broke off, waiting for an introduction.

Werner stepped towards her till they were barely a pace apart. German polite society was punctilious about this greeting, particularly the first of the day. It would have been instilled into her psyche. He offered his hand. '*Guten Tag*,' he said quickly. There was an involuntary half-word of her own.

'Gut...' she uttered, just the first syllable, then silence. But she had betrayed herself.

'*Frau* Margaret, my name is Werner Scholz,' he began in German, not unkindly, before switching to English. 'I am from London, and we know who you are. Perhaps we might all sit down?'

Margaret was appalled at the stupidity of her indiscretion. She and Robert sat close together on one side of the kitchen table. Werner and Sergeant Wilkins sat opposite, but further apart. Margaret clasped her hands together, apprehensive, but trying not to look too concerned. Robert wondered whether the sky was about to fall in on his world, which, in a way, it was.

'Margaret,' Werner began gently, 'we know that you are a spy for Germany. You accompanied the Wagners when they returned home from Belfast. The *Abwehr* recruited you, but we failed to pick you up when you were dropped into the United Kingdom. We have finally traced you to Snettisham. We have recovered your radio and code book. They are in the back of Sergeant Wilkins' car outside.'

Robert was aghast. He placed his hand over Margaret's. 'Darling, tell me it's not true,' he burst out.

Instead of answering her husband, she asked quietly, 'How did you find out?'

'All I am going to tell you,' Werner replied, 'is that I have spoken to a former colleague of *Herr* Wagner's in Germany, and not long ago, I found your picture in a photograph on the grand piano of their family home in Hamburg.'

Her shoulders slumped. She turned to Robert, choosing her words carefully. 'I'm so, so sorry, my love, but it's true. I set out to use you when we first met, but then I fell in love. That much, at least, I beg of you to believe.' She turned back to Werner. 'So what happens now?' she asked, with what little confidence she could manage.

'That depends,' he replied, still speaking softly, 'on where we go from here. But I should tell you that you are by no means the first agent that we have apprehended. For the most part, the penalty is death by hanging.'

Robert jumped to his feet, pushing his chair back so that it crashed onto the flagstones. 'You can't,' he said, his voice raised in anger. He placed one arm protectively around her shoulders and pulled her towards him. 'I'm British, and Margaret's now my wife.'

It was Sergeant Wilkins' turn to intervene. 'Robert,' he ordered evenly. 'I think you should hear what the gentleman has to say.'

'Your loyalties must be confused and divided,' Werner told her. 'A father killed by protestant riots, befriended by a German family, taken back to a new life in their homeland, then finally recruited by the *Abwehr*, not least because of your ability to return to the United Kingdom and blend into the background. But do you really hate the British?' he asked bluntly.

'I think I did, back then,' she replied after a few moments' hesitation. 'But I can't now, can I? Not after I have fallen in love with Robert.' He moved to stand behind her chair, both hands on her shoulders, offering support.

'The only agents that have not been executed,' Werner stated, his voice now quietly matter-of-fact, 'are those that have agreed to work for us.' He let the silence hang.

Robert retrieved his chair, set it back next to Margaret's, resumed his seat and placed one hand over both of hers. 'You have to, darling,' he pleaded, his voice an urgent but audible whisper, 'there's no choice…' He turned to face Werner. 'What would that mean?'

But Werner continued to address the now silent Margaret. 'We are working with the Americans,' he told her, 'and their main interest is a man we believe to be a German agent at the former RAF Swanton. He came on the scene quite some time after you first arrived in Snettisham, so we have every reason to believe that you must have been in some way involved with his entry into this country. For your own and Robert's sake, Margaret, tell me what you know.'

There was another long silence. Werner was only too aware that her thoughts had to be in turmoil. He watched as Robert squeezed her hands, then rocked them from side to side. 'Please, my love...' he implored her.

She exhaled audibly, looking first at Robert and then directly at Werner, seemingly having come to a decision.

'His first name is Max,' she said eventually, 'Max Staunton. We were briefed by the same officer in Berlin, so he has to be *Abwehr*.'

'Thank God,' said Robert quietly.

'He's still calling himself Max Staunton,' Werner responded. 'The real Max Staunton was a British-American journalist working for a USA newspaper, the *Boston Daily Record*, which means that he's almost certainly no longer alive. And our Max Staunton looks nothing like the original.'

'What do you want from me?' asked Margaret in a flat monotone, entirely without expression, which told Werner that she had accepted defeat. The former Margaret Minogue had been successfully, to use the jargon of his trade, "turned". She was his to do with as they wished.

'We are going to use Max to send a series of false reports back to Berlin,' he told her. 'But it is important that we vet the contents. Presumably, he has his own radio?'

A slow, double nod of her head confirmed that he did.

'But if his own radio were out of action, what would he do?' Werner pressed on.

She thought, but only for a moment. 'Almost certainly, he would have to come to me,' she replied carefully. 'I doubt he knows the identity and whereabouts of any other agents, but he knows I have a radio.' She glanced at Sergeant Wilkins. 'Or I did, before you put it in the back of your car. Anyway, I sent a message for him when he first arrived. So yes, I think he would have no choice but to contact me.'

'And you would know the content of any such message sent on his behalf?' queried Werner.

'Only if we used my code book, and I made the transcription,' she replied. She told him about the *Ladurner* code. 'Otherwise, I wouldn't.'

'You will have to make sure that you do,' Werner responded sharply. 'In fact,' he said more slowly, 'that's the price of your continued freedom. No, I stand corrected' – he paused – 'that's the price of your life.'

* * * *

Two days later, Sam Heimy picked up the receiver. 'I work for the director you met the day before yesterday,' the caller announced. 'Can you meet me off-base? I'll be at the village tearoom. And please don't tell anyone; just turn up there.'

'Uh-huh,' responded Sam. In truth, he was not sure what to say. And now the caller had hung up.

Ten minutes later, he pushed open the door. Several tables were occupied by lady shoppers enjoying a mid-morning break. From one, in the far corner of the room, a single male rose to beckon him over. None of the adjacent tables were occupied. A fair-haired individual extended his hand. The civilian clothes were British, not American. He had to be in his late twenties or early thirties, Sam thought. Average height, regular looks. There was absolutely nothing remarkable about him. He wore a sports jacket and flannels, a white shirt and a plain tie – nothing that would stand out in a crowd. It was as if his entire persona had been designed to blend, unnoticed, into the background.

'Mark Weyland,' he offered, by way of introduction, 'thanks for coming.' The accent was in stark contrast to his appearance. Gruff Midwestern – Chicago, Sam guessed if he had to put a finger on it. 'And yes,' Weyland added, 'before you ask, I work for Director Casey. I'm also O.S.S.'

'I told your Director Casey everything I know about Max Staunton,' Sam responded, 'so I'm curious… why telephone me again this morning?'

'Because we need your cooperation,' came the reply, 'and also that of your colonel, so you will need to bring him in on the situation. But you two must be the only people on base who know about this operation. Absolute secrecy. Otherwise, many lives will be at risk. Some of them your own aircrew.'

'Go on,' invited Sam, a gentle nod of the head indicating assent.

'There's a lot of concern about losses,' Weyland began. 'You will have seen it with your aircrew, but the higher-ups are also acutely worried. The present, twelve-plane, staggered, three-layer combat box formation gives some protection, but only to a limited extent. As you know, LeMay, among others, has been developing the concept of a three-box combat group, thirty-six B-17s, again staggered, both vertically and horizontally. Better defence and a higher bombing intensity.' The name came as no surprise to Sam. He had once served under the highly intelligent and forward-thinking Major – now Colonel – Curtis LeMay.

'At the moment, we are mostly bombing France,' Weyland went on. 'But we want to use these massive formations for deep penetration, daylight raids, into France *and* Germany. And they are going to have to do it without fighter cover – our pursuit squadrons don't have the range.

'But first things first.' Weyland paused, then, 'For now, I would like you to confirm when Staunton is on base and devise some way of keeping him there for a while. I want to find his radio. As he has no idea that we know who he really is, it's almost certainly somewhere in his accommodation. I'm going to search for it, and you are welcome to join me. In fact, I'd welcome your help. But don't wear uniform. How would tomorrow sound? Would that be too soon?'

'Just give me a number where I can reach you,' Sam replied.

Later that day, the transport section warrant officer called Mr Staunton to tell him that his jeep was overdue a service. They would collect it as soon as he had arrived on base tomorrow morning. Once safely on base, he was going nowhere for the next two or three hours.

Sam was waiting for Mark Weyland by the main barrier and climbed into the front passenger seat of an inconspicuous Morris 8. It was ten miles to Staunton's cottage, which had no immediate neighbours, and they parked behind it, out of sight from the road.

'Probably chose somewhere like this deliberately,' Weyland observed, taking a wallet from his pocket and extracting one of several lock picks. He had the kitchen door open in under a minute. So confident had Staunton been of his cover that the radio was not even concealed. Once upstairs, they found it almost immediately, in its suitcase, on top of the wardrobe in a spare bedroom at the rear of the property.

'So he can just throw the aerial out of the back window,' Sam remarked.

He watched as Weyland removed the radio and unscrewed the back cover to expose its innards. Removing two of the valves, he shook them hard till he could see through the clear glass that the filaments were broken, then replaced them and reassembled the set.

'That should do it,' he said without explanation before carefully returning the suitcase to the top of the wardrobe, positioned precisely as he had found it. The whole exercise had taken little more than an hour and a half. Back at the base, Sam made a brief phone call to the transport office.

Chapter 18

Mark Weyland and Werner met, at his suggestion, for lunch in Town. By mutual agreement, Werner would continue to 'run' Margaret, whilst Mark would handle the American end, with Sam Heimy's assistance. The two professionals were forming an easy working relationship. They exchanged details of both *Abwehr* agents, photographs, addresses and so forth.

'Never know when they might come in handy,' said Werner. 'Avoid any crossed wires and all that.'

'You don't think that there's a risk,' queried Mark, 'leaving the Irish girl her freedom?'

'No choice,' Werner replied bluntly. 'She has to be available to Max Staunton at any time. But no, I don't think she'll do a runner. She's heavily invested in her future with Robert Chapman. And I was at pains to point out that if she settled anywhere in the United Kingdom or the Irish Republic, we would find her eventually, and she would hang. Plus, in the unlikely event that she made it back to Germany, we would let the *Abwehr* know that she had also been working for us. Either way, she knows she would finish up on the end of a rope.'

'And how's her husband, this farmer fellow, Chapman, I think you said his name was, taking it all?' asked Mark. 'Must have been a hell of a shock, finding out that what he thought was an ordinary Irish girl turned out to be a German agent.'

'Way out of his depth, still reeling from the news,' said Werner. 'But Sergeant Wilkins, the local bobby I've been working with, has known Robert all his life. Used to be a friend of his parents when they were still alive, so he's a bit of a father figure. He's stopping by at the farm pretty much daily to keep an eye on things.'

He twirled the stem of his wineglass. 'I have briefed him on a point of English common law, and he's passed it on to Robert. Historically, it was known as "Pleading the Belly".' Mark raised his eyebrows, inviting further explanation.

'I gather it goes back to the late fourteenth century,' said Werner. 'If an obviously pregnant woman was convicted of a crime punishable by death, the sentence could be delayed until after she had given birth to the child. It was still the law until not long ago, when the 1931 Sentence of Death (Expectant Mothers) Act came into being. Now, a death sentence would automatically be commuted to one of life imprisonment with hard labour.'

'Still a pretty rough deal for the Chapmans, now that they're married,' observed Mark.

Werner shook his head. 'Robert has been told that the people I work for have regular contact with the highest levels of government, which is true,' he added. 'The head of our organisation has direct access to Winston. So he knows that all being well, if she cooperates fully and everything goes according to plan, Margaret's *Abwehr* activity will remain a state secret. After the war she should be able to resume a normal life. But if his wife were to become pregnant, that could only strengthen their hand. He was told to think of it as no more than an additional insurance policy.'

'Jeez,' said Mark, 'how on earth did he take that?'

'Rather calmly, so I'm told,' said Werner with just the faintest hint of a smile. 'To quote Sergeant Wilkins, he thinks young Robert has every intention of killing two birds with one stone.'

'I have a feeling,' came the reply, 'that the action is going to be divided between our base at Swanton and in Snettisham. I'm travelling down to Swanton tomorrow to discuss the next phase with Sam and Colonel Hofmeyer.'

* * * *

Spencer heard the news from a buddy who was assigned to the detail that cleaned up the headquarters.

'We is bein' transferred back stateside!'

The men were cock-a-hoop. Although had they known what eventually awaited them in the Asia Pacific war, they would have been less exultant. Planning for the American offensive in the Far East was still in the early stages, and the priority had always been first to defeat Hitler in Europe. But now assets were being transferred to support the 1942 US offensive on Guadalcanal in the Solomon Islands. Construction units would always be at the forefront of this campaign.

For Spencer, it was a disaster. He had to admit that their work on the Swanton base, apart from ongoing maintenance and occasional runway repairs, was finished. But life in England was good. His talent had blossomed. He was now the lead singer for Isaac Hofmeyer's musicians, who were developing rapidly to produce a smaller but equally effective version of the big band sound. He had a steady if – for him – an overly platonic relationship with Flossie Harding and a life off-base that was the envy of his friends. Sundays, they usually went for a walk, sometimes a drink in The King's Head, before whatever Gladys could manage to produce for a Sunday lunch – a meal more often than not enhanced by his contribution to their rations.

That afternoon, Gladys excused her daughter-in-law from the washing up. The weather was sunny and still warm.

'Go, take a walk,' she suggested, shooing the two of them towards the door. 'Make the most of the fine weather – it wasn't that good a summer, but we're having a decent enough autumn so far.' They followed a public footpath, little used at this time of year, across a local farm, eventually stopping in a copse that overlooked a small stream. Spencer took off his uniform coat and spread it on the grass.

'Something's wrong,' she said when they were seated side by side. Spencer hadn't put his arm around her or even held her hand. She did her best to put on a brave face.

'I have never known you so quiet. You haven't had much to say all morning. Be honest,' she asked anxiously, 'are you growing tired of me?'

He turned to look at her, arms round his knees, hands clasped together. 'I'm black; you're white,' he began hesitantly. 'But I think we feel somethin' fo each othah. Got some bad news, though. We is bein' sent stateside. Probably before we git deployed someplace else. From what I hears, Far East is probably next. An' derr was meh – tryin' to git up da courage to ask if you would marry meh…' In his anxiety, he had reverted entirely to the Georgia dialect.

Flossie was silent for several seconds, thinking furiously about what he had said, what those few words must have cost him. And beyond the colour of his skin, not for the first time she saw the quiet courage of a man prepared to stand for his rights, his beliefs.

'But what about Jimmy?' she asked hesitantly.

'I'm nevah gonna be able to tell folks he's mine,' he said with a smile, 'but ah would be mighty proud to help raise him into a fine young man. Reckon I would owe dat to Edward Hardin'.'

It was a momentous decision. But she knew it was the right one, that her secret inner soul had fallen for this quiet mountain of kindness. Making a creditable attempt to copy him, she said, 'If yo still axin', then da answer's "yes".'

They had kissed before, but this time, it was different. His hand was on her breast, albeit outside her warm jacket. She left it there for a few seconds before gently pushing him away.

'Not in the middle of a wood,' she said softly, but smiling at him. 'The sun might be shining, but it's not that warm. And besides, we might not be the only people taking an afternoon walk.' She rose to her feet. Spencer followed, brushing bits of grass and dirt off his coat. Flossie looked around. Then they were kissing again, holding each other tight. Finally, she took and squeezed his hand. 'Come on,' she said, giving it a gentle tug, 'you don't have to ask Gladys' permission, but we have to tell her. And that's not going to be easy.'

She took it calmly. Their news, apparently, had not been entirely unexpected. But she was not smiling. Spencer admitted that he wasn't sure whether he needed official permission to get married. He would have to find out. Gladys was kind enough to say that she was pleased her daughter-in-law had found happiness again, but she was going to have to live at home until after the war because Spencer could be posted anywhere. And she was, she confessed, not looking forward to the prospect of eventually being separated from her grandson, the only child of her fallen son. They talked for well into the evening, but it was not quite the happy occasion for which Flossie had hoped. When he finally left to walk back to base, Spencer realised that there were more problems than answers.

His troubles began the following lunchtime when he was ordered to report to his company commander, a white civil engineer recruited for the duration. Spencer had hardly spoken to the major – his orders were handed down through non-commissioned officers. Rusty Irwin, who still had some of his red hair left, had not found life easy in the post-Depression years, but the war had given him status and fair pay. He planned to apply for a permanent commission. So, no way was he going to blot his copybook.

Spencer saluted and stood to attention, taking in the slightly crumpled uniform and the somewhat overweight figure inside it. The major could have been good-looking. But a fondness for food and drink, plus an aversion to exercise, had given him a bit too much stomach for his early thirties, not to mention facial features bordering on the podgy. His jowls moved as he shook his head in disapproval, at the same time ordering Spencer to stand easy.

'I'm told you have been asking about permission to marry,' he began.

'Sir,' Spencer responded in a flat monotone. It was the stock-in-trade answer used by every soldier when he wished to give nothing away but wasn't sure where the conversation was heading, or why he had been summoned.

'So, who's the woman?' asked Irwin.

Spencer rather resented the tone of the question. Flossie, to his mind, should have been referred to with more respect.

'A local *lady*, sir,' he replied, putting just the slightest emphasis on the word. If he sensed the correction, Rusty Irwin ignored it.

'And she's white?'

Another flat 'sir'.

'Is she pregnant?'

Spencer could hardly believe his ears. He made the only gesture he could. Stamping to attention, he roared out a 'No sir!' before re-assuming the at-ease position.

'Don't shout at me, soldier. I'm your company commander, in case you had forgotten,' the major replied evenly. 'And it's a court-martial offence for a US soldier to marry without permission,' he added bluntly. 'It is the policy of the United States government that we do not allow black G.I.s to marry white British women. It causes social tension and inevitably leads to what I believe you people call "brown babies". The Brits here call them "half-caste". And don't bother getting her pregnant, either. It won't make any difference, and she will not be allowed to claim any paternity support. So, permission denied.' He nodded his head sharply. 'Dismissed.'

For a moment, Spencer was rooted to the spot. Afterwards, he could not remember coming back to attention, saluting, and turning to take his leave. From the greatest happiness he had ever known, within twenty-four hours, his world had fallen apart. Fortunately, as a member of the construction crew, he knew where he could slip under the fence and leave the base without a pass. That night, almost in tears, he gave Flossie the news.

'Take my advice,' said Gladys. 'Do nothing and wait a while. Carry on seeing each other, but quietly, not too obvious. It's outrageous, but the war can't last forever. You won't always be in the military, Spencer.' She stood and placed a sympathetic hand on his shoulder. It was the first overt friendly gesture she had ever offered. But it did little to lift his spirits before he announced that he had to return to base.

'They can't do this to us,' Flossie said vehemently, the knuckles of one hand pressed to her teeth. 'I'll find a way... I'm going to fight,' she finished ominously. Spencer pulled on his coat and kissed her goodbye at the front door, his thumbs wiping sideways the tears on her cheeks.

She did not work on Sunday or Monday evenings. For the pub, they were the quietest nights of the week. But on Tuesday,

Flossie told Uncle Bill of her troubles. Even serving the occasional drink failed to take her mind off things.

'One of my regulars is a local, name of Mikey Greenwood,' her uncle told her. 'More to the point, he's a reporter on the *Peterborough Examiner*. If you can hold the bar, I'll go and give him a ring.' He was back inside five minutes. 'Mikey is sensing a good story,' he told his niece. 'He says if you don't mind waiting, he'll be here in half an hour, and he would love to talk to you.'

Greenwood, Flossie guessed, was in his early thirties. He was tall, as thin as a rake, and despite his lack of years, he walked with a stick.

'Polio,' he explained, easing himself into an upright wooden armchair. 'Lucky to be able to get about as well as I can. Now, what's all this your Uncle Bill's been telling me about?' Flossie gave him her story. He did not, she noticed, take notes. Perhaps nature had compensated for his disease with a good memory.

She began by telling him what she had learned about the way black soldiers were treated by their white fellow Americans, their different living conditions, and the denial of facilities. She told him how she had been asked to serve a white airman first, and did not mince her words when she described the events of that Saturday night's violence. However, she was at pains to point out how Colonel Hofmeyer had corrected the injustice.

'But it's just not right,' she concluded. 'Here Spencer is, an American serviceman, a volunteer, fighting a war away from home, yet he's not allowed to marry me because he's black and I'm white. This is England,' she slapped her palm on the table. 'Where's the justice in that?'

Greenwood knew that he had the makings of one hell of a story. He promised to stay in touch. 'But give me a few days,' he asked, 'then I should have some news for you.'

It was Thursday evening, not long after opening time, when Uncle Bill told her that some woman called Monica Everleigh wanted to talk to her on the 'phone.

She was, she announced, a member of the Peterborough Council local affairs office. Flossie agreed to be at home for a meeting on Saturday afternoon.

Although Flossie had been expecting an older woman, Everleigh was about the same age. She introduced herself with a handshake and an, 'I'm Monica'. Flossie knew that Gladys had not taken to their visitor. She did not offer tea, just left them seated around the table.

'I have been asked to talk to you, Miss Harding,' she began, 'because of your relationship with an American serviceman. I gather Spencer Almeter is his name.'

Flossie knew immediately that this was some sort of official reaction and that "Monica", despite her false camaraderie, was not on her side. 'Go on...' she replied, and left it at that. It was not her intention to be helpful.

'This is a much wider issue,' Everleigh continued, apparently intent on some sort of explanation. 'In fact, it embraces many important aspects of our war. First off,' she touched one index finger with the other, 'we have many members of the Empire fighting alongside us. Many Indian troops, as well as a good number from the Caribbean. All of whom, of course, are black or brown. But that's only one side of the coin.'

Flossie was not in a mood to be lectured. 'What has that to do with me and Spencer?' she asked bluntly.

'Everything. I'm afraid, my dear,' came the reply. The patronising, upper-class accent annoyed Flossie even more, but she held her tongue.

'You see, we really can't fight this war without the help of our Empire.' The woman pressed on, seemingly unaware of Flossie's feelings. 'And then, thank the Lord, the Americans entered the conflict. Without them, our next generation would probably grow up speaking German. Initially, our government did ask them not to send over black troops. But they refused. They had to, for their own political reasons. But by the same token, many of the states in America do not allow the marriage of black men to white women, so for that reason, the American authorities are not prepared to sanction a mixed marriage over here.

'Frankly, the whole thing is a mess and a fudge,' Everleigh admitted. 'If we support the American view and forbid mixed marriages, we offend our own Empire servicemen. But if we oppose it, there is the risk we might endanger the alliance and the whole future of our survival. In the end, we had no choice.'

'Which is...?' asked Flossie.

'To allow the Americans to do as they wish,' Everleigh confided. 'They remain here. We do not forbid a mixed marriage, but they do not allow their black servicemen to marry our white women. I can tell you here and now that after the war, not one black G.I. will be allowed to sail home with a white wife. Our churchmen and civilian registrars have been made aware that no black American serviceman can be married here without a letter of official permission. And that permission is not being granted. Nothing has been written down,' she said finally, 'but that situation has been adopted unofficially as the firm policy of the United States forces stationed over here.'

'And we turn a blind eye,' said Flossie bitterly. 'So are you telling me that I can never marry Spencer?' she demanded.

'I'm sorry,' said Everleigh simply. 'Thank you for hearing me out. I know it will be hard to take on board. Perhaps I should leave… I can show myself to the door.'

It was Uncle Bill who provided the final, damning evidence.

'Greenwood's been in touch,' he told her. 'I told him about your meeting. His editor has warned him off. The story has been spiked, and if he pushes it any further, he's not only out of a job, he'll be blacklisted from the entire British newspaper industry. Says he's sorry and all that, but he has a wife and a young family. But he did give me one other piece of information,' her uncle added. 'There is no district department for home affairs. And no one called Monica Everleigh is employed anywhere within the entire Peterborough Council.'

Chapter 19

Isaac Hofmeyer opened a file. Its cover carried the security classification of "Secret". The only other officer present in his office was Sam Heimy. Max Staunton was not on base. He had an appointment in Peterborough – Sam had checked. As an additional precaution, the inter-connecting door to the adjoining office had been left open. They would know instantly if he returned.

'It's a week today, Sam,' he told his intelligence officer. 'And the target is in Limoges, Southwest France, just beyond the occupied zone. The *Gnome et Rhone* factory used to make motorcycles and aero-engines before the war. But now the Krauts have retooled to make BMW 801 radial engines. They go in the Focke-Wulf Fw 190 fighter, so you can see why it's a high-priority target. And it's going to be a big wing job, a Maximum Effort. Nothing we can do about the flak, but it's the fighter cover that the top brass are worried about. We could get savaged, particularly on the way back.'

Sam was clearly impressed. 'An M.E. – every last aeroplane we can shove into the sky.'

'Mix of H.E. and incendiary,' Isaac added bluntly. 'High explosive fused to go through the roof and blow the walls out, then incendiary to set fire to whatever's left.'

'So where do I come in?' asked Sam. 'I won't be doing the target planning – on a mission like this, my job usually starts after the crews get back.'

'This is going to be our first effort at a Staunton deception,' the colonel told him with something of a wicked grin. 'It's got top-level approval. If we can convince the Krauts that the target is not Limoges but someplace else, we reckon they will have to reposition at least some of their fighters.

'We're going to tell them it's the marshalling yards at Strasbourg, three hundred and sixty miles to the north-east,' he went on. 'It's a good choice. Right up against what used to be the Franco-German border, so it's not going to look good back home in Krautland if we can plaster them right on their doorstep. And they won't want to take fighter assets from Germany or from further west, where they are facing the UK coastline and protecting Paris. So, drawing them up from the south makes absolute sense.

'It all looks plausible,' he added. 'Strasbourg's a juicy target. If we can get them to pull a few of their fighter squadrons, maybe even more, away from their southern sector whilst we knock seven bells out of Limoges, it could save a lot of American lives.'

'So you want me to plant a false trail for Staunton to send back home,' Sam surmised.

'On the button,' said Hofmeyer approvingly. 'Talk to the planners at Group, then draft me a folder similar to this,' he tapped the file on his desk, 'but for Strasbourg. Then think up a way of letting Staunton have just a glimpse of it. Once you have done that, liaise with Weyland from O.S.S. and this Werner Scholtz person, and come up with a plan. Let me know if you need any more resources. In the meantime, I'll go back to Group and tell them that it's all in hand.'

It was not difficult to put the file together. Sam took the original Limoges brief and simply built in all the changes needed for a raid on Strasbourg. He presented the file to the colonel. The problem, as Sam saw it, was how to pass the information to Staunton. It had to be him who had leaked the arrival of the B-

17s because they knew now that he was a German spy. But how had he come by the information in the first place?

'Apart from the senior NCO who runs the outer office, I was the only one who had access to that file,' said Hofmeyer. 'Ryder wouldn't have left it lying around. As chief clerk in the orderly room, he runs a tight ship. No way would he ever set a bad example to the rest of the staff.' He paused, thinking things through. 'When I ask for a secret file, he takes it from the secure cabinet and brings it to me. When I'm done with it, he returns it straight away. I hate to admit it,' he concluded reluctantly, 'but I reckon Staunton looked at that file when it was on my desk. Been thinking about it long and hard. There was only one time I left it there – remember that afternoon when we all dashed out to watch that damaged bird?' His fingers hard-tapped the desktop. 'It was here, goddamnit. Staunton joined us outside, but he had time to take a ten-second look on the way.'

'That has to be it, Colonel,' Sam agreed. 'But don't blame yourself,' he added tactfully, 'we didn't know then what we know now. There was no reason to suspect a spy. And at least there were no American casualties when the B-17s arrived, apart from one minor shrapnel wound. No lives were lost.'

'Valuable aircraft, though,' countered Hofmeyer with regret. 'But where does that leave us?' He indicated Sam's Strasbourg file on his desk. 'We still have to get this information to Staunton.'

'I think what happened back then helps,' Sam replied, 'because it tells us what not to do. If we staged a similar stunt – all dashing out to watch a landing, the file on your desk – it would look too obvious. Staunton would smell a rat. So we find another way.'

Sam had always been Staunton's first point of contact if he needed something on base. Initially, Sam Heimy authorised his pass and then his transport. He had arranged membership of the Officers' Club and even signed off Max's admission to the PX. The workshop section warrant officer was only too happy to oblige. Later that afternoon, Max Staunton's jeep stubbornly refused to start. The warrant officer offered to provide a vehicle to take him home. But he was not optimistic about getting it repaired.

'Got an important Maximum Effort on next week, sir,' he said politely. 'All my men are working overtime as it is. We can do your jeep first thing the day after, though, as soon as it's over.'

It was enough to arouse Staunton's interest. 'A Maximum Effort?' he asked idly as if it were a casual query. 'What's that?'

'For an M.E.,' came the reply. 'We have to get every aeroplane we can fit to fly. But we could start on your vehicle on Friday, sir. Have you fixed up for the weekend.' And no, the warrant officer replied in response to the next question. Unfortunately, he didn't have a replacement vehicle that he could make available to Mr Staunton in the meantime.

The seed had been planted skilfully. The prospect of no wheels for the best part of a week was not good news to Max Staunton. He knocked on Sam Heimy's office door. Sam quickly drew an opened file from across his desk so that it sat in front of him, before shouting for his visitor to come in. On the top of the first page, right underneath the central security classification, and in big red letters large enough to be read upside down by someone standing in front of the desk, was the single word "STRASBOURG", followed underneath by the date in same-sized numerals: "MONTH/DAY/YEAR".

Sam reflected afterwards that he should have trained for the theatre. He watched as Staunton's eyes were drawn to it as if by a magnet, and for just too many seconds than would have been innocent. Ostentatiously, he folded over the front cover as if to deny sight of the contents, then pushed the file to one side, But he was confident that Staunton had put two and two together.

'Sit down, Max,' he invited.

'I'm sorry to bother you,' Staunton began, 'but it's about my transport...'

Sam promised dutifully to have a word with the warrant officer. That evening, Staunton had the privilege of driving home in a khaki Buick with a big white star painted on the rear doors. The senior officers, he had been told, would always have first call on their small staff car pool. But the warrant officer was happy to make this one available for now. And he should be able to find another jeep for him sometime soon.

All suspicions were confirmed when Staunton returned the car the following morning but asked if he could kindly be given a lift to Peterborough station later that same day. Sam telephoned Weyland, who in turn contacted Werner. He took the Tube into Town, and the two of them set off by road. All three of them would arrive in Norfolk at about the same time.

Parked further along the lane, Mark and Werner watched as Staunton, with a small grip in hand, stepped from a bus and opened the garden gate to Margaret's cottage. Once he was inside, Mark started the engine. It was time for a good supper and a couple of pints at The Feathers.

* * * *

She drove over to Dersingham. 'Glad you warned me - I had a 'phone call earlier this morning,' she told them. 'He's installed himself in my old place and wants to make a transmission tonight. I agreed to meet him there earlier this evening. I'm taking the Austin, and as far as Staunton is concerned, I have told Robert that I need to spend a couple of hours sorting out a few papers and belongings still at the cottage. Though I shall be going back to the farm for the night.'

'Your radio and code book are back where we found them,' Werner confirmed. 'The rest is up to you.'

The front of the cottage was in darkness, but a faint glow from the back garden told her that there was a light on in the kitchen.

'It's me,' she called out, not bothering to use her German and closing the front door behind her. In the kitchen, she set down a shopping bag on the table. She noticed a 9mm Walther on the draining board. 'I've brought you a few supplies,' she told him. 'A bit of shopping from the village. I didn't leave much food behind, but the drinks cupboard is still quite well stocked.'

'The radio?' he asked.

'Buried in the greenhouse at the bottom of the garden.' She took a flash lamp from one of the cupboards. 'You can hold this whilst I retrieve it.' She also removed a small hand brush. 'Save bringing a load of dry earth into the kitchen,' she added.

Had she not known, Margaret would have assumed the radio had lain untouched since she had last hidden it there. Back in the kitchen, she wiped off the few bits of soil that had survived her original brush-over and removed the code book.

Max picked it up. '*Hauptmann Ladurner,* by Luis Trenker,' he read from the cover. 'But I have brought my own code book. I am more familiar with it – I know where to find at least some of the words I shall need.'

Margaret had anticipated this. 'Your security isn't that good,' she said with more than a hint of criticism. 'You can sign on with your code name, so they will know which book to use, but before I left, I took the precaution of arranging that if a message was sent over my radio using any other code name than mine, they were to assume that I no longer had full control over it and that the message was either false or being sent by me under duress. I'm surprised you didn't think to do the same,' she added flatly.

It was a bluff, but he did not object when she took her book gently from his hand. 'And I'll do the transcription,' she said firmly, with heavy emphasis on the "I".

'Like you,' she pressed home her argument, 'I've used my code book often enough to know where to find most of the words we'll need; otherwise, we are going to be here for hours whilst you either look for them or spell them out letter by letter. And I haven't got all night – Robert thinks I'm just sorting out a few personal papers and things. He'll be expecting me back at a reasonable hour.'

Max shrugged his shoulders, seemingly accepting what she had said. Or perhaps he had allowed himself to be coerced by a bossy woman. Either way, Margaret didn't care. She sat at the table, opened a notebook and waited for him to speak.

'How long are you staying?' she asked. They were back in the kitchen, having sent the message from an upstairs room and then returned the suitcase to its hiding place. Margaret had also made the transmission because, as she insisted, they would be expecting her 'fist'. But he had listened carefully as she tapped out her code name. Now, she tore the transcription pages from her notebook, plus several blank ones underneath. 'I don't want to light a fire here,' she told him, 'and leave bits of burnt ash lying around. I'll throw them into the kitchen stove back at the farmhouse.' She had decided to stay for just one drink to be sure that he was now more relaxed and there were no signs of suspicion.

'I'll go back in the morning,' he replied evenly. 'I don't keep regular hours, so it's unlikely anyone on base will have missed me.'

Obviously, he was fine. 'I'll give you a spare key,' Margaret told him, pulling on her coat, 'so that you won't need to pick the lock next time. I assume there will be a next time,' she queried, by way of confirmation, 'seeing as you'll want to use my radio again.' She rinsed her glass and left it upside down on the draining board. 'Just be sure to leave the place secure in the morning.'

She found Robert, Mark and Werner in the kitchen, each with a tumbler of PX whiskey to hand. 'How did it go?' Robert asked nervously as soon as she was inside the room. Two pairs of raised eyebrows indicated that they, too, were anxious to hear her news.

'I'm all right,' she replied irritably, 'but thanks for asking, the three of you.' She pulled out a chair and slumped down. 'Sorry darling,' she told Robert, 'but I didn't realise it would be such a tense evening.' She nodded towards his glass. 'You can pour me one of those, and better make it a large one. Then I'll tell you all about it.'

'Meanwhile,' she turned to Werner, 'whilst he's pouring me a drink, here's a present for you.' She took the torn-out pages from her pocket and pushed them across the table.

* * * *

'Thank you for agreeing to see me, Colonel,' said Flossie. Isaac Hofmeyer had risen and moved to greet her, offering his hand, after which he invited her to be seated on one of the two easy chairs.

'Can I offer you anything, Miss Harding?'

Flossie declined. It might turn out to be a difficult meeting. She did not want to be distracted by accepting hospitality.

'It's about me and Spencer, Colonel,' she began, 'as you must have guessed.'

'I haven't spoken to Private Almeter,' he told her gently, 'but after you asked for this meeting, I did speak to his company commander. Major Irwin has briefed me on a recent interview, after your…' he hesitated, then, '…just for now, shall we say close friend, had enquired about permission to marry.'

'And it was denied.' she replied flatly.

He repeated, as sympathetically as possible, the argument given to Flossie by Monica Everleigh. 'I'm afraid, Miss Harding, he concluded, that much as I dislike the obvious hypocrisy, and believe me, I do, our hands are tied. It might not be written down as official doctrine, but there is a very heavy hand over us commanders on this issue.'

She held eye contact. 'Colonel, there's nothing personal in this. You and I have always got on pretty well, and you know Uncle Bill has always tried to cooperate and help you out in the past.'

'Which I have appreciated,' he responded.

'That's as maybe,' she pressed on. 'But this marriage thing is not right, and we both know it. It hurts me to make a threat, but there's nothing Spencer can do, so I'm fighting for both of us, for our future happiness.' She paused to inhale, as if summoning up courage. 'If Spencer isn't given permission, then I'll have to go to the newspapers. There's a story for them – for us – here. I'm sorry, but that's how it is,' she finished, looking down into her lap.

Hofmeyer realised how difficult it must have been to make that statement and challenge the US Air Army. He admired her courage.

'But you must know, Miss Harding,' he said softly, 'that the British press has already censored the story in the interests of national security. "Spiked" is, I believe, their word for it.'

Flossie lifted her head defiantly. 'I'm aware of that, Colonel Hofmeyer,' she replied, looking up at him again. 'But I'm not talking about our press over here. I refer to your own newspapers back home. Particularly those that support, and in some cases are run by, the Negro population.' This time, she did not look down, although inwardly, she was nervous at the way their confrontation was playing out. 'I believe the last thing your government would wish for is what I have heard Spencer refer to as "a right Goddamn ruckus" back home.'

To her surprise, he did not react other than with a faint smile. He stood, walked to the connecting door, and called into the outer office.

'Chief, bring us a pot of coffee. And two glasses of sherry. We are going to be here for a while.'

In truth, Isaac Hofmeyer did not particularly want a glass of sherry when there was still an hour to go before lunch, but he sensed that Flossie Harding's nerves were stretched tight. He had more news to impart, and it wasn't all good.

'While we are waiting,' he went on, 'let me tell you about the situation with the press back in the States.

'In December '41,' he began, 'President Roosevelt signed Executive Order 8985. It created the Office of Censorship, and it covers all the ways Americans receive news information – newspapers, radio, the lot. I have to tell you that it is supported enthusiastically by the industries concerned. It also has the power to look at all letters and communications that cross into or out of USA borders. Even if you wrote to *The Daily Worker* in Chicago, which actually supports Stalin's communism, I'm afraid there is no way your story would ever see the light of day.'

There was a knock on the door. He held up a hand to forestall any reply whilst drinks were set down on the coffee table. He raised his glass of sherry in salute, but Flossie left hers untouched.

'I'm sorry, Miss Harding,' he said, taking a quick sip before setting down his glass, 'but what you have proposed is just not possible.'

Flossie was silent for a moment. 'So we have no chance,' she said eventually before picking up her glass and tipping back half of it in one gulp. 'All we can do is wait until the end of the war, see what happens, and just hope for the best. And in the meantime, we are going to be separated. It's not right, but you have won, haven't you?' she finished bitterly.

'It's not all bad news, Miss Harding,' he replied. She looked up at him, her face still flushed with indignation. 'Please hear me out,' the colonel continued. 'If I could sign off Private Almeter's request, I would. Morally, it would be the right thing to do. If I did, I doubt my masters would sack me, but I would certainly be overruled.'

'That's all very well,' Flossie said quietly, 'I appreciate your view, but it doesn't help me and Spencer...'

'As I said,' he interrupted, 'please let me finish. Here's what I am going to do.

'Spencer was quite correct, when he told you about the rumour sending his construction battalion back stateside. But I shall also retain a small unit here on base, mainly to fix up any bomb damage to our runways, but also for general maintenance. Only a small detachment, and it exists already, separate from Spencer's battalion, so I am going to have him transferred.

'As base commander, I'm not entirely without influence,' he went on. 'Last evening, knowing that you had asked for this meeting, I made a phone call. The guy I needed to speak to is a buddy of mine. What I think you Brits call "the old boys club". We Americans place a huge emphasis on building good relations with local communities here in England. The socials we hold, the dances on and off base, they all make a major contribution to that effort.'

He paused, then picked up his glass again. 'My former buddy is aware of your situation,' he said with a smile. 'But he then agreed to forget what I had told him. After which, I asked him, as a huge favour, not to send home my only vocalist. All it needed, we agreed, was a simple signature on a piece of paper. Quite frankly,' he said sadly, 'if I had asked on moral and compassionate grounds, I would probably have been turned down. But for my only vocalist...' His shoulders lifted in a gesture that said it all.

'A couple of instrumentalists will join him, just to avoid any suspicion of favouritism. And besides, I could do with keeping them, too. But basically, Spencer will not be transferred stateside with the construction battalion. He will stay here, under my command,' he concluded emphatically.

'We are going to win this war, Miss Harding,' he added confidently. 'I don't know how long it will take. Maybe a year or two yet. But the day it's over, and if you are both of the same mind, I'll sign the papers and the hell with the consequences. Spencer will be given a couple of weeks leave, and you can get married. Best I can do,' he said evenly and picked up his glass again.

Flossie had listened intently. She had to dab at tears glistening in her eyes. Eventually, she said, 'Colonel, you're a good man.' She stood. 'If it were not inappropriate, I'd give you a hug and a great big kiss.'

* * * *

Weyland had driven to the base to confer with Sam Heimy. Then he intended to go back to London, at least for the time being. Werner wanted to stay on at The Feathers, at least for an extra day, and have a final chat with Robert and Margaret that afternoon. He was sort of enjoying a late morning Camp coffee when the landlord beckoned him to the telephone.

'Mr Scholz?' she began. 'It's me. I don't want to talk over the 'phone, but can you come round to the cottage?'

Fortunately, Sergeant Wilkins was at the station and agreed to pick him up straight away. Margaret met them at the door and showed them into her lounge.

'I came round to check the place over,' she told them, 'and to make sure he had locked up as I told him to. Then, just as a precaution, I went to see that we had hidden the radio away properly. It was dark last night, and we only had a flash lamp.

'Well,' she slapped the arm of her chair, 'the bloody thing's not there. He's stolen it. Left me a note under a piece of brick in the greenhouse.' She passed a scrap of paper to Werner. On it, Staunton had written: "My need is more important than yours". 'And I gave him a load of rubbish about having to use my code book so that I could give you those pages afterwards. The dryshite's taken that as well,' she added, her Irish accent well to the fore.

Werner sat quietly for a moment, then, 'He'll be halfway back to Swanton by now,' he said, thinking out loud. 'But maybe this doesn't change things too much. He can still send our deception messages. Or maybe we'll help you to steal it back. Either way, let me think about it,' he offered.

At least, thought Margaret, she was still in play with the British. Possibly, they still needed her. So, she was not about to be arrested.

After a quick lunch at The Feathers, Werner asked Charlie Wilkins to drive him to the station at King's Lynn.

Chapter 20

It was a clear day. Limoges was a deep penetration raid, nearly five hundred miles, and most of it over enemy territory without a fighter escort. The wing assembled at its forming up point over Norfolk and set course. Their height of twenty thousand feet not only put them within the ceiling of flak but also well under the thirty-nine thousand capability of Messerschmitt Bf 109 fighters. And the braver German pilots would dive through them, trying to scatter the formation.

They reached the target area without incident. Bombardiers took over, the top-secret Norden bombsight accurately measuring ground speed and direction to target. But German radar and controllers had hastily assembled squadrons that had not, the day previous, been redeployed to more north-easterly airfields. The formation suffered some casualties on the home run, although the Staunton deception undoubtedly saved lives. Of the 30 aircraft that set out on the mission, twenty-eight returned, although others were damaged by flak and cannon fire, which also claimed the lives of aircrew.

Isaac Hofmeyer watched his squadrons return. He did not get to fly much these days; promotion and his duties as base commander more than claimed his time. Besides, it was discouraged. *Righteous Rosie* looked pretty shot up, but she made a landing of sorts. He learned only afterwards that Rudy Ansbach had brought the ship home. Curtis James' shredded body had been pulled from his seat somewhere over Nantes. Somehow, Rudy had flown the stricken aircraft with one engine shot to pieces and the cockpit a mess of blood, brains and smashed instruments – Johnny Carstairs, the flight engineer, transferred to the still-wet pilot's seat, had to press dressing after dressing over Rudy's left eye, pierced by a splinter of metal.

'How is he, Doc?' Isaac asked later after a tour of the medical centre.

'He'll come round soon enough,' came the reply, 'and we've given him morphine. I managed to get the splinter out, but I doubt he'll see much out of that eye again. Frankly, Colonel, I think his flying days may be over.'

Not for the first time, Isaac Hofmeyer had too many letters to write.

* * * *

His routine schedule time was nine in the evening. Max took his stolen radio into the back bedroom and suspended the aerial out of the window. He used Margaret's code name and transcription book. It was a brief message, just his best estimate of the number of aircraft lost and damaged. He had expected Berlin simply to acknowledge and sign off. But they did not. Their reply, transcribed, was short and to the point: "Target Limoges not Strasbourg. Investigate".

Obviously, he realised, valuable German fighter assets had been moved to the wrong place. And although the Americans had suffered losses, they had on reflection, been much lighter than usual. Only two aircraft from Swanton had been lost with all crew, although five had been damaged, one of them seriously. He had overheard talk of an injured co-pilot miraculously bringing it home.

With the radio packed away, he went downstairs, settled into an armchair, poured himself a large brandy and stared into the lounge fire as it crackled into a respectable blaze. There were, he mused, only two possibilities. The first was that the target had

221

been changed because of unfavourable Met. over their first choice. But this he discounted. He could listen to German as well as British radio stations. There had been high pressure and clear skies over England, and there had been no mention of adverse weather conditions above the continent. Which had to at least suggest that the Americans might have found out who – or what – he was and had used him to transmit a false destination. Could that have been why Margaret Chapman had been so insistent on encoding and transmitting his message? Was it possible that she had to be sure the correct disinformation had been sent... that she was working for the other side? He didn't think so, but...

Still mulling it over, he went into the kitchen and made himself a simple supper of ham and eggs bought from the PX. Back in the lounge, he turned on the radio and found an opera playing on the Third Programme. After a few bars, he recognised Giacomo Puccini's *Madame Butterfly* and left the volume low whilst he poured a second drink and brooded over the situation.

Could the Americans have discovered who he was? The more he thought about it, the less he was certain. Thus far, apart from some regular loss reporting, he thought he'd had two major successes: the raid on the newly arrived B-17s and now the Strasbourg message. Could they have run a security check after the former and deliberately misled him over the latter? He didn't think so, but it wasn't out of the question. The trouble was, he had no way of finding out.

Then the thought hit him like a mental brick, just after he had poured a final post-prandial nightcap. Margaret had claimed that unless she used her code book, they would assume she was no longer in control of her radio... *But that meant that they had to know which code book and radio set was being used for a particular transmission!* His technical wireless knowledge was limited, although he had done the three sciences at school, but he doubted she had very much at all. Provided they received a signal, how on earth could the operator at the other end recognise one radio from another? He almost bounded back upstairs. Aerial out of the window and using his own book, he sent his code name and requested a radio check. It was acknowledged immediately. Max sent two more words: "Snettisham tomorrow". Again, an immediate "ack". As a final check, he requested confirmation of the target in France. It was re-sent immediately. No sign of hesitation or suspicion. Normal radio traffic. He signed off. For whatever reason, it looked as if she had been lying.

* * * *

Max needed his own transport. True to his word, the workshop warrant officer had returned his own jeep that morning. They had worked on it whilst the B-17s were over Limoges. He could hardly drive it to Snettisham, but it did offer one huge advantage. He could fill up at the transport pool on the base. And no one was going to notice if he occasionally transferred a small amount of fuel from its tank.

He found the answer that Friday evening in the weekly advertising section of the local paper. There were several motorcycles for sale, but he opted for a 249 c.c. 1938 BSA B21. And it was conveniently nearby – he could walk to the next village. It was being sold by a war widow. She did not know what her late husband had paid for it, but she was happy to accept what Max suspected was a generous offer of fifty pounds. The tank was still a quarter full, although the ration of petrol for civilians had been abolished in July. A military mackintosh and cap stolen from the officers' club cloakroom would make him look like some sort of despatch rider. A satchel slung over one shoulder would complete the illusion. And he had his base pass if stopped and questioned. It should be enough for the average village bobby.

Apparently, the seller's father had run the engine from time to time, for it started third kick. Max was not an experienced rider, but he soon worked out the foot-operated gear lever. Fortunately, he still had his goggles from the arrival jump. He wobbled a bit at first but soon had the hang of it, and its single-cylinder overhead valve engine pushed it along nicely at a steady 35 miles an hour. It was a credit to the Birmingham Small Arms Company at Small Heath in Britain's second-largest city. When he lifted the machine onto its stand inside the garden shed, he felt pleased with his evening's work.

Next morning he packed the small case that had once held his now useless radio with a few clothes and his Walther. His officer's pattern mackintosh and a pair of gloves would offer reasonable protection. The weather was fine and dry if a little on the chilly side. He quite enjoyed the ride to the cottage, which proved to be empty when he let himself in that afternoon. He was cold after the journey, notwithstanding a thick pullover. Max poured himself a brandy and settled at the kitchen table to strip, check, oil and reassemble the Walther.

Chambering a parabellum cartridge, he ejected the magazine, added a replacement, and finally slid home a full eight rounds. He remembered his instructor at Vögelsang, 'The name comes from the Latin motto of the German factory that first made them,' he had told them. '"*Si vis pacem, para bellum*": if you want peace, prepare for war!' He used the safety-decocking lever to lower the hammer. A long, double-action trigger pull would fire the first round. It was pure habit. He liked the peace-of-mind insurance of that one extra.

* * * *

Max rode slowly past the entrance to the farm. The gate was wide open, and light from a window threw a soft glow into the yard. He parked the bike in the next field, where it would not be seen from the road, and walked back. Standing well away from the window, Walther now in hand, he saw the two of them seated at a kitchen table. He approached the farmhouse on the other side of the kitchen door from the window, past another window to a room still in darkness. Light music playing on a wireless somewhere inside the kitchen was just audible in the yard. Max placed his left hand on the doorknob. It turned smoothly. The gentlest of pressure, and it moved inwards a fraction. Relieved that it wasn't locked or bolted, he stepped into the room.

The man – it had to be Robert – who had been sitting facing the window saw him first. His, 'What the...' was cut off by Margaret's shout of 'Max!' as she turned to look in the same direction. Then she noticed the Walther. 'What's the meaning of this,' she demanded, 'and why are you here?'

'You,' he said sharply, pointing the weapon at Robert and ignoring her question, 'go stand next to her. In front of the sink.' Max slowly moved opposite them as Robert hesitantly complied. He pulled the vacant chair further back from the table and sat down, the Walther still pointing towards them.

'You haven't been entirely honest with me,' he said, looking at Margaret. 'So it's time we had a little chat. Why did you insist on using your own code book?'

Margaret was taken aback. She hesitated, just long enough for Max to think that she was struggling to assemble her thoughts. 'I told you,' she replied eventually, 'it was a security issue.'

'That is not true,' he stated evenly. 'I have checked with Germany.'

'Then there has to be some mistake,' she blurted hastily. Then, more calmly, 'It was arranged before I left. Perhaps the person you messaged back home was simply unaware of that.'

He switched track to keep her off guard. 'The message was false,' he told her. 'There was no raid on Strasbourg. The target two nights ago was an important aero-engine factory in Limoges. A big raid, and thanks to that message, the *Luftwaffe* redeployed some of their fighters. The target area had nothing like the cover that should have been there, and although the Americans took casualties, far too many enemy aircraft made it back to base.'

'Hardly my fault,' she countered. 'You told me Strasbourg. That's what I transmitted.'

Max might be suspicious, but he had no hard evidence against her. She was beginning to feel a little more confident now. Until his next train of argument.

'I had to ask myself,' he began slowly, 'why you had to be involved at all. I should have been able to send that false message routinely from my own radio. It was working fine. Then suddenly, two valves are blown. Yes, I opened up the radio and checked for myself,' he added when Margaret lifted her head to look at him. 'Two valves failed to light up. One, I might have accepted, but more than that – too much of a coincidence. And German valves that I can't easily replace over here, if at all,' he stated bluntly.

'It wouldn't have been difficult to put my radio out of action,' he went on. 'I had no reason to think that they were on to me, so it would have been easy enough to locate in my cottage.

'But what would be the purpose of doing that?' It was a rhetorical question – he wasn't looking for an answer. 'Obviously,' he developed his argument, 'it forced me to use the only other radio to which I had access. And that was yours. So why, I ask myself, would anyone want to do that?'

'Stands to reason,' he told her, his voice less whimsical now. 'Someone had to know for sure exactly what had been transmitted. It was a big raid, not some small-time operation, so if the Americans had sold me what I believe they call a bum steer, in order to give their aircraft the best possible chance of survival, they had to be sure their deception really had been sent as intended.

'And how else to do that,' he reasoned, 'than to ask Little Miss Margaret here to insist on coding and transmitting it for me. It's the only possible explanation,' he concluded, a note of triumph in his voice. 'So now, you are going to tell me exactly what your role is in all this and why you are working for the Americans.'

'It's not what you think,' she replied, a hint of desperation in her rebuttal. 'I know how it looks, but you have to admit, it's all circumstantial. There's no proof that anyone buggered about with your bloody radio, any more than there is about me supposedly working for the Americans. It's rubbish,' she almost shouted, her hand slapping the table in apparent frustration.

Her reaction was entirely expected. But Max had thought long and hard about the probability. And he had to be sure. There was too much at stake, not least his own survival.

He stood and adjusted his aim. 'Margaret,' he said evenly, 'you had better tell me the truth. If you persist with this ridiculous denial, I shall put the first round into your husband's kneecap. After that, if you continue to deny me, I shall put the second one into his other leg. If that fails to persuade you, my third round will go into your stomach. And my last one into Robert's. You will both take a long time to die. Now, I shall count to five…'

Already, his finger had tightened visibly on the trigger, ready for what she knew would have to be a long first pull. He got no further than "two".

This time both hands slapped the table as she jumped to her feet. 'I'll tell you,' she shouted, panic in her voice, begging for him to stop. 'Just don't do that to him, to us,' Max knew that from now on, she would be telling the truth – she blinked… tears were beginning to form in her eyes.

He signalled with the Walther's barrel for them both to sit down. She told him everything, about the Coopers from The Feathers… Sergeant Wilkins… Werner… at first with the occasional catch in her voice, but then more in control. 'It was either that or hang,' she said flatly. 'And I didn't betray you. They already knew who you were. The fact that they told you it was Strasbourg and not Limoges is proof of that. All I did was provide them with confirmation of what had been sent – the notes I told you I'd put into the kitchen stove.

'What the hell am I supposed to do now?' she demanded. 'And come to that, what about you? They could pull you in any time. Seems to me you're much nearer the end of a rope than I am.'

Max put the Walther down on the table, sliding it to his right so that it was still in hand but now less of a threat. He looked at Robert. 'After what's just happened,' he said, 'I have no right to request your hospitality. But we all have the same problem. It might be a good idea if we could try to talk this through over a glass of something to drink.'

A still-shaken Robert pushed himself upright from the kitchen table. He was a civilian farmer. It had been bad enough that first time, with Werner. Now, being confronted with a firearm in his own kitchen was an even less pleasant experience. But despite the threat that had been made, it seemed that the person opposite was prepared to try to find a way through this mess of spying that endangered them all.

'Do you have a name?' he asked calmly, his voice belying his inner feelings.

'He's Max Staunton,' said Margaret. 'At least, that's what he calls himself. I have no idea if it's true or what his real name might be.'

'So, Max whoever-you-are,' Robert responded. 'There are glasses in the cupboard behind you. Margaret will have to go into the lounge to fetch a bottle of plum brandy – it's a sort of liqueur, but it's all we have.'

Max picked up his weapon and half-turned to open the cupboard door. He held up a glass. 'This do?' he asked. Margaret nodded. He set that one plus two more on the table. 'Thank you,' he said quietly, and nodded towards Margaret. When she came back, bottle in hand, he was still holding the Walther, which was pointing in her direction as she came through the door. And he also had sight of Robert, albeit from the corner of his eye. Neither trusting nor taking chances, she thought. A trained professional… but nothing she would have done differently.

He raised his glass but did not offer a toast. 'The problem, as I see it,' he began, 'is that we both – by which I mean Margaret and me – are surviving for the moment only because the British and also the Americans think that we can be of further use to them. The Americans need me so that they can send false information. And they can only confirm what was sent using Margaret. They need the certainty of that confirmation to be sure that a major raid will probably avoid heavy casualties.'

'But from what you have said,' Margaret pointed out, 'our masters at *Tirpitzufer* are already suspicious, which is why they have asked you to investigate.'

Max sipped his drink and raised his eyebrows in appreciation. Then he stared into his glass, obviously thinking.

'It seems to me,' he said at last, 'that we need each other. You,' He looked at Margaret, 'are safe whilst they need to confirm what is being sent to Germany. I know the British. If you continue to do this, you will probably earn your pardon from the rope.' He emphasised the "probably". She winced at his choice of words but silently agreed. There was every chance that, eventually, she and Robert would be allowed to live out their lives together on the farm. She had to cling to that – their only hope.

'For me,' he went on, 'the situation is different. Our *Abwehr* masters do not know that my cover has been blown. On the other hand, the Americans do not know that I am aware of this or that they are already suspicious back home. I think they will continue to send deception messages, at least until they are sure that they are no longer working.' He twirled the stem of his glass. 'But once that happens,' he added, 'I have no bargaining chips. My fate is sealed. At that point, if they can catch me, I shall be arrested and hanged.'

'So what do you propose?' asked Robert, who had taken no part in the discussion until now.

'I am under orders to investigate the target issue,' he replied. 'I can tell them US Intelligence decided at the last minute that Limoges was more important to counter the Focke-Wulf threat, especially to their bombers. That will give us both breathing space. I will almost certainly be asked to send more messages, which I will denounce as false, to give our defensive forces, not least our fighters, the best possible chance to destroy the American aircraft when they try to attack the Fatherland. But in the meantime, I shall make preparations – as foolproof as possible – to return to Germany at a time of my own choosing.

'Does that make sense?' he demanded. Margaret and Robert looked at each other. Both slowly nodded their approval.

'In which case,' said Max, 'you say nothing further about me to this Werner person, and I will not mention your situation to Germany. They will assume you are still an asset, as normal, and you can continue to earn your pardon over here. Are we agreed?'

They were. 'Then let us drink to our survival,' said Max, raising his glass. After which, unbidden, Robert poured them all a refill before Max finally disappeared into the night.

He left the cottage the next morning, still quietly pleased with the outcome of last evening. Back at home that afternoon, he spent quite some time working on a transmission. It had to be as short as possible. Anything over three minutes risked detection. Satisfied at last, he made himself a meal and then waited for his schedule time.

That couple at Snettisham were fools. Germany had a war to win. "Contact established," he began to transmit. "Target probably a deception. Believe I am suspect with US so safe and operational only for now. Needed for more messages. Snettisham turned but now safely under my control. Please advise."

The answer, when it came, was clear enough. "Return here your judgement. If possible, eliminate Snettisham and Werner Scholtz. Latter the prime target."

Max switched off and set down his headset. Time now for a decent drink, whilst he pondered the way ahead.

Chapter 21

A few days later, Berlin provided a good head and shoulders photograph of Werner Scholtz together with background notes, posted from London and probably sent via Dublin. The problem was Max had absolutely no idea where to find him. All he knew was that Scholtz, almost certainly now part of British intelligence, had been running Margaret as an agent. She would not, he was fairly certain, have told him about her latest confession – that would have seriously undermined her usefulness to the British, not to mention her hopes for a future pardon. So, somehow, he had to persuade Scholtz to a specific place from where he could be recognised and followed. Then, with Scholtz out of the way, Max reasoned, she could be disposed of, probably without raising much interest or alarm amongst the British intelligence services as and when they became aware of her demise.

But Scholtz and Margaret would have to wait. In the days leading up to Christmas 1942, Max found himself busy helping to organise the festivities. The colonel had managed to book a proper Army band and wanted a combined concert and carol service open to both his serving personnel and the local populace. Their base padre joined forces with the vicar of Swanton, and the parish church was packed to overflowing, which did not matter too much as American engineers had wired loudspeakers playing into the churchyard and out to the lane beyond.

There was also a Christmas dance on the base. Max had augmented the supply of village dance partners with an invitation to the nurses at the Peterborough hospital, who were bussed to the event. This time, there was just Colonel Isaac's Band, as they had come to be known, but by now, they were playing to semi-professional standards. The food, not to mention the drinks, were a godsend to local inhabitants of a wartime-rationed Britain.

But the main event, in the colonel's opinion, was the children's Christmas party. Max was ordered to invite every child within a ten-mile radius, which included three village schools. They were collected by bus, and on arrival, each child was met by an airman who had volunteered to be an honorary guardian for the day. Most had done so because they had children of their own back home. A massive tea was served, again an absolute feast for children who had suffered food shortages for the past three years. And for the first time, they tasted Coca-Cola. There were games, and afterwards, a well-padded Santa handed out presents: dolls for the girls, flown in from America and of a size and quality no longer seen in British stores; model tanks and aircraft for the boys; and a book for every child.

Busy as he had been, helping organise the events in the run-up to Christmas, Max could not help noticing a gradual change in the adult population. It was too soon to talk of victory, but no longer was there a constant fear of defeat. Air raids persisted, but not as intensely as during the blitz. People were beginning to hope that they would not be hiding in cellars or shelters for much longer. And the tide of the war was starting to turn. Montgomery's victory at the second battle of El Alamein, at the end of October and the beginning of November, was still a recent and welcome memory. It eliminated the threat to Egypt, the Suez Canal, and the Persian oil fields. And the Allied invasion of French North Africa had opened a second front in the desert. There was even speculation about a threat to the soft underbelly of Europe. Staff officers laid plans for deep penetration bombing raids over Germany itself early in the coming year.

Saturday nights, when Uncle Bill could spare her by taking on another girl from the village, Spencer usually took Flossie out, often for a drink, sometimes to the cinema, but not for another meal. Ten days before Christmas, Gladys suggested instead that Flossie ask him round for supper. She offered to blind bake a shortcrust pastry base for an open homity pie, a popular wartime recipe. Flossie would have to make the filling because that evening, the local branch of the Women's Institute was hosting a Christmas function in the village hall. The four of them went for a walk that afternoon, after which Miz Gladys, as Spencer had taken to calling her, retired to her room to change for the festivities. They enjoyed a glass of sherry together before she kissed all three of them on the cheek, wished them a nice evening and let herself out of the front door.

With both seated at the kitchen table, Spencer read Jimmy a story whilst Flossie made the pie. Thanks to Spencer's access to the PX, Gladys' larder was better stocked than most. Their usual homity pie was filled with potatoes and other vegetables and topped with cheese. Tasty enough, but thanks to Spencer, this pre-Christmas version was enriched with a generous portion of cubed bacon. And even if French wines were no longer available, the Californian vineyards produced a good, if *ordinaire*, alternative. Spencer had turned up with a bottle under each arm.

Flossie placed a couple of candles in the middle of the kitchen table. The pie was delicious. Afterwards, bribed with the promise of another Hershey bar in the morning, Jimmy was happy to be tucked up in bed. They washed and dried in companionable silence. At Flossie's request, Spencer opened the second bottle and took it, together with their glasses, into the small lounge. Flossie coaxed the open fire back to life and then soon had it burning well. Wood collected from local farmland gave off a perfume that reminded Spencer of home. Gladys did not own a sofa – just two wooden-armed but upholstered easy chairs, one either side of the fireplace. A fender and fire guard protected the thick, homemade rag rug between them.

She noticed a tear forming in the corner of one eye. After a while, it was large enough to run down over his cheek. Spencer ignored it and took another sip from his wine.

'What's the matter, love?' She asked softly.

'Thinkin' of mah folks back home. How they is treated, togethah wit wat I gots foun' ovah here. Fo da first time in mah life, I'm treated as an ordinary human bein'. A person in mah own right, not just a niggah. You know, no white woman back there be like you been wit meh.' Whether it was the wine or the depth of his feelings, she didn't know, but Spencer's speech had reverted to the deep black vernacular of his native Georgia.

She sensed an overwhelming unhappiness. Not with the here and now, but more from the past and for the future. She longed to comfort him. Flossie set down her glass and moved to sit on the rug at his knees, her head resting on one arm over his thigh.

'It's not going to be easy, even over here,' she said gently. 'I was lucky with Edward; he was a good man. But if he taught me one thing, it was how to recognise another one. You're a good man, too, Spencer love. I can't tell you how touched I was when you told me you felt you owed it to Edward to help bring up his son.'

She looked up at him. He put his hands under her arms and effortlessly lifted her onto his knees. 'The hell with the rest of them. We can make something of this,' she said firmly, and wiped away the damp line from his tear.

Her mind made up, Flossie stood and walked back to stand, facing him, in front of her own chair. She unbuttoned her cardigan and set it behind her. When she started to unbutton her blouse, he, too, stood, took off his tie and unbuttoned his uniform shirt. By the time he had unbuttoned what he called his pants, she was naked. Afterwards, she could remember only that they were together, on the rug, when she encircled his manhood in her hand and guided him towards and inside her.

* * * *

Max's morale moved in inverse proportion to the rising optimism of those around him. And there was still the problem of Werner Scholtz and Snettisham. After Christmas, it rained almost non-stop for the rest of the month. The base was quiet: flying was often scrubbed for the day – more often than not, the pilots wouldn't be able to see the target. Sometimes, with the cloud base under five hundred feet, it would have been difficult, if not impossible, for a returning bomber to find the home airbase. Christmas festivities were a fading memory, so no one thought twice about it when Max announced that he was going to take a few days' leave. Having fine-tuned his plan, he sent instructions to Berlin using his own code, which he was confident the Allies would not have broken.

At his request, Berlin, in turn transmitted to Margaret, using her code – details of which he knew she had mentioned to Werner Scholtz whilst planning the Strasbourg message. This one was long enough to have a reasonable chance of being intercepted but not so long as to be obvious. "Shamrock" would be ordered to meet and assist. As he had her radio, he would have to 'phone on the message in the morning. Scholz almost certainly knew about this, but that would not matter. It would serve only to reinforce his deception. And he was confident that she would pass on the message. If she did not, and it *had* been intercepted and decoded by the British, she might be signing her own death warrant.

The intercept found its way to Quentin Frobisher's office. 'What do you think?' he asked Werner.

'Took us a while to track down a copy of the *Ladurner* book,' he replied, 'but I'm pretty sure it's genuine. We have a time and date but not the location,' he added. 'On the other hand, we know that "Shamrock" is Margaret Chapman. Almost certainly, this new agent is to be dropped into the DZ she uses on the edge of the Sandringham estate. I'll take a small team and welcome him – or her – to the United Kingdom.'

Margaret talked it over with Robert at length. But in the end, she argued, there was no choice. If her message from Berlin had been intercepted, and she failed to act, she would hang. She trusted Werner. In accordance with his instructions, she made a phone call to the one contact telephone number he had given her.

He pre-empted her message. 'Am I right,' he broke in, 'that you have been sent an instruction?'

Margaret confirmed that she had.

'Do nothing,' she was told. 'Stand down. We will handle it. There will be no comeback on you. Your former employers will inevitably assume we have broken your code and there was an intercept. I doubt there will ever be any questions, but your fallback is that you were there but discovered that you were not alone. You had to back off to save yourself.'

* * * *

He arrived at the farm in a large vehicle that looked like a cross between a shooting brake and a small lorry. 'It's a Humber Box,' Werner replied in response to Robert's question. 'The Army uses them as a command vehicle. It's heavy and slow. Even with a four-litre engine, you'd be lucky to push it much over fifty. But the great thing is, it's four-wheeled drive. So if we need to go cross country to catch our man, that's not a problem.'

'And who might "we" be?' asked Margaret.

'The rest of my team, there's four of us, will arrive by train tomorrow,' he told her. 'Our kit's in the back of the wagon, and we will be staying at The Feathers. Convenient if we need to liaise with Sergeant Wilkins.

'We'll settle in, then the following morning, we want to do a recce of the DZ,' he added. 'I'd appreciate it if you would come with us. Not least because you've used it before, you know the lie of the land, and your input could well be useful.'

'What about the night of the drop?' she asked him. 'Will you need me there for that?'

'Negative,' came the immediate response. 'We'll meet Jerry, bang him up for the night, and next morning take him to enjoy His Majesty's hospitality in the Tower of London. After we have extracted every last ounce of information from him, that is,' he finished with a grim smile.

Max had requested, and Berlin signalled, a drop time a couple of hours after last light. It made sense. A parachutist would have the rest of the night to be well clear of the area. The weather played ball. There was enough rain and squalls for conditions to be possible but perhaps marginal. Werner and his team would stake out the area but would not be overly surprised if the agent failed to materialise. Max would spend the evening at her cottage, although he did not make contact. And he already knew where Werner stayed when he visited Snettisham.

Three hours after the appointed time, wet and extremely cold, they called it a night and returned to The Feathers and a couple of bottles of Scotch that Werner had left in his room.

Max waited until well past midnight before riding his motorcycle the two-and-a-half miles from Snettisham to Dersingham. Sure enough, a big Humber was in the pub car park, some twenty-five yards ahead. He turned the bike round, pulled it up onto its stand well clear of the road, and walked the rest of the way. In his hand was a rolled-up strip of leather. Inside, a number of pocket slots contained a selection of hand tools.

The two vented side panels of the bonnet lifted up and folded back over the top. With the aid of a small flash lamp, he found the distributor cap, lifted it off and removed the rotor arm. He fractured it, then carefully put the two pieces back, holding them in place with one hand as he replaced the cap with the other. When the Humber failed to start, that would be one of the first checks a driver would make. Removing the arm would have raised an alarm. But finding two broken pieces... he smiled at his own ingenuity. With the side panel replaced, he checked that he had all his tools, rolled up the leather and walked back to the BSA. At the cottage, he set an alarm clock. He did not want to miss the early bus to King's Lynn.

At the station, he bought a second-class ticket and a newspaper. Max was fairly certain Werner would have seen at least one photograph, but with his collar turned up and his face behind a copy of *The Daily Mirror*, he was reasonably confident he would not be recognised. Besides, the trip to Snettisham had been to capture an agent being met by Margaret. Werner would not expect Max to be in Norfolk, so he would not be looking out for him.

It was mid-morning before he appeared, carrying a small holdall. Probably had a quick debrief with Margaret, thought Max. He was alone, which made life easier. The rest of the team had presumably been left behind to fix the Humber and follow on later that day or tomorrow, depending on when they could locate and fit the spare part.

Werner disappeared into the station buffet. After about half an hour, following an announcement of the platform and departure time of the next service to London Kings Cross, he reappeared. Max watched as he boarded a first-class carriage, then made his way to the more crowded second. He found a window seat from where he could observe any departure, but once past Cambridge, he was confident that Werner's destination was the capital. Well before their arrival, he made a point of staking an early exit position near the carriage door.

At Kings Cross, Max, secure within the press of second-class passengers on the platform, had no difficulty following Werner to the Tube station and onto the westbound platform of the Piccadilly line. He took an adjacent carriage. Again, it was easy enough to follow at a safe distance when Werner alighted at Barons Court, where a few Londoners had already established a pitch for the night on the platform. He followed Werner to the District line and its Richmond terminus.

Max had to hang well back now, but after a twenty-minute walk, Werner opened the garden gate of a small, detached cottage. Max waited for a few minutes, but his target did not reappear. A pick-up vehicle was parked in the drive, in front of closed garage doors – what the British Army called a Car Light Utility 4 x 2, or "Tilly" for short. As Max moved closer, a small child ran around the side of the building onto the front lawn. Werner knelt to hug him, after which a tall, fair-haired woman, who had chased after the toddler, scooped him up in her arms and carried him inside through the front door. Max crossed the road and retraced his steps to the station. He was exultant. So this was where his quarry lived. From now on, his task should not be too difficult.

Back in central London and using a public 'phone box and coded speech, he placed his order. A male voice with a hint of the Irish confirmed that what he needed would take a few days, but it would be delivered by courier. Well-satisfied with his day's work, Max asked a taxi driver to take him to a decent but modest hotel. Tomorrow, he would travel back to Snettisham, collect his motorcycle, and perhaps return to Swanton the day after. For now, the Margaret woman would have to wait her turn.

* * * *

He was listening to the early evening news when there was a knock on the door. As soon as he opened it, a car parked in the lane pulled away. At his feet was a package in plain brown paper. Carefully, despite the fact that he knew it would be safe, he carried it to the kitchen table. There was a block of what looked to be trinitrotoluene, or TNT, a detonator, and a battery, all substantially cloth-wrapped to be insulated from each other. He pushed the explosive gently with the tip of his forefinger. It had been mixed with some form of plasticiser. They had even provided a generous supply of wire.

All he needed were a soldering iron, which he would purchase in the morning, and a form of tilt switch, which would act as a motion detector. They had been taught how to improvise during basic training.

He soldered a length of wire to a copper connector fashioned from an ordinary domestic electricity plug and pushed the wire out through the end of a matchbox. He glued the connector inside the box. A second one, free to move from side to side, would be placed opposite but not touching the first. Movement would inevitably swing them together, completing the circuit. All he had to do was make sure that the connectors were kept apart when he placed the bomb. A wooden "separator", acting as a combined safety and arming device, could be pulled out through a slit in the matchbox once the bomb was in place...

Chapter 22

They were allowed one fresh egg per person per week. Anneliese and Werner took it in turns to donate theirs to Charles Dieter so that he had two, although they referred to him only as Charles these days to avoid awkward questions. This morning, it was his favourite, soft-boiled with "soldiers".

Werner announced that he had to attend a meeting in Baker Street, a follow-up conference with their people and the Americans after the no-show in Norfolk. He had breakfasted already. It was a bit chilly for the Ariel. And as he wanted to avoid being delayed by traffic and any bomb damage, he would leave the Tilly in the drive and take the Tube. Hopefully, he would be back some time after lunch.

He had been gone for a good hour when there was a knock on the front door. It was Virginia, her next-door neighbour. 'Virginia, darling, not Ginny,' she had said when they were first introduced. Anneliese was always amused by Virginia. Her husband was somewhere in North Africa on Montgomery's staff, a fact that she never lost an opportunity to mention – as with the fact that she had been presented at court before the war. But tall, blonde, willowy Virginia had a kind heart and had taken the trouble to befriend and help her foreign neighbours when they had first settled into the cottage. Anneliese suspected that she was lonely and rather envied the fact that Werner lived at home. She had simply told Virginia that they were both Swiss nationals and that, as a fluent German speaker, her husband worked for the government.

She accepted Anneliese's offer. As usual, Virginia screwed up her nose at what she referred to as "that dreadful stuff out of a bottle", but Camp "coffee" was all anyone had these days.

'Doing anything today?' she asked. 'Wondered if you fancied a walk to the pub and a lunchtime drink? Be lucky to get anything but beer, and I reckon they've watered that down to save on sugar,' she added. 'Give my eye teeth for a decent gin fizz.'

'If we had the gin, the lemon juice, the syrup and an egg white, you might stand a chance,' Anneliese replied. 'But I think there's still something in the soda siphon if that makes you feel any better.' Much as she liked her neighbour, she could not afford to reveal her own family background. But it tickled her fancy to let Virginia know that she was not entirely unsophisticated.

'Got to do a bit of shopping,' Anneliese informed her, 'just local, but I can do that this morning. Then a walk sounds fine.'

'Leave Charles with me,' Virginia offered. 'He can play with my Helen. You can get round more quickly, and they are both less trouble when they amuse each other.'

'You're on,' Anneliese accepted gratefully, 'finish your coffee, then I'll bring him round. Anything you need?'

There wasn't. So half an hour later, clutching her string bag, she was ready to set off for the village.

But Werner had, as usual, parked that dratted Tilly thing, as he called it, far too close to the garage doors. She needed to reverse it so that she could take out Charles' pushchair and wheel him as far as Virginia's house. There simply wasn't room for it in their tiny hallway. Fortunately, he always hung up the keys, next to those for his motorcycle, in a box on the kitchen wall. Her MG TA, which had belonged to her late husband and had been very kindly gifted to her by his parents after he died in the

London blitz, was up on blocks in the garage. The pushchair was right behind it, alongside the Ariel.

She inserted the ignition key and started the engine. Just a couple of yards back would do. She was a competent driver, but the clutch snatched. She was conscious, for a millisecond, of a blinding white flash before her life ended with the merciful, painless blackness of instant death.

* * * *

He had nowhere else to go, so Werner accepted Sir Manners' invitation to spend some time at Stonebrook Hall. Not without misgivings because it was where he had first met and then courted his late wife. But Sir Manners and Madeleine, Lady Fitzgibbon, could not have been kinder or more considerate.

The memory of arriving back at the cottage near Richmond was burned into his conscience. The police cars in the distance, then running towards the still smoking remains... An elderly constable, brought out of retirement for the duration, breaking the dreadful news... Virginia rushing out of her house to tell him that Charles was safe and she would look after him for the time being... it was obvious what had happened... if only he hadn't parked so near to the bloody doors.

A statement to the police... then the most awful task of formally identifying Anneliese's remains. Fortunately, the mortuary attendant lowered the sheet only as far as her chin. What was under the rest of it, Werner could not bear to think about, for it was clear from the contours that not everything was joined together.

Sir Manners had phoned, telling him to sit tight whilst he sent his car and driver to collect him. It had been approaching midnight when they finally arrived in Leicestershire. Forewarned, Madeleine had stayed up to offer refreshment, but he had no appetite. Sir Manners said very little. Just set down a bottle of brandy and two glasses. Brook, their butler, eventually helped Werner to bed.

He reappeared mid-morning with two Aspirin tablets, a glass of Alka Seltzer and a cup of strong black coffee. 'You will find shaving accoutrements in the bathroom, sir,' he announced. 'And there is a robe over the chair,' he looked across the room towards the window, 'for when you have finished your coffee. The master has returned to London but will be back later today. For now, please join Lady Madeleine in the dining room when you are ready.' When Werner returned from his ablutions, laundered and brush-cleaned clothing had been placed on the bed.

He breakfasted on more coffee and just toast. Madeleine kept him company but did not offer condolences again, for which he was grateful. She had simply placed one hand over his and squeezed gently.

'I have taken the liberty of engaging a nursemaid from the village,' she said when he finally set down his napkin. 'Maureen's on standby until you decide what to do next. She's a cheerful soul if a bit of a plum pudding, but when her mother died, she brought up her younger sisters, so she's competent. If you wish, I can take you to the station in the pony and trap, and the two of you can collect Charles and bring him back here...' she trailed off.

'I can't afford to pay for a nanny...' Werner protested, but Madeleine simply held up a hand. 'Manners said he has access to certain funds,' she told him, 'and it's the least the government can do.'

*　*　*　*

Charles toddled to his father but seemed happy enough to return almost immediately to play with Helen. Leaving him where he was, he and Maureen went next door, she to Charles' room to sort through and pack his things, whilst Werner somehow found the courage to enter what had been their bedroom. He looked at the nightdress folded on their bed but resisted the temptation to pick it up and press it to his face. It was almost as if she were still there, telling him what had to be done. He selected the things he needed for the next few days, plus Anneliese's jewellery case, and carried his duffel bag downstairs. He found Maureen sitting in the kitchen. There were no windows left in the front rooms of the cottage.

Werner asked her to wait for him next door. The Tilly had been taken away for forensic examination. The garage doors were badly scorched and blown in, hanging half off their hinges, but apart from being covered in dust and bits of debris, the MG looked to be undamaged, although one of the garage doors had crushed Charles' pushchair against the rear bumper. When he reconnected the battery, there was enough juice left to turn over the engine, which burst into life. The MG's tank had been almost full when he'd put it up on blocks. With wire wheels and central wing nuts, it was the work of minutes to re-commission her.

He accepted gratefully Virginia's offer of coffee. She also promised to find someone to board up the windows. 'We can settle up later,' she told him. 'Presumably, you'll have to come back for the rest of your things.'

'As you probably know, we rented furnished,' he replied. 'But I'll phone you and let you know what's happening.' He turned to Maureen. 'If I tie everything on the luggage rack and put the hood up, could you cope with Charles Dieter on your lap?' he asked. He had consciously used their son's full name. Somehow, he felt he owed it to Anneliese. 'It'll be a lot quicker than the train, and driving will take my mind off things,' he added.

She responded that, of course, she could. He thanked Virginia, who gave him a kiss on the cheek and a squeeze on both arms. Werner used their washing line to secure the luggage, then pushed the doors wide open and set the Ariel and Charles Dieter's now badly dented pushchair to one side. He reversed out the MG, replaced them both and shoved the doors back almost together, leaving them hanging drunkenly in place.

It was an uneventful journey. Charles Dieter obligingly slept for most of the way. Werner was glad of his decision to drive. It proved a welcome distraction but also gave him time to think, during a companionable silence, about who might have been responsible for his wife's murder.

He was pleased to see Sir Manners' Bentley when they pulled up in the drive. Madeleine came out with her husband and Brook to tell them that she had opened up the former nursery, with an adjacent room for Maureen, and Cook was still on hand to provide whatever Maureen might need. Sir Manners took Werner's elbow and led him towards the steps. 'We'll talk tomorrow,' he told him. 'You must have had a harrowing day. Madeleine and I were very fond of Anneliese. What we all need is a stiff drink before dinner. Afterwards, there's a decanter of port, if you would care to join me. It might help you to sleep.'

* * * *

They breakfasted together. But as Madeleine was also present, shop talk was put off till just the two of them were settled in Sir Manners' study, with a fresh pot of coffee for Werner and Earl Grey for his host.

'Well, dear chap, how are you bearing up?' opened Sir Manners kindly.

Werner did not wish to appear discourteous, but it was difficult to exchange pleasantries after the horror of what had happened.

'I've had plenty of time to think,' he responded. 'That bomb was obviously meant for me. There are only two *Abwehr* players in this game, Margaret and Staunton. She doesn't have a motive – there was already the promise of a pardon in exchange for her cooperation. It must have been that bastard Staunton.

'Either he placed the bomb, or he organised someone else to do it for him,' he said flatly. 'Possibly, he was acting off his own bat, but more likely, it would have been on the orders of Berlin. Margaret has no idea where I live, so either he or somebody working for him must have followed me home from Norfolk. The drop was probably a set-up, so they could be sure either I or someone from my organisation would be there. After that, all they had to do was follow…' He broke off. It was too painful to talk about it.

Sir Manners steepled his fingers. 'I'm inclined to agree,' he said at length. 'I spoke to our American friends again yesterday. Max Staunton's been on leave for a couple of weeks. They haven't had him under close surveillance. Partly resources, but also because we asked them to back off so as not to prejudice our own investigation in Norfolk. So, although he's a prime suspect, we can't be sure what he's been up to. But,' he added, 'the Americans still want to try sending more false raid information back to Germany. They still view him as an asset.'

'We contrived for Margaret to send the last message for a perfectly good reason – we had to be sure precisely what was sent,' countered Werner. 'So there's no reason why she can't send the next one. All we have to do is retrieve her radio. With the benefit of hindsight, Staunton's now redundant,' he finished ominously.

There had been times in his life when Sir Manners Fitzgibbon had deployed the technique of masterly inactivity. Now, it was a time for silence and an equally masterly blind eye. There was no need to tell the cousins, but he could neither counsel nor forbid Werner. Max Staunton was a dead man. He lowered his head towards the grieving widower in silent understanding.

'It might be wise to let Staunton think he's succeeded,' he said after a few moments. 'We don't want him nosing around the village to check up, then perhaps having another go. I'll have a news item put out on the Home Service – "a man was killed in a vehicle explosion near Richmond yesterday, police are investigating, they have yet to name the driver" – something like that should do the trick.'

It was time for a change of subject. 'What about Charles Dieter?' he asked. 'Any thoughts about his future? Don't worry about paying for the nanny; it's all taken care of for as long as you need.'

'I'm really grateful, both to you and Madeleine,' Werner replied. 'Maureen's a lovely young person, but I don't see her as the permanent solution. Back home, there's only my father – assuming he's still alive, that is. But over here, Charles Dieter has grandparents. I haven't met Charles Kaye-Stevens' mother and father. Anneliese did invite them to our wedding, but they didn't feel able to attend. I think it's only right that I involve them in any decisions about their grandson's future.'

'Couldn't agree more,' Sir Manners nodded vigorously. 'Do you want to give them a ring, then perhaps go and see them?'

'If I may, I'll 'phone them this morning,' Werner replied. 'Then, if Maureen is agreeable, perhaps we could go and see them tomorrow.'

'I'll take a train to the ministry in the morning,' Manners offered. 'Take my Humber and driver.'

Werner had intended to tell them the news once he had arrived. All he wanted to do for now was arrange to call on James and Muriel. The conversation did not go entirely as planned. James took the call.

'Sir, it's Anneliese's husband, Werner Scholtz,' he began. 'And before we go on,' he added quickly, 'please don't be concerned. Charles Dieter is fine.'

He knew that Anneliese had stayed in contact with her late husband's parents, setting aside time to write once a month on a Sunday afternoon, regular as clockwork, and occasionally enclosing a photograph.

'If Charles Dieter is fine, and you are telephoning us, then there is news about Anneliese,' came the response. 'Is she all right?' Werner could almost feel the anxiety behind the question.

He could not speak for several seconds, then, 'I'm sorry to have to tell you, Mr Kaye-Stevens, that Anneliese has passed away… she is no longer with us.' Despite his resolve, Werner could do nothing to stop the tears running down his face.

'Werner, I am so sorry for you,' said Kaye-Stevens eventually. Then, after a while, 'How did it happen?'

He tried hard to speak naturally. 'It was an accident,' he replied, 'involving a motor vehicle. Please, I can't say much more on the 'phone. Would it be possible for me to come and see you, perhaps tomorrow?'

'Come for lunch,' James replied. 'Bring Charles Dieter, if you can. You know where we are?'

'Thank you. Yes,' he managed, but then had to replace the receiver. He did not trust himself to say anything more. Werner lowered his face to his hands and, for the first time since Anneliese's death, wept uncontrollably.

* * * *

The Humber drew up in the drive of a small country house between Bromsgrove and Redditch, just inside the county of Worcestershire in the West Midlands. Werner asked Maureen to wait with their driver. He gathered up Charles Dieter but was barely out of the car when the front door opened. Charles' parents had not seen their grandson for over a year, when Anneliese had been able to pay them a short visit. James stood back, but Muriel rushed towards them, suddenly stopping short when she realised that she might alarm her grandson, who was clinging to his "father", one arm around his neck and his face now buried anxiously in Werner's shoulder.

'Say "hello" to your Grandmamma,' he said softly.

'Hello, Charles Dieter,' said Muriel quietly, brushing his cheek gently with the back of her forefinger. 'And bless you, Werner. We're so desperately sorry. But thank you for coming to see us and bringing Charles Dieter with you.'

James had advanced to stand next to his wife. 'Werner, come inside,' he welcomed him, then nodded towards Charles Dieter. 'He'll soon get used to us.'

'His nanny and our driver are in the car,' Werner replied. 'Would it be all right if I asked them to come back…' he looked at his watch, '– say about half past two? I promised to stand them lunch and a drink in a local hostelry. Or Maureen could stay if you prefer, Mrs Kaye-Stevens?'

'It's Muriel, and I shall call you Werner. No,' she added, 'carry on with what you have arranged. I'm not so old that I have forgotten how to look after this young man.'

James invited Werner to a chair. He and his wife settled on a sofa. Charles Dieter sat on the floor, totally engrossed in a box of toys produced by his grandmother. Werner tried to keep his voice level as he told them what had happened only forty-eight hours ago. Emotionally, it was hard pounding, hiding his feelings as best he could, although he was not entirely successful.

'It was meant for me,' he concluded. 'As you know, I am German, and I work for the British government. Anneliese is – was – entirely innocent. Because of *dies verdammte Krieg*, this damned war, you have lost a son and now your daughter-in-law. And I have lost my wife and Charles Dieter, his mother.'

It was a measure of his depth of despair that Werner had made a rare lapse into his native German. These days he used his own language only for the purpose of interrogation. There was a tense moment of silence as they watched an oblivious Charles Dieter playing on the floor.

'There's still a little time before I have to look at lunch,' Muriel said eventually. 'Can we talk about the future? What are your thoughts, Werner?' She tried to disguise it, but he could feel the anxiety in her question. She and James must have talked about little else since his 'phone call yesterday.

'I, too, have given it much thought,' he responded. A frown creased his brow as he managed just the faintest hint of a pained smile. 'Until two days ago, we were a happy family. I have grown to love Charles Dieter, and I would have brought him up as my son. We were also hoping for another child of our own,' he added sadly, 'but...' he trailed off.

He had to get a grip of himself, not least for the sake of these two, kind people hanging on his every word. Werner took a deep breath.

'I am not Charles Dieter's immediate family,' he pressed on. 'We are not directly related, although it would never have made any difference. That said, you are his grandparents. If you wish, I can continue to be a father to him. But I think the decision has to be yours. What is it that *you* wish to happen?' The last bit had come out more bluntly than he intended, but it had been a painful question.

James looked at his wife, then back to Werner. 'As you must imagine, we have spent hours talking about it,' he began gently. One hand settled on his wife's knee. 'We were childhood sweethearts,' he told Werner. 'We married the day after I qualified. So we feel we are still young enough to look after our son's only child…'

'You would always be able to come and see him,' put in Muriel quickly – she hesitated – 'but our dearest wish is to be allowed to bring up our grandson.'

He had prepared himself for this. Picking up his stepson, who was playing with a scruffy teddy bear that must have once belonged to his father and still holding him so that he would not fret, Werner bent down to place Charles Dieter gently on Muriel's knee.

'It is not easy for me,' he said quietly, standing upright, 'but this has to be for the best.'

Muriel hugged Charles Dieter, who was more interested in trying to pull an ear off teddy. One arm still held her grandson, then her free hand flapped upside down on her husband's knee. She was streaming tears. 'Handkerchief' was all she could manage.

Werner returned to his chair, quickly wiping away his own tears whilst his back was turned. James moved to stand beside Werner's chair, one hand softly patting his shoulder.

'Thank you, dear boy, thank you,' he said, almost in a whisper. 'You don't know how much this means to us…'

When they moved to the dining room, Werner was surprised to see a wooden highchair. 'It was Charles',' explained James. 'After you phoned, I gave it a good clean-up and once-over. It's fine.'

'We kept all his things,' Muriel added. 'The cot's already back upstairs, and this afternoon, James can bring in the playpen. After Charles, we were hoping for more children, but sadly, we were not blessed.'

Lunch was a hearty vegetable soup with rolls baked by Muriel that morning. She expertly lowered Charles Dieter into the chair and, in between taking spoonsful of soup, fed him puréed and strained vegetable. 'Charles only ever had homemade food,' she announced to Werner, 'and so will Charles Dieter.'

After lunch he was put down for a nap. They had just finished what passed for coffee when the Humber returned.

'Don't wake him,' said Werner, rising to leave. 'I'll come back from time to time, if I may, but it's better this way.'

Outside, Werner took a suitcase from the Humber's boot. 'I felt I already knew you from what Anneliese had told me,' he said. 'I expected that this would happen. His things are in here.' He set the case on the ground.

Muriel gave him a huge hug and kissed him on both cheeks. For some time, James Kaye-Stevens slowly shook his hand, placing his other one on top. It was an emotional parting.

'I know he's in safe hands,' said Werner. 'When he's old enough, tell him about his mother and me.' Quickly, he slid onto the back seat next to Maureen. 'Go,' he said abruptly to their driver, looking up for just the briefest wave. It was a good five minutes into their return journey before he felt able to speak.

'I'm sorry,' he turned to Maureen, 'but I have just deprived you of your employment.'

She shook her head. 'Her Ladyship warned me what was likely to happen, so I always expected it would only be for a day or two. And don't worry, sir,' she added. 'Sir Manners has already promised me a generous bonus.'

Werner said almost nothing for the rest of the way. Maureen had a good idea of what he was feeling and left him to his thoughts.

She was only partially right. Werner's thinking passed from Charles Dieter to the man who was responsible for this tragedy in his life. He had to try to put sadness behind him. Back in Germany, he had killed the man responsible for the death of his mother. A fleeting memory... the back seat of a German staff car, where he had executed Kurt Roth. The *SS-Sturmbannführer* had thoroughly deserved his fate. Max Staunton could expect no less.

Chapter 23

Dinner that evening was a subdued affair. Madeleine was at pains to reassure Werner that he had done the right thing. Charles Dieter would be brought up by loving grandparents in the relative safety of rural Worcestershire. With a stepfather still at war, and no matter how kind Maureen might have been as his nanny, this was surely by far the better option.

Sensing Werner's sadness, she excused herself after dessert and left the two of them to a decanter of port. Werner broached the subject of his future. 'I think I should return to Germany,' he said evenly.

'I had rather expected that you would carry on as you are, working with Quentin Frobisher,' Sir Manners responded.

'There's still some unfinished business there,' Werner admitted, 'not least the situation in Snettisham. But Colonel Frobisher won't need me for much longer. We are pretty much back to the *status quo ante*. The *Abwehr* operation over here has been virtually closed down. And any new ones they send over are promptly arrested. I suspect that's why they haven't tried to insert anyone else for quite some time.'

'What are you proposing?' asked Sir Manners.

'I would be grateful if you would talk to the colonel,' Werner replied, 'but in the not-too-distant future, I think I could do something much more useful. I know a lot of our agents in Holland have been arrested. That circuit has been leaking like a sieve. And we don't have much cover in Germany, either. I want to fight Hitler and, in a way, avenge Anneliese. Now that I don't have to worry about Charles Dieter, how do you feel about me wanting to go back over there?'

'You are right about the situation with our agents,' Sir Manners agreed after having thought for a moment. 'But what do you see yourself doing?'

'Munich's a prime target,' Werner responded. 'It was bombed by the RAF in 1940, but it was, and still is, protected by distance from the United Kingdom. Consequently, it hasn't received much attention. There's the Dornier factory at nearby Augsburg, and BMW make aero-engines in Munich. Then there's the huge industrial area. I would have thought having someone on the ground who could identify and pinpoint targets would be a huge help as we develop our German bombing campaign.'

'Useful, very useful, in fact,' conceded Sir Manners.

'But there's more,' Werner told him. 'Munich is the spiritual home of the Nazi Party. We are also hearing rumours of an anti-Hitler movement there, based on the University. If they are still in existence, and I can make contact, they could form the basis of a very useful resistance cell. Certainly worth a look.'

'If we agree, and I say *if*, where would you base yourself?' queried Sit Manners. 'I know your family home, Buchbach Manor, is not far from there.'

'I have to declare a personal interest,' Werner admitted. 'I haven't seen or heard from my father since I was last there almost two years ago. Back then, I was able to visit and stay at the manor without any difficulty. As for now, I have no idea. I would have to play it by ear. But it's important to me, Sir Manners.' He paused for a moment. 'Now that I have lost my family over here, if he is still alive, the general is my only living relative. Clearly, the operation takes priority. But if I could help him in any way, even just see him, it would mean a very great deal.'

'No promises, but I'll have a word with Quentin Frobisher in the morning.'

* * * *

Werner reluctantly moved back into the cottage. He had little choice. Other than the village pub or lodgings, he had nowhere else to go. But Virginia had been as good as her word. The downstairs windows had been replaced, not just boarded up, and the garage doors were no longer hanging half off their hinges. To his surprise, someone had also cleaned up the downstairs rooms. All traces of glass and bits of debris had been removed. He blessed the stone construction of the old building. It had survived for more than two hundred years. The blast had marked but not damaged the walls.

'My "daily" did that for you, darling,' Virginia informed him when he went round to thank her. 'Here are the bills from the builder and glazier, but Mrs Kelly did it for free in her own time.' Werner made a mental note to organise some suitable recompense. To his relief, someone had also tidied the bedrooms and remade their – now his – bed with freshly laundered sheets. Anneliese's nightdress had been folded away into a drawer.

Werner gently pushed it shut. Tomorrow, he would purchase a suitcase and then ask Virginia if she could donate Anneliese's things to charity. For now, he needed to report for duty. There wasn't a bus at this time in the morning, and he was not in the mood to wait. It would have to be the Ariel.

'I can't tell you how sorry I am,' Quentin Frobisher said immediately when Werner knocked on his office door and walked in, 'but I'll say no more.' Werner was grateful for the brevity. He brought the colonel up to date, including his firm belief that Staunton was responsible. And it was only courteous to mention that Sir Manners would be calling, and why.

'Let's say I don't want to lose you, but I can't argue the logic,' he responded. 'In the meantime, you have arrangements to make. I'll wait until I see what he has to say, but the important thing for you, laddie,' he added in his soft Scottish burr, 'is that you take some leave. Stay in touch, but if you can, try to get away. You look exhausted. A break might do you the world of good. Don't come back until you are good and ready. And, er... you'll let me know about the funeral. Jennifer and I would like to pay our respects.'

There was a knock on his front door that evening. The stranger wore a white dog collar on a black shirt and introduced himself as Alan Palmer. 'I'm the vicar of Saint Phillip's in the village,' he added. Werner invited him in, and they settled in the lounge.

'My local competition is Father O'connor,' he said after offering his condolences. 'We haven't seen your good self or your late wife within either congregation, but I volunteered to call and ask if one of us could help in any way.'

'Anneliese was not a religious person,' Werner replied. 'Neither am I. But she did mention that her family back home sometimes attended the *Deutsche Evangelische Kirche*, which, as you probably know, is more or less the equivalent of the British protestant church.'

'Perhaps then, a service, in celebration of her life,' suggested the Reverend Palmer.

Would that be wise... he wondered? *Staunton thought he was dead... but just as a precaution, he could ask Sir Manners to make sure that nothing reached the press.* 'I think she would have liked that,' said Werner after a moment's reflection.

'And would you like to say a prayer, now?' asked the vicar.

Werner thought of his intentions for Max Staunton. 'Thank you, but if you don't mind, I would prefer not… it's too soon, Padre,' he responded, automatically using the military form of address.

'But I am fortunate to have a supply of whisky,' he deflected. 'Would you be kind enough to join me in a toast to my late wife?' *It was difficult to read the expression on the padre's face*, thought Werner. *It might have been one of religious zeal. More likely, he suspected, one of unexpected but pleasurable anticipation.*

The funeral was surprisingly well attended. Sir Manners and Lady Fitzgibbon were there – his Bentley caused a few tongues to comment. He had also very kindly arranged transport for James and Muriel Kaye-Stevens, who sat with Werner on the other front pew. The colonel and his wife, whom Dieter had not previously met, sat behind them. Virginia stationed herself at the back of the church, with Charles Dieter and Helen, both in pushchairs. They were as good as gold. But what surprised Werner most was the number of villagers who attended, nearly all of them complete strangers, just a few with whom he had exchanged a friendly wave. There had been talk. They did not know precisely what the foreign gentleman did for a living, but motor vehicles did not blow up on their own accord. It was a very British expression of solidarity and local support.

Somehow, Werner, accompanied by just the principal mourners, stood through the internment in the peaceful village churchyard. He had to close his eyes at the exact moment when Anneliese was laid to rest, just hearing the words of the padre and the twitter of birds in the hedgerow, last year's hatchings. Mother Nature did not pause to mourn. Then, thankfully, it was over. Virginia had arranged tea and a few sandwiches in her cottage before those who had been at the graveside took their leave. James and Muriel were the last to go, which gave Werner precious minutes and a hug with Charles Dieter before they waved gently from the back of the Humber. At least Anneliese's son had been entirely content and at ease with his grandparents. Back inside, Virginia handed him a hefty three fingers in a crystal glass.

'It's pusser's rum,' she announced. 'Giles brought back a few bottles last time he was home on leave. It's all I have these days.' She nodded towards the bottle on the table. 'No rush, but take that one next door with you when you go. You look as if you might need it.'

* * * *

He had access to their small armoury but could not risk drawing a weapon. Travel was also a problem. The Ariel didn't have the range even to reach Swanton, never mind the return journey, and he could hardly leave a refuelling trail along military bases, there and back. It would have to be weaponless and public transport. Werner disguised himself as best he could. He bought a pair of workman's overalls and a cap and travelled second class to Peterborough, booking into a cheap bed and breakfast and paying cash. He took the Swanton bus next morning, mixing with other workers heading for the airbase but stepping off at the stop after Staunton's village.

The drive was empty. Had Staunton been at home, there would have been a jeep parked outside. Werner walked round the back of the house. He cut two separate lengths from the washing line, rolled them into a ball and stuffed it into his overall pocket. It was the work of seconds to slip a blade under the latch of a kitchen window. Closing it behind him, he set out to search the house. It did not take long to discover the two radios and code books – the one used by the American and the other stolen from Margaret. When he left, he would take both with him.

Margaret would need hers to send any future messages on behalf of the airbase. Staunton's radio he was quite sure the boffins would be able to fix.

Werner was in for a long vigil. There was food in the larder, for which he was grateful, and he listened to the wireless in the lounge, from where he had a good view of the drive. But as dusk fell, he first heard and then saw the jeep as it pulled up outside. He picked up his sap, simply a pair of socks, one inside the other and filled with sand and a tyre lever. Ducking below the window, he took station behind the kitchen door.

He did not have long to wait. Werner heard the key in the lock of the front door. It closed. A pause, then footsteps echoed along the hall. Staunton took a step into the kitchen then halted, as if some sixth sense told him that all was not right. Something thudded, very hard, into the back of his head. Then, a blinding pain ripped into his spine as he was rabbit-punched in the kidneys. Only half conscious, he staggered forward, arms reaching out for support from the kitchen table. But they were grabbed below the elbow and pulled behind him. Werner slipped a prepared noose of washing line over Staunton's wrists and pulled it tight. Then, for good measure, he slammed his face down, hard, onto an inch-thick surface of solid deal. It was the work of seconds to finish off the noose with a couple of extra knots.

He turned Staunton around. His nose was broken. Blood was running onto his lips. At first, he seemed to be having trouble trying to focus.

'You,' he said at last. 'You're supposed to be dead!' The blood around his mouth bubbled on the "p" sound of "supposed".

'You're going to walk upstairs,' said Werner. 'I shall be right behind you, pressing the blade of this knife against your arse.

Anything untoward, like trying to kick back, and I'll shove it as far as I can up your backside. It won't kill you, at least not for a long time, but it'll sure as hell hurt.' He grabbed Staunton's shoulder with his left hand and pulled him away from the table before goading the tip of the blade firmly into the seat of his trousers.

'Move!'

Werner noticed that the keys to the jeep had been tossed onto a narrow hall table. Staunton's military cap and American-style jacket were hanging over the knob at the foot of the bannister. He pushed and prodded him up the stairs and into the main bedroom. Another even more savage blow to the head from the sap rendered him unconscious. By the time he shook his head and regained his sight, Werner had bound his ankles. Worse still, his arms had been pulled above his head, and the line securing his wrists lashed to the bedpost. He tried to draw up his legs. They were pulled tight, similarly tied at the other end. Werner was sitting in a chair, watching.

'Going to search your property,' he announced. 'Any noise and banging from up here, and I'll be right back.' He unbuttoned Staunton's fly, pushed the blade into his undershorts and flicked out his penis.

Staunton's mind flashed back to the horrors of bullying at boarding school. 'Please...' he cried out, clearly panicking.

'If you want to keep it, lie still,' said Werner evenly.

He took the two radios and code books from the spare room and set them outside the front door. Leaving it open, he placed as much paper and soft furnishing as he could find at the foot of the stairs, making sure there was just enough room to step past, before pulling the stuffing half out from three cushions and tossing two of them to the bottom of the pile. He put the last cushion alongside the radios, picked up the keys, together with Staunton's cap and coat from the bannister, and placed everything but the last cushion in the jeep.

There had been no noise from upstairs. Werner could see from the doorway that Staunton had hardly moved.

'Good boy,' he said. 'Now listen carefully. Your bomb went off all right, but it did not kill me. My wife needed to move the pick-up back from the garage. She died instantly.'

'The... that w-was not...' stammered Staunton.

'Shut up,' interrupted Werner. 'You also left a little boy without his mother. I'm going now. As I leave, I shall set fire to this cottage. If you are lucky, the smoke will kill you before the flames. Frankly, either way, I don't give a shit. But scream all you want. No one will hear you.'

He turned on his heels and left the room. Staunton was babbling something as he tugged frantically, without success, at his bindings, but Werner ignored him. At the bottom of the stairs, he put a match to the cushion stuffing. The fire was soon well alight and spreading into the staircase. Outside, leaving the door open to create a decent draft, he lit the stuffing still attached to the last cushion. The makeshift torch he threw up and onto the low thatch above the front bedroom window.

Werner reversed the jeep away from the cottage and watched for a while. Soon, the tinder-dry staircase and roof were blazing furiously. The first patch of flaming straw disappeared as the roof began to fall in. Within seconds, there were high-pitched screams coming from the bedroom.

'That was for you, Anneliese, my love,' he said softly as he reversed into the lane and left what remained of Max Staunton within his funeral pyre.

Werner parked up in a wood overnight, and early next morning, he spent some time wiping the jeep carefully in a corner of the station car park at Royal Leamington Spa. The keys he left in the ignition. The Americans might get their jeep back; they might not. Pulling the collar of his coat up and his cap well down, he bought a ticket to Birmingham. From there, he travelled, again second class, to Bristol. It was late in the evening when he finally turned the key in the door of the cottage.

The Americans would find out about the fire soon enough. Then, there would have to be a meeting with Mark Weyland, who could tell Sam Heimy that deceptions were still possible. He would also have to travel to Snettisham sometime soon to brief Margaret and return her radio.

Although still officially on leave, Werner decided to ask for a meeting with Sir Manners Fitzgibbon. He took the Ariel up to town.

'Lovely service,' he complimented Werner once they had settled with a cup of coffee. 'If ever these things can ever be said to do so, I thought everything went very well. A fitting tribute. So how are you keeping?' he asked kindly. 'And what can I do for you? I should tell you that the O.S.S. have already been on the 'phone this morning. Director Bill Casey himself, no less. Apparently, there was a bad fire near Swanton the night before last...' he left it at that.

Werner had thought it through very carefully. There were four players in this: the O.S.S., the Americans at Swanton, the British intelligence services and the police. He gave Sir Manners a complete account of events.

'Appreciate your honesty,' was the immediate reply. 'I'll talk to Bill Casey. No one's going to shed any tears over Staunton, especially when I let Bill know that we have a turned agent who can still send messages to the *Abwehr*. I'll leave him to brief the people at Swanton. Up to him how much he wants to tell Hofmeyer.

'And I'll speak to Quentin, a word in his shell-like, as it were. Just in case the police should contact him. Frankly,' he dipped his head at Werner, 'I think you've done a damn fine job. I doubt the police will ever have any idea what really happened. But if they start sniffing around, I'll speak to the Chief Constable. After that, they'll soon lose all interest.'

'Thank you,' said Werner simply. 'And my wish to return to Germany?'

'Looking good,' responded Sir Manners encouragingly. 'Still have to talk to a few people, but in the meantime, stay on leave. If and when you go back, everything has to be as secure as possible. You're ex-*SS*, so it's a hell of a risk. You don't need me to tell you what's likely to happen if you were caught. You have had a dreadfully bad time of it lately, so I want you fully rested and restored.'

'Then I have a request,' Werner told him. 'I was very well trained by the *SS*. But I suspect that there are other skills that I might need. And my physical fitness is not as I would wish. I know from speaking to colleagues that you have a commando training base somewhere in Scotland. Spending some time up there would also take my mind off everything that has happened.'

'Stay on leave for now,' said Sir Manners. 'But it's a capital idea.'

* * * *

'Brought it back,' he announced, setting it down on the kitchen table.

Margaret opened the suitcase. 'It seems fine,' she said, peering carefully at the radio, 'I don't think it's been damaged.'

'It was working before I put it in the car,' he told her. 'So I think you can assume that it's all right now.'

'How did you manage to persuade Staunton to part with it?' asked Robert.

Werner paused for a moment. 'I didn't have to,' he replied. 'All you need to know is that Staunton is dead and that if – or more likely when – the Americans want to send another message to the *Abwehr*, we will ask you to pass it on, same as before.'

'What happened to him?' asked Margaret, looking up from her radio.

'There was a fire – he died in his cottage. We had already retrieved your set, although he was unaware of that at the time. That's probably all you need to know,' he added.

Margaret sat down. A huge feeling of relief washed over her. If Staunton had died in a fire rather than having been arrested and interrogated, then he could not have told them about their meeting. She and Robert were in the clear.

'One more thing,' said Werner.

Her heart skipped a beat. *Did he know, after all?*

'My days of *Abwehr* hunting in this country are about over,' he told her. 'We have rounded up almost all their agents and, in part thanks to you, they have been unable to set up an alternative organisation. I am to be transferred. I can't tell you where, but my successor will contact you as and when we need your services.

'My people are aware of your history,' he went on, 'and in return for what you have done in the past, as well as for your future cooperation, rest assured that our agreement will be honoured when the war is over. The tide has turned,' he told her. 'We had our victory in North Africa. On the Eastern front, the battle of Stalingrad is over. Hitler cannot fight the Soviets, the Americans and the British Empire forever. I can't tell you when, but eventually, the Allies will be victorious in Europe.'

Robert offered his hand. 'Thank you for what you have done for us,' he said sincerely. 'Good luck with your next appointment, and if you can, look us up after the war. There will always be a glass of plum brandy waiting for you.'

It was Margaret's turn to shake his hand. 'Thank you, and good luck from me too,' she said simply. At last, she could look forward to a life as Mrs Robert Chapman and bury Margarete Wagner in the past.

* * * *

For the rest of his leave, he concentrated on improving his physical fitness. It had been at its peak after his *SS* recruit training. Good living in Paris had taken its toll, as had the relatively sedentary nature of his duties with the British intelligence services. But his days now started with an early morning run, weather regardless, to be repeated late afternoon. He mapped out a five-mile course, then pushed it to ten. He was still working on bringing the time down when Sir Manners summoned him to a meeting.

'Been talking to the United States bomber people, as well as the RAF,' Werner was told. 'They are both enthusiastic about having a man on the ground identifying targets. Not only that, this is a part of Germany that has been pretty much left alone till now. What's more, we have people in Holland and Germany who will help downed airmen. But we have nothing in the Munich area. Buchbach Manor would be ideal.

'The problem is,' he continued, 'last time you were able to travel light, as a civilian, without incriminating luggage. An insertion by train was relatively straightforward. This time, if you are going to achieve anything, you will need a fair amount of equipment – weapons, explosives and so forth.'

Sir Manners paused, marshalling his thoughts. 'We can hardly send you off from Switzerland with a couple of suitcases holding a small arsenal. We're still working on it, but it looks as though you are going to have to go in by air. Ever done any parachute training?'

Werner confessed that he hadn't. 'Then we'll arrange that for you, as well,' Sir Manners replied.

'I want you to start with a few days at Ringwood, near Manchester. It's where we parachute-train our agents. The instruction will be one-on-one. There's a rail warrant for you in my outer office.'

He mistook Werner's look of surprise for one of concern. 'Don't worry,' he added blandly. 'They say if anything goes wrong, it's only the last half-inch that hurts.'

Would he ever fully understand the British sense of humour, Werner wondered, as he kick-started the Ariel.

For the second part of his training, he was sent to a country manse in the Highlands of Scotland. Physically, it was arduous, but no more so than when he joined the *SS*. He coasted through the weapons, explosives and unarmed combat phases and enjoyed the experience of using British equipment. Most important, though, was the agent instruction, where he learned the techniques of identifying and then losing a tail, of brush passes and dead letter boxes, the use of explosives, and not least, Morse code and operating his radio. 'Practice every day,' they instructed. 'The faster you transmit, the less chance of detection.'

The last month had seemed something of a whirlwind. But when, back at the cottage, Werner finally settled into an armchair and poured himself a decent, stiff drink, he felt that he had at least a chance of surviving the next phase of his war.

Chapter 24

It was a warm and sunny early May morning in London. At times he still grieved for Anneliese, but physically had never felt in better shape after weeks of arduous training in Scotland. The Russian Army was winning the war in the East, and now the mood of the nation had been lifted further by the news that the German Army had surrendered to the Allies in North Africa. Werner was anxious to return home and to take the war to Hitler's régime. Hence this planning meeting in Baker Street with Doreen Jackman and Bill Ives.

'The problem,' she opened after they had been served coffee, 'is one of insertion. Last time, it was easy enough: all you needed was a set of false papers. But now you have to go in with a radio, not to mention a weapon, ammunition, and at least a small supply of explosives. The trouble is, we have absolutely no assets on the ground in that part of Germany, so it's very much a start-up-from-nothing exercise.'

'It looks as though it will have to be a parachute with a drop bag,' put in Bill Ives. 'But a lone aircraft is out of the question – it would be a suicide mission. It needs to be part of a raid. The RAF don't plan to bomb anywhere near Munich for the foreseeable future, but I have checked with the cousins, and they tell me they are looking at Augsburg. There's a Man factory there making diesel engines, mostly for U-boats, so it's a high-priority target.

'The RAF had a go at it in April last year,' he went on, 'but it had to be a low-level daylight raid for reasons of accuracy. They hit the target, but out of twelve aircraft, seven were shot down. Thirty-seven airmen killed and twelve taken prisoner,' he finished bluntly.

'The Americans believe Man are back in full production,' Doreen took up the narrative, 'and with the Norden bombsight, a high-level daylight raid is now feasible. It's a hell of a long way into German airspace. The Americans don't want to risk a big wing operation at this stage of the war, but they are looking at sending in a single squadron of thirteen aircraft. The aim is to interrupt production, at least for a while, until there is sufficient air superiority to mount a massed bomber attack. That probably won't be before sometime next year, when the new Mustang fighter will have the range and firepower to offer the bombers much better protection whilst they are over enemy territory.'

Werner thought for a moment. 'Augsburg, you say,' he observed eventually. 'That's still thirty-five miles short of Munich, and our estate is on the other side of the city.'

'For this mission, the Americans won't have the advantage of several squadrons at different levels.' Bill added. 'Even so, a single B-17 formation is designed for collective security. But any stragglers would be lucky to make it home without being pounced on by German fighters. I'm told they can't risk a bomber and ten crew to take you on to Buchbach. They'll overfly Augsburg, and you are welcome to jump into open country as they turn off the bombing run, but that's the best they can do.

'And there's another problem,' Bill continued. 'The RAF are bombing Germany by night, but the Americans are making only daylight raids. And what's more, they'll be at somewhere around twenty thousand feet. They won't risk dropping a B-17 out of formation, so you would have to make a high-altitude exit.'

'But there isn't enough oxygen at that height,' countered Werner.

'Nor there is,' agreed Bill. 'But when I was talking to them, I asked how they managed if their own aircrew had to jump from way up there in an emergency. It seems they have what they call a bailout bottle attached to their parachute harness. It'll give you enough oxygen to see you down to about ten thousand feet, after which you should be able to breathe normally.'

Werner was quiet for a while, thinking things over.

'It all sounds too risky for me,' put in Doreen. 'I'm beginning to think we should be looking at another way of sending you home.'

'No,' Werner replied. 'We all know there isn't any realistic alternative. I don't much fancy the parachute drop, but American airmen face the same risks every day.'

'We could give you an American identity and uniform,' suggested Doreen. 'That way, if it all goes wrong, the worst thing that could happen would be a prisoner of war camp.'

'If I don't take at least some equipment with me,' he argued, 'then I'm not going to achieve anything when I get there. And if I do, that immediately defeats the deception of a uniform. No… I won't take a drop bag, but I'll jump in German clothes and lower as much as I can in a large rucksack. I had several practice jumps at Ringwood. Much as I dislike the idea of a daylight jump, I'll open as low as I can, so I won't be using a static line. I'm not so much worried about being seen by the locals – I can play that by ear. But at least I'll be armed, and they won't.'

'And if you are seen by a military patrol…?' Doreen let the question hang.

'Then let's hope I can put my expensive training to good use,' he replied. 'It has to be worth a try.'

But he could see that she wasn't convinced. And neither, if he was honest with himself, was he.

* * * *

It was a Saturday evening. Spencer was enjoying a quick conversation with Flossie during her break when the door opened, and a *Snowdrop*, as they called their military police, stepped inside and looked around the bar. He was an older man with the rank of sergeant on his arm.

'Private Almeter?' he enquired politely enough. 'Colonel Hofmeyer's orders, he wants you back at base.' The sergeant took in Spencer's almost empty glass and shrugged his shoulders as if to suggest that he had no idea why. 'Drink up, soldier,' he added sympathetically, 'and follow me – transport's outside.'

'Got nah choice, baby, somethin' must gots come up. We talk sum more tomorrow.' Spencer stood, gently patted her shoulder and followed the sergeant. Outside, the Snowdrop moved briskly to take the driver's seat. Spencer got in alongside him.

They drove quickly from The King's Arms and turned towards the base. But something didn't seem quite right. For a start, on reflection, Spencer couldn't think of a single reason why the commanding officer should need to summon him from a public house at this time of night. He looked around the jeep. Then it came to him... this wasn't a military police vehicle... for a start, there was no radio or any of the other usual police equipment. He turned to face the sergeant.

'Hey, wait a minute...'

He had to push out an arm to brace himself when the jeep braked sharply before crossing the lane and driving through an open gate to stop a few yards inside a field. Alarmed now,

Spencer looked at the driver, then turned to put his legs over the side. They must have been standing behind the hedge. Six more figures had moved to stand in front of him near the vehicle.

They were not robed, but above their uniform jackets, they wore the white, high-pointy conical hood masks of the Klu Klux Klan.

Spencer was booted forward from behind by the driver. Not a word was spoken. The circle closed. They had truncheons, and the beating began.

* * * *

They were helping themselves to breakfast in the mess hall. 'I wouldn't touch those little fart-fuckers,' advised Hal Parsons, newly promoted and today's aircraft captain of a much-repaired *Righteous Rosie*, as Werner paused in front of a container of baked beans. 'You don't want flatulence at twenty thousand feet.' Conscious that he had no idea when and where his next meal might be, he stocked up instead with bacon and sausages. And just one spoonful of powdered egg, *surely that couldn't hurt?* Hal made no comment. Werner took silence for assent and added another. By the standards of wartime Britain, this was a breakfast feast. But he limited himself to just a couple of mouthfuls of coffee.

Hal reduced power to idling, fully depressed the brake pedals and released the parking brake handle. Brakes off, and he advanced all four throttles with his inverted right hand till *Righteous Rosie* was moving, then reduced power. At the runway, a brief touch on the starboard engines brought her into a gentle turn. He braked and pulled off the power whilst String Roper, his lanky, newly arrived co-pilot, radioed for final clearance.

Werner sat with the gunners just aft of bulkhead number six. One of the waist gunners – he wasn't sure which – was on comms with the interphone. To max the trim, they would stay there until they were clear of the field, and it was flaps and gear up.

Hal held *Rosie* on station with the brakes and set the throttles for one thousand revolutions per minute. Clearance given, both he and String made a final check of all instruments and he released the brakes.

'We're away.'

Again, he advanced all four throttles together, gently building engine speed. He felt his co-pilot's hand backing him up. They were beginning to drift offline in the crosswind, but at this stage, there was no bite in the rudder. He corrected with a gentle push of two throttles, then levelled all four again to build speed as fast as possible. With acceleration came rudder control. As soon as the throttles reached the stops, String set the friction lock to prevent them from creeping.

At seventy-five miles per hour, he had elevator control and was able to ease back, taking pressure off the nose wheel. With a full load of bombs and fuel, *Rosie* was heavy, but with the wings now at the optimum angle of attack, she would literally fly herself off the ground. String watched as Hal made altitude, letting her climb away gently, knowing the trick was never to lower the nose for more speed. That would set the wings at the wrong angle, and the loss of lift would dump them back onto the tarmac – probably with disastrous results. *Rosie* was up to one hundred and forty miles per hour now and at a safe height. Hal gave the order for String to raise the gear.

He brought the flaps up in stages, gradually raising the nose to maintain lift, and *Righteous Rosie* settled into a steady climb, banking gently whilst the rest of the squadron took station behind her. The gunners assumed their airborne positions, made a last check of the feed belts and tested their weapons. Leaning back against the bulkhead, Werner was left to his thoughts. Soon, it would be time to re-activate his heated suit and oxygen supply. Hopefully, he was in for a quiet, if boring ride, as *Rosie* thundered on towards her target. He had been briefed to exit through the bomb doors. But it was what happened afterwards that concerned him most.

* * * *

Something caught her eye. Flossie glanced out of the window – a huge American car had drawn up outside. She recognised the passenger as Sam Heimy, the station intelligence officer. Before she could reach it, there was a knock on the door.

'Mrs Harding,' he said quietly. 'We have met. May I come in?'

She opened the door wider and stepped back to allow him entry into their front room. Already, she was fearing the worst.

'Has something happened?' Flossie asked anxiously. 'Why are you here?'

'Spencer is all right, ma'am,' he said quickly, anxious to placate her obvious concern. 'But there has been an incident. Pfc Almeter is in our base infirmary. He's been attacked.'

'How can you say he's all right if he's been attacked? And now he's in your hospital…' Her words came fast and furious.

Sam held up a hand, palm towards her. 'He's been hurt, beaten quite bad,' he told her, deliberately speaking softly, trying to allay her fears. 'The medics were worried at first, but now they think that in time, he'll make a good recovery. I've come to offer you a ride to the base if you would like to visit with him.'

Flossie thought for a moment. Gladys was out shopping, but she was due back any time now. Jimmy was next door, playing with his friend.

'Give me a minute,' she said quickly. 'I need to speak with my neighbour. Then I'll be with you.' She pulled on her coat. 'Can you wait for me in the car?'

Unsure whether or not Gladys had taken her keys, Flossie did not lock the door.

'So tell me...' she said abruptly, settling herself into the rear seat alongside Sam Heimy.

'We haven't been able to question him,' he began, 'and anyway, docs want us to wait a while. But he was lucky. We know from a trail of blood in the field where it happened that he managed to crawl to a grass verge in the lane. A passer-by, a local gentleman living not far away, was out walking his dog last thing at night. Found him unconscious at the side of the road. He ran home and called for an ambulance. Spencer was in uniform, and the base was the nearest facility, so the crew brought him to us.'

'How bad is he?' she asked again. Then, 'I want the truth.'

'He's not well enough to talk to our military police,' Sam told her gently. 'The doc thinks he'll make it OK, but there are injuries, some of them serious. But even only half conscious, he kept repeating your name – *Flossie* – and when this was reported to the station commander, Colonel Hofmeyer knew straight away that he had been asking for you. He ordered me to make contact and let you know what has happened.'

The guards at the gate were obviously expecting the Packard. Up went the barrier, and there were no identity checks. Flossie's anxiety did not diminish as they carried on, surely above the base speed limit, to a building in the administrative area. There was a huge red cross on a white circle above the double doors. Sam accompanied Flossie to an office, where she was greeted by a surprisingly young medic wearing scrubs.

'I'm Doctor Anderson,' he introduced himself, rising to stand behind a desk. He waved a hand. 'Won't you please be seated?' Sam Heimy took the other chair in front of the desk.

'I know who you are and of your relationship with Pfc Almeter,' he told her. 'Our base commander filled me in, so I'll level with you. Your man is lucky to be alive. If he hadn't made it off the field to where he was found, I doubt he would have survived.'

Flossie's hand flew to her mouth, knuckles pressed to her teeth.

'He was brought in late last evening,' he continued. 'We took X-rays, and fortunately, his skull is intact, but there's severe bruising and concussion. I had to operate, a splenorrhaphy – stitches to repair his spleen. He still hasn't fully come round.

'I also had to set breaks in both arms,' he added, 'probably from when he was trying to protect himself. Plus, there is severe body bruising. With you and me, this would show up as purple-red from blood vessel damage. But with Spencer's skin colour, it looks black. Most of the damage appears to be from blunt instruments. A truncheon comes to mind, with the rest probably from being kicked when he was on the ground.'

Flossie was quiet for a moment, taking all this in. Anderson had spoken quietly, as if trying to lessen the impact. She was looking down into her lap. He glanced at Heimy as if to say, *I put it as gently as I could. But this is not good.*

Finally, she lifted her head. There were tears in her eyes.

'Why…?' she whispered to herself, then to Anderson, 'Can I see him? He will be all right, won't he?'

'Yes, you can see him,' came the reply, 'but there might not be much response. And please don't be alarmed by the machinery. Rest assured,' he went on, 'we have all the latest equipment here. Sometimes, our airmen come back with every conceivable injury. Pfc Almeter will get the best care available in this country.'

His hand moved to an intercom on his desk. 'I'll have one of our orderlies take you to his bedside. If you need to speak to me again after your visit, I'll still be here.'

'Me too,' added Sam Heimy. 'Please let me know whether you want to stay, or I can offer you a lift back home.'

A male orderly escorted her to a small, private ward. Flossie gasped when he opened the door. Spencer was surrounded by machines. There was some sort of drip into his left arm, and a mask half covered his face. The orderly stayed respectfully by the door, offering her a degree of privacy. She stepped quickly to his bedside. Parts of his face and ears were a mass of bruises and cuts, the worst of which had been stitched together. His hands were horribly swollen, and both arms were in plaster.

Flossie drew up a chair and sat by his bedside, tentatively taking hold of his one free hand. Gently, she stroked its back, as lightly as she could, with just two fingers. His eyelids were closed.

'Spencer, my darling,' she whispered, 'what have they done to you? I'm here, love. It's your Flossie.'

His eyes remained shut, but her thumb had slid under his palm. *Surely, hadn't she just felt the faintest of pressure?* Then it was gone.

'He knows I'm here,' she said, turning to the orderly. 'I definitely felt something just then.'

'That's a good sign, Mrs Harding,' the enlisted man said politely. 'Maybe the best thing is just to let him rest quietly. I've seen this sort of head injury before. It's not unusual with aircrew. Could be hours, though, maybe even days.'

Flossie thought quickly. Every instinct told her to stay. Till the orderly came over, looked at Spencer, and placed a comforting hand on her shoulder.

'Maybe we should let Mother Nature take care of his recovery, ma'am,' he suggested. 'You can visit with him again later today if you wish. And in any case, we will contact you the moment he wakes up. Transportation won't be a problem.'

She nodded slowly, kissed Spencer as gently as she could, her lips barely touching his forehead, then turned to leave. Sam escorted her back home in the Packard, for which she was grateful, promising to return so that she could visit again for an update later in the day.

The afternoon passed in a daze, but he was back just as they were finishing their tea. The smile on Sam's face when she opened the door said it all.

'He's come round,' he said simply, 'and he's talking, if a bit groggy.'

'Thank God,' said Flossie softly to herself.

'You want to get your coat, ma'am? I'll wait in the car.'

On the way to the base, she learned that Spencer had been able to give the military police a brief outline of what had happened but had left it at that.

'He'll probably be able to give them a proper statement tomorrow,' he added. 'For now, best I let him tell you himself.'

He escorted her directly to Spencer's room. To Flossie's surprise, there was an armed military policeman in the corridor by his door.

'Colonel Hofmeyer would like to speak with you after your visit,' Sam told her. 'Just ring the bell when you're ready, and I'll collect you.' He opened the door but closed it behind her.

He was awake and no longer wearing a mask, just looking at her – as if unable to speak. But she could sense the love in his eyes.

'Flossie,' he croaked eventually, his voice hoarse from a damaged throat.

She rushed to the chair on the other side of his bed from the drip tube, took his free hand in both of hers and tried her hardest to smile. But she knew it was a pale imitation.

'My dearest man, what have they done to you?' she whispered sadly, bewildered, shaking her head slowly from side to side. 'Why…? Was it because of me?'

'I couldn't fight them all,' he said softly, 'but it wasn't you – it was cuz I fell in love wit a beautiful white lady. They were Klan, wearin' hoods. At least it was just a beatin'. Back crib they would gots hung meh.'

He pulled his hand away and placed it over hers, then winced from the pain. 'Changes nothin. I still love you, Flossie. They git meh patched up, I'm out of here.'

They talked for about ten minutes. Inconsequential things… how was Jimmy… there would be a celebration lunch the day he was discharged, but she could tell that he was tiring.

'Going to leave you in peace now, darling,' she told him. 'You need to rest, and I'll come and see you again tomorrow. Colonel Hofmeyer wants to see me before I go…' she went on, but already his eyes were closing. Spencer was drifting off to sleep.

'I was hoping,' Isaac Hofmeyer said to Flossie, 'that when we came to fight a common enemy, we had left the worst of our racial violence back home. But I'm afraid this is an appalling reaction to the equality enjoyed by black servicemen over here – the use of the same off-base facilities and jealousy of friendship with local ladies…' he trailed off, but she sensed the sadness in his voice.

'He said something rather strange…' said Flossie after a short pause. '*Back crib, they would have hung me.*'

'Back home,' Hofmeyer translated succinctly. 'Sadly, yes. Racial terror killing, as well as mutilation, is all too common in some of our southern states. No one knows the exact number, but rather than the hundreds, it's probably well into the low thousands,' he admitted.

'What will happen now, about Spencer, I mean?' she asked.

'We have a military police unit on base,' came the reply, 'and they have begun an investigation into what happened to Pfc Almeter. So far, he has been able to tell them that he was ordered from The King's Head by a uniformed sergeant. After that, he doesn't remember much, except that he was driven into a nearby field, surrounded by hooded Klansmen, and badly beaten up. Not much to go on,' he confessed.

'But surely, you can identify the sergeant?' asked Flossie, frustration evident in her voice.

'We intend to show Pfc Almeter a photograph of every sergeant on this base,' said the colonel. 'But since this is the one person that could be recognised – he emphasised the *could* – it's possible they used someone from another outfit, or maybe even just dressed up someone who isn't a sergeant at all. Rest assured, we'll do our damnedest,' he went on, 'and we'll just have to see how the investigation progresses, but I'm afraid that, at the moment, it's not looking too hopeful.'

'So what happens,' Flossie replied, having thought for a moment, 'if you can't find out who did this dreadful thing? My uncle, Mr Harding, thinks that Spencer should, at the very least, be entitled to some form of compensation. After all, the US government is ultimately responsible. Surely, Spencer would have a legal case? He could even go to the press.'

Hofmeyer said nothing for quite some time, then placed one palm on his desk as if having come to a decision.

'We have spoken about the press back home already,' he said eventually. 'I would still strongly advise against attempting any such course of action. It would not be in his best interest.'

'Not in *his* best interest,' she replied, exasperated. 'He gets badly beaten by his own side, you can't find out who did it, and then there's absolutely nothing he can do about it? No compensation – no redress at all. How come that's not in his best interest?'

Again, a long pause, 'Flossie,' he said eventually, 'I'm going to level with you. But in return, I need you to respect my position. If what I'm about to tell you were repeated outside this room, it would seriously jeopardise my situation. Do you understand?'

'I think so, yes,' she replied more quietly. 'Please go on, Colonel.'

'According to Doctor Anderson, Pfc Almeter will probably make a full recovery. There might be some residual damage, but it's unlikely to be enough to warrant a medical discharge. Are you with me so far?'

Flossie nodded her agreement.

'So,' Colonel Hofmeyer continued, 'he serves to the end of the war. We're confident enough now of an Allied victory. Eventually, along with all the other volunteers and enlisted men, your Pfc Almeter will be demobilised.

'At the moment,' he explained, 'benefits for ex-servicemen are a bit of a hotchpotch. Usually, they get preferential treatment for jobs in government service or the defence industry. But Roosevelt's got the US Veterans Bureau looking at a proper range of rewards for war service: college grants, family financial support, partial or full disability pensions – all sorts of things. It's going to be called the GI Bill. As part of this development process, senior commanders are being consulted – myself included.'

'I don't see what this has got to do with my Spencer and his case,' Flossie put in.

'It has everything to do with you both,' he shot back more quickly than he had intended. 'Look,' he said more gently, 'the golden key to all these benefits will be an honourable discharge certificate. But do you know what a Blue Discharge is?'

Flossie shook her head. 'It's called a Blue because of the colour of the paper it's printed on,' he told her. 'Basically, it's *not* an honourable one. We're told it will be given to anyone whose service the government considers has not been absolutely one hundred per cent, according to the book. But it goes beyond that. I'll give you two examples. Homosexuals will not be given an honourable discharge. Neither will any black servicemen who have opposed the system in any way – whether in the cause of equal rights, or criticism of official policy… anything.' He paused for a moment, then added finally, 'I have the distinct impression that many more Blues will be given to coloured airmen than to whites.'

He paused to let this sink in. 'Flossie,' he said, his voice as gentle as he could make it, 'you remember when you wanted to go public about marriage. The papers here wouldn't touch it. You took my advice and backed off. The same would happen if you try to sue for compensation,' he added.

'Sure, there is a black press in America, but even if you could get through to them, white people don't read it. What I do know,' he told her, 'is that the government is using the threat of a Blue Discharge to frighten off any civil rights opposition. If Spencer goes public,' – she noticed that this was the first time he had used his Christian name – 'I guarantee he'll not get an honourable one. He'll be thrown out on his ear, with no help whatsoever for any wounds or injuries sustained during his time in the military. No pension, no college fees, no family support, no disability payments, no vets medical care... *nada*...' His hand slapped the table. 'Nothing.'

'It isn't right, but that's why you have to let this go,' he finished quietly.

Chapter 25

They had agreed that he would choose when to jump. The squadron turned north after bombing their target. He watched through the bomb doors as the tip of Augsburg passed under the belly of the aircraft. Far below, and through thin wisps of cloud, came open countryside. He waited till they were well clear of the built-up area, then switched to his bailout bottle. With one hand firmly on the ripcord handle and the other gripping his rucksack strop, he took a step forward into thin air.

Werner was aware that he was tumbling out of control. Also, the strop was slipping through his fingers. He let it slide. Keeping his hand firmly on the ripcord handle, he tried to curl himself into a ball. When he let go of the strop, the weight beneath him had a steadying effect; although acting as a pendulum, it also swung him from side to side. Allowing for time to reach terminal velocity, which he could only guess at anyway, he had calculated that it would take somewhere around two minutes, perhaps fractionally less, for a human body without a parachute to reach the ground. He had intended to release as low as possible but realised with a panic that he was beginning to black out.

Werner was not sure how long the feeling lasted, but suddenly, the ground looked dangerously close. He ripped away his mouthpiece and pulled the handle. To his intense relief, there was a satisfying crack from above his head but also a nasty snatch into his crotch. The overwhelming sensation was suddenly one of silence. He did his best to look around. It had been a good call. He was heading for a wooded area and in sight of only a handful of farmhouses.

He was dropping into a field, yards from the trees. His rucksack touched, and then his feet. He rolled as he had been taught. *Thanks, Hathaway and Ringwood,* he thought to himself. He had landed from twenty thousand feet without even a sprain.

There was very little wind. Werner gathered in his parachute, removed his heated suit and rolled everything into a ball. Shouldering his rucksack, he carried everything else to the edge of the wood and stuffed it under some bushes. It was barely concealed, but that was the intention. If his landing had been noticed, any search party would assume that they were looking for someone in an American flyer's uniform. Not someone in civilian clothes.

The rucksack was a different issue. If Werner were caught, its contents would guarantee his execution. Ideally, he needed to conceal it somewhere, make his way to Buchbach Manor, then retrieve it when any search activity was long since over.

He took his bearing from the partly cloud-covered lightness in the sky and set off east, cross country. With the remaining daylight, he needed to be something between five and ten kilometres from where he had landed. Shortly before last light, he crested a low rise to look down on a substantial farmhouse surrounded by several outbuildings. If he could conceal his rucksack and perhaps find somewhere to spend the night under cover, tomorrow, he would find some way of moving on to Buchbach – an innocent civilian with all the right papers and unencumbered with damning evidence.

The largest outbuilding by far was a barn across the cobbled yard from the main house, which, in the early evening light, was still in darkness. He ignored the barn's double doors and tested a smaller pedestrian one set to one side. It was unlocked. There was a strong ammonia smell inside. Cattle had only recently been let out to spring pasture. But a stout wooden ladder made from cut branches leant against a hayloft. It was ideal for his purpose.

He was halfway up when there was a loud click from behind. He turned his head to see a young woman who had snapped up both barrels of a shotgun, now aimed directly at his head.

'Down,' she ordered confidently. He complied and turned to face her. They were about ten paces apart. Even unencumbered by his rucksack, there was no way he could reach her in time. He slowly off-shouldered it and set it down on the floor beside him.

'Who are you,' she demanded, 'and what are you doing in my barn?'

'I mean no harm,' he said evenly. 'I am trying to reach my home. All I need is somewhere dry and warm for the night.'

She studied him for several seconds. 'You're not in uniform,' she said eventually, 'so you must be a deserter.'

He was saved a response by the sound of a vehicle pulling into the farmyard. She kept the shotgun pointing in his direction and stepped sideways to where she could look from behind the door. The sound of a large dog barking furiously came from the main house.

'It's a *Kübelwagen*,' she said. 'Four men in it. I think they're *SS*.' The woman took a pace to the rear, swung the shotgun to point at the intruders and walked into the yard. Werner dived into his rucksack, extracted a Browning HP automatic from a side pocket, and rammed home a 13-round magazine. A second magazine he stuffed into his jacket pocket. But against four – he accepted that this was probably over-optimistic. He had to hope that they were carrying rifles and not the *Maschinenpistole 40* submachine gun.

He moved to stand behind the door. At least he could be sure of taking the first man to enter the barn. After that, it would be just three against one, assuming the woman stayed out of it. He listened.

'What do you lot want?' he heard her shout. Presumably, she had not moved far from the door.

'Please, dear lady, do not point that thing at us,' came the response. But the voice did not sound angry.

'I live here on my own,' she replied, 'and I've met your sort before. So it stays where it is. Now, I've asked you once, and there won't be a third time. What do you want?'

A junior non-commissioned officer came into Werner's view through the crack below the top hinge on the door. Unfortunately, an *MP40* was hanging from his shoulder.

'We are looking for someone, an enemy parachutist,' came the reply. 'We have a report that he bailed out not far from here, this side of Augsburg.'

She had noticed that her visitor in the barn wasn't in uniform, which meant that... An idea formed instantly in her mind. It might just be possible... 'If he had landed anywhere near here,' Werner heard her say, 'either I would have shot him, or Otto Von Bismarck there' – her head indicated the incessant, frantic barking of a large hound – 'would have chewed him to pieces. I've only just shut him indoors for the night. No way anyone could have approached the house or hidden on the farm.'

The soldier looked at her for a moment. Reassured by the sight of the shotgun and the noise of the dog, he said, 'Then I guess *Herr* Bismarck has saved us the trouble, *Fraulein*. *Heil Hitler!*' Werner watched as his arm stiffed out and his heels came together.

'*Heil Hitler,*' she replied, 'and good luck with your search.'

He disappeared from view. Seconds later, an engine started and the *Kübelwagen* left the farmyard.

'You can come out,' she called to him. 'They've gone.'

He left the barn, Browning still in hand but pointing at the ground. She broke open the shotgun and extracted two cartridges. He ejected the magazine and racked the slide to remove the chambered round, which he picked up from the cobblestones.

'It seems we are not going to shoot each other,' he said with a half-smile. It was not returned.

'Put it away, pick up your bag and come into the house,' she said, turning away from him and walking towards the door.

A large, wet nose thumped into his stomach, but Otto's tail was wagging furiously. 'He had them fooled,' she said. 'He barks at anything and everything, so he's a good watchdog, but otherwise, he's just an old softy.'

It was a large kitchen and well furnished. A long, pine table and six chairs still left plenty of room to walk around. Cupboards lined one wall, with a sink opposite, underneath a window looking out onto the farmyard. A fire in a range at the far end took the chill off the evening.

'Sit down,' she told him. 'It's you they're looking for, isn't it?'

He held her look but said nothing. She was, he supposed, about his age. Her almost white-blonde hair and blue eyes would meet with Aryan approval. A weathered tan and lines around her eyes suggested time out of doors. It was a plain, rather square and ordinary face, and her dungarees failed to hide a perhaps over-generous figure.

'If it was you,' she said after a moment's hesitation, 'you're no airman. Not in those clothes. And out there, you had an automatic. You obviously know how to use it. Armed... plain clothes... there's only one logical explanation.'

Werner chose to ignore the implied question. 'Why didn't you report me to that patrol?' he asked.

'I might have said *Heil Hitler*,' she responded, 'but our *Führer* is a load of shit. My husband was a reservist, called up even though that left only me to manage the farm. Last I heard, he was on the Eastern front. Stalingrad – I have no idea whether he's alive or dead. And even if he is, alive, that is, I doubt he'll survive the war as a prisoner of the Russians.'

'Even so...' he trailed off, suggesting that there had to be more if she chose to reveal it.

'The *Weiße Rose* mean anything to you?' she queried by way of an answer.

'I have heard of the White Rose, yes,' he admitted.

'I have a sister. She's older than me, but we have always been close. Her daughter, my niece, was a student at Munich University. Just a teenager. She was a member. They caught her with some anti-Nazi leaflets. She goes on trial in a couple of weeks – a *Volksgerichtshof*, a so-called people's court, a jumped-up, self-important load of puppets answerable to no one but the Nazi state.'

Her voice was rising with emotion. 'Do you know what they did with some of the others?' she asked. 'Threatening the security of the nation, they said. At the trial, the defendants were not even allowed to speak. Guilty! They cut off their heads with a guillotine. A guillotine!' she exclaimed with horror. 'Not since the French revolution... Gerda's only a young girl...'

'But at least she's alive now, so there has to be a chance,' he said quietly.

'She'll be damned lucky to get away with her life, they say, and even if she does, it'll be at least twelve years. Not even twenty years old... just for having pieces of paper...' *Heil Hitler?* I fucking hate them,' she said vehemently before slamming the shotgun down on the table.

Werner gave her a few moments to quieten down. 'So that's why you didn't tell them,' he said eventually.

'What are you going to do next?' she asked, her voice more normal now. 'And I can't keep saying "you". Don't you have a name?'

He had papers identifying him as Erich Hahn. 'Call me Erich,' he replied.

'And I'm Ilse,' she said simply.

'As I said before,' he went on, 'all I'm looking for is somewhere to spend the night. I'll be on my way in the morning. Although ideally, it would be good if I could hide my rucksack for a while, then collect it later, after all the hue and cry has died down.'

'No need to sleep in the barn. There are plenty of spare rooms in the house,' she offered. 'But why leave in the morning? There will be patrols all over the place checking transport and everything. Even if you set off on foot, cross country, you stand a good chance of getting caught.'

'Makes sense,' he replied. 'But that's going to put you in danger. At the very least, you could get carted off to one of the camps. More likely, though, it would be a firing squad.'

'My sister and her husband have been left alone since poor Gerda was incarcerated, and *she* certainly won't have told them about me. No… the patrol's been here, and they have no reason to come back. And if they do, I'll just tell them that you were in the barn with a gun at my back.' Her shoulders lifted, then dropped. 'But I can't see that happening. The farm's been ticked off their list.'

'Then if you're content, Ilse,' he said, 'I'll accept gratefully. I won't risk going out to work in the fields, but I can try to earn my keep. Perhaps spend some time building up your log pile. Or anything else you can think of. Also, I am well provided with funds, so I am more than happy to pay my way. And I have ration cards.'

'I don't need your money or your cards,' she replied. 'I don't know if you are aware, but our bread, meat and fat rations were reduced just over a year ago. I am all right, though, here on the farm. I made a large bowl of stew this morning. I can heat it up for tonight. It's rabbit, snared the other day, and there's plenty of bread. At least we're not reduced to *Daschschwein.*'

He raised his eyebrows. 'Roof pigs,' she explained. 'Rumour has it that in the cities, they are raising cats for food in roof cages. Come on,' she said, changing the subject. 'I'll show you to your room and where you can wash up whilst I sort out the supper.'

Ilse announced the next morning, over a breakfast of an egg and buttered bread, that she would be out for most of the day, doing the last of the spring sowing in a field on the edge of the farm. But he was to make himself at home. As she left, Werner was standing well back from the kitchen window, probably not visible from outside. He was surprised to see her wheel a bicycle from the barn. She appeared to take an anxious look at the house before riding away.

She had quite a ride ahead of her. At the police station, a disbelieving officer was eventually persuaded to her story. He made a telephone call, and half an hour later, a military officer appeared, introducing himself as *Major* Berger. He tried to bully her into giving away the information there and then, but she stood her ground. She had deliberately not brought any identification with her, rules or no rules. And if they detained her and tried to force his whereabouts from her, she told him, that would take time. Unless she returned reasonably promptly, he would assume the worst and almost certainly do a runner. The Major eventually spoke to the head of the Munich *Volksgerichtshof.* There appeared to be some sort of argument over the 'phone, but from the tone of his voice, the officer was making it very clear who had the authority to make the final decision. Only at the end of their conversation did he return to a more civil exchange.

'You have my word as a German officer,' he said to her afterwards, in a rather more conciliatory tone. 'Gerda Schafer will not be executed and will receive only a very light, token sentence.'

She had no choice but to accept.

Chapter 26

It was late afternoon, and Ilse still wasn't back. He'd helped himself to some cheese from the meat safe on the cold slab in the larder and listened to the wireless, but by now, Werner was bored with being boxed up indoors.

He'd kept a good eye on the drive, but no one had approached the farm all day – the only vehicle access led into the farmyard. He couldn't watch the other sides of the house, but the door into the yard was open, and he trusted Otto to warn him if anyone approached.

Werner needed to stretch his legs. He couldn't risk working out in the open fields, but taking Otto for a brisk walk would do him the world of good. Be better to leave the precious rucksack behind, but he could take out the Browning and Mr Wilkinson Sword's Fairbairn-Sykes commando knife, to which he had been introduced in Scotland. This latter, inside its scabbard, he strapped to his calf. The rucksack, together with the rest of its contents, he would leave in the hayloft.

He was enjoying the walk, not pushing the pace, when he crested the rise from where he had first overlooked the farmhouse yesterday. A *Wehrmacht* lorry followed a *Kübelwagen* drove into the farmyard. Both skidded to a halt. Werner melted into nearby woodland, from where he could still see the farm. A squad leapt from the lorry and surrounded the house. An officer, pistol in hand, entered through the kitchen door accompanied by two *MP40*-armed soldiers. Otto bounded away from him.

The dog raced back down the hill and into the yard, barking furiously. As he approached the soldiers, one of them fired a short burst, and the hound skidded on his knees before collapsing motionless onto his side. There was a scream. Ilse emerged from the back of the *Kübelwagen* and ran to kneel beside him. From a distance, she appeared to be sobbing uncontrollably before raising her head to shout invective at the man who had shot and killed her pet.

The major and his two soldiers emerged from the kitchen door. He must have given an order because his men began to enter the outbuildings. They did not find the rucksack, probably because Werner had hidden it under a low pile of empty sacks too small to conceal anyone. After about five minutes of activity, the men reassembled in the yard. One of them lifted Ilse's bicycle from the back of the lorry and leant it against a wall. Two men detached themselves and, carrying a radio, walked into a stable alongside the barn. The rest mounted up and drove away.

The officer obviously knew his tradecraft. He had left behind an observation post in case Werner returned. Almost certainly, if nothing happened, they would be collected in the morning. Ilse approached the stable door, and the two soldiers carried Otto into the barn for her, presumably to be buried the following day. They returned to the stable, and as twilight settled over the farm, a light came on in the kitchen. Werner moved back down the slope and settled himself behind the barn, but from where he could see the entrance to the stable. It could be only a matter of time.

A couple of hours later, the stable door was pushed open a little wider, and one of the soldiers emerged. He walked around the side of the building and began to urinate against the wall. He felt almost nothing as a hand clamped over his mouth, and the stiletto blade of the Fairbairn-Sykes pierced his throat and was pushed forward, eviscerating his carotid arteries and larynx. He fell with barely a sound. Werner wiped the blade on the man's uniform and contemplated his next step.

If he did nothing, the soldier inside would eventually come looking, but he would be alert and suspicious. Werner sheathed the knife and pulled the Browning from his coat pocket, walking further away before working the slide to chamber a round. The click would have been inaudible inside the stable.

The low, ambient light in the yard would be behind him – his body and face would be in deep shadow. He could just make out the shape of the second soldier sitting on an upturned box, the radio and his *MP40* on the floor. He lifted his head as Werner stood in the doorway.

'*Hände hoch!*' he commanded briskly, at the same time taking a half step inside and turning so that the soldier could see clearly the outline of the Browning. There was the briefest movement of his arm, no more than a flicker as if making a reflex move for his weapon. Werner extended his arm into the aim, and the threat from a barrel not much more than a metre away, pointing at his chest, made the soldier change his mind. Slowly, he raised his hands.

'Who are you, what do you want, and where is Hans?' he asked.

Werner said nothing, just walked behind his prisoner and hit him hard on the back of his head with the butt of the Browning. The soldier was out cold.

He kicked the *MP40* a short distance away. It was a struggle, and it took some time, but he took off the soldier's greatcoat and uniform jacket and trousers, setting them aside. They were pretty much the right size. His man was beginning to regain consciousness. Much as he hated doing it, he dragged the soldier away from his box and used his knife, this time expertly into the ribcage and from side to side, cutting off the heart. Less blood to stain the floor.

The door to the kitchen was locked, which was hardly surprising. Ilse must have assumed that it was one of the soldiers, because she did not cry out, just unlocked and opened it.

'You... she gasped in surprise, a hand flying to her mouth when she saw the Browning in his hand. 'We thought you were long gone,' she said. He advanced into the kitchen, one palm against her shoulder, pushing her back but gently, then half-turned and nudged the door shut behind him.

'"We" being you and those two in the barn,' he suggested, not unpleasantly. 'Well, I'm sorry to tell you that they will not be coming to your assistance. Sit down. You have some explaining to do.'

Hesitantly she took a seat, her back to the window. Werner sat down opposite. 'You did not help me because you dislike the Nazis,' he began. 'In fact, as we both now know, you betrayed me.'

Her hands, in front of her on the table, were wringing. 'I... I'm s-so s-sorry,' she stammered. 'I didn't want to do it. I've got nothing against you, and I m-meant what I said about the N-Nazis, I mean. I hate them.' She gulped, a tear forming at the corner of each eye. 'But I had to try to save Gerda. It was all I had to bargain with, and they promised...' she trailed off, looking down at her hands.

'You might – or you might not – have saved your niece,' he told her. 'It depends where we go from here. But I have just had to kill two men, and you have lost Otto. So did that *major* tell you what happens next? About his two men in the barn, I mean?'

'If you turned up again, they were to radio in and sit tight,' she replied. 'Presumably, *Major* Berger – that's his name – intends to return and surround the house again.'

'No instructions to make regular radio reports, otherwise?' he asked her.

'Not as far as I know,' she offered. 'And I was there when he gave them their orders.'

'And if it's "nothing heard", as far as the *major* is concerned?'

'He told them they would be collected in the morning,' she answered.

'If so, he'll send a vehicle, just one or two men,' Werner observed. 'No need for anything more.'

Initially, he had thought that a soldier's uniform might come in handy. Now, a plan was forming in his mind.

'Already, your *major* friend is two men down,' he said flatly. 'I have an *SS* uniform I can put on, and I could really use a vehicle. That gets me away from here. But there are two dead soldiers outside. If you are implicated in any way, I know these people. Your niece will hang, and most likely, you with her.'

She was clearly shocked by his words. Tears began to roll down her face. He ignored them. 'What can we do?' she whispered desperately. 'Anything…'

'There's only one way out of this,' he told her. His voice was uncompromising. 'When that vehicle comes in the morning, the occupants cannot be allowed to survive. If we dispose of the bodies and I take the vehicle, you can tell the *major* that there has been no sign of me, and all of them left together in the *Kübelwagen*, or whatever turns up.'

'Will he believe me?' she asked anxiously.

'Depends how good an actress you are,' he replied. 'But from what I've seen so far, you ought to manage. He's far more likely to think that I might have had something to do with it rather than you. So where do we put the bodies?'

She thought for a moment. 'There are plenty of wild boar in the forest. They would get rid of any remains,' she said eventually, her face grimacing at the thought.

'So we strip them, burn the rest of the uniforms, and I'll dump them a kilometre or two away from the farm,' he announced, in a tone of voice that brooked no argument.

Werner borrowed a couple of blankets and slept fully clothed in the kitchen. She was awake and dressed before dawn and made them both some breakfast and a cup of *ersatz* coffee. At least it was a hot drink. Before he left for the stable to await the arrival of the collection vehicle, she handed him a piece of paper.

'Four names,' she told him. 'Best if you memorise them. Two men, two women. Friends of Gerda's,' she added. 'If they still have their freedom, they might help you with whatever you intend to do in this part of Germany.'

He glanced at the paper, folded it and put it in his back pocket. 'It's not much… but it's all I can do to make amends,' she said hesitantly.

* * * *

Things had gone well enough that morning, Werner reflected. The driver, the only occupant of a *Kübelwagen*, called at the kitchen, spoke with Ilse and then crossed the yard, calling out as he entered the stable. He'd knocked him unconscious from behind the door, stripped off his uniform and despatched him with the Fairbairn-Sykes. Having put on the larger of the unmarked uniforms, he reminded Ilse to rake out and get rid of the buttons after she'd burnt the bloodstained one from last night.

She had given him good directions, and the bodies were in the forest, well beyond any search area centred on the farm. It wasn't much consolation, but they had been *SS*, not ordinary conscripts whose only misfortune would have been a compulsory call-up into Hitler's war. And now he had an extra uniform, an *MP40* beside him, his rucksack on the floor in front of the passenger seat, plus two more *MP40s* and spare magazines in the foot well behind.

His original plan had been to reach Augsburg and then take a train to Munich. But now, in uniform and with a military vehicle, he could transport himself and his newly augmented armoury all the way to Buchbach. Approaching Augsburg, there was a police car checking the few vehicles on the road. He slowed but overtook the column, half-saluting the two patrolmen standing alongside a van at the head of the queue. They waved him through. He was not surprised. He doubted there were many military stationed in the town. Munich was the spiritual home of the Nazis. They would have *SS* stationed there in force, but not that many locally. Berger's small force from yesterday was probably almost the entire Augsburg garrison. Additional roadblock or search personnel would have to come from the police and any civilian manpower resources. They were not much of a threat.

There was no need to risk driving through Munich, and the further he was from the farm, on the other side of Augsburg, the less he worried about being stopped. He took a northerly loop round the city and approached Buchbach Manor from its far side, the northeast. It was early afternoon. He turned onto the track from where he had originally hidden in the hope of meeting his mother, backed off under some trees, where the *Kübelwagen* was shielded by undergrowth from the track and concealed from the air, and switched off the engine with a sigh of relief.

Neither was there any point in waiting till Anna returned to her cottage, assuming she was still working for his father. He would not be able to stay at Buchbach for more than a day or so without her knowledge, and he needed longer than that. He took an *MP40* and a spare magazine and set off on foot towards the house. The front door was closed, and there was no sign of activity. But there was a wisp of smoke coming from one of the chimneys, which he knew served the range in the kitchen at the rear.

Through the window, he saw Anna seated at her kitchen table, a cup of something before her. Not wishing to startle her, he knocked gently on the door and took a pace back.

'*Wer ist es?*' he heard her call as the latch lifted.

'Anna, it's me, Werner,' he replied.

His former nanny ran forward and threw her arms around him, sobbing uncontrollably. '*Mein Gott*, Werner,' she managed eventually, dabbing at her eyes with a handkerchief, 'we did not know whether you were still alive. Your father said you had been here, but that's all he would tell me, and it's been almost two years...'

His hands held her gently as he kissed her on the cheek. 'And father?' he asked. Before she could answer, the other door into the kitchen opened, and over her shoulder, he saw the old general holding a shotgun.

'I heard voices,' he said.

'It's Werner, General,' she replied, stepping to one side.

The old man quickly broke open the weapon and set it on the kitchen table. 'My son, my son,' he said, choking up and half walking, half staggering forward. They embraced. His father pushed him back, a hand on each shoulder, his grip still strong. 'And what the hell are you doing here in the uniform of an *unterscharführer*, with an *MP40* hanging from your shoulder?'

'I'll be with you in a few minutes,' Werner replied. 'It's a long story. But first, I need to hide a *Kübelwagen* that – er – doesn't quite belong to me. All right if I put it in the barn?'

'*Ja, ja,*' his father replied joyfully. 'Anna, my dear, a bottle of schnapps and three glasses, if you please.' Then, turning to Werner, 'We'll wait for you at the kitchen table.'

'We have to bring down Hitler, and I am working for British intelligence,' he told them on his return, essentially for Anna's benefit. 'I have a mission to complete in Munich, and that's really all you need to know. Except,' he added, 'that I would like to use Buchbach as a base whilst I am here, which could be for quite some time.'

'I shall make up your old room,' Anna announced happily.

'Been thinking about it. I'm not sure that's such a good idea.'

'What then?' his father asked.

'The future is uncertain to the point of being dangerous,' he responded. 'If I'm caught, Father, you would almost certainly be assumed guilty by association.'

'I'm an old man,' his father growled. 'My Johanna's gone. There's nothing more they can do to me... I'll take my chances.'

'I'm grateful,' said Werner. He hesitated, then, 'There is something more I must tell you both. I, too, have lost a loved one. My wife, Anneliese, died not long ago. Our son – although I am not his natural father, we were a family – is now being raised by his grandparents.'

'My boy, I'm so sorry,' his father whispered. Anna placed a comforting hand on Werner's forearm. 'How did it happen?' she asked gently.

'It was the war,' Werner said bluntly, and left it at that. They did not question him further. He would doubtless tell them with the passing of time.

'But now we have to think of Anna,' he went on. 'My survival is by no means guaranteed. If I am caught, you and I might have to face their so-called justice, but if I don't live in the manor house, Anna would be able to deny all knowledge. As just an employee,' he placed a hand over her's – 'and we all know you are much more than that to both of us,' he reassured her, – 'she would have every chance of convincing them of her innocence, that she had no idea I was even here.'

'What do you propose?' asked his father.

'There are several empty cottages on the estate,' he replied. 'The one I have in mind used to be allocated to our head forester. It's isolated, in the middle of a wood, and pretty much overgrown. If I can push the *Kübelwagen* through the undergrowth, it would be ideal.'

'But it's almost derelict,' his father exclaimed. 'Last time I looked, bits of the roof were missing.'

'Then that's where we start, first thing in the morning,' said Werner. He filled their glasses. '*Prost!*'

Chapter 27

Spencer made a gradual but good recovery. Captain Anderson kept him in hospital for the first week, after which Colonel Hofmeyer gave him permission to live off-base for his month of sick leave. Gladys' house was a two-up, two-down, but there was a small attic that, like the bedrooms, had its own fireplace. Uncle Bill lent her a bed and some furniture from The King's Head. They turned the attic into a cosy room for Spencer.

At first, he did little more than rest by day in one of the lounge's two easy chairs. It was another week before he could walk, slowly, without too much pain and discomfort from cracked and bruised ribs, and only in the third week after the attack could he take a cautious, deeper breath. It was towards the end of that week, when he was looking forward to a return to light duties that Gladys announced a visitor.

'Mr Almeter, you're a hard man to track down. I eventually managed to persuade Captain Heimy to tell me where I might find you.' His visitor handed over a card bearing the crest of The Manor Hotel, Peterborough – the one much favoured by the officers and senior ranks of the base – and underneath: Robert Arbuthnot, Manager.

The hotel's manager was of medium height, perhaps five foot seven or eight, middle-aged, with black, Brylcreemed hair combed sideways to cover one-half of a widow's peak. Perhaps hardly surprising for a hotel manager, he was carrying enough spare weight to give his face a slightly plump appearance. Still, his smile was genuine, and his suit was certainly beyond the quality worn by the majority of men in wartime Britain.

'Please,' he said, offering a hand, 'don't get up. I understand you have recently been incapacitated.

'Mr Arbuthnot,' Spencer replied cautiously, standing nevertheless so that he towered over his visitor, 'wat be it dat you want wit meh?'

'In words of one syllable,' Mr Almeter, 'I need your help.'

Not knowing quite what to say, Spencer sat down again and just looked at him.

'For some time now,' Robert Arbuthnot began to explain, 'We… that is at the hotel… have been planning a dinner dance aimed mainly at our American friends, to celebrate the Fourth of July. That's a Sunday, but we will start the previous evening, and the party will go on till well after midnight.'

'Nice idea,' responded Spencer, but left it at that.

'Well, as you know,' Arbuthnot pressed on regardless, 'we have a resident orchestra at the hotel.'

'No, I wouldn't, I'm afraid.' Spencer responded flatly. 'Us coloured folks is not welcome at da Manor, so we don't go there.'

Robert Arbuthnot had the good grace to look embarrassed. He cleared his throat to cover his confusion.

'If I might be allowed to elaborate,' he continued. 'Our little orchestra is what the manor's usual clientele expect. They are more of the waltz, foxtrot and quickstep persuasion,' he explained. 'But this event is for our American friends, a much younger audience, as will be their partners. The idea is to put on an evening of what I believe you call big band or swing music. Something along the lines of a Glen Miller night. We need a different musical ensemble.'

He paused to allow Spencer to take this in. 'I have been talking to Colonel Hofmeyer, and he has agreed to provide the musicians. I heard them not long ago when I was a guest at an airbase function,' he confided, 'and for our Fourth of July evening, they are just what we need. Absolutely tickety-boo,' he finished enthusiastically.

'Sho' you is quite right,' said Spencer, 'but how does dat involve meh?'

They were interrupted by the return of Flossie, hefting two bulging string bags of shopping which she set down on the table. After introductions, she settled on the other chair to listen to their conversation. Arbuthnot gave her a one-liner update.

'The problem is,' he went on, 'that Vera, our rather mature lady vocalist, same name, not quite the same talent,' he confided, 'absolutely refuses to take part. Says it's just not her style at all. The bottom line,' he concluded, 'is that I have come to ask if you will be our star singer for the evening.'

Spencer stood up again and took a deep breath. It twinged, but not too much.

'It's too soon, he's not well enough,' put in Flossie, seeing the slight reaction on his face.

He took another deep breath. 'It'll be all right, Flossie, love,' he told her. 'There's still more than a week to go.'

She was about to argue, but he held up his hand.

'I'll do it, Mr Arbuthnot,' he replied. 'But derr is two conditions.'

'If it's a question of payment,' he answered, 'the hotel will reimburse you handsomely. It will have to be in pounds sterling, but we would be looking at twenty-five for the evening.'

Flossie gasped. That was five times the average weekly wage, just for one night's work.

'It's not the money, although that's fine,' said Spencer. 'Derr is othah conditions.'

'And they are?'

'First, if mah construction boys want to be derr, they gots to be admitted. Nah coloured boys, no meh,' he said bluntly.

'Captain Heimy told me you would say that,' Arbuthnot responded with a grin. 'Also, that Colonel Hofmeyer has already said he would not allow it any other way. And your second condition?' he asked.

'When it's da "Apple Tree" number, someone else does da vocal. Or you go without. Meh, I gets to jitterbug wit mah Flossie.'

* * * *

The "we" restoring the cottage turned out to be just Werner. As his father pointed out, the few hectares of the estate that were not let to tenants still had to be farmed. All the male hands had been called up. Women from the village were only too happy to put in a few days' work in exchange for a share of the produce. And he was just grateful, even at his age, to be able to work some of the land himself. Production was way down from pre-war figures, but that was just one more stupidity of Hitler's war.

Besides, the general had argued, better that he was seen to be following his normal routine rather than disappearing to help with fixing the cottage roof. And anyway, he was too old to be up and down a ladder. At least there was no shortage of materials. Werner took all that he needed from other abandoned cottages on the estate.

It was not too comfortable at first, but he found a dry spot where rain did not drip down through the roof. And the iron range was still serviceable, so he was able to cook, collecting rations from the manor kitchen a couple of evenings a week after Anna had gone home and enjoying drinks with his father. Hard labour kept him fit, and after the first week, when he had patch-thatched the roof, Werner raised a glass of schnapps to the first night when not a drop from driving wind and rain penetrated the small loft.

The cottage had been stripped almost bare. The only furniture still there was an old kitchen table, which Werner scrubbed clean. But a couple of trips from the main house with a hand cart added surplus furniture and utensils, unused since pre-war days when it had been a bustling and thriving estate. And it had not been shot over since before the war. The younger men had been called up, and the threat of his father's shotgun had discouraged the occasional older poacher. Werner found that an *MP40* was equally effective against deer. He had gralloched a small hind the day before yesterday, and the first hint of aroma from a large pot of stew was beginning to fill the warm kitchen. With a bottle of red from his father's cellar, it would be a feast. He took a sip from his glass and contemplated the way ahead.

He had to reach the city, where he could operate from the flat. The estate was thirty kilometres from Munich. There was a bus and a train service from the village, but that would be too risky. There was every likelihood he would be recognised. He could just imagine the gossip... 'Guess what? I'm sure I saw that *Sturmbannführer* Scholz on the way to work this morning. He wasn't wearing his uniform, though. Isn't he supposed to be wanted for something...?"

Neither could he take the *Kübelwagen*. There was no room for it in his garage, and if it fell back into the hands of the military, they would trace it to Augsburg and then shift their search for him to Munich. He discussed the problem with his father.

'It will have to be a push bike,' the old general advised. 'Anna has her own, but she did mention she was thinking of selling the one that belonged to her late husband. I'll ask her about it.'

Which was how, a few days later, Werner found himself the owner of a 1930's *Stadion Herrenrad*, an ancient boneshaker that had neither gears nor a pannier. At least it had a sprung saddle, although the old-fashioned handlebars, curved back at each end, were decidedly uncomfortable. Werner oiled the wheels and chain and checked it over as best he could. It would have to do.

He waited for a fine day. It would not do to arrive at the apartment looking like a drowned rat. There might also be a new concierge in the entrance hall, so he chose a respectable but non-descript outfit of jacket and flannels. All weapons and his radio he left at Buchbach. If he were stopped, they would find nothing incriminating,

It was a reasonable enough journey. Werner pushed his bicycle up the steeper hills, and it was late afternoon before he arrived at the city. Still protected from the United Kingdom by distance, it was as yet undamaged. He went first to his garage, relieved to see that the lock-up was untouched and the Mercedes and BMW R12 were as he had left them. Leaving the bicycle inside, he walked the short distance to his apartment block. Heinz was still there, inside his glass-fronted cubicle. Seeing Werner, he slid open the window.

'Spot of leave, Heinz,' he said cheerfully. 'How are you keeping?'

'It's a pleasure to see you again, sir,' came the automatic response. Obviously, after all this time, the slight change of hair colouring had not been noticed. 'Not too badly, sir,' he added, 'and thank you for asking. I trust you will find everything in order, but please don't hesitate to ask if there is anything I can do to assist.'

'Thank you, Heinz,' Werner replied, turning towards the penthouse elevator. He stepped out into a small hallway and used his key to open the door. A quick inspection confirmed that the apartment had not been entered since he had last used it. It was wartime: as far as Heinz was aware, he was still in the *SS*. Werner's absence for such a long time would be by no means unusual.

He ate out that evening in a local restaurant that he had frequented occasionally before the war. Women had replaced the male waiters. There was a moment of anxiety when he proffered the ration card provided by London, but it was accepted, and his waitress removed the appropriate stamps without comment. At least the notes on the plate covering the bill were genuine, and his modest tip earned a quiet word of thanks.

Travelling around the city presented Werner with a choice: he could use either his bicycle or the *Münchner Straßenbahnen* service. Next morning, he took the tram to the University district. The war had certainly changed the demographic – there were far more female students in the cafés and bars than young men. Conscious that he stood out within this student community by virtue of his age; nevertheless, he saw little alternative. He had long since memorised the names given to him by Ilse and had chosen one of the two women at random.

He used the same query over and over: 'I'm trying to trace a distant relative, Irmgard Stein. We used to play together as children. Do you by any chance know of her?'

By late morning, he had all but given up hope. He found a *Bierstube* patronised by workmen as well as students and ordered a beer and *Wurst*. If there was any meat in the sausage, it wasn't obvious. He had just finished his lunch when a young woman of student age seated herself uninvited at his table.

'You have been asking about Irmgard,' she said without preamble. 'When I leave, follow me at a safe distance.'

His pulse quickened, but before he could reply, she stood and walked from the bar. He paid hastily at the counter, handed over his coupons and followed outside. She had paused about twenty-five metres away but walked on as soon as he emerged.

The woman turned down an alley between two shops. It led out onto another street, but she stopped halfway and turned to face him. Behind her, two men approached from the other end, walking towards her. Werner looked over his shoulder. Two more followed, but they were not students. From their clothing, all four were working men, perhaps just above the age of conscription. They took their time. Each pulled a wooden cosh from under his jacket. Werner backed up against a wall to keep them all in view. The young woman made no attempt to move. Werner had been well trained, but he was unarmed. Odds of four to one were not good.

Chapter 28

These people were not German police or military. The four men formed a rough semi-circle about three metres away, two on each side of her, but made no move to attack. The woman advanced halfway towards him. 'Why have you been asking after Irmgard Stein?' she demanded.

'I may be able to help her,' he replied evenly, 'and she may be able to help me.'

'And you are...?'

'My name is Hahn,' he responded, 'Erich Hahn.'

'And what would be the nature of this *help* that you can offer?' she queried.

'That would be a private matter between me and *Fraulein* Stein,' he stated bluntly.

'I could order these men to beat the truth out of you,' she said, but he sensed that there was no real menace behind the threat.

'You could,' he admitted but offered nothing further. One of the men behind her began to tap the end of his cosh against his palm, as if to reinforce what she had just said. But it was too theatrical. Werner's instincts told him that he, too, was bluffing. A suspicion formed in his mind.

'Irmgard says that you are lying,' she went on. 'You did not play together as children. She has never seen you before in her life. So, who gave you her name?'

'Someone who knows that you are a friend of Gerda's, Irmgard,' he said softly, 'and also that you are no supporter of the present régime.'

'Very clever,' was all she said at first. Then, after a pause, 'So why do you think you can help me?'

'I need to speak with you alone,' he told her. 'So call off your hired help. For both of our sakes, what I have to say is for your ears only. I am no threat to you or your organisation. But unless you are prepared to trust me, our conversation is over, and you will not see me again. As for them,' his head indicated her escort, 'I'll take my chances. But it would be a pity if a couple of them were seriously injured, all to no purpose.'

The cosh tapper moved forward to stand alongside her, but she quickly placed the back of her hand in front of his chest. 'It's all right,' she told them. 'I'll talk to him. Thank you all very much for your help, but please leave us now.' Then, turning back to Werner, 'Come with me,' she beckoned.

'We'll go back to the bar where I found you,' she said. 'I'm known there, and it will be safe.'

'Two beers, Johann, please,' she called out as they entered. Werner noticed that she chose a corner table from where they could see the door. She took off her jacket and rested it across her lap. Irmgard Stein did not have the classic, Aryan, blonde-and-blue-eyes look. Her complexion would be defined as white, but he thought he detected just the faintest hint of golden olive. Her black hair was pulled back in a ponytail, and she had almost jet-black eyes. Perhaps, he thought, there might be a hint of Jewish or even Romany blood, which could account for her hatred of the régime. A black jumper made no secret of a lithe, athletic figure. She was a little above average height, and her only make-up was a dark red shade of lipstick. Irmgard lit a cigarette but said nothing whilst they waited for their drinks to be served. The word *exotic* came to Werner's mind.

He pushed the thought aside. 'The more I tell you about myself,' he opened, 'the more danger I am in if ever you are interrogated. But can you accept that I am aware of the White Rose organisation and that I am just as opposed to Hitler and his Nazi régime as you are?'

'But you're not from the university, and you are German,' she replied. 'At least you sound as if you are.'

'The White Rose is not the only anti-Hitler organisation in this country,' he told her. 'Many of the older, traditional families feel the same way. Let's just say we are a parallel organisation, and we have the same aims, but we have more resources.'

'So I assume you want us to work together,' she concluded.

'Only if you want to,' he replied. 'But yes, I believe we can help each other.'

'In what way? What would you want from us?'

'So far, you have distributed anti-government propaganda in the form of pamphlets,' he responded. 'But that has achieved little more than having at least three of your people arrested and executed after a farce of a trial. I meant to ask you,' he added quickly, 'what has become of your friend Gerda? I'm sorry, I don't have a second name,'

'Apparently, her lawyer has been allowed access,' Irmgard reported. 'They have said that she will go to trial, but as she was not heavily involved, she can expect a more lenient sentence.'

That was good news – Werner was relieved for Ilse's sake. She had obviously proved herself a convincing actress.

'Do you wish to escalate your activities, at least in part, to avenge the three who were guillotined?' he asked bluntly.

'There are many in our organisation who do. I am one of them,' she added, 'but we lack weapons and equipment, not to mention training.'

'I can provide all of those things,' he told her.

She looked at him. 'You're not just an ordinary civilian, are you?' she said at length.

'No, I'm not,' he admitted. 'But best you don't press for any more information.'

She paused to consider this. 'So, let's just assume that we work together,' she offered eventually. 'What must we do in return for your help?'

'Let me give you an example,' he said by way of explanation. 'And I got this from a Polish lady who was a member of the resistance after the Germans invaded her country back in thirty-nine. Attractive young women would meet German soldiers in bars, then go with them outside, seemingly for sex. It's a classic formula: dick leads, brain follows. The braver ones used a knife. The more squeamish had a male accomplice to do the deed. Either way, if you are interested, a little training would help.'

He watched carefully for a reaction. Her face was deadpan.

'It wouldn't work in Poland now,' he went on. 'They're wise to it. But here, in Munich, with German girls, not Poles… They would not be suspicious. You could target only the SS and the Gestapo, people in the organisation that murdered your friends…'

She thought about this for a moment but did not react, one way or the other. 'Can you also provide explosives?' she asked abruptly. 'We know the bars which are always crowded with these people.'

'That, also, would be possible,' he said. 'I can construct devices for you, and I imagine you have members whose degree subject is such that they would need little more than to be provided with materials? But again, if necessary, I can offer training.'

She nodded. 'And what else would we have to do for you in return for all this?' she insisted.

'For a start, you have to go back to basics,' he told her. 'The White Rose is finished. You can guarantee it will have been infiltrated. Three of your leaders are dead, and you have no way of knowing who you can trust or who will sell you out to the Gestapo. Unless you regroup, were I to help you along the lines we are discussing, like as not someone would be lifted within a week.'

Irmgard did not disagree. 'What do you propose?' she asked.

'You abandon White Rose. Let it wither on the vine,' he told her. 'We build a new organisation. Far fewer people, just a small, hard core drawn from those closest to you. People you will trust with your life. This has to be a true resistance organisation, not an overly large club of pamphlet pushers. And think carefully about those you ask,' he added. 'This is going to be a nasty business. They have to have the stomach for it, and it is perfectly possible not all of us will see the end of the war.'

She held his gaze. 'Point taken,' was all she said.

'As for what I want,' he said, 'there is more to my presence here than just setting up a new partisan cell. Munich is a major industrial city. For example, we understand that BMW has a major plant in the Allach district, just a few kilometres northwest of the city centre. A refugee told us that a concentration camp has been built to house slave labour, and the whole complex is camouflaged in the surrounding forest.

'The important point,' he went on, 'is that we believe the Allach plant is one of the two main production units in Germany for BMW aero-engines. We need a precise map reference, preferably also with photographs or a sketch of the area. Then, we can plan a bombing raid. What I also need, and this is where you and your friends come in,' he added, 'is information on as many Munich factories engaged in wartime production as you can find: electronics, instruments, ball bearings, vehicles, rolling stock for railways, any fuel processing plants, particularly if they are making synthetic product – just about anything you think might be considered essential to the war effort.'

'So you want that we obtain this information for you,' Irmgard surmised.

'It's too big a task for one person,' Werner told her. 'I will be involved, but on my own, it would take me too long. And just one person permanently doing all this reconnaissance would bound to be noticed, sooner or later. That said, a small team, different people, varied places, could put this information together in a matter of weeks… a couple of months at most.'

What he did not tell her, but it had been part of his briefing for this mission, was that an American P51 Mustang, fitted with lightweight, paper-mâché drop tanks, was about to enter service. It would have the range to escort bombers deep into Germany. And a photo-reconnaissance version, with wing cameras, would also be able to fly missions over Munich. A dossier of potential targets, plus supporting aerial views, was a pre-requisite for the United States Army Air Corps to blast the industrial capacity of this major city into oblivion.

She finished her beer and stubbed out the cigarette. 'I shall have to think,' she said at last. 'Then perhaps we should have another meeting. How do I contact you?'

Werner had expected this. 'You don't,' he replied. 'Suggest a time and place, and if it's suitable, I will be there. Would you like another drink, whilst you are thinking about it?'

She nodded and lit a second cigarette. He went to the bar to give her time and space. The barman swept the froth from above the two small glasses into a copper tray and topped them up.

'*Wohnung sechs, Mozart Straße vierundzwanzig,*' she told him. 'A week today, mid-afternoon.'

'This apartment six, 24 Mozart Street, who lives there?' he asked her.

'I do,' she replied. 'It's a fairly upmarket address not far from the university. My parents bought it before the war, but now, like others who can afford it, they have moved out into the country. What I suggest is that I contact just three or four very close friends for now,' she went on. 'You can meet them, and we will talk about the way ahead. We can have coffee and cake,' she said evenly as if this were no more than a casual, social invitation. 'Stay on after they have left, and you can tell me what you think of them.'

'You're taking a risk,' he told her, 'giving me your address. Why didn't you choose some neutral ground?'

'Two reasons,' she replied. 'First, I don't know my neighbours all that well. They are older than me – it's not your usual student accommodation, and I'm the only one in the block. They – the neighbours, I mean – were a bit concerned when I first moved in, but I kept them sweet by never having noisy parties or doing anything to disturb them. So now, they are friendly enough. I have no reason to distrust any of them, and they are quite used to me having my student friends around from time to time. Just a few people for coffee and cake on a Sunday afternoon will be quite normal. Won't even raise an eyebrow.

'It has to be a lot safer,' she continued, 'than choosing somewhere we might be noticed. I wouldn't even risk it here, even though I have been something of a regular for ages. And trying to book a private room wouldn't be safe, either. You never know who might report a meeting of some new, unknown group to the authorities. Since White Rose, they have had eyes everywhere.'

'Fair enough,' he agreed, 'but that wasn't what I meant. What about the risk of giving your address to a stranger, one about whom you know absolutely nothing?'

'That's not entirely true,' she said. Werner could not help but raise his eyebrows. 'I knew what name to expect, and I had a very detailed description, right down to your speech, in plummy *Hochdeutsch*. Ilse didn't even risk a phone call. She went to see Gerda's parents, and they came to see me.

'They both asked me to pass on their heartfelt thanks,' she added. 'And they both said that if there is ever anything they can do to repay your trust, and they asked me to emphasise the *anything*, you have only to ask.'

She gave a brief, disarming smile. 'I had to put you through your paces,' she explained, 'make absolutely sure you were the genuine article. Also, I wanted to see how good you were.' She shrugged her shoulders. 'My friends and I are not professionals at this filthy business, but I know one when I see one. You might be German,' she said flatly, 'but you're a British spy.'

She finished her drink and stood to leave. '*Bis nächste Woche, Erich. Tschüs.*'

He raised his almost empty glass. "Til next week, Irmgard. Cheerio,' he responded.

Chapter 29

With a week to go before his next meeting with Irmgard, Werner did not relish a cycle ride to Buchbach and then all the way back again. For now, he preferred to think of his cottage on the estate as a retreat for an emergency. Besides, he felt safe enough at the apartment. The Gestapo had absolutely no reason to research its ownership, even if the documents showing that it had been purchased by the steward of the Buchbach estate well before the war were still in existence.

He had taken the precaution of filling up the Mercedes' tank before putting it up on blocks, so there was no shortage of fuel for the motorbike, but he preferred not to take the risk of using it. He might as well make a start on his target research, either riding his push bike or taking the trams to explore the city area, starting with Allach.

First listed as a municipality towards the end of the eighth century, it was on the extreme northwest of the city, some fifteen kilometres from its centre. Known originally as Ahaloh, which meant "forest by the water", it was now the most heavily industrialised area of Munich. The district was still well-wooded, not least with the *Allacher* Forest. Werner hoped that the BMW aero-engine facility, together with its sub-camp for slave labour, provided from the conveniently close main concentration camp at Dachau, would not be too difficult to find.

Much as he hated pedalling the old bone shaker, it was not as bad as the journey from Buchbach. Werner reasoned that there had to be civilian workers at the camp, men too old for military service but with specialist skills unlikely to be found from within the ranks of camp inmates. If the facility was camouflaged, it was almost certainly in the forest district. And since this was well away from the residential area of the Allach district, the workers would need to use public transport. So he pedalled first to the main tram station.

Trams throughout the city announced their destination on a notice displayed on the front, at the top of the car above the driver. Sure enough, he found one heading for the *Allacher Forst*. Pedalling furiously and taking advantage of the occasional stop to catch up, he was able to follow for quite some distance before losing sight of it. But he continued along what appeared to be a main thoroughfare until he came to the terminus. Not far away, a line of trees marked the edge of the forest.

Left or right? Werner thought about waiting for the arrival of the next tram to see which way most of the passengers went, but he was reluctant to hang around in what had to be a sensitive area for the authorities. He set off left but after about a kilometre or so had found nothing. The terminus had to be reasonably convenient for the camp if, indeed, that was its purpose, so Werner pedalled back and set off in the other direction. After only a few hundred metres, he came across a road off to the left leading into the forest, just wide enough for a single vehicle. It was hard-surfaced, so this was no forestry track.

Werner pushed his bicycle into the trees until it could not be seen, either from the main road or the forest one. He went forward on foot, parallel to the forest road but far enough away to be able to hide from any passing vehicle. It was not all easy going, and several times, he had to detour around patches of impenetrable undergrowth. But as he advanced, he became aware of the noise: a low hum at first, possibly from diesel generators, but then muffled sounds of machinery, even the odd shout from a human voice.

He moved more cautiously now until, in the distance, he could make out, through the trees, a high fence, it's top inward sloping for a metre or so and consisting of strands of barbed wire. It was designed not to keep people out but to prevent the escape of those within. Beyond lay a number of huge sheds, like aircraft hangars, from which came the machinery noise and, as he edged closer, the sounds of banging, metal on metal, as if from hand tools. Almost certainly, this was the BMW aero-engine complex.

If he could just get closer, it might be possible to confirm his find, although he was not expecting a sign announcing the name of the establishment. He stopped about forty metres from the fence and waited. From this distance, he could see that the area was well camouflaged, although not completely invisible from the air. But this part of Munich had not been over-flown by the Allies, and even if it were, unless a pilot knew exactly what to look for and where, it would probably not be noticed. Werner suspected that those inside the plant felt relatively safe and secure.

An armed guard walked past just inside the compound, left to right, but then the relative quiet of the forest was shattered by two or three barking coughs, followed by an unmistakable sound coming from one of the nearby workshops: the crescendo roar of an aero-engine being run up and tested to full revs. The noise held for a minute or so, then slowly died down. Werner was absolutely sure – he had found it! All he had to do now was note the grid reference and description, ready to transmit to the United Kingdom, together with whatever additional targets his embryo cell might identify.

He was about to turn back when another guard walked into view, this time just outside the fence, walking in the other direction. On a leash was a large Alsatian. Werner froze and, to his dismay, realised that the faint breeze was blowing onto the back of his neck. The dog stopped, its ears erect, nose pointing directly towards where Werner was crouched beside a tree. It has been trained not to bark. The handler was looking from side to side at the forest, but Werner felt sure he would not be seen through the undergrowth.

After a minute or so, the guard stopped looking and turned to move on, perhaps thinking that his dog had scented something of the local wildlife. He gave a firm tug on the leash, but the Alsatian refused to budge, instead emitting an involuntary whine, trying to pull away from its handler, who seemed to come to a decision. He slipped the leash. Without giving voice, the dog bounded forward, directly towards where Werner was hidden.

* * * *

Pfc Tremayne Thompson, "T-T" to his friends, had been an electrician before the war. His father still ran the family's second-hand electric goods store in Kentucky. True, he hadn't been admitted to college, so he had no formal qualifications, but taught by T-T senior, there was nothing that Junior couldn't fix. At least the Army had recognised his skills, with rapid promotion to Private First Class.

The roof of the single-storey building allocated to senior non-commissioned ranks' accommodation had been repaired by fellow members of the maintenance crew, but heavy rain had shorted the electric wiring, which had also been found to be in a bad state of repair – a fire risk. T-T had been ordered to fix it. The re-wiring had to be a daylight job when the occupants were either flying missions or absent on other duties. The power needed to be back on by nightfall, when light bulbs and wireless sets provided an element of comfort for the inhabitants, most of whom enjoyed the privilege either of a room to themselves or, in the case of the more junior sergeants, at least sharing with only one other.

Which meant that, after each new connection in the loft, T-T had to have access to the room below to check that the lights and sockets still worked. In some of the rooms the occupant, or occupants, had metal lockers. But for the most part, they had been happy to use the ancient wooden furniture left over from former RAF days, including the old-fashioned wardrobes.

The return of Spencer Almeter, albeit on light duties, had re-ignited the sense of injustice amongst the coloured servicemen, not least because apparently there had been no success in bringing the perpetrators of the assault to justice. T-T had an idea. Acting purely on his own initiative, he searched every room. And there, soon enough, he found what he was looking for. On a top shelf, underneath folded shirts, he discovered a high-peaked hooded mask. Sergeant Chuck Hoskings was a member of the Klan. Eventually, he found another mask in the room of Sergeant Franklin Wilder.

Feeling the need for older and perhaps wiser counsel, T-T confided in his sergeant. Also an enlisted man, George Slatman had been something of a human rights activist before the war but, fearful of the Blue Discharge, had kept his head down during his military service. He listened carefully to what T-T had to say.

'Leave it wit meh,' he told him. 'I gots to think about this, an' maybe talk to Spencer.'

'We can make him tell us,' he said to Spencer and Flossie in The King's Head later in the week. 'Poun' to a pinch, he was in on da gang dat beat you up.'

'Don't see how we can do it on da airbase,' Spencer replied. 'We gots to git him alone, an' dat's not gonna be easy.'

'It's the big dance at The Manor tomorrow night,' said Flossie. 'All the senior ranks not on duty will want to be there to celebrate your Fourth of July. And both of our suspects are aircrew. They won't be flying on Saturday night, so this is what we do....'

* * * *

Flossie had always admired her friend Susie: just a little on the plump side, with a generous figure, but her height carried it well. She had a beguilingly innocent look with short blonde hair cut to her chin and very kissable lips. Flossie and Susie had been at school together and remained close ever since. Married to a warrant officer in the Royal Tank Regiment, currently training in the North of England, Susie was a hairdresser and certainly knew how to make the best of herself. She had met Spencer a couple of times in their local and had been horrified by what had happened to him. When Flossie outlined her plan, she was only too eager to help.

Spencer was in full voice, a version of Jimmy Dorsey's "Tangerine". It was late in the evening, and the slow foxtrot number had couples dancing cheek to cheek. Susie had walked past Sergeant Hoskings on her way to the powder room, and he had most certainly noticed her. The borrowed dress was a little tighter than she would normally have worn, with an alluring décolletage, but Susie knew it had caught his eye. She gave him a deliberately faint, hesitant half-smile on the way back to the table she was sharing with Flossie. Sure enough, after a few minutes and a word to his three friends, he set down his drink and walked over to ask her to dance.

They danced twice, the next time to Glenn Miller's hit "Kalamazoo". Spencer was certainly earning his twenty-five pounds. 'Name's Chuck,' he had told her, and after the second dance, he asked if she and Flossie would like to join their small group, seeing as they appeared to be on their own. Susie smiled, turned away from her partner and beckoned Flossie over, giving her friend a wink of confirmation as she walked towards them.

Drinks were offered and accepted. Both girls danced with all four Sergeants, but Susie made a point of pulling Chuck Hoskings to his feet several times over the next hour. At the stroke of midnight, the room stood to attention as Isaac Hofmeyer led his musicians through "God Save the King", followed by "The Star-Spangled Banner", after which there was a thunderous round of applause.

The next number was much quieter, a slow version of Miller's "Moonlight Cocktail". Susie was dancing with her cheek on Chuck Hoskings's shoulder. She deliberately let her body press to his.

'Take me outside, Chuck. I need some fresh air,' she whispered. There were other couples on the front steps of the hotel.

'Let's walk aways,' offered Hoskings, sensing that something more than fresh air might be on offer. Susie did not reply, just placed her arm through his and led him towards the darkness of the hotel car park.

Once round the corner and out of sight of the others, he turned her shoulders for a kiss, his lips on hers, his hand on her bottom, pulling her towards him. She could feel his arousal through her dress. But Chuck had failed to notice four balaclava-covered figures that emerged from the shadows. She stepped back as hands gripped his upper arms, and a ball of cloth was thrust into his mouth. Someone bound a strip of something over it, and his hands were tied behind his back before a sack was thrust down over his upper torso. An engine started, and

Sergeant Hoskings was picked up bodily and thrown into the back of a covered Studebaker light truck.

They drove for what he guessed to be about twenty minutes. At first, he tried to sit up, but a sharp kick to the stomach discouraged any further attempts. Eventually, the truck took a turning, and he was jolted as it drove over rough ground. Finally, it came to a halt. Sergeant Hoskings was seriously worried. He wondered whether this was connected with what they had done to that coloured boy. His fears were confirmed when he was pulled from the truck, the sack was lifted, and he saw eyes surrounded only by light and dark brown complexions. His feet were kicked from under him, and he landed heavily face down on the grass. Hands roughly turned him over.

'You are goin' to give us the names,' said one of the five. He wasn't from the South; it was more of an East Coast accent.

'What names?' he blustered, concern now bordering on fear. Chuck Hoskings was no coward. He prided himself on doing his duty as a dorsal gunner and flight engineer. But the four who had taken him, now plus their driver, had him at their mercy. And they could do serious damage. The name came back to him. He had no wish to suffer Spencer Almeter's fate. The duty medic had said the man was lucky to be alive.

'First off,' said the voice from within the balaclava, 'you are going to admit that you are Klan, and you were one of them that beat up our buddy.'

'No, not me,' he said desperately. 'I was never in the Klan.'

But his interrogator ignored the denial.

'We know different,' he said. 'So you are lyin'.' He nodded to the others. Two of them pinned down his shoulders, kneeling on his chest and upper arms. Two more went for his legs. They were big men, heavier than he was. He could barely move. No orders had been given. Clearly, they had discussed whatever it was they were about to do.

The fifth man, the one who had spoken to him, knelt alongside his waist and produced a standard US Army M3 fighting knife. It was razor sharp along both edges and at its point. He undid the bottom buttons on Hoskings's tunic jacket, exposing the trouser belt. Despite Chuck's futile attempts to writhe from side to side, he undid the belt and cut down through the cloth before pulling down his pants and undershorts.

'Want the truth,' he said quietly, which made the words sound all the more menacing. 'So goin' to nick into that little sack there. I'll only cut one out, for starters, then I'll ask you the same question again. I gets the truth; maybe I leave you the other one. Maybe not… Either way, you fly better next time 'cause you won't weigh so much.' He grabbed the top of Hoskings's scrotum, pulled it up, and, pushing aside his penis, squeezed the spare flesh so that the rest of it bulged. He pressed the tip of the knife against his skin, just hard enough to break through.

Hoskings broke, wetting himself and screaming for him to stop. Minutes later, they had not only his confession but the names of all seven men responsible for putting Spencer Almeter in hospital.

'Any of this turns out not to be true, we goin' to have this conversation again,' said the voice. 'But next time, we cut you good. Probably bleed to death.' A splashed hand wiped itself off on his clothing.

They left him there, in the field. Hoskings managed to stand and, with his trousers round his ankles, took tiny steps to the edge of the field. It took him several minutes to fray the cord binding his hands on the gatepost so that he could pull up and belt his trousers. There was nothing he could do about the knife damage, but his jacket concealed it. Out in the lane, he thought he recognised where he was. Unless he could hitch a ride, it was a hell of a long walk back to base.

Chapter 30

The guard dog seemed to be bounding towards him in slow motion. Amidst a rush of adrenalin, his mind went blank. He could not, for a split second, remember his training. Then, a frantic memory: close combat on the course in Scotland, a short and wiry instructor, who introduced himself as a "Weegie", which Werner eventually discovered meant that he came from Glasgow – a Glaswegian. The man's speech, with its *diz'nae* and *hav'nae*, was hard to follow for someone whose first language was not English, but there was no doubting the quality of his instruction.

Werner put his back a metre or so in front of a large tree. According to Weegie, as he still thought of him, he had a choice. Either way, he had to grip the very tops of the animal's forepaws as high as possible. From there, at the same time keeping his head down, he could twist and push outwards as hard as he could – which, he had been told, would mash up its insides. The alternative was to swivel and try to bang its head into a solid object – in this case, the tree. Werner liked dogs; they had always kept them on the estate. The first choice was the more certain, the more sensible. He chose the latter. The Alsatian thudded into the trunk. There was a half whimper, then silence. But its chest was still moving.

Werner ran for his bicycle. The guard could not be far behind. Breaking out of the wood, he leapt onto the saddle and peddled furiously towards the terminus. A shot rang out, but he was able to swerve in front of a parked, horse-drawn delivery cart, which covered him 'til he could turn onto the main road leading back to the city. There were no more shots. Perhaps the guard had gone back to tend to his dog.

Either way, Werner did not slow down till he had put a good kilometre behind him. He left the main thoroughfare, against the unlikely event that there was a vehicle search for him, and wound a tortuous way back to the city centre. With the bicycle returned to its garage, he let himself into the building – for some reason, Heinz had not been at his post in the hall. Safely back inside the apartment, Werner pulled a cold beer from the refrigerator and sank gratefully into an armchair.

That evening, he treated himself to a meal in the *Pinkus Mühler*, a local beer-hall-come-restaurant named after the Westphalia strong lager it also served. But, he noticed, many of the usual choices he would have enjoyed were no longer available. There was still the best part of a week to go before his next meeting with Irmgard Stein. He felt he deserved a few days to unwind after the stress of his arrival and the events of today. But by the end of the week, he was bored with walking, eating, reading, listening to the wireless – and drinking, although he was careful to sustain his level of physical fitness.

He arrived early on Sunday and watched the entrance to 24 Mozart Street from a nearby park. Three young individuals entered together shortly after lunch, two men and a woman. Older people – residents or visitors, mostly couples – came and went, but they were neither students nor had they the appearance of members of any security, military or police organisation. Fairly confident that neither he nor the building was under surveillance, he pressed the button. 'Ja?' intoned a metallic female voice through the intercom. 'Erich,' he replied. There was a buzz, and the door opened. Apartment number six was on the first floor, where a half-hidden Irmgard beckoned to him urgently from behind a barely opened door. The three young people he had seen entering from the street were seated on a sofa. None rose to greet him.

'As I mentioned earlier, I have asked you here this afternoon because there is someone I want you to meet,' she said to them: 'This is Erich'. Then, 'That's Horst on the left, Gerhard in the middle, and Ursula.' She did not offer surnames, but Ursula had been the other girl's Christian name on the piece of paper Ilse had given him.

'Ursula and I were at school together,' Irmgard went on, 'the other two I met here in Munich. We have all been members of the White Rose from the very beginning of last year. They are the only ones I trust enough to be here today,' she added, 'although until this afternoon they did not know you were also coming. And I haven't told them the purpose of our meeting.' Werner approved of her caution.

'So who are you, Erich?' asked Horst abruptly, not sounding too pleased by the presence of a stranger. He was tall and thin, probably in his late teens, Werner guessed, with an over-large, thin nose and jet-black straight hair brushed back from a high forehead without a parting. Dark eyes were deep-set, giving him an almost cadaverous appearance.

'I'll tell you in a moment,' replied Werner evenly. 'But who are you, and more to the point, why aren't the pair of you in uniform?'

'We are second-year medical students,' said Horst, his hand indicating himself and Gerhard. 'The *Wehrmacht* urgently needs more doctors, so I doubt we will be allowed to complete our studies and fully qualify before we, also, are called up. But that's why we are still allowed to be students. For now,' he added contemptuously. Gerhard, shorter and fair-haired with a rather more pleasant and open face, nodded in agreement.

'And you, Ursula?' asked Werner gently.

'Languages,' she said simply. 'English and French, like Irmgard. We both want to teach, although the Party will probably decide they have other uses for our talents.'

'And we are all opposed to Hitler and his fascist régime,' Werner surmised. There was a general murmur of consent.

'The White Rose is not the only organisation opposed to Hitler and the Nazis,' Werner told them. 'I am a member of another group – much larger, better resourced and able to mount a much more effective resistance.

'Hitler is losing this war,' he went on, 'and he is destroying Germany in the process. The only way to save the Fatherland, for our children and future generations of Germans, is to end the war as quickly as possible. Only then can we begin to rebuild under a régime at peace with the rest of the world.'

'We have not been told that we are losing the war,' offered Ursula, more in surprise than by way of challenge or contradiction. 'On the wireless, they say we are resisting the enemies of the Reich.'

'Earlier this year,' countered Werner, 'in Russia, the Sixth Army under *Generalfeldmarschall* Paulus surrendered at Stalingrad, and our forces in the East are in retreat. Rommel has been defeated in North Africa – the Allies took a quarter of a million prisoners. We have invaded Sicily, and our air forces are bombing mainland Italy prior to the inevitable invasion. German cities are being raised to the ground by the RAF and the Americans, and the Ruhr is still largely without power after the destruction of the damns in May. At sea, we have lost the battle of the Atlantic, and America is now supplying the British and their own forces almost at will. And the tide has turned against Japan in the Far East.'

'How is it that you know all this?' Horst demanded.

'Because I work for the Allies,' said Werner bluntly. 'And I have access to accurate information, not propaganda. But before we can rebuild Germany, Hitler has to be defeated.'

'We know of the bombing of our cities,' Irmgard put in, 'but we did not know the war against Hitler was so… advanced,' she finished after a pause.

'Which brings me to my point,' said Werner. 'We have to destroy his industrial base so that he can no longer prosecute this war. As I have already explained to Irmgard, Munich has, by and large, been saved from heavy bombing because of its distance from Allied airfields. But this situation is about to change. Your old White Rose organisation is riddled with informers. I am here to set up a new, much smaller cell in order to identify industrial targets for our air forces.' There was a stunned silence at the realisation that he was a spy.

'But there will be civilian casualties,' objected Gerhard eventually.

'There will,' Werner conceded. 'And also amongst the slave labour, many of them Poles, from our concentration camp at Dachau. But there has to be a choice. Do nothing and allow Hitler to prolong the war until Germany is wiped out, or oppose Hitler, help end the war and begin to rebuild our nation.' There was no reply for several seconds until Horst surprised him.

'My father is a military doctor,' he began thoughtfully. 'We have both read Carl von Clausewitz: "War is the continuation of policy with other means",' he quoted. 'I suppose our White Rose leaflets were politics. Now, you are just asking us to do something different. For my part, I am prepared to help you.'

'Thank you,' said Werner simply. Heads from the other two indicated that they, too, were agreed. Werner spent some time advising them on how to proceed – particularly, warning them against arousing suspicion by overt questioning. They all agreed to meet again when they had something to report. Irmgard disappeared into her kitchen to return with a sponge cake rich with jam and cream.

'I went home on Friday night,' she told them. 'Came back this morning. This is courtesy of ingredients from our place in the country. Cut yourselves a decent slice. I'll make coffee, but I'm sorry, it's only *ersatz*. If we could grow coffee beans, we would.'

After her friends left, Irmgard produced a bottle of something and two glasses. 'Homemade,' she said, pouring, 'from apples. – all we have these days.' Werner sipped cautiously. It had quite a kick.

'When last we spoke,' she said, 'you told me about Poland – how the girls enticed German soldiers and all that.'

'Do you have anyone specifically in mind?' he queried. 'Or, is this just a general question?'

'I haven't mentioned this before,' she replied, 'but obviously, I knew Sophie and Hans Scholl quite well. I don't know what those bastards did to them before they were guillotined, but the fact that I'm talking to you today means that I was not betrayed.'

'And so…' said Werner, leaving the question hanging.

'They were not the only ones executed,' she said, with something of a catch in her voice. 'I was introduced to them by my boyfriend – we met soon after I arrived here at university.'

'He was already a member of the organisation,' stated Werner by way of confirmation.

'*Was* is the operative word,' she said sadly, her head making small movements from side to side. 'Manfred was also caught and executed. We had been going steady for a couple of years – he had already invited me to meet his parents. Nothing had been finalised, but we both knew that it would not be too long before he spoke to my father... we would become engaged to be married.' Irmgard tried to blink away incipient tears.

'I'm so sorry,' said Werner.

'That day, when we were passing out leaflets at Ludwig Maximilian – that's the name of our university here,' she explained, 'it was a caretaker, Jakob Schmid, who told the Gestapo.'

'So you mean you want to kill Schmid?' he asked.

She shook her head. 'I have no way of reaching him. And in any case, we all knew he was a Gestapo informer. But,' she emphasised, 'he would not have known that we were going to be distributing leaflets that day unless someone told him.'

'And you know who that was?' queried Werner.

'His name is Franz Klein,' she said flatly. 'He's even been boasting about it in the *Bierstube* where we first met. Him and his girlfriend, Wilma. She's a leading member of the *Bund Deutscher Mädel* in Munich. The BDM, or League of German Girls, is our female section of the Hitler Youth,' she explained. 'To join, you have to have German parents, unquestioning support for Third Reich, be in good health and conform to Nazi racial rules. They also have to dedicate themselves to becoming dutiful housewives whose sole purpose in life is to produce children for the State,' she finished contemptuously.

Werner was well aware of this. 'So what are you saying...' he asked eventually.

'We used to have drinks with them, a group of us, back in the early days,' she replied. 'He tried several times to get familiar, even when Wilma was around. I made it clear that I was with Manfred, so eventually he gave up. Recently, he's tried his luck again. *Ich denke, er mag mich sehr*,' she reflected. 'I said to him not long ago that it's too soon. But I know it would work.'

So, he still had strong feelings for her. 'What exactly do you mean?' queried Werner.

'I want revenge,' she said, bitterness giving a sharp edge to her voice. 'Mostly for me and Manfred... for what might have been and what we will now never have. But also for Sophie and Hans and the others.

'I'm not interested in bloody Wilma,' she announced emphatically. 'She's just a Nazi cow. But Franz deserves everything that should be coming to him. I'm frightened to do it on my own,' she admitted, 'but it's no use asking Horst or Gerhard. They can pedal around on bicycles looking for targets, but at the end of the day, they're just students. I need somebody who has had training. If I try the Polish thing with Franz Klein, would you be able to watch over me in case anything goes wrong? Be a backup, just in case?'

Somewhat taken aback by her bitterness and determination, Werner agreed that he could.

'You will have to play it carefully,' he advised, 'nothing too sudden or too obvious. Let's meet up again in a couple of weeks. And in the meantime, try to find an opportunity to offer this Franz person a hint of encouragement but nothing more. Gently does it at first, but come the day, you want him panting for what he thinks might be on offer...'

* * * *

Werner decided to return to Buchbach the following day. Tempted though he was to use the motorcycle, in the end, he settled for the push bike, vowing to try to find a more up-to-date and comfortable model, preferably with a set of gears. Despite setting out in bright sunshine, there was a summer shower when he was still half an hour from home. He arrived at the cottage wet, tired and irritable. It would be a stiff aperitif, a hot meal, a bottle of wine and an early night. He would make contact with his father in the morning.

His other task for the morrow would be to radio the information on the BMW factory back to England. The rest of the target information would have to follow later. For now, it was simply a matter of using a grid reference. They would have the same map, marked with vertical and horizontal lines. The complex occupied a whole square, so he would just send "grid" followed by the top number first and the one from the side second. But he was too tired to encode tonight – that, too, could wait till morning.

* * * *

Irmgard spent some time thinking about Franz Klein. They both frequented the *Bierstube,* where she had first met Erich. But to turn up alone and attract his attention, if Wilma were with him, would be too obvious. She asked Gerhard to accompany her for a drink. Shorter than she was and not particularly good-looking, even though his features were pleasant enough, he would not come across as serious competition. She did not tell him why, but he was happy enough to be asked, particularly when she told him that she would pay for everything – Erich had provided her with what she called "research funds".

Irmgard knew that Franz would not be there at the beginning of the week. Habitually, he turned up on a Wednesday and then again on Fridays and Saturdays. She told Gerhard she would meet him there. She dressed carefully – a wide-waisted but modest *dirndl* skirt and a close-fitting bodice, with a low neckline blouse underneath. The traditional Bavarian dress allowed her to show off her breasts without arousing suspicion. She joined a crowd of students seated at a long table, Franz and Wilma more or less but not quite opposite. Gerhard, she noticed, could hardly lift his eyes. Franz, too, but as Wilma was with him, he tried to be less obvious.

They drank beer, the boys from *Humpen*, the traditional grey beer mug, the girls from smaller, rather more elegant glasses. Bread and *Würstchen* appeared, although what was in the sausages at this stage of the war was anyone's guess. Eventually, Irmgard stood to leave. 'Maybe see you all on Friday,' she said.

The next time, she went on her own. Not, this time, in traditional dress, but wearing a soft, woollen top with a vee-neck that offered a glimpse of the swelling beneath, only partly obscured by her eighteenth birthday pearls, a gift from her parents. It was early evening, and only a few students sat at their usual table. On Friday, significantly, not only was Franz already there, but he was unaccompanied and made a point of beckoning her to a space beside him. He was, she thought, stepping over the bench to sit down and showing a generous amount of leg in the process, a well-built young man, although not much taller and quite good-looking. He was also generally amusing and pleasant company. She was sure it was a façade, a veneer. Underneath, from the occasional chance remark, Irmgard detected an odour of blind acceptance – of enthusiastic support for the fascist views of The Party.

She stayed for an hour and a half, insisting at first on paying for own beer but then accepting his offer of a second. Finally, she stepped back over the bench and announced that she was off.

'It's early yet,' he suggested. 'Would you like to go somewhere else, or can I walk you home?'

Standing behind the bench, she placed a hand on his shoulder and gave it no more than a gentle squeeze. 'I'm meeting a girlfriend,' she explained, 'but I'll be here again next Friday.'

Franz watched her backside before turning away and taking a long pull from his beer. She was an exotic little piece, better fitted out and a lot more interesting than his Wilma, who only tried to agree with everything he said. He was well-satisfied with his evening but keen for more. His thoughts turned to lifting that skirt, his hand between her thighs...

Chapter 31

Flossie, Spencer, and Sergeant George Slatman were huddled around a table in a corner of the bar in The King's Head.

'We got to decide,' said George, 'what to do with Chuck Hoskings' information. We could always make a plan, pay da others back with a beating, one by one.'

There was silence for a moment whilst they thought about it.

'Not right,' said Flossie eventually. 'I can't help feeling that it would be wrong to sink to their level. And besides, after the first one or two, the others would be on their guard, so it probably wouldn't work anyway.'

'You got a bettah idea?' asked Spencer.

'Will you let me think about it… trust me to do the right thing?' asked Flossie.

The two men nodded their agreement. The conversation turned to Major League Baseball. Flossie left them to it, still thinking.

The following morning, she was shown into Isaac Hofmeyer's office. Courteous as always, he rose to greet her and indicated one of two easy chairs beside the coffee table.

'Thank you for agreeing to see me yet again, Colonel,' she began. 'I have something to give you.' She handed over an envelope. As he opened it, she said, 'There are seven names on that list. They are the men, all sergeants, who administered the beating to Spencer Almeter. Five from this airbase, two from another – it's all down there.'

'How did you come by this information, Miss Harding?' he asked evenly. 'And how can I know it is accurate?'

'It is,' she replied flatly. 'And before you ask, I know for a fact that Spencer was not involved when it was obtained. At the time, he didn't even know about it.'

'If this is true,' he said slowly, 'there is only one way someone else could have come by it.'

She did not answer.

He tried another tack. 'Do you know who *was* involved in obtaining it?' he asked gently.

Flossie shook her head. 'No. And I understand that the men who seized the informant were all masked, so he can't identify them.'

'How do you know *that*?' he asked more sharply.

'The girl he was with at the time told me. Apparently, they only met that night at the Fourth of July dance. She came back inside the dance hall after he was taken, then she went home.'

He pondered this for a moment. 'And this girl...'

If it was a question, he had left it hanging. 'She's entirely innocent, Colonel,' she responded, 'and couldn't tell you anything anyway. So better you don't ask. Please...' she added.

'But you know who she was with,' he replied. It was a statement rather than a question.

'Chuck Hoskings, one of your sergeants. His name's on that list,' she told him bluntly.

He folded the document and placed it on the coffee table. 'I think, Miss Harding,' he said eventually, 'that someone has been extremely clever. And I don't mean that unkindly or by way of criticism. At least not at this stage. Which begs the next question... what do you expect me to do about it?'

Flossie lifted her head to look at him directly. 'Spencer and I have discussed this, Colonel,' she responded. 'You're the base commander. You have been very good to us in the past, even though your hands are tied, and you can't give us permission to marry. We look to you for some form of justice, but beyond that, we are content to leave the matter entirely in your hands.'

'Thank you,' he said simply, but Flossie could tell that it was heartfelt. She stood to leave. 'I have a few thoughts,' he added. 'and I shall need to make a few phone calls, but you and Pfc Almeter will be fully informed of the outcome.'

As soon as she had left, he summoned his chief clerk. 'I need to see Sergeant Hoskings,' he said curtly.

'I believe he may be airborne, Colonel,' came the reply.

'My office, as soon as his wheels are on the ground.'

'I'll pass the word, sir.' *Something tells me*, he thought, *that the sergeant is not going to enjoy a rather one-sided conversation.*

Isaac put through a call to the base medical officer. Dr Anderson was able to confirm that Spencer Almeter had made a good recovery. 'No permanent damage,' he stated confidently, 'but make no mistake, Colonel,' he added, 'he's a lucky man, and he's been through a pretty unpleasant experience.'

'Thanks, Doctor,' Isaac replied. 'That's all I needed to know.'

Later that day, the colonel learned that Hoskings had not told his fellow conspirators, partly out of embarrassment but also for fear of reprisal. And given the choice of a court-martial, followed by a custodial sentence and dishonourable discharge, or turning witness for the prosecution, he chose the latter. JAG lawyers were good, although Isaac was not sure whether the

Judge Advocate General's Corps would have been able to secure a conviction against Sergeant Hoskings. But that no longer mattered. The bluff had worked, and he had his plan.

* * * *

Beside him sat Colonel Russell Hammond. Isaac had known of Russ Hammond, a fellow base commander, but they had met only that morning. A tall, square-jawed aviator from St. Paul, Minnesota, he looked older than his thirty-eight years. But a full tour of missions did that to a bomber pilot. He had only recently been promoted into his appointment. And he had been only too keen to accede to his fellow commander's request.

Chief Master Sergeant of the Air Force Roderick Foxton marched in all seven sergeants. Halted in front of the colonel's desk, they were not invited to stand at ease. Both the driver of the jeep and one of the other six were under Russ' command. He had been quite content to allow Isaac to take the lead. Ominously, for the seven sergeants, the Chief Master Sergeant had not remained in the office – he had saluted and left the room, making a point of not closing the door quietly. Seven men waited nervously, sensing an unorthodox hearing.

'Gentlemen,' he began, 'although the term is hardly appropriate in this case, you are guilty of abducting and administering a beating to one of my coloured airmen. So badly that he required surgery on an injured spleen and suffered several broken bones. Had he not been found by a passer-by, the charge would have been one of homicide, that is to say murder in the first degree.'

He had spoken crisply but quietly, which made the accusation sound even more venomous. Eyes flickered left and right as if they were trying to gauge a fellow accused's reaction. Hofmeyer allowed his words to sink in for a few moments.

'One of you has been offered a choice,' he continued. 'Either a full confession and a willingness to turn witness for the prosecution, or a court-martial. He has chosen the former. I know who he is, but I am not going to tell you.' He scanned their faces. 'But that means we can court-martial every man jack of you, although as a plea bargain, that man will not serve time, and he will not be discharged dishonourably, with no benefits.'

His right hand turned over; palm now uppermost on his desk. 'Maybe you think I'm bluffing,' he pointed out, his voice still quietly calm and reasonable… but deadly. 'So hear this, Sergeant Brewer – he looked directly at one of Russell Hammond's men – you were first contacted by telephone on June sixth by a Sergeant Jameson, who is under my command. The two of you met two days later at The Lamb and Flag, a few hundred yards from your base. If you think I'm bluffing, ask yourselves, how come I know all this? Believe me, we can put six of you away for life.

'But that would not be ideal,' he went on, 'for two reasons. And on this, Colonel Hammond and I are in complete agreement. First, the trial would not be good for the reputation of the United States Air Army in this country. And second, neither Colonel Hammond nor I wish to lose personnel when there's a war on.' He was vehement now, his voice rising in anger: 'Not even a lousy bunch of Ku Klux Klan racist motherfuckers like y'all.

'So here's the deal,' he said, his speech now back to normal. 'If you want a court-martial, we are both,' his hand moved to include Colonel Hammond at his side, 'quite prepared to oblige. The alternative,' he paused for effect, 'is that you make major financial recompense to the victim of this cowardly assault. I will tell you the details, then you miserable specimens of humanity can make your choice. And believe me… Pfc Almeter is going to get justice, and whatever which way it goes, personally, I don't give a flying fuck!'

They were visibly shaken, not least by his un-military choice of words, which served only to emphasise that he felt free to act totally out with all convention. They were entirely at his mercy, to do with as he saw fit. And they knew it.

'This is what's going to happen,' he told them. 'A private first class makes a basic fifty-four bucks a month. Add on his twenty per cent for foreign service, and we'll call it sixty-five. That's seven hundred eighty a year. Or, at the official exchange rate agreed between our governments, just over one hundred-and-ninety-three pounds sterling. I'm rounding it up to two hundred, or eight hundred and six dollars. I am arranging for this sum to be made available now to Pfc Almeter.

'You sergeants are on ninety-four dollars a month,' he went on. 'For the next six months, you will each repay nineteen dollars and nineteen cents to the compensation fund. Major Heimy will take care of the administration. Fortunately, only two of you are aircrew, so in the unfortunate event that you do not complete that length of service, the debt will be cancelled. It will not be taken from any benefits passed on to your family.'

He did not tell them that he would be making the initial payment from his personal funds and would be making up any shortfall if the worst happened. However, the sum was not a major consideration for someone from his financial background.

'You all have to agree,' he continued, 'or it's the court-martial option. And one final condition,' he concluded. 'You get rid of that stupid Klan headgear and take no further part in any such activities. If you want time to think it over, I'll give you fifteen minutes to talk amongst yourselves in the office next door.'

There was a prolonged silence, then, 'Permission to speak, sir?' It came from Sergeant Brewer.

A curt nod. 'Way I see it, sir, we got no choice. If any man objects, let him say so now. For my part, I'm in, and I'm grateful to you, sir.'

He looked the row of sergeants in the eye, each in turn. 'I take it silence means you all agree to my terms?'

There was a chorus of "sirs", accompanied by murmurs and nods of acceptance.

'Report now to Major Heimy,' ordered Isaac Hofmeyer. 'Dismiss.'

* * * *

Isaac Hofmeyer knew that what he had set up was outside the code of approved military procedures. And he was reluctant to attract attention to the fact that something might be going on by holding a further meeting with Pfc Almeter and Flossie Harding in his office. He drove himself, out of uniform, to Gladys Harding's house. According to Major Heimy, who had made the arrangements on his behalf, Flossie and Spencer would be waiting. Neighbours might remark on a US Army Packard parked in the street, but there would be nothing untoward or unusual to be seen on the base.

Gladys offered him a cup of tea, which he politely declined, then excused herself and made a tactful retreat into the kitchen. He began by thanking them both for allowing him to resolve matters as he thought best.

'I had three aims,' he continued by way of explanation. 'The first and the most important one was to secure some form of justice for what Spencer and you, too, Miss Harding, have had to endure. I have taken advice from the base medical officer, and

I know that Spencer has made a full recovery, but it has all been extremely unpleasant.'

The use of his Christian name was not lost on either of them.

'It was also necessary,' he went on, 'to inflict some form of retribution on the perpetrators. They had to be made to undergo some form of punishment for what they had done.

'Finally,' he said, 'I had to think of the war effort, and I admit to you privately, both I and the commander of the two other sergeants involved were reluctant to deprive Uncle Sam of the services of seven very useful sergeants when we are just beginning to turn the tide of the air war against Hitler. Also, it would have been very damaging to the reputation of the US Army Air Force if this matter had resulted in an open court-martial. Very damaging,' he repeated.

Spencer nodded his agreement. He could see the rationale.

'I came to the decision,' he explained, 'that they should remain in the Air Army, continue to serve, but make a major financial contribution to the two of you by way of compensation for what you have suffered. I do hope that you will understand why I came to this conclusion.'

Flossie sensed that Spencer was nervous about voicing an opinion to his commanding officer. She decided to speak for both of them.

'I think we understand very well, Colonel,' she said, at the same time looking at Spencer, who was more than content to nod his agreement. Isaac turned to him.

'Pfc Almeter,' he said rather formally, 'and you too, Miss Harding, I thought that a year's pay would be substantial and reasonable recompense for what you have endured. I have rounded up the figures,' he went on. 'And you are to receive, now, a sum of either eight hundred and six dollars or two hundred English pounds, whichever you prefer. And I can assure you, Spencer, that there will be no comeback from any of those who assaulted you.'

He let this rest for a moment. 'My thinking,' he said eventually, 'was that it looks as though you will be able to marry as soon as this war is over. I have no idea whether you will settle over here or return stateside. But either way, at today's prices, in this area, that sum will buy you a small house. Back home, there will be G.I. benefits, including a college education, but even if you have to delay the wedding for a short time, eight hundred bucks should still give you a useful start-up to married life.'

Flossie decided to speak again for both of them. But first, she looked at Spencer, who had lowered his head, accepting what his colonel had said.

'I still wish this had never happened in the first place,' she replied. 'But I understand that you must have faced something of a dilemma. I think you have been very wise, very fair, and perhaps just a little bit generous. So thank you. And yes, we are very content to accept your decision.'

A man much relieved, Isaac Hofmeyer stood to take his leave. 'Please thank Mrs Harding senior for allowing me to visit tonight,' he told Flossie. 'Major Heimy will be in touch to sort out the details. I'll wish you both a good night.'

On hearing the front door close, Gladys came out of the kitchen.

'Not sure 'bout both of us goin' back stateside,' said Spencer. 'Got too used to bein' treated like a human bein' over here. Miz Gladys,' he turned to her, 'you are renting this house, right?'

She nodded her agreement.

'Ask him if he'll take two hundred for it,' he said, 'cash on da nail. We can all be together after the war.'

Chapter 32

Irmgard was expecting Werner to turn up again towards the weekend, which would be two weeks since their first Sunday afternoon meeting at her flat. Thus it came as no surprise when he met her in the street, a few yards from her apartment building, as she returned from her last lecture of the week at midday on Friday. He was carrying a small basket.

'Come on up,' she invited, pushing her key into the door. Inside the apartment, he followed her into the lounge, where she dropped a briefcase onto the sofa.

'I have brought some lunch,' he said, offering her the basket. She placed it on a low table. Under a drying up cloth, and resting on a much thicker one beneath, were two bottles of beer and a large, square parcel, wrapped in brown paper and tied loosely with string.

'Egg sandwiches,' he said. 'I made them this morning – came back to Munich yesterday and brought a supply with me. I'm sorry, but there's no mayonnaise.'

'Then you must have come from the country,' she observed, 'because we don't see eggs in the city shops these days.'

He made no comment, just untied the string, opened the parcel, and, with a wave of his hand, invited her to help herself. After they had eaten and were enjoying the beer, he asked if she had heard from the other three.

'Slow progress,' she replied, 'but I ran into Ursula the other day. She's making a map of all the marshalling yards and railway junction boxes. She pointed out that if you destroy a piece of track, they can mend it quite quickly, but if you disable all the switching gear, the system takes a long time to repair, and the railway doesn't work at all well in the meantime. She's also noting down bridges, particularly those that carry railway lines over rivers. I don't know how much progress the boys have made, but I was going to wait until you were back before asking them round again.'

'And this Franz Klein person,' he asked gently. 'Are you still of the same mind?'

'I've said I'll be at the beer hall tonight, the one where you and I first met,' she told him, nodding her head by way of confirmation. 'I went there on the Wednesday after we last spoke, and he was there with his girlfriend Wilma. I was there again two days later, on my own, and she wasn't with him. I think he had deliberately not invited her because he asked me out. I put him off but said that I'd be there again tonight. He's most definitely interested…'

Werner crumpled up the brown paper and set it aside before lifting the remaining cloth. She gave a small gasp. Nestled underneath were an automatic pistol and a wicked-looking knife. Werner picked it up and put it on the table in front of her.

'The Browning is mine,' he said. 'I made the knife for you whilst I was away. Originally, it was a kitchen knife, but I ground it down so that, as you can see, it now has a very narrow stiletto blade.'

She lifted it gingerly by the handle with just two fingers and her thumb. The blade, about eighteen centimetres long, had been sharpened on both sides and to a point. Werner had put a new, wooden handle on the slightly shorter shank, narrow in the middle but generously bulbous at either end so that the weapon could be pushed or pulled into or out from its victim. Irmgard looked at it for a moment, then all her fingers closed round the handle, and she hefted it with a firm grip.

'You still want to do this? It won't be pleasant.'

'For Manfred, as well as Sophie and Hans Scholl,' she said unflinchingly, looking him in the eye. 'I was going to let him buy me dinner tonight, but now that you're here…' she trailed off, but the suggestion was obvious.

He was quiet for a moment, then, 'Let's give it some thought,' he offered. 'When they find the body, there's going to be a police investigation, even with a war on. You can't be seen leaving some public place with Klein, only for him to be found dead somewhere else soon afterwards.'

'I have an idea…' she said.

After their discussion, Werner suggested that he knew the ideal place. 'We'll take a walk this afternoon,' he said. 'Do a reconnaissance…'

* * * *

It was early in the evening when Irmgard entered the *Bierstube* to find Franz seated at a long table with several of his friends. He rose to meet her, but instead of rejoining the table, he took her elbow and escorted her to a small, unoccupied one further into the room. They sat side by side, and a waitress she knew only by sight served them beers.

After a few light pleasantries, he asked what she would like to do for the evening. 'I'm meeting a girlfriend for a drink later,' she replied, 'same as last time.'

He did not try to hide his disappointment. 'I had rather hoped,' he told her, 'that we might spend the entire evening together.' A hand, she noticed, had settled on her knee.

'I wasn't sure what you might have in mind,' she offered, 'but I could always put Helga off – have a quick drink with her, perhaps two, then meet up again with you later.'

'Have you eaten?' he asked.

'Of course not, it's far too early,' she replied, 'although I had been thinking I might go somewhere with Helga.' The implication was not lost on him.

'Have a drink with your friend Helga, but then have dinner with me,' he suggested.

She pretended to think about this for a moment or two. 'All right,' she said eventually.

'And can I walk you home afterwards?' He persisted.

They had finished their drink. He had ordered only two small glasses. 'Another one, before you go?' he offered.

Without waiting for her reply, Franz signalled for the waitress. 'It's a lovely evening,' she told him after their drinks had been served. 'I'll meet you in the park near the university, so I won't have too far to walk. Wait for me on a bench near the bandstand, then you can take me to dinner. If you want to walk me home, I might even ask you in for a nightcap,' She patted his arm with a smile of encouragement. His hand moved further up her thigh, although it was outside her skirt. It was as much as she was prepared to allow. She lifted it off and placed it on the table.

'I have my reputation to think of,' she said gently, 'so don't be impatient.' She finished her drink and set down the glass. *Bis später, Franz. Tschüs.*

So, until later... He watched her walk to the door. There would be time for a couple more beers now, then something to eat, not too expensive, and they would go back to her place, wherever that was. But the invitation, the promise, even, was obvious...

Irmgard hurried home. As they had agreed, she did not let herself in but rang the bell for *Frau* Huber's apartment, nearest to the door on the ground floor. She was a kindly if nosey old lady who lived alone and, on occasion, had let Irmgard in when she had forgotten her key. She announced who she was and apologised. As expected, *Frau* Huber cracked open her door as she entered the hallway. She said 'Sorry' again and received an indulgent smile in return before the door closed. But if asked, *Frau* Huber would recall that she had admitted Irmgard and at roughly what time.

The lower floor of the block was a below-ground basement area containing the heating boiler, a huge coal store, and a small, lockable storage compartment for each resident. She and Werner were careful to step quietly through the hall – they could hear music through *Frau* Huber's front door – down the basement steps, and out through its side door, leaving it unlatched behind them.

Irmgard was determined, but she had a hot, sickly-sweet feeling in the pit of her stomach. She was sweating despite the cool evening air. Werner was anxious for her. 'You don't *have* to do this,' he said gently as they walked towards the park. 'I can do it for you.'

She swallowed hard. He wondered if she was about to be sick. 'You have done enough,' she said at last. 'I couldn't live with myself if I betrayed their memory by backing out now.'

They were early. But few people walked in the park at this hour in the evening. It was almost empty. She settled on a bench to wait for him. On the other side of the path, in front of the bench, was an ornate display of flowering shrubs. There was a similar display not far behind her, leaving a soft scent on the evening air. Werner settled himself well down, opposite the bench, on the earth. He would be virtually invisible in the gathering gloaming. Path lights, none of them anywhere near the bench, added to the deep shadows under the foliage. He took the Browning from his waistband, cocked it, and waited.

Franz strolled towards her, hands in pockets, then stopped a metre or so away. 'I wasn't sure you'd still be here,' he said. 'Sorry if I'm a few minutes late. I had no sooner gone back to my original table when Wilma turned up, almost immediately after you left. Just as well you missed her – might have been a bit awkward. She might have made a scene.'

Irmgard breathed a sigh of relief. Their one concern had been that Franz might have boasted to his friends that he was seeing her later. If Wilma had been there, he would definitely have kept his mouth shut.

'Anyway,' he said, sitting next to her and putting an arm around her shoulders, 'what happens next?'

She rested her head on his shoulder and then looked up, inviting him to kiss her, which he did. A hand slipped under her jacket, which she had not fastened, and onto her breast. She made a conscious effort not to resist his attentions. His tongue pushed into her mouth. He smelled of beer, but she made herself suck on it, then, for good measure, her own pushed back.

She placed a hand on his chest and restrained him so that they broke apart. He was breathing heavily. But she was able to glance from left to right. They were alone on this stretch of the footpath. 'That's as far as we go on a park bench,' she said lightly, standing up. 'And besides, I'm hungry. So just one more kiss…'

He stood to face her. Fortunately, she was tall enough to be able to look over his shoulder, but now she could see only in one direction, behind him. He pulled her towards him. She felt his tongue. One hand stayed on her back, the other moved to her bottom. Then he was lifting her skirt, a hand slipping inside her knickers and down onto bare flesh.

There was nothing she could do about it. She had to get both hands behind Franz's head. The sheathed stiletto was strapped to her left arm, inside her jacket, the tip of the handle just above her wrist.

He took her lack of resistance for encouragement and began to rub himself against her, his erect penis hard against her stomach. Her hands came together. She touched the handle, at first with just her thumb and the tips of two fingers... out a little... and then it was firmly in her grasp. She placed one hand behind his neck to hold it firm, but as if welcoming the embrace, urgent for a coupling.

Franz groaned, almost out of control. She wondered whether he intended to ravish her out in the open, here in the park. But that was never going to happen. She remembered Werner's careful instruction and the training he had given her that afternoon. She aligned the point of the stiletto just forward of the centre of his neck, on the left-hand side, and pushed with all her strength. It went in surprisingly easily.

He seemed to freeze as if unsure of what had happened. Then he tried to speak, but she had already sliced forward and stepped away, the stiletto cutting itself free. His muted throat filled with blood. She moved aside as he fell to the ground. Gore was pumping freely now; some of it had fallen on her skirt and shoes. His eyes were still open, but he was barely alive.

She knelt, her face a metre or so above his. 'That was for Manfred,' she hissed. Maybe he had understood, perhaps not, before his eyes stopped moving. She was conscious of Werner at her side, a hand under her armpit, pulling her urgently to her feet.

He sat her back on the bench, pushed the Browning into his waistband, took the stiletto from her hand and wiped the blade on Franz's jacket. Another glance in both directions confirmed that they were still alone. Grabbing Franz's feet, he dragged him well back into the undergrowth where he would be hidden, at least till morning. A quick search revealed a wallet and watch, both of which he removed to make it look like a robbery.

Back in front of the bench, he took Irmgard's arm and quickly unstrapped the sheath, replaced the stiletto and shoved it into his trouser pocket. She was sobbing quietly. 'Come on,' he said gently, 'we can't stay here. Take deep breaths. Try to look as though you are all right. Here,' he passed her a handkerchief, which she used to wipe her eyes and nose. As they walked back towards one of the entrances, she seemed to be recovering her composure.

On the way out they met only one person – a middle-aged woman walking a small dog, but she barely glanced at a couple, the man with his arm around a girlfriend's shoulders. Once safely in the street, he took her hand as they walked away. Werner did not want to take a tram anywhere near the park, but after walking for ten minutes or so, he deemed it safe. Irmgard was outwardly calm but not speaking. He thought it better to leave her to her thoughts, rather than risk the attention of their fellow passengers by saying anything that might cause another outburst of tears.

They returned to the apartment block by the same basement entrance, and he dropped the latch to lock the door behind them. Safely inside her front door, her eyes were glistening as Irmgard removed her jacket. She turned back to him and threw her arms around his chest, hugging him tightly. He rocked her gently, patting the back of her head. Eventually, she took a step back and looked at his face.

'My God, but that was awful…'

She blew her nose and looked down at her shoes and the bottom of her skirt. 'I'll have to get rid of them,' she said, turning towards her bedroom door, which was half open. 'But I have to take a bath first before I do anything else,' she added, disgust plainly evident in her voice. 'There are drinks in the sideboard. Help yourself, and pour something strong for me.'

He found a bottle of schnapps, open but almost full, poured a couple of stiff measures and downed his own in one before pouring a refill. He thought about the events of the evening... she had left the bar early, on her own... Wilma had arrived, so he had not told anybody... *Frau* Huber would provide an alibi... and they had met only the woman with her dog. Everything had happened as well as he could possibly have hoped.

He turned on her wireless, found some classical music – it sounded like a string quartet, Mozart or Haydn, he could never tell – and sat back, enjoying the warmth of the schnapps and the music. The door opened. Irmgard, now in a pink bathrobe, picked up her glass, raised it in salute, and said, 'To Manfred, Sophie and Hans.' She, too, emptied her glass in one and turned back to the sideboard to pour another. She settled at the other end of the sofa, half facing him.

'Thank you for tonight,' she said simply. 'I couldn't have done it had I not known that you were there.'

They sat in silence for a while. 'Where do we go from here?' Werner asked eventually. 'It would be helpful to know how the others are getting on. Apart from Ursula, that is.'

'Would you like me to ask them here on Sunday afternoon?' she suggested.

'If you wouldn't mind,' he responded. 'That would be very helpful.'

He noticed that the top of her robe had shifted, showing half of one breast. She caught his glance and slowly untied the knot at her waist. The invitation was obvious.

'You must have been in action lots of times,' she said. 'Is it normal, after something like that, to want sex?'

Chapter 33

'I'm afraid there's no cake – I haven't been home,' Irmgard announced, setting a tray of coffee on the low table. 'And it's *ersatz* again. I swear they grind it from acorns. So, what do you have to report?'

'There's a Dornier factory,' said Gerhard. 'I've got it marked down, and Horst has found one making parts for Junkers aero-engines, but so far, that's all.'

'And you have been careful not to arouse suspicion?' Werner confirmed.

'I have been able to help,' put in Ursula. 'I think Irmgard may have mentioned my railway project?'

He nodded to confirm that she had.

'Also, I live at home,' she went on, 'and my father is a member of the town council. As a family, we are not supporters of the régime. I have been asking him about the industries based in Munich. That's how I was able to tip the boys off about the two aircraft facilities based locally. He's promised to talk to some of his colleagues, those he's sure he can trust, and find out who is making anything that might be important for the war effort.'

'And he didn't suspect anything?' queried Werner.

'Of course he did,' she replied. 'But he didn't ask questions. He knows I was involved with White Rose. Just urged me to be very cautious, as he intends to be, that's all.'

'This is not going to be an instant process, compiling a really good target list,' Werner observed. 'I don't have anything like enough to send back as of yet. Let's meet again, say in two weeks' time.' They agreed, and conversation turned to more general matters. They asked if he had any information that might not have been reported in the German news.

'Well,' he replied, 'I can tell you that earlier this month we – by which I mean Germany – retreated from Sicily to the Italian mainland, and on August the seventeenth, the Seventh US Army, under General George Patton, met up with the Eighth British Army under Field Marshal Montgomery in Messina, completing the Allied invasion of Sicily. I suspect that sometime next year,' he went on, 'Germany will find itself fighting on three fronts – in Russia, Italy and hopefully France as well.'

After the other three had left, Irmgard returned from taking the coffee tray into the kitchen and sat opposite him in the other easy chair. 'I haven't had much chance to apologise,' she began, 'but I'm still embarrassed about Friday night. When you told me that your wife had lost her life not too long ago, it made my behaviour seem ten times worse. What must you think of me? But thank you for putting me right so gently... that was kind of you... sorry...' she trailed off.

'There's nothing to apologise for,' he said quietly. 'People respond to extreme stress in different ways. But there's nearly always some evidence of intense psychological tension. One of the more usual signs is what a complete outsider might see as highly inappropriate humour. Yours was just another form of the same adrenalin-fuelled reaction. Rest assured, I have nothing but admiration for your courage and for what you achieved, despite your fears.'

'Thank you,' she said again quietly.

* * * *

In 76/78 Tirpitzufer, *Gerneralmajor* Hans Oster was discussing the situation in England with *Oberst* Hans Piekenbrock, his Head of *Abwehr* Department One, responsible for foreign intelligence collection.

'As you ordered, *Herr Generalmajor*, said the colonel, 'we have tried repeatedly to re-establish contact with agent Staunton, but it's been a failure – there has been no response.'

'His radio might be faulty,' observed the general.

'But he was in contact with Shamrock,' the colonel pointed out. 'He could have reported using her radio. And the chances of two sets being unserviceable at the same time…' he left the statement hanging.

'So what's to be done?' asked the general bluntly.

'I'm going to ask Ernst Gericke to try to find out,' Pieckenbrock replied. 'He's still active, doing good work. We know where Staunton was living, so it shouldn't be too difficult. What's more, he knows what the Wagner woman looks like because she was his reception agent. We also know she had been turned but was still being controlled by Staunton. She might be involved in all this. Staunton had been ordered to eliminate Werner Scholz first and Margarete Wagner afterwards, so the finger of suspicion has to point in her direction.'

'Let us proceed,' confirmed the general. 'Get an order off to Gericke on his next schedule.'

* * * *

He had taken the not-too-dissimilar name of Ernest Gerard. His journey to Birmingham, two years previous, had proved uneventful. His late father had been an academic who taught English at Leipzig, Germany's second-oldest university. He had studied for a year at Oxford, but his reception, too soon after The Great War, had been mixed, to put it politely. He was only too happy to return to the Fatherland. But in the meantime, he met and eventually married an English girl. Grace had learned to speak excellent German, but she spoke only English with Ernst at home, knowing that her husband could hardly object. As a result, Ernst was fluent, with – as Margaret had noticed – absolutely no trace of an accent.

Once in Birmingham, he had taken lodgings. The landlady, Mrs Florence Wilson, was a widow, her husband, who had been much older, having died in an industrial accident at Fort Dunlop, the tyre factory. Their terraced house had four bedrooms, and she took in commercial travellers or theatre people and the suchlike in order to make ends meet.

Thanks to the support of the Party, who were not short of funds, rather than seeking employment, he opened a small bookshop. It saved having his background probed by any potential employer. At first, the business had barely broken even, but he was a personable individual, and it slowly began to turn a profit – albeit small.

Florence Wilson looked critically at herself in the mirror. She had undressed, ready to slip into her nightdress. *Not bad*, she thought, even though she was somewhat older than her new lodger. Her breasts were not that large, but they were a nice shape and holding up well. And her waist was still trim. She made a point of wearing clothes that made the best of her figure. Several times, she found him looking at her with interest, although he always glanced away when he thought she might have noticed.

The hints were subtle: a touch on his shoulder, when she set a plate of food before him, sometimes just a smile. One night, she treated herself to two large glasses of gin, hoarded since before the war, brushed her teeth twice with toothpowder, and knocked on his door. He had been reading in bed. In response to his "Come in", she had opened the door and walked to his bedside. When he smiled and, with a nod of encouragement, turned back a corner of the bedclothes, she dropped her robe and climbed in beside him.

Their coupling had been a mix of frustration, lust and sheer pleasure. But it had been good. Ernest moved into her room, a much better one at the front of the house, and after a few weeks, the turnover of guests meant that no one suspected they were not man and wife. His radio, previously in a locked case on top of his wardrobe and untouched as evidenced by the telltale he had left behind, now went inside a waterproof wrapper and into the shed in the garden. Florence no longer needed to go there – she was only too glad to have someone else push what she thought of as that bloody lawnmower over the back lawn.

Ernest was not too pleased when, after so much time, his world was invaded by an instruction to find out what had happened to some agent in the wilds of Norfolk. He told Florence that he was going to talk to some book publishers in London. But first, he took the precaution of giving the lawn what he hoped would be a last cut before the onset of winter.

He took a train from Snow Hill to Paddington and from King's Cross to Peterborough. A bus took him to within a few yards of Staunton's address. It was a burnt-out ruin with a "For Sale" sign nailed to a tree in the front garden. He rang the estate agents, who confirmed that the plot was indeed for sale.

'What happened to the original property?' he enquired, adding that he was not from "round here".

'A tragedy,' came the reply, a man's voice. 'There was a fire. The person living there sadly lost his life. Traces of human remains were found in what was once a bedroom, although the building had collapsed internally. The coroner took the view that, mercifully, he had probably been overcome by smoke fumes before he died. The verdict was "accidental death". But it's still a prime location for anyone contemplating a rebuild on the same site, Mr...?'

Ernest replaced the receiver.

He rode into the country to meet his schedule and simply reported what he had discovered. Berlin called him off. They already knew that Shamrock had been turned, so any further messages could be a valuable warning to the Fatherland, to be interpreted as suggesting they should do the opposite of what the Allies were trying to achieve. There was no evidence that she had in any way been involved with the fire, so there was no point in risking the exposure of another agent in order to secure her execution. Berlin decided to try to exploit whatever she might send in the future and, for now, to take no further action. Ernest was grateful that the matter had been dropped. He returned to his activity of identifying targets for the *Luftwaffe*, reporting on bomb damage, running a now gently prosperous business, and the pleasures of Florence's bed.

* * * *

Spencer's former battalion was recalled to the United States prior to re-deployment to the Pacific theatre. Robert Arbuthnot knew he could not regularly lay claim to the services of the base commander. Still, he was able to employ his musicians, who were far more popular than The Manor Hotel's previous, ageing ensemble.

As well as crooner, Spencer found himself promoted to the role of band leader, which he loved – he had watched Colonel Hofmeyer often enough to copy exactly his style of conducting, and he could continue to enjoy standing in front of the mike for the vocals. He found another clarinettist to replace Isaac Hofmeyer, a retired theatre musician who was not quite as good at improvisation but could otherwise play the dots. They never failed to pull in a good crowd when Arbuthnot put on what he billed as "An American Dance Night".

In Norfolk, a Mrs Margaret Chapman was looking forward to their first Christmas as man and wife. They had not had a honeymoon. As Robert pointed out, no farmer could take a holiday at harvest time, and there was little point in going away afterwards as nearly all the local beaches were mined and wired off from the general public. She'd had that final visit from Werner, returning her radio, checking up on her – indicating that his successor might ask her to send more messages to Berlin some time in the new year.

The tide of war had turned for the Allies. The Russians had liberated their North Caucasus and, in the west, had forced the Germans from the city of Kiev. At the end of November, the mighty triumvirate of Churchill, Roosevelt and Stalin met in Tehran to plan the future of the war in Europe. And by way of a belated Christmas present, on Boxing Day, the British battleship HMS Duke of York and her escorts sank the German battleship *Scharnhorst*, the pride of the German Navy.

Of greater importance to Margaret was that she was able to tell Robert she was pregnant with their first child: he or she would be a summer baby.

* * * *

Werner spent a quiet Christmas with his father. He felt safer living in his small cottage in the forest than in the Munich apartment. Anna had prepared a Bavarian *Schweinshaxe* that morning before leaving to spend the day with her sister. The general, who had learned to look after himself with military fortitude, cooked the pork hock in a rich beer gravy till the meat was tender and the crackling perfect. He served it with *sauerkraut* and fried potatoes, together with a cold *Stein* of beer. They finished their Christmas evening with a bottle of brandy.

In the week after Christmas Werner's first visit to Irmgard produced a surprise. She told him that her father wanted to meet him.

'Don't worry, I'm not going to introduce you as a potential boyfriend,' she reassured him. 'But I told you that my parents are opposed to the régime.'

Werner assumed that this had something to do with providing a list of targets and agreed to travel with her on Friday. 'We'll see in the New Year with my parents,' she told him, 'so bring a few things and stay overnight. We can come back on Saturday morning.'

They took a tram to the outskirts of the city, then waited for a bus to take them the last fifteen or so kilometres. 'We could have caught the bus in the city centre,' he pointed out.

'Just a precaution,' she said. 'I was never sure whether the police found out who I was during the White Rose days. Back then, if anyone else got off the tram and waited at the same bus stop, I was probably being followed. So I'd have walked round a few shops and then gone back into the city, rather than lead them to my parents' place. Seeing as I have a good idea who or what you are, it seemed like a good idea to take the same precaution.'

Werner heartily approved. The family home had once been a farmhouse, she told him as they rattled and swayed along country roads, but most of the land had been sold off, keeping just a few hectares and outbuildings which the previous owners had used as an equestrian centre. Her mother still taught equitation and ran a sizeable smallholding, complete with a few chickens and farm animals.

Irmgard's father opened the door, and she rushed to give him a hug before introducing Werner. They shook hands, Werner taking in a middle-aged, bespectacled man of his own height with a rather sparse build and thinning black hair. He was ushered into a comfortably furnished lounge made pleasantly warm by a log fire. An older version of Irmgard was seated on a sofa. She, too, had an exotic appeal but with a complexion a shade darker than her daughter's. It reinforced Werner's thought that there was some foreign, possibly Romany heritage in the family.

Herr Stein told Werner that he had moved out of the city so that he and his wife could live quietly, in relative isolation in the countryside.

'I am from Armenia,' *Frau* Stein put in, 'although I no longer have family there. They were killed in the Turkish genocide after The Great War. Fortunately, I had been sent to study in Germany, where I met my husband.'

'I'm sorry,' said Werner.

She lifted her shoulders. 'It was a long time ago. But the Nazis are also very racist. We think I am safer living out here. My husband is now the headmaster of a local school.'

'Forgive me,' *Herr* Stein intervened, 'but Irmgard has told me a little about you.'

Werner looked at her. This disclosure was not good news. To his surprise, she stood and left the room. 'Don't be concerned,' her father hastened to reassure him. 'It was very recently, and only then because she knew we had a serious problem on our hands, and she thinks you may be able to help.'

The door opened, and Irmgard returned, followed by a young man in ill-fitting clothes who could not have been much more than twenty years old.

'*Und Sie sind..?*' asked Werner, demanding to know who he was.

'Sorry, pal,' came the response. 'Haven't been here long enough to learn the lingo.'

The accent was pure American. 'Sergeant Joe Roots, United States Air Army,' he added, extending a hand.

Chapter 34

'Well, we hit Augsburg a while back,' explained Roots in response to Werner's question. 'But Mustang long-range reconnaissance suggested that they had rebuilt part of the facility and that the Man submarine diesel engine plant was probably back in production, at least in part. Or so we were told at the mission briefing. The brass decided to bomb it with another squadron-sized raid. I was our B17's rear gunner. We were hit bad, and the skipper shouted for a bail out. I went through the exit right behind and forward of my turret but didn't see any other 'chutes after I jumped. Then the ship exploded, a fireball...' his voice drifted off.

No doubt, thought Werner, *he was thinking about the rest of his crew.*

'Joe had the good fortune to land near our property,' put in *Herr* Stein, speaking excellent English and sensing the airman's discomfort. 'He asked for our help. We have given him some old clothes of mine, although they don't fit very well. The problem is, we don't know how to arrange his escape from here – he needs to be put in touch with a resistance pipeline, but we don't have any contact with that sort of organisation. Irmgard thought that with your background, you might just know of someone...'

'Not really, but let me think about it,' Werner replied. 'The trouble is, I don't believe such a pipeline exists this far south. They do in northern Germany and the Netherlands, as well as in France, but I have never heard of one in Bavaria – in the Nazi's backyard. Have there been any signs of a search locally, looking for Joe?' he asked.

Herr Stein shook his head. 'I think I would know if there had,' he replied.

'Which suggests the jump probably wasn't reported,' said Werner. 'Makes life a lot easier. Perhaps I might be able to come up with something in a day or two…'

Frau Stein rose to her feet. 'That is enough talk of war,' she announced in passable English. 'It is the last night of the year. Heinrich,' she turned to her husband, 'open some of that wine you have been hoarding in the cellar. Irmgard, come with me, child. We shall prepare Bavarian *Leberkäse* – that's a liver meatloaf,' she added for Joe's benefit, 'and there will be *Sauerkraut* and *Spaetzle* noodles. It's a good thing we have plenty of eggs – there has to be some benefit in living on the edge of beyond. It will put some flesh on your bones,' she said pointedly, looking at her daughter.

It was a convivial evening, with a fine supper and several bottles of wine. *Herr* Stein asked Werner how he might be able to help Joe, but Werner demurred politely. 'The less you know, the safer for all of you,' he said to his hosts. 'Just keep well hidden for a day or two,' he told the American, 'and I'll come back for you.' The following morning, he thanked *Herr* and *Frau* Stein, and he and Irmgard returned to the city.

* * * *

This time, Werner did not pedal back to Buchbach. The boneshaker was getting past a joke. He chose mid-evening, whilst there were still plenty of people and some light traffic about, and he was out of the city in almost no time at all. He had his Browning HP tucked into his raincoat, the BMW had a full tank, thanks to a top-up from the Mercedes, and he was confident he could shoot his way out of any casual police road check. But the journey proved uneventful.

That evening, Werner discussed his plan with the general over supper at the manor house. He had the spare uniform from Ilse's farm. It was smaller than his own, but it would be an adequate fit for Joe. The next morning, Werner set off in the *Kübelwagen*, wearing the same captured uniform that he had used to reach Buchbach, to arrive unchallenged at the Stein residence. Seated at the kitchen table, with a cup of hot *ersatz* coffee to warm his bones, Werner placed an *MP40* on the table, barrel facing safely away from them all, and announced that he had come to collect Joe.

'He can't stay here indefinitely,' he said to all three of them. 'It's too dangerous, not just for you, Joe, but for *Herr* and *Frau* Stein as well. Unfortunately, as I mentioned the night before last – and thank you again for a splendid New Year's Evening – I am unable to put Joe in touch with any local resistance organisation that might be able to smuggle him back to England. But what I can do is offer a place of safety until we can work out something else. How does that sound?' he concluded.

'Where would that be?' asked Joe.

'Again, the less I say now, the better,' said Werner. 'The choice is: stay here, with an ever-increasing risk of discovery, with all that it would mean for *Herr* and *Frau* Stein, or take your chances and come with me. No guarantees, but hopefully, at least these good people will not be put at any more risk.'

'Thank you,' said Joe sincerely to his hosts, 'but Werner is right. I have to go.'

'There's a spare uniform in the *Kübelwagen* outside,' he told him. 'You'll look like any other military type swanning around with a driver – Munich's full of them. We ought to be able to get away with it. But if not…' he pulled a Browning HP from his jacket pocket and pushed it across the table. Joe picked it up, turned it from side to side, clipped out the magazine and checked the chamber. Werner had not racked in an extra round. 'You seem to know what you are doing,' he said, somewhat relieved.

'Been around guns all my life,' he said, in his Smoky Mountains accent. 'Never used this one before, but that ain't a problem.'

'You can always reach me through Irmgard,' Werner told the Steins whilst Joe was getting changed. They both thanked them again before taking their leave.

'So where are we heading?' asked the American once they were on their way. He had to raise his voice in the open vehicle.

'Buchbach,' Werner replied. 'Not much more than half an hour away. My father's a retired general and in touch with a number of people who don't support the Hitler régime. There's a manor house, but I'm living in a cottage on the estate,' he went on. 'You can stay with me. It'll be a lot safer than the Stein place – for a start, it's deep inside woodland, and nobody ever comes anywhere near.'

'Sounds great,' said Joe, 'but for how long. What'll I do all day if you can't put me in touch with the resistance?'

'In a way, you already are,' Werner explained. 'I am setting up a new cell in this part of Germany. I'll tell you more later, over a drink and a meal, but it occurred to me when we were at the Stein's place over New Year: with someone else to help me, I could achieve a lot more than just persuading a few former White Rose students to find targets for the RAF and your Air Army.'

'White Rose?' queried Joe.

'Oh shit,' exclaimed Werner. They had just rounded a bend. Fifty metres ahead was a *Kübelwagen* in the green colours of the *Schutzpolizei des Reiches*, or the *Schupo*, the state protection police of Nazi Germany and a branch of the *Ordnungspolizei*, or *Orpo*, the uniformed police force. It was facing them, blocking their side of the road. One uniformed man stood in front of the bonnet, another immediately to its right in the offside lane. However, their side arms were still holstered, presumably because they did not perceive a threat from the approaching vehicle. Nevertheless, the one in front of them raised a hand, palm forward, in the unmistakable, universal gesture to stop.

Werner's thoughts were racing. If he spoke to him, they might be able to bluff their way through. But if they said anything at all to Joe, they were in trouble. Joe had the Browning, but if they stopped and the police decided to draw their weapons, he would almost certainly be shot before he could use it. The *MP40* was on the floor, under Joe's legs. Werner doubted whether he would have time to pick it up, and he wasn't sure whether Joe knew how to use it. Besides, even if he did, that meant only one weapon against two. 'We can't stop,' he said quickly. 'I'll slow down, then hit the throttle.'

He kept the *Kübelwagen* in second gear as they approached the checkpoint. One of the policemen stepped further into the offside lane, ready to walk forward and approach the driver's door. The other stayed in front of their vehicle. From almost at a standstill, Werner floored the accelerator, pulling out to aim at the policeman on his left, who dived for the verge to save his life. In his peripheral vision, Werner saw the other one spinning to watch them, unfastening his holster flap. As they shot past the roadblock, one man was struggling to his feet, and as he swerved back into their own lane, the police *Kübelwagen* blocked off the view of the other.

'Duck,' he shouted at Joe. They were a good twenty metres beyond the checkpoint, almost out of range for a handgun, before the first shot was fired. Werner had no idea where the bullet went, and he didn't care. They were far enough away now, although inevitably, the *Schutzpolizei* would give chase. Seconds later, they were in fourth gear and flat out at around eighty kilometres an hour, but Joe turned in his seat and shouted that the other *Kübel* was in sight, about a quarter of a mile behind them.

'Listen up,' Werner had to raise his voice above the noise of the wind, 'this is what we are going to do...'

* * * *

Flossie had arranged to meet Spencer and a couple of his friends at The King's Head. She wasn't working that night; it would be just a couple of quiet drinks. His friends Joshua, a trumpet player who had been transferred with him from the construction battalion, and the electrician Tremayne Thompson, who had always been a member of the base maintenance team, would also be there. But she was running late. Jimmy had developed a nasty cold, and despite Gladys' reassurances, she had wanted to be sure he was settled before leaving the house.

She was surprised to see her friend seated at a far table with the three Americans. She had spoken only once with Susie since the night she had delivered up Sergeant Chuck Hoskings, to thank her for what she had done. They had not seen her arrive, and she was a little surprised to see Susie's hand on top of one of Spencer's, apparently giving him an affectionate squeeze as she waggled them both from side to side.

Seeing Flossie approaching their table, she pulled her hand away quickly. Both she and Spencer looked a little guilty. Without explanation, he rose to draw back a chair for Flossie and went to the bar to buy her a drink. Announcing that she had to go, Susie drained her glass and took her leave. Spencer set down Flossie's drink and rejoined their table, still without saying anything. Flossie did not think too much about it at the time. Susie had always been a bit flighty.

But the following evening brought another surprise. As Flossie was peeling vegetables, Gladys remarked that she had seen Spencer earlier that evening. Coming home, her bus had passed through the village.

'I don't know what he was doing there,' she remarked, obviously trying to keep her tone even, 'but I saw him leaving Susan Hall's house. I thought he might be on his way here, but he hasn't turned up, so presumably, he has either gone to The King's Head or back to the base.'

'I'll have to ask him,' she replied and left it at that. But the thought kept coming to mind all evening. Susie had a bit of a reputation back in the day before she married. She had confessed to Flossie that she hadn't been a virgin. She had let the then Staff Sergeant Hall have his way with her after they got engaged. But he had been away from home for months now, and when a woman like Susie had been used to a regular sex life…

She had dismissed the incident in the pub as just a mild flirtation on Susie's part, but could Spencer be playing around? Surely not… but he was an American from a very different background. Perhaps his culture took a different view of fidelity. Yet he had always seemed such a kind, decent person. She would have to find some way of discovering the truth, but she was reluctant to ask him directly for fear of putting their relationship at risk. Still undecided, she spent a restless two hours in bed before finally falling into a troubled sleep.

Chapter 35

They were driving through a wooded area. Eventually, Werner saw what they needed: a forest track leading off their country road, although he couldn't see very far beyond the entrance. Once they had turned off, it would be too late. If the track did not suit their purpose, there could be no question of turning around and regaining the road before the *Polizei* vehicle was on them. He braked and swung hard left across the offside lane.

It looked all right. He gave it twenty-five metres and slammed on the brakes, handbrake included. Joe was already out of the *Kübel*, running back a few yards to take a position to one side of the track. Werner grabbed the *MP40* and cocked it. Any second now, and the *Polizei* would be there. He ran back as far as he dared and dived into the undergrowth on the opposite side of the track from Joe. They just had to hope that the *Polizei*, too, would make the turn.

No doubt thinking that the driver of the escaping *Kübelwagen* would try to lose them in the forest, the police vehicle had braked equally harshly and turned onto the track. Seeing the other vehicle at a standstill, the driver stamped on the brakes. It was an ambush. He screamed 'Jump' to his partner, who leapt from the still-moving vehicle and rolled into the trees before Joe could take a shot.

As the driver, too, jumped clear, a three-round burst from Werner's *MP40* took him in the chest. His partner put down his weapon and stepped from the undergrowth, hands raised, back onto the track. Joe's round took him centre face.

Werner and Joe approached their victims, but the result was obvious. 'No choice,' said Joe reluctantly. 'Pity, but he could have identified us. And that was for the crew of *Flying Florence*,' he added.

'Let's get the uniform off this one before he bleeds too much,' Werner said, indicating the dead passenger. 'We'll pull the bodies into the trees. We now have another vehicle and uniform plus a couple of extra semi-automatics. You happy to follow me for the rest of the way?'

'Sure am,' came the reply.

They reached Buchbach without further incident. Werner drove his vehicle into its hide, then helped Joe construct a similar one to camouflage their police trophy. Once they were satisfied, he led Joe into his cottage. He put their prizes of weapons and uniform on the table. 'These are going to come in very useful,' he remarked, 'but we can find somewhere safe for them later.' He went to a cupboard and produced a bottle of his father's brandy and two glasses. 'I think we have earned this,' he said, splashing out generously.

Later that evening, after he was sure Anna would have gone home, he took Joe to the manor house, introduced him to his father and related the day's events.

The general, who had spent time in London as an assistant defence attaché in the early 1930s, spoke excellent English. He welcomed Joe warmly to Buchbach and congratulated them both – Joe on his survival and the pair of them on their escape. After a bottle of wine, he set down a pot of rabbit stew prepared that day by Anna, together with a loaf of fresh bread. They shared an adequate, if not over-generous, meal.

For Joe's benefit, Werner outlined his mission and recent activity in Munich but then went on with his thoughts for the future. He hoped that the list for a raid on Munich's industrial base would be ready by the end of the month or some time in February at the latest. In the meantime, he proposed a sabotage attack on the main railway signal box in Munich's marshalling yard, which would put the entire goods system out of action. 'Would have been difficult on my own,' he told Joe, 'but with two of us, it ought to be possible.'

The general observed that if Joe moved off the estate, he would always be vulnerable because he did not speak German. He offered to obtain a set of papers, an *Ausweiß* identity document, plus a letter on official medical headed paper that would declare him to be unfit for military service because of profound deafness. This latter document would also state that he could sometimes lip read but that his only sure means of communication was through sign language. Hopefully, the average policeman or soldier would give up and just wave him on.

'You can do this?' Joe asked.

The general confirmed that they could. 'We have a number of members in senior positions in the régime's administrative and medical departments,' he replied. 'The documents will be authentic. They will not bear in-depth investigation, but they should survive a casual inspection. You will be able to walk the streets with at least a modicum of safety.' He would bring a camera to the cottage the following morning.

And as Werner pointed out, any reconnaissance would have to be conducted in civilian clothes.

* * * *

To her frustration, Flossie had to work that Saturday evening. Uncle Bill's usual stand-in had a bad cold and wasn't available. Spencer came into the pub, and she was able to sit with him from time to time, but Joshua and T-T were with him, and in any case, there would not have been time for a serious conversation. He came to the house for lunch on Sunday, but either Jimmy or Gladys was always within earshot, so yet again, she had to hold her tongue. Taking his leave, he announced that he would call for her the following Saturday, and they could spend the evening in The King's Head. And it did not help that he made no effort to contact her for the whole of that week. He did not even call in for a drink whilst she was working.

Next Saturday would be her birthday, but Flossie could not remember feeling so miserable. Gladys had used some of her precious coupons to buy her a much-needed cardigan, and Jimmy had coloured a homemade card, but there was nothing from Spencer. No doubt assuming that he would be taking her out for a celebration, her mother-in-law announced that she would be spending the evening with friends. But she had arranged a babysitter, and a teenager who occasionally looked after young Jimmy turned up shortly before Spencer was due to arrive. Glancing at her watch, Gladys wished her a pleasant evening and let herself out of the house.

It was hardly the sort of evening for which she would have wished. Time was when he would have risked a table somewhere for a quiet dinner. She was feeling very insecure when he turned up, chatting with the babysitter while she put her coat on so that they could walk to the pub. Obviously, whatever he had to say, her reaction would have to be muted by the presence of others, although she thought that this was a cowardly way out. Flossie had this ever-growing feeling that when she finally had the chance to talk to him properly, their relationship would fall over a precipice.

She steeled herself for what was about to come. Flossie knew she had to stay strong, not least for Jimmy James. She had survived the death of his father, although it had never been confirmed, and she would survive what she now saw as a betrayal of her love for Spencer.

As they approached The King's Head, he took her elbow and steered her away from the door leading into the lounge bar. 'We're heading for the snug,' he announced. *So that was it,* she thought. Like as not, it would be almost empty this early on a Saturday night. Much the best venue for whatever he was about to say.

He pushed open the door and propelled her into the room. In one corner, a small group from the air base band burst into a rendition of "Happy Birthday to You". Gladys, Susie and a bunch of his friends, all with glass in hand, were singing their heads off. Even Uncle Bill had popped through for a moment from next door.

To one side of the snug was a long trestle table laden with food, a buffet the like of which had not been seen in the pub since before the war, and in the centre of the room, on a separate, round table, was a huge birthday cake covered with tiny candles. T-T handed her a glass of what looked to be champagne, with another for Spencer. He put an arm around her shoulders, gave her a huge hug followed by a kiss on the cheek and said, 'Happy birthday, my love.'

Flossie burst into tears. Had Spencer not held her up, she would have fallen to her knees. He offered his handkerchief, and to empathetic 'aahs', she blew her nose and wiped her eyes, but they still glistened freely as she accepted her well-wishers' greetings and congratulations.

It was a lively evening. After Flossie had blown out the candles and cut and served the cake, and during a welcome break from the dancing, several of them were having a quiet drink together. Spencer mentioned that he had asked Susie to make the cake. 'But I couldn't have done it if Spencer hadn't brought me the sugar and butter and dried fruits,' she admitted. So that was what he had been doing round at Susie's house, Flossie realised and immediately felt guilty for ever having doubted him.

'Where have you been all week,' she asked him, 'apart from organising this lovely party?'

'Tell you later,' he said mysteriously.

'Aren't you worried about closing time?' Flossie asked Uncle Bill, who had come through again to join the party. It was well past ten o'clock, nearer eleven.

'Shut the doors half an hour ago, after drinking up time,' he replied. 'Constable Hargreaves knows it's your birthday party. He's next door with one or two others, having a quiet after-hours pint. Says he won't be off on his bike for a while yet!' At eleven o'clock, the group played a last waltz and packed away their instruments, which was the signal for the revellers to wish Flossie and Spencer goodnight. The three of them walked home together. Flossie realised she had gone from being utterly miserable to not having felt so happy in a long time.

Gladys announced that it had been a lovely party, but she was dead on her feet. 'Goodnight, you two,' she announced, and even Spencer also got a kiss on the cheek. 'Wow, dat was a first,' he exclaimed once they were alone together. Taking a small, blue box from his jacket pocket, he opened it and went down on one knee.

'Maybe we got to wait, but time I asked properly...' he said.

* * * *

Apart from a couple of air raids that had been aimed at specific aircraft factories, Munich had been substantially untouched by the war. The cafés, bars and restaurants had less to offer, but the good citizens enjoyed their leisure, each according to his – or her husband's – income and status. A two-section guard had been allocated to the station and marshalling yard, which they patrolled to a routine pattern, but the main signal box, which was some two hundred metres along the line from the nearest platform, did not have anyone permanently on post alongside it.

They had used the motorcycle to travel from Buchbach earlier that morning. Werner decided that there was little risk in making the journey. He had a pistol in his raincoat pocket, and Joe, riding pillion, had an *MP40* concealed between them. They could not afford to be stopped and searched: the panniers contained weapons and explosives, either dropped in Werner's rucksack or acquired subsequently along the way. However, the trip proved uneventful, although Joe was open-mouthed at Werner's beautiful Mercedes and almost as impressed by the luxury of his apartment.

Two unarmed civilians, the two of them walked away from the station along the pavement parallel with the railway lines, which had eventually disappeared behind a row of industrial buildings.

'Be easy enough to find a way through and onto the tracks,' noted Werner.

Back at the apartment, Joe watched nervously as Werner unwrapped and examined explosives, a detonator, a timing device and wiring. 'Only take a minute or two to put this lot together,' he told the American. 'You been keeping up with the war in Italy?'

Wondering why he had asked, Joe confessed that he hadn't.

'Well, when the Allies invaded last July,' Werner explained, 'Italy signed an armistice, but the Germans decided to fight on. Now, Kesselring has lines of fortified positions in the mountainous region south of Rome, and at the moment, it's hard pounding. Munich's an important resupply line for northern Italy, so anything we can do to damage Hitler's ability to move men and materiel into that theatre has to be worth a try.' He looked up at the American. 'We can't do much about the marshalling yards, and if we blow the lines, they'll get repaired soon enough, so the signalling system has to be the best option,' he concluded.

'And that,' he added as an afterthought, 'was pointed out to me by a young female student at the university here.'

'Smart kid,' agreed Joe. It was past midnight. It would soon be time…

* * * *

'So what have you been up to all week?' asked Flossie, sitting on his knee, now that they were alone, with an arm around his shoulders. She had used soap to remove her wedding ring, albeit with difficulty, and it now rested on the fourth finger of her right hand. On her left hand was Spencer's shiny new engagement ring, with its single diamond. And quite a generous one, she realised.

'Been spendin' as much free time as I can at Fred Laxham's place,' he told her.

'What, that run-down old garage in the village on the other side of the airbase?' she replied.

He nodded. 'There's virtually nah car repair work, wat wit da war an' everythin'. It's mostly mendin' farm machinery. Da odd tractor, a bit of welding, sum blacksmith jobs,' he explained. 'But Fred's an old man. He wants out. An' he hasn't seen dat aftah da war motorin' gonna be a boom industry. I know motors, I can fix tractors, an' I can weld, even though I can't shoe horses,' he admitted. 'but first off, I wanted to show you this.'

He produced a document from his inside pocket. Flossie looked at it, and her hand flew to her mouth. It was the title deed to the house where her mother had been the tenant. And it was amended to show the joint names of Flossie Harding and Spencer Almeter.

'Spencer, my love...' she said and buried her head into his shoulder. Eventually, she stopped almost squeezing the life out of him, wiped her eyes, not for the first time that evening, and looked at him. 'Nobody has ever done anything like this for me before,' she whispered simply. But it was heartfelt.

'Wat I reckon be this,' he told her, 'we use the house as security to borrow nuff from da bank to buy Fred's business. We don't need a lot, far less than this place be worth. I've been makin' good money singin' at da Manor. Twenty-five a Saturday night, fo a couple of months now. Mrs Higgins at da post office let meh open a savings account. There's a fair bit in da book. I could borrow da rest, buy out Fred, keep him on till he wants to retire, an' there's a business just waitin' to be developed aftah da war. Da land be derr – wouldn't take much to add on a showroom. Take on an agency, sell new cars... there's a good life here fo you an' meh, Flossie love. An' Gladys would still be able to help raise young Jimmy.'

* * * *

It was easy enough to access the track. They were about a hundred metres beyond the signal box. Werner and Joe had dressed in dark clothing, and each carried an *MP40*. Werner had the makings of the bomb divided between his pockets. They walked slowly towards the box, the platform and the marshalling yard complex. A low light inside the box enabled the signalman to operate his bank of switches but still have some vision of the area outside. A line of wooden steps led up to the door on the opposite side from their approach.

It took a while – they had to wait from time to time until their man inside was otherwise occupied, moving the giant levers and, on one occasion, answering a phone call from a receiver at the other end of the box, which meant that he had his back to them. But finally, they were at the bottom of the steps, no longer visible from above. Werner nodded at Joe and began the ascent.

Willi Krauser was looking forward to retirement. He had worked for the now-renamed *Deutsche Reichsbahn* all his life. In 1937, Hitler's Germany assumed full control over the railways, but they still operated as a civilian organisation. A survivor of The Great War, he was a loyal Party member. He had supported the Nazi rebirth and regeneration of his Fatherland ever since the collapse of the Weimar Republic, following the devastating terms imposed under the Treaty of Versailles, after what had effectively been a crushing defeat in 1918.

He was completely surprised when two civilians aiming submachine guns walked into his signal box. Automatically, for an old soldier, he raised his hands.

'Go with my colleague,' said the older of the two men. 'You will walk in front, along the line,' his head indicated over his shoulder, 'away from the station. Don't bother trying to talk to him, because he has been deaf since birth. But he will obey my last order without question.'

'Which was?' asked Willi, his voice less confident and more hoarse than he had intended.

'If you try to run, he will put a round into your spine. *Alles klar?*'

Willi could only nod his head in agreement. All was, indeed, very clear. Joe nudged sideways with the end of his muzzle, and with Willi in the lead, they descended the steps.

Werner set to work. It took no more than a couple of minutes to assemble the explosive device. He placed it in the centre of the box, on the floor between the two rows of levers.

He was about to switch on the timer, set for ten minutes, when there was the unmistakable sound of a single shot from the direction of their approach along the line. Seconds later, a whistle sounded, and two soldiers began running along the platform. They jumped off the end and advanced towards the signal box.

Ten minutes was out of the question. He reset the timer instead for two minutes – hardly safe practice, but he couldn't leave it for the soldiers to find and disarm. He was down the steps when the first shots rang out from the direction of the platform, but firing from a standing position after a short run did little to improve marksmanship. Werner dropped, pinned down in the shadow beside the box, and waited, only too conscious of what was about to happen immediately above.

From somewhere behind the box, two short bursts rang out, and both soldiers went down. 'Run,' shouted Joe desperately. They both sprinted away, only to be engulfed by the blast as an almighty explosion ripped the box to pieces, sheets of flame lighting up what little remained. Werner had thought that they might make it, but everything went black.

Chapter 36

Werner could hear the sound of gunfire. He thought he'd only been out for a few seconds. Joe's *MP40* was firing single shots. The weapon had just one setting, automatic, but with a touch of skill on the trigger, it could be made to fire one round at a time – useful if it was necessary to conserve ammunition.

Joe had been in front, less affected by the blast. Now, he had taken cover behind the foundations of the signal box. Werner crawled round alongside him. The soldiers advancing from the platform were silhouetted by light behind them. Werner and Joe were in darkness. He was holding them off – they were less than anxious to mount an assault.

Werner shook his head, still groggy. 'Fire and movement,' he said to Joe. 'I'll cover you. Sprint back about fifty yards, using the box as cover, then move into a fire position whilst I do the same.'

Joe nodded his understanding, patted Werner on the shoulder and turned to run. When he heard a three-round burst from Joe, Werner ran back to a position a further fifty yards behind him. At first, he was weaving a bit from side to side, but then his legs were more under control. He dropped to the ground in almost pitch blackness, rolled sideways, and loosed off a single round vaguely in the right direction to keep their heads down and let Joe know that he was clear for another run. Joe flew past him, and Werner fired again as two more of the enemy ran towards the shelter of the signal box.

Eventually they were down, side by side, almost at the point where they had walked through the factory yard to the railway lines. 'Go start the bike engine,' Joe shouted. 'As soon as I hear it, I'll run and join you.'

The BMW fired up first kick. Werner gave it a good burst of revs. Joe loosed off half a magazine, just to keep their heads down for a bit longer, then sprinted away at ninety degrees. Shielded by the buildings, he joined Werner on pillion, and they accelerated out of the yard. They were well away, out of sight, before the first of the soldiers emerged to look left and right along an empty road.

With the BMW safely in its garage, they both breathed a sigh of relief but agreed to postpone any further discussion till they were back at the apartment.

Werner produced a bottle of Ansbach and poured two generous helpings. 'What in Christ's name happened back at the signal box?' he asked.

'The signalman had been watching too many movies,' Joe replied. 'Tried the trick of stopping, in the hope my *MP40* would be up against his back, which it was almost, then tried to pirouette like a damn ballet dancer and sweep it away. But he was too slow and made the mistake of grabbing the end of the barrel. My finger was on the trigger, and the gun went off. I think the bullet went into his side 'cause he fell, clutching it. Knew it would cause trouble, so I turned back towards the box, saw two soldiers and took them out to give us a chance to get clear.'

'Thank God you did,' said Werner. 'I had to set a short fuse – only a couple minutes – then I got trapped alongside the signal box till you came to the rescue.'

'I was in front when we started running,' Joe added, 'so the blast didn't knock me out. Good thing you came round quickly, though. The others didn't have time to form up properly and assault *en masse*.'

Werner thought for a few moments. 'I doubt anyone saw the motorbike,' he observed, 'but just in case, we'll take the rest of today off and not go back to Buchbach until tomorrow, Monday. We'll leave it for a couple of weeks, then Irmgard should have enough target info for me to send back to England.'

* * * *

He saw no reason to take Joe with him. He was safer left behind on the estate. With the papers provided by the general's contacts, he was able to help out on the farm. The authorities would never be able to disprove his cover documents: not with a false address in Dusseldorf that had been blown to pieces linked to a public building in which all the associated administrative records had been destroyed by an air raid incendiary. Anna suspected that he might not be who the general said he was. When her employer introduced him as a casual worker, and she served them both a midday meal, she noticed that he cut it up first and then used just a fork. But Anna was fiercely loyal to the general and Werner. She kept her thoughts to herself.

Werner's early evening call on Irmgard was unannounced, but she welcomed him warmly. 'Be another week, but the list's coming along nicely,' she told him as they enjoyed a glass of blackberry and apple wine made from the produce of her parents' smallholding. 'But you will have it by the third week in March.'

'Do you have plans for this evening?' he asked. 'Be happy to offer you supper if you know somewhere nearby that can still serve a decent meal.'

'I went home for the weekend,' she replied. 'Came back with half a dozen bottles of wine, but also some chicken and vegetables. I was going to make chicken schnitzel, but there's enough for two.'

'That's a kind offer,' said Werner, 'and if you're sure…'

'Let's take our wine into the kitchen,' she suggested, 'and I'll get started.'

Werner sat at a small table whilst she flattened two chicken breasts and set out the flour, eggs and breadcrumbs. He could not help but watch as she worked. Irmgard had jet-black hair cut to the shape of her head. Her skirt and blouse made no secret of an elfin figure. And, he noticed that evening, she had lovely, slightly almond-shaped eyes, the darkest he had ever seen. Definitely a throwback to her Armenian Romany heritage and exotic, in sharp contrast to his own blond, Aryan looks. She was, he realised, extremely attractive, but he told himself not to be ridiculous; there had to be at least ten years between them.

She fried together some potatoes with chopped onions and dressed a small bowl of mixed salad. 'At least our hothouse has survived the war – so far,' she said, setting supper on the table. 'Father worries that if a bomb comes down anywhere near, he'll never be able to replace all the glass.'

Simple though it was, the meal was delicious, far better than anything they would have been served in a restaurant, and he told her so. She seemed pleased by his compliment. 'My mother taught me, of course,' she told him. Afterwards, they sat in the lounge finishing their wine before he announced that, much as he was enjoying her company, he would have to take his leave to catch the last tram.

She hesitated before standing up. 'I don't even know where you live,' she told him.

'Safer that way.'

She opened the apartment door. 'Thank you for a delightful supper,' he said, then kissed her, a chaste brush of his lips on her cheek, and turned to go.

Irmgard closed the door behind him and leant back against it for several seconds, deep in thought. She had been on the cusp of inviting him to stay...

* * * *

'There's been a complication,' the general said to Werner and Joe over dinner on Werner's first night back at Buchbach. He turned towards his son. 'I had a visit from a senior *Reich* official whilst you were away. It seems that Buchbach Manor is to be requisitioned – our government needs it for a hospital. We have so many wounded and not enough bed spaces where they can complete their recovery, once they have survived surgery and are on the mend.'

'Ouch,' said Werner, 'that's going to make life difficult. When is all this supposed to happen?'

'They have given me a week,' said the general, 'but that was a couple of days ago. So, I've had time to give it some thought.

'It's hardly ideal,' he went on, 'but perhaps not the disaster it might seem at first sight. Although I have closed off the two wings, this house is still too big for me alone. The lodge has been empty for a long time, since the war began. It might only be a three-bedroom gate-side cottage, but it's still in a good state of repair – cosy and easy enough to heat. Anna lives out, so she can just as easily look after me down there at the end of the drive.' He managed a half-smile. 'And there's a bonus: the *Sanitätsdienst Heer* will take over responsibility for the upkeep of this pile. It's been quite a drain on my resources now that the estate's no longer making a profit because of the war.'

Werner thought about this for a moment or two. 'So how do you see this working out for us two?' he asked, his index finger moving to indicate himself and Joe.

'Thought about that, too,' the general replied. 'This place will be a hospital, not a *Wehrmacht* unit in the usual sense. The only activity will be in and around the manor house. I don't see sick inmates or medical staff wandering around the woods, over half a kilometre away on the other side of the estate. You should be safe enough there, and in the unlikely event that you are asked, you are simply casual workers in a tied cottage.'

'We have some pretty compromising equipment there,' pointed out Werner. 'A pair of *Kübelwagen*, not to mention a few uniforms and a small arsenal.'

'Had time on my hands while you were away,' put in Joe. 'There's an old stone storage room, like a small barn, not far from the cottage. There's some rusting forestry machinery inside, plus an old horse-drawn cart that looks like it hasn't been used for years. The doors are hanging off. We could pull everything out, put the *Kübelwagen* and the other stuff inside, fix up the doors and put on a decent padlock to keep out any casual passers-by.'

'Good thinking,' said Werner.

'Let us know if you want any furniture shifting,' he said to his father. 'And ask Anna to put out anything she wants from the kitchen – they might be taking our manor house, but it doesn't have to come fully equipped. And I'll remove the old *SS* uniforms still hanging in my wardrobe. They can go with the rest of my clothes in the cottage.'

It took two days, by which time the general was comfortably installed in the lodge. Anna had spring-cleaned the place and declared the kitchen operational with everything from the main house that she needed. The following day, the *Kübelwagen* were driven to their new home, and Joe proved himself to be a competent carpenter, refitting two now refurbished and stout, heavy-duty doors. A week after the initial visit, a uniformed colonel of the *Sanitätsdienst Heer* accepted the keys to the manor house from the general, saluted again, and thanked him profusely for his courtesy and cooperation.

* * * *

There was no response when he pressed the buzzer for Irmgard's apartment. On impulse, he tried the bar where they had first met, and she was there with Gerhard, Horst and Ursula.

'I know what you have come for,' she said as he approached their table. 'We can collect it after you have bought us all a drink as a reward for our hard work.' He was only too happy to buy them several rounds of drinks, although he raised a finger to his lips when Ursula began to mention what they had been doing. It was early evening before they left the bar, the other three heading back towards the university whilst Werner and Irmgard set off for her apartment.

She took the paperwork from a desk drawer and set it out on the table, unfolding two large maps. One was of Munich and the surrounding countryside, while the other was a street plan of the greater city area. 'You know Ursula's father is on the city council,' she explained, 'and he's had these since before the war. On the former, they had marked all the local airfields, including the small ones used by flying clubs and now emergency landing strips; the Augsburg diesel plant 51 kilometres west of the city; an airfield in Erding, 31 kilometres to the northeast, used to train *Luftwaffe* pilots; and a factory at Oberfaffenhofen, also to the west of the city, where Dornier was preparing to make the new Do335 heavy fighter, as well as producing blades for the Junkers turbojet engine.

'Now,' she said, unfolding the second map, 'on this one, I've numbered various locations, then using the grid reference system you taught us, the precise positions and what the factories make are listed on a separate piece of paper.

'This is gold dust,' Werner exclaimed. 'How on earth did you come by all this information?'

'Some of it from Ursula's father,' she explained. 'He talked to his counterparts in and around the city. Believe it or not, even in wartime, factories still notify the authorities about what they are doing, even if they don't have to ask for formal planning permission. Horst got lucky, too,' she added. 'His family are pretty brainy. One of them, an aero-engineer, works for Junkers. The two families often have Sunday lunch together, and the odd snippet comes out. Also, both boys spent ages hanging around in the local bars, picking up snatches of conversation from factory workers. That's one of the reasons this all took so long.

'By the way, there's also the railway station on this street plan,' she indicated. 'They have had to replace the signal box. Did you have anything to do with that, by any chance?'

'I'll assume that as a suspicious "yes",' she said when Werner did not answer immediately. 'Also, we have marked the most important railway bridges, and this here,' her finger indicated a large, circled zone, 'is the general industrial area. A lot of the smaller factories do something or other for the war effort, so this would be ideal for *Flächenbombardierung* – surface bombardment, what I think you call carpet bombing.'

She produced a bottle of wine whilst he studied the maps and paperwork. 'I'll have to convert all this to numerals and text, then encode it,' he told her as she poured. 'I'll leave for the country tomorrow; it's a lot safer than transmitting from the city centre.'

Irmgard folded the documents and placed them in a large envelope. She moved to sit on a sofa, patting a cushion for him to be beside her. '*Prost,*' she said, and they clinked glasses. 'I know next to nothing about you,' she went on. 'That time you were here when I made a fool of myself, you mentioned that your wife had died. Was it the bombing?'

He shook his head. 'No,' he said, 'it was last year, back in England. A bomb was meant for me, but she moved the vehicle to get at a pushchair in the garage. It went off,' he said simply.

'So you have children,' she assumed.

'Again, no,' he told her. 'Charles Dieter is Anneliese's son by her first husband, but he *was* killed in the bombing early in the war. I came along later. The boy is with his grandparents now. It was the best way…' he trailed off. She could feel the sadness in his voice. They sat in silence, sipping their wine.

'Life hasn't been very kind to you,' she said, eventually. Then, 'You speak German perfectly… in fact, you sound German,' she observed. 'Where did you learn our language?'

'I am German,' he replied bluntly. 'But the only way to save Germany is to oppose Hitler. So I work for the British,' he stated by way of explanation. 'But please don't ask me any more…'

Werner finished his wine and set down the glass. 'Thank you for the drink,' he said, rising to his feet and picking up the envelope from the table, 'and I can't tell you how grateful I am for this. Tell the boys the next time I see them that I will underwrite every *pfennig* they spent in and around the bars gathering the information.'

'They'll love that,' she said with a smile, moving to stand in front of him. 'But you don't have to go. You are welcome to stay if you want…'

Werner hesitated, then put down the envelope and held her gently by the shoulders.

'Irmgard,' he said softly, 'you're a beautiful young woman. I'm older than you, but any man could so easily...' She looked up at him. He saw that her eyes were glistening. 'You, too, have suffered the loss of a loved one,' he went on. 'I would like to rule nothing out, but it would have to be for all the right reasons. I'm honoured by what you have just said, but for both our sakes, can we take things slowly, one step at a time?'

He kissed her, but quite chastely on the lips, then picked up the envelope and let himself out without another word. Yet again, she was leaning against the door. Most young men of her acquaintance would never have turned down a chance to get inside her knickers. Perhaps... just maybe... after all that had happened to both of them, she had found someone special.

* * * *

'The planning is well underway,' said Sir Manners to Bill and Doreen, tapping a folder containing a transcript of Werner's encoded information. It's to be later this month but before the beginning of May. The US Air Army will bomb by day, followed immediately by the RAF that same night. A massive raid.

'We should send a diversion message,' observed Bill. 'See if we can draw some of their fighter squadrons further north, away from Munich.'

'Already in hand,' said Sir Manners. 'Our planners will talk to the Americans; we'll agree on a form of words, and Quentin Frobisher will send a replacement to brief Margaret Chapman at Snettisham. Should all be quite straightforward now that Staunton's out of the way.'

'We should warn Werner,' said Doreen Jackman. 'He might be all right if he's back home at the manor; Buchbach's probably far enough away, but from what he's sent us, he has to have been spending a lot of time in Munich itself. We know the family has an apartment there. Be dreadful if he were killed by the RAF – I gather that between them, they and the Americans plan on destroying a large part of the city.'

'We can't afford to take the risk,' Sir Manners said slowly. 'If the message were decoded, it could cost hundreds of aircrew their lives. His schedule will be days before the raid. And if he were discovered and made to talk...' he let the question hang.

'It's a horrible decision to have to take,' he went on eventually, 'but one for which I take sole responsibility. Our man Werner will just have to take his chances.' The other two remained silent. Sadly, they knew he was right.

Margaret, now very obviously pregnant, had been inactive for some months. But she was only too happy to make the transmission. It was acknowledged. The message had been received. But not for one moment was it taken at face value in 76/78 Tirpitzufer. 'We know she has been turned,' said *Gerneralmajor* Hans Oster to *Oberst* Hans Piekenbrock. 'If the British and Americans are saying Berlin, the target is probably somewhere further south.'

He turned to a map of Europe mounted on his office wall. 'Let's draw a line from the British and American airfields to the capital,' he suggested, 'then look for a likely angle to a target elsewhere, roughly the same distance for a deep penetration raid.' His finger stabbed the wall. 'It stands out like a dog's bollocks,' he said to Piekenbrock. 'A *Reichsmark* to a pinch of shit: they're going for Munich. And our *Luftwaffe* fighters will be waiting for them!'

Chapter 37

Isaac Hofmeyer's alarm went off at a quarter to two on the morning of 24th April 1944. His hand slammed the top to shut it off. It was what he thought of as a "two-three-four" morning: awake and up by two, breakfast at three, and briefing at four.

He forced himself to swing his legs over the side of his bed. Today was an M.E., a Maximum Effort. Every last ship the base could put into the air. But first, he had time to wash, shave, dress and take a decent breakfast. There were fresh eggs today, better than the dreaded powdered jobs. Much as he enjoyed them, it wasn't a good omen. Somehow, the better the breakfast, the shittier the mission. And Isaac knew already what his airplane crews would not learn until the 4am briefing. Both the 8th and 9th Air Forces, together with the Royal Air Force, would mount a massive raid on the city and surrounding area of Munich: the former by day, the latter that same night – heavy bombers and their escorts penetrating deep into the heart of Nazi Germany.

That day, over seven hundred B-17 Flying Fortress and B-24 Liberators, together with their mainly Mustang fighter escorts, would attack the city and area so historically important to Hitler's régime. There was also a personal dimension for Isaac Hofmeyer. Since the death of Max Staubin, he had been increasingly grounded by the duties of base commander. So, he had decided to dump most of Staubin's duties on Sam Heimy. He had come to realise how much he resented sending men to their deaths whilst he was flying nothing more than a desk. Today, he would fly the lead ship.

String Roper had proved himself an excellent number two in the cockpit of *Righteous Rosie*, so much so that he had been selected to be sent back stateside next month for a conversion course. The B-24 was more demanding to fly than the Fortress. When he returned, it would be as delivery captain of one of the newer Liberators. String had not welcomed the news: the B-24 was not as robust as the Flying Fortress, and it had a lower ceiling and not such a good lower airspeed performance. But it carried a heavier bomb load. Aircrew preferred the Fortress, the general staff the Liberator. As Isaac had been obliged to point out, the course and appointment – and promotion – were a testament to String's ability as a pilot. And the clincher was, the United States Air Army was not a democracy.

But that was all in the future. Since the injury to Rudy Ansbach, a permanent captain had yet to be appointed to *Rosie*. Rudy's former crew had not much welcomed their recent missions, with different officers under whom they had not previously flown, no matter how competent they proved to be. A ship needed a captain bonded with his crew.

After Isaac had informed String Roper that he would fly the mission, his fellow crew members welcomed the news. They knew he had mentored and flight-checked Rudy Ansbach, and Isaac's experience and tutelage had given them a first-class skipper. The Colonel would fly as captain and command pilot. But whilst the entire crew had the greatest respect for Isaac, they all knew that flying front and centre would make them a prime target for enemy fighters.

Isaac received the green flare, and Rosie began her take-off run, always a tense moment, as was the landing. With a full fuel and bomb load, *Rosie* was slow to accelerate. Perhaps there had been some deterioration, or it had been nicked by a bullet or a piece of shrapnel on a previous mission, but just over halfway down the runway and at barely ninety miles an hour, there was a loud bang, and *Rosie* began to pull to one side. The left-hand tyre had blown. As best, they would veer off the runway and ground loop, the wingtip catching the grass and swinging the aircraft violently round and round to crash and burn. At worst, they could block the runway and abort the take-off for every airplane on the mission – an absolute disaster for the raid.

Isaac had long thought about this nightmare possibility. It was either fly or die, and he didn't hesitate. 'Dropping one-third flaps,' he shouted to String, easing back just enough to lift her off. To his immense relief, *Rosie* inched herself free from the runway. They were airborne and gathering speed. With flaps and gear up, they climbed safely away.

'Great job, Colonel,' said String tersely. Isaac's instant reaction had saved them all. It was a lesson in airmanship he would never forget.

'Now for the boring bit,' said Isaac, his heart rate still not quite back to normal. 'We circle round and round till everyone else forms up. And we'll have to be last to land, so we don't foul up the runway.'

Assuming we get back at all after a start like that, was String's unspoken thought.

Flak was accurate over the continent, but much of it was now radar-guided. Batteries tended to fire all together once the target had been acquired. The crew were briefed to watch for the pronounced flash, and their warning gave Isaac time to bank away. For minutes on end, he danced *Rosie* to one side or the other, left or right, away from the point of aim.

Their escort fighters were doing a great job of keeping enemy fighters at bay as they droned across Belgium, Luxembourg and into the skies over Germany itself. Only once did a flight of Bf 109s break through the cordon. They were ahead and high, the brave German pilots intending to dive through the formation in a frontal attack, with the aim of both shooting down aircraft and scattering the formation.

Isaac shouted a warning, but Rich Ruddich had already picked them up in the nose and Johnny Carstairs in the upper Sperry turret. Their sights were set to one thousand yards, but the two experienced gunners waited till they were approaching six hundred, the maximum effective range for the paired 50-Cal Brownings at each station. Isaac and String watched the line of tracer from the leading Messerschmitt as it swooped towards *Righteous Rosie*, both of them taking an involuntary duck below the instrument panel. But return fire from the dorsal and nose gunners caught the fighter, a piece of metal breaking off and spinning away, as it was forced to jink from a deadly response. Then it was diving to pass underneath.

'Yours, Brad,' shouted Rich to the ball turret gunner, who had already lined up his guns on where he expected the enemy to appear. He followed through with a burst that used a precious five seconds of the one-minute firing time that was all each weapon on *Rosie* could carry. He was rewarded with a burst of flame from the 109, possibly a hit on the fuel tank, for seconds later it inverted into a roll then dived vertically before exploding in a fireball. Isaac called for damage reports, but with apparently nothing more than a few more draughty holes in her fuselage, *Righteous Rosie* pressed on to her target.

They reached the IP, the Initial Point of their bombing run, without injury or any further damage, as now the enemy fighters had pulled off as the bombers came under attack from Munich's defensive flak. Rich Ruddich, the bombardier, had the con with his AFCE, or Automatic Flight Control Equipment. Their target was in the centre of a large industrial complex. Both Isaac and String were holding their breath... the bombing run was six seconds, two longer than they would have wished. Fragments rattled against the fuselage, but *Rosie* flew on till they heard the blessed "bombs away", and Rosie lifted and increased her speed as twelve times five-hundred-pound bombs released from her bay. Doors up, and Isaac was hands and feet back on as he turned *Rosie* away from the murderous line of anti-aircraft fire. 'Spot on,' shouted Carstairs from below. Ruddich had creamed their target.

* * * *

Werner had returned to his apartment in order to meet up and discuss with Irmgard how best they could develop their embryo cell and what future assignments they could undertake. Most of the bombs seemed to be landing on the industrial area, but some were closer, on the city centre. Whether they were deliberate or simply strays, off-target, he had no way of knowing. But he *was* aware of the general strategic thrust of the Allied bombing campaign. The Americans, using their Norden bomb sights and H2S – Height to Slope ground scanning radar – would high-level attack specific targets by day, regardless of cloud cover, and the RAF would carpet bomb by night, with the aim of flattening residential areas, destroying civilian morale with thousands of casualties. He had to get out of the city, and take Irmgard with him, or there was every chance neither of them would be alive tomorrow morning.

Much as he hated the idea, it would be safer to leave the Mercedes behind. He collected the BMW, locked up the garage and arrived unchallenged outside Irmgard's apartment. Like Werner, she was only too aware of the close and almost continuous whistle and *crump, crump* of exploding ordnance. He hauled the BMW onto its stand and rushed to try the buzzer, but to his frustration, there was no response. *Of course! The residents would have taken shelter in the basement.* Running to the side of the building, he was relieved to see that the door was open, presumably in case the occupants had to try to evacuate the cellar. He found her inside, huddled up with a group of neighbours. She looked up in surprise. He held out a hand to help her stand.

'Come with me; we have to get out of here.'

Irmgard neither argued nor asked questions; she simply allowed him to half-pull her into the street and to the motorcycle. 'Get on,' he shouted as a near miss whistled down to explode only a couple of blocks away. Fortunately, she was wearing a pair of slacks and a warm jacket. It would be cold, but she would survive the ride well enough. The bike started first kick, and they were away, riding dangerously fast from the city centre and into the relative safety of the suburbs. There were few other vehicles, just the occasional ambulance, fire truck or police car, not one of which took the slightest interest in a trench-coated motorcyclist fleeing the city with a girl riding pillion – not that any of them could have caught up with them anyway. There were even fewer pedestrians, just the odd one walking quickly, shoulder almost pressed to a wall, as if that could somehow protect them till they found shelter. When they reached the surrounding countryside, well away from the worst of the danger zone, Werner stopped briefly.

'Munich's going to get plastered,' he told her, shouting over his shoulder above the noise of the bike's tick-over. 'We have to get to my place at Buchbach.' She knew where the village was, but this was the first she had heard of "my place". This was no time to ask questions; she just thumped his back with her acceptance, and they were off again.

The lodge was out of the question. He would have to use the main gates, there could well be a guard, and there was always the chance that someone from the manor hospital would call on his father during daylight hours. He took the track from the lane and pulled up outside the cottage. Hearing the noise from the BMW, Joe Roots opened the door, Walther in hand, which he turned back to set down on the kitchen table before coming out to meet them.

'Thank God, you made it,' he said with obvious relief. 'You can see and hear from here that Munich's getting a pounding.'

'It's only the beginning,' said Werner. 'The Americans are going for industrial targets, but I reckon tonight the RAF will carpet bomb the city itself.'

Joe followed them into the cottage's one living-room-come-kitchen. 'You'll have to stay here,' Werner said to Irmgard, 'at least until we know what's happened. And that might not be for a day or two.'

'There's only two bedrooms,' pointed out Joe. 'If you want, Irmgard can have mine.'

'But what will you do?' asked Werner. 'I suppose you could bunk down in here,' he said, his hand indicating the living area where they were standing. Joe shook his head. 'Been thinking about that old barn with the vehicles in it,' he replied. 'Don't seem right, somehow, that all the stuff we have in there is just left unattended. I've fixed up the doors, and the place is dry and secure. I could take a wood stove from one of the other cottages and set myself up real comfortable, like. You and Irmgard stay here, and I look after the other place. Makes sense…'

'Grateful, and thanks,' said Werner, after a moment's thought. 'I'll tell Father about Irmgard after dark; then, perhaps in a day or two, we can go and see what's left of Munich.'

'Can I come with you when you go to meet your father?' asked Irmgard.

'Don't see why not,' said Werner eventually. 'I think the old general would enjoy meeting you. And don't be put off by his manner. There's a saying I learned in England: his bark is worse than his bite.'

* * * *

They were out of the Munich flak zone, and the escort fighters were keeping off some of the German Fw 190s and Messerschmitt Bf 109s, but it appeared to Isaac that the *Luftwaffe* had managed to put a hell of a lot of extra squadrons into the air. The fighters on the approach and flak on the bombing run had already taken a toll. Now, on their home run, the B-17s were no longer flying in big-box formations but in isolated groups of four to six aircraft, huddled together for mutual support as they tried to fight their way back to England. But with so many smaller formations from which to choose, too many of the enemy fighters were getting through their screen to attack the now more vulnerable bombers.

Isaac knew it was time for a course change, to put them on a different route back to the coast, but his head felt thick and heavy, his thoughts sluggish. He couldn't for the life of him work out what was wrong.

'Pilot to Navigator…'

No response.

'Pilot to Navigator, do you read, over…'

Nothing.

He glanced sideways at his co-pilot. String's head was slumped on his chest as if he were asleep.

Isaac shook his head violently from side to side, trying to clear his thoughts. *It had to be asphyxia!* The condition in which an extreme decrease in the concentration of oxygen in the body, accompanied by an increase in the volume of carbon dioxide, leads to loss of consciousness and death. One of the hits they had taken must have damaged the oxygen storage area directly behind the cockpit. If he didn't get *Rosie* down to breathable air damn fast, they were all going to die.

He pushed forward, and the B-17 went into a frantic dive, way past VNE, or Velocity Never Exceed. Isaac managed to reach over and pull off String's mask before settling back into his seat, all the while blessing the designers and construction engineers who had put *Rosie* into the air, which was screaming over her airframe. Fifteen thousand... fourteen... thirteen... at this altitude, the air was breathable.

'Roper,' he yelled as String's head lifted and he looked woozily around the cockpit. 'Help me!' Isaac was sweating hard with the effort of trying to haul Rosie out of her near-suicidal dive.

String's hands were back on, and slowly, slowly, they levelled her out at twelve thousand feet. They were safe for the moment but alone in the sky.

'Get back,' Isaac shouted to Roper. 'Pull their masks off so they can breathe.' String nodded his understanding and staggered out of his seat. He was back a few minutes later, giving a thumbs up. 'They're all awake,' he shouted back. With their oxygen off and masks only half back on, Isaac once more had control of his crew.

But below, a lone B-17, smoke pouring from two dead engines, was surrounded by a swarm of fighters. On her own, the craft and her crew would not survive for long. Isaac could have held his height and course, but he could not leave the other aircraft to her inevitable fate. Two could mount a better defence than one. 'Hang on,' said Isaac over the intercom. 'Stand by all guns, we're going down again.'

Chapter 38

They were barely halfway to the stricken bomber when a burst from one of the fighters must have entered the cockpit. The nose pitched up, a sure sign that the pilot had been hit, probably the co-pilot as well because the B-17 half-rolled onto a wingtip then dived vertically to the ground. There were no parachutes. The aircraft fire-balled into a field. Sadly, Isaac levelled out *Righteous Rosie* and began to climb for height and safety. But they had been seen. Four fighters from the previous attack were climbing towards them. They were experienced pilots: not flying directly towards them, but to a point above and astern, from where they could execute a high-speed dive onto his ship. He knew Johnny Carstairs, his engineer and dorsal gunner, and Dutchy Holland, the tail gunner, would do what they could. But against this sort of odds, on her own in the sky, *Rosie* was in trouble.

They flew on, Dutchy providing the occasional report as the fighters positioned for their attack. Suddenly, there was an excited whoop from the tail gunner.

'We got company, Captain,' he yelled. 'Five 17s, diving on the fighters, screaming down towards us. They're flying them 17s like they was frickin' pursuit Mustangs. And they got one of them Kraut bastards...'

Isaac realised that the diving bombers could only be those they had been flying with before the oxygen emergency. Against all standing orders and protocol, they had sacrificed their own height and safety to box up with his command ship. He blessed them for their courage. Now, it was six B-17s in a safety box against three fighters.

'They're not going to mix it!' Johnny exulted, his voice a mix of triumph and relief. 'They're breaking off to look for easier prey.'

'Thank you, gentlemen,' said Isaac quietly to the other captains over the command net.

'We know you got a crap navigator,' said an undeclared callsign. 'Thought you might need us to show you the way home.'

Isaac double-clicked an ack and smiled appreciatively at the humour. The box was on its own, but now they were over Luxembourg. Soon, it would be Belgium and then the coast. They were approached on the way by a lone fighter, but the sheer volume of fire from the massed 50-cals of a group of B-17s persuaded the enemy pilot to sheer away. Once over the channel, they eased the formation apart for more relaxed flying, till they entered a holding pattern over their Swanton Field.

Isaac alerted the tower to his problem of the blown tyre and ordered the remaining aircraft to land first. Fortunately, there was a good crosswind, which helped him hold *Rosie* level with aileron as they finally touched down. Eventually there was nothing more he could do. The flat tyre shredded itself on the tarmac and the wheel started to dig in. At first, he fought the turn with full rudder, till *Rosie* slowed to a safe speed, before allowing her to ease off the runway and onto the grass, safely out of the way. Half a gentle ground loop from the stately old lady, her wings level, till she slewed to an otherwise undamaged halt. The fire tender and ambulance waited for a few minutes before returning to their station. Isaac looked at his watch. They had been airborne for just under eleven hours.

* * * *

Werner opened the kitchen door to the lodge, which his father had indicated would be left unlocked until he retired for the night and, as they had agreed, called out to announce his presence. They joined the general, a half-full brandy balloon on a table beside his fireside armchair in his small but cosy drawing room. Irmgard stood somewhat hesitantly in the doorway. Werner took her hand to draw her into the room alongside him.

'Father, this is *Fraulein* Irmgard Stein,' he said quietly. 'She has been helping with the resistance. I managed to rescue her when the Americans were bombing the industrial sector. I'm pretty sure the RAF will flatten the city tonight.'

The old general levered himself to his feet, offering his hand. 'Welcome to Buchbach, *Fraulein* Stein,' he said courteously. 'Werner, help yourself and the young lady to a drink, then tell me your news.'

So his real Christian name is Werner, Irmgard noted. *So much for the Erich Hahn.*

They had been talking for about twenty minutes when there was a knock on the door. '*Herr General*,' called a voice. 'It is *Leutnant* Schneider from the hospital. I hope I am not disturbing... you have company.'

'He must have heard voices,' said the general very quietly. 'There is no point in making a run for it. You will have to stay here.'

He opened the door to see an *Oberartz*, or senior physician, in the uniform of a senior lieutenant of the *Wehrmacht* medical corps. '*General* Scholtz, I am Wilhelm Schneider,' he introduced himself. 'I come with a message from our commandant.'

So he's Werner Sholtz, she realised.

The general could have asked what it was, leaving him on the doorstep. But that would have been unconscionably discourteous, quite out of character, not to mention suspicious.

General Scholtz managed an amiable smile. 'You had better come in, *Herr Oberartz*,' he invited, stepping back from the door. 'We are enjoying a drink,' he said over his shoulder, leading the way into the drawing room, 'but you are welcome to join us.'

As the general had hoped, Schneider was a little embarrassed. 'That is most kind of you, *Herr General*,' he replied. 'But I simply wish to extend an invitation. The officers are having a small drinks party on Saturday evening to celebrate the successful opening of the hospital. You have been most generous in helping to transform Buchbach Manor. *Commandant* Volkmar extends a warm invitation for you to join us. But you have guests...'

The general thought quickly. '*Fraulein* Stein,' he offered, 'and her companion – '

'*Major* Schumann,' interrupted Werner quickly, using the first name that came into his head. 'Also a family friend. We are just visiting briefly. I shall be returning to the front in Italy the day after tomorrow.'

This appeared to satisfy the doctor. He turned back towards the general, who said, 'Please thank your commandant for his kind invitation and say to him that I am delighted to accept.'

Schneider formally clicked his heels and bowed his head. 'Allow me to show you to the door,' offered Werner politely.

'I hope everything will be all right,' Irmgard whispered as Werner rejoined them.

'I think so,' responded the general. 'You are both well away from the hospital for now, on the other side of the estate. And even if he wanted to, which is highly unlikely, there is no way he can prove there is no *Major* Schumann fighting somewhere in northern Italy. Quick thinking, Werner, my boy.'

'Either way, we'll finish our drinks and then I think perhaps we should be going,' Werner announced. 'If my suspicions are correct, I would like to be back in the cottage before the next raid starts.'

* * * *

Hours later, they were woken by the sound of explosions as 234 Lancaster bombers and 16 Mosquito fighter-bombers pounded the city of Munich. Werner put on his dressing gown and lent his overcoat to Irmgard, who had emerged from her room sleeping in the only clothes she had with her. They watched in horror as an orange glow developed, wider and wider, above the central and residential part of the city. Eventually, the explosions and flak died away and the drone of aircraft engines faded into the night. Joe called out as he arrived to join them.

'Thank your lucky stars you weren't underneath that lot,' he said to Irmgard, who just shuddered at the sight of what had to be massive and widespread destruction.

'We'll give it forty-eight hours then go take a look,' said Werner. 'Later this morning, I think we should visit Irmgard's parents. They must be worried sick by now.'

'Can I come with you?' she asked.

Werner shook his head. 'Best not. There is less risk if Joe and I use a couple of uniforms and take a *Kübelwagen*. If the worst comes to the worst, we can always shoot our way out, like we did last time, but there's no sense in exposing yourself to danger.'

Disappointed, she nevertheless accepted that he was right. 'We might as well stay up now,' Irmgard observed, 'I'd never get back to sleep. Werner, why don't you get dressed, and I'll make us all some breakfast.' Her use of his correct first name raised an eyebrow, but he made no comment.

Mid-morning, Werner and Joe arrived at the Stein smallholding without incident. As Werner had remarked, pretty much all civil personnel and resources would have been summoned to help with the devastation inflicted on the city and the people of Munich. As they parked in the yard, *Frau* Stein emerged from the kitchen door and threw her arms around Werner.

'*Meine Tochter*...' she shouted, tears streaming from her eyes.

'Your daughter is safe and well,' Werner replied quickly. 'I was able to collect Irmgard from her apartment building during the first raid, when the Americans were attacking the industrial area. By the time the RAF began their night attack, we were safely out of the city, at my home in the country. I left her there only an hour or so ago.

'But I am to ask if you would kindly pack her clothes and things,' he added. 'At the moment, she has only what she was wearing when we fled the city.'

Herr Stein appeared at the doorway. 'Josef,' she cried, running to her husband. 'She is alive! Our Irmgard is out of the city, safe and well with *Herr* Erich.'

Werner walked towards the couple, now standing in an embrace, arms around each other. *Frau* Stein had tears running down her cheeks. Josef's eyes were glistening.

'Thank you from the bottom of our hearts, *Herr* Erich,' he managed. 'We could see the destruction... we have been so worried, fearing that we might have lost our daughter, our only child. I am in your debt... we cannot thank you enough for taking the risk to bring us this wonderful news.'

'We'll leave you in peace,' said Werner, also indicating Joe, who had remained in the *Kübelwagen*.

'You most certainly will not,' ordered *Frau* Stein, drying her eyes and taking firm hold of Werner's upper arm. 'You will both come inside. Not *ersatz* coffee, Josef, something stronger to bless this wonderful news!'

* * * *

They decided to stick with the *Kübelwagen* and their uniforms disguise for the journey into the city. He suspected that there would have been heavy aircraft casualties on both sides, so Werner doubted the RAF would risk a single photo-reconnaissance mission so far behind enemy lines. That being so, he was sure a first-hand report on the aftermath of the raids would be appreciated by both the British and American air forces.

There was a risk in taking Joe, who did not speak German, and his medical exemption papers would be of no use if he were in uniform. But Werner opined – and Joe agreed – that the extra firepower, if they ran into trouble, outweighed this concern.

Irmgard was anxious to know if her apartment had survived the raid, so Werner undertook to try to find out. She was also worried for the safety of her friends, Ursula, Horst and Gerhard. She gave him their addresses. Not knowing what they would find, Werner said they would do what they could.

There was some isolated damage on the edge of the city – the occasional bomb load off-target or released from a stricken aircraft. But as they approached the city centre, they encountered almost a wall of destruction. They were flagged down by two police officers standing alongside their vehicle.

'Afraid you can't go any further,' one of the officers told Werner. 'The roads are full of rubble. We think the city centre was the target area for last night's raid. Initial estimates are that something over eighty per cent of all buildings have been destroyed.'

'Can we go forward on foot?' asked Werner.

'Where are you two from?' asked the policemen. To Werner he did not sound suspicious, more like idle curiosity.

'We're stationed in Augsburg,' he replied. 'Our boss, *Major* Berger, said he wasn't getting much news over the *Reichs-Rundfunk-Geselschaft*. He thinks either the *RRG* doesn't know what's really happening or our national network of regional public radio is deliberately censoring the news. Either way, a lot of our men in Augsburg have families in Munich, so he told me to get over here and find out what's really been going on.'

'It's bad,' the officer shrugged his shoulders. 'In fact, it couldn't be worse. Probably over a quarter of a million have lost their homes. A lot killed; thousands injured.'

'So can we go forward on foot?' repeated Werner.

'Help yourself,' came the reply. 'But it's at your own risk – falling masonry as well as the occasional unexploded bomb.'

'Would you mind keeping an eye on our vehicle?' he asked.

'No problem,' came the genial response. 'What's up with him?' said the second policeman as Werner beckoned over Joe, who had a scarf wrapped around his mouth.

'Had a tooth extracted this morning,' Werner told him. 'No dentist, so it had to be done by a nurse. I gather she made a bit of a botch of it. You can try talking to him, but you won't get a very polite reply.'

'See you later,' said the first officer with a sympathetic grin. Shouldering their weapons, Werner and Joe set off into the city centre.

Over the next hour and a half they made five discoveries: Werner's apartment building was a pile of rubble, as was Irmgard's; Ursula's was untouched, although they did not attempt to make contact; the lock-up containing the Mercedes was undamaged – more important than the apartment, said Werner, because it contained their only source of petrol for the BMW or the *Kübelwagen*; and sadly, they were still digging bodies out of the collapsed remains of the house in which Horst and Gerhard had shared rooms.

Fortunately, the two *Polizei* were still on station, keeping traffic and non-essential personnel out of the city centre. Joe went straight to the *Kübelwagen*. Werner thanked the officers but, in response to a question, just shook his head from side to side. The Allies would welcome his report, but they would be taking sad news back to Buchbach.

Chapter 39

Fred Laxham was pushing seventy. A widower, he and his late wife Vera had not been blessed with children. Fred lived in a small cottage on the edge of Swanton village. He knew his health was failing but could not give up a lifelong habit of lighting up yet another Capstan Navy Cut medium strength. So he had no intention of paying the doctor to tell him what he already knew. Before the war, trade had been good. Now, with civilian motoring virtually non-existent, the garage was barely surviving. He had some savings. If he could sell the business, that little extra would allow him to see out his days tending his beloved vegetable garden.

It had come as quite a surprise when the black American man had asked if he wanted any help with the garage.

'Can't afford to pay you,' he responded bluntly.

'Been asking around,' came the reply. 'Folks tell me you want to retire. No family to take over. I gots to think of my future, after the war. If you let me work with you for a while, in my free time, I gets to look at da business. Maybe even make you an offer. Very least, you gets some free help, so you got nothing to lose. If ah's interested, we kin talk. If not, ah just walks away.'

It had quickly been obvious, from the low volume of poor-quality work coming in, that financially, the garage was in a parlous state.

'But you have to look at the books, understand the finances,' Flossie had insisted, 'if you're thinking of taking it over for after the war.' Whilst she admired his vision and ambition, she knew he was an infant when it came to the practicalities of putting a value on the Laxham garage.

'Look,' she said. 'I told you I had a clerical job before I was married. You never asked, and I had no reason to tell you, but before my Edward came along, I worked for a company with its own accounts department. Originally, I was only hired as a cleaner and tea girl, fourteen years old, straight from school and with no qualifications: sweeping the floor and pushing the refreshments trolley around mid-morning and afternoon.'

'Go on,' Spencer encouraged her, keen to know more of Flossie's past.

'You remember my friend Susie – the one who helped with Sergeant Hoskings,' she reminded him. 'Well, her mother had been a shorthand typist. Mrs Hall even had her own typewriter, a Royal portable, in a suitcase. She was going to teach Susie, and she said I could learn as well. After a few months, we were quite good at it.

'Back then,' she went on, 'I was seeing one of the young clerks at the firm. Nothing came of it because I wouldn't let him have what he wanted, but he knew the lady who was in charge of female personnel administration quite well. I think they were neighbours or something. Anyway, whilst we were still walking out, he told her about me. Mrs Clarke was a really nice lady – a spinster, so she had always been independent, financially. She asked me in for an interview. Said I *could* apply to be employed as a typist, but she liked my ambition to better myself and get on in the world and offered to give me a chance as a trainee bookkeeper. Explained that it paid more and was a much better career. A lot of bookkeepers were women back in those days between the wars. I jumped at it.'

'So what happened?' asked Spencer.

'I never qualified,' she admitted, 'because after a while, I met Edward, and he proposed. You had to leave work once you were married. But provided I can have access to the books, I'm sure I picked up enough to find out what the business is really worth – save you from making a mistake with your savings.'

Anxious as he was to be rid of what he now saw as a burden, Fred Laxham made no objection. One Saturday morning in late May, Spencer and Flossie walked into the small area of the main shed that had been partitioned off as an office. It was the only warm part of the building, but there was an unhealthy smell from the fumes of a paraffin heater.

'It's all there, Miss,' said Fred, indicating a pile of ledgers and a mass of paperwork. 'Spencer's going to help me with a tractor gearbox, so we'll leave you to it.'

The accounts were in a terrible state. For a start, there had been no entries for the last two months. The work was all low-value, agricultural stuff. When she compared the entries in Fred's booking-in diary with invoices sent out, she realised he had not even billed for all of it. Flossie prepared a profit and loss assessment covering the past twelve months. As she told Spencer later that evening, the garage was barely making enough to cover its basic outgoings. As a business, it was worthless.

'So,' he said eventually, having spent some time looking at the figures, 'the only value be in da property an' equipment: a forecourt wit pumps sellin' virtually nah fuel, a shed wit nothin' more than a few tools an' two inspection pits, an' all surrounded by da best part of a field. But it's on a busy road. Add in fuel sales, aftah da war, plus a dealership – I still think it's a prime site.' His analysis, Flossie had to agree, was spot on. She was pleasantly impressed with his grasp of the potential.

'If you agreed to take ovah da books,' suggested Spencer, 'and we made sho' everyone paid fo wat da garage be doin' now, would derr be 'nuff income to keep Fred on till da end of da war, maybe just part-time? From wat I'm hearin' on da base, we is probably lookin' at a year at most, maybe less. I can help out, but I'm still committed to da US Air Army.'

It was a friendly enough negotiation, conducted over a couple of pints in the snug of The King's Head. Fred was only too happy to receive a small income in exchange for reduced hours, and they agreed the sum of one hundred and fifty pounds for the freehold of the property and contents, which, Flossie told Spencer, was a fair price but still a bargain. Swanton Garage would be under new ownership. All they had to do now was raise the finance.

'Can't be a problem,' she suggested, 'after all, we have the house as security.'

Spencer surprised her by announcing that he had half of what they needed anyway in his Post Office savings account. He had been content to live on his pay, sending home or banking money from his appearances at The Manor. He would ask his sergeant for a half day off and see a bank manager in Peterborough to arrange everything else.

* * * *

Spencer was surprised to be summoned to Isaac Hofmeyer's office, where a uniformed major introduced himself as Robert Holdsworth. Colonel Hofmeyer announced that he had a meeting with his engineering officers, so he was leaving them to talk.

'Sit down, soldier,' said Major Holdsworth, indicating one of the two chairs round the coffee table. This was even more unusual. Pfcs did not sit to talk with majors. Spencer seated himself rather nervously on the edge of the chair, knuckled hands on his knees, back upright. If the military had a position for "sitting to attention", this was it.

'Ever heard of my outfit?' opened Bob Holdsworth. 'I'm with the United Service Organisation – the USO for short.'

'Sir, heard you provide entertainment fo our troops, shows an' things, but nevah seen one,' Spencer replied, wondering where this conversation was leading.

'We were formed in 1941,' the major began, by way of explanation, 'on the orders of President Franklin D. Roosevelt. I'm part of the Special Services Division. You have probably listened to our radio programmes. We also manage the Army Exchange System, which you know as the PX. I'm here because the entertainment branch produces shows for our servicemen worldwide. Priority has been for soldiers in the field, mostly up till now in the Pacific theatre. You may have read in the *Stars and Stripes* that many show business celebrities have volunteered their services: Glenn Miller, Marlene Dietrich, Mario Lanza, Pete Seeger – big names like that.'

Spencer nodded his agreement.

'But what people don't realise,' Holdsworth continued, 'is that most of our entertainment is provided by talent drawn from our own service personnel. My remit is to establish a more widespread set-up for personnel based in the United Kingdom. I know up till now, you guys here have enjoyed yourselves within the local communities, but some good 'ol American music and a few dancing girls with the right accent to chat to would definitely be good news. Remind everyone over here what they're fighting for back home.

'We sent out an information request to our unit commanders,' he went on. 'Colonel Hofmeyer has spoken very highly of you. I want you as part of our organisation. Would you be prepared to join us?'

'Doin' what, sir?' asked Spencer.

'I attended your last show at The Manor,' said Holdsworth. 'You have an ace combo, but more to the point, you're a great crooner. Best I've heard in a long time. And believe me, son, I've heard a few in my time. I was a showbiz agent before the war.

'I want you to set up a USO club here on the base,' he explained. 'Colonel Hofmeyer has kindly agreed to provide the necessary office accommodation, and he is already using hangar space for dances, so no problem doing the same for concerts. His maintenance section can put up some extra huts for female personnel – they're volunteer entertainers, but they also mess with the men, as well as providing free coffee and donuts. They talk to the boys in their off-duty time. It's a huge morale booster.'

'So, who will I report to?' Spencer queried, still somewhat confused by this turn of events.

'Colonel Hofmeyer's the base commander,' Major Holdsworth replied. 'So ultimately he has the right to approve or veto anything you do here. But technically, you transfer to my outfit. You won't be bringing your musicians with you. Hofmeyer says he can't afford to lose almost half his entire maintenance team, but you will be able to call on them for entertainment here, which is a huge plus: a ready-made band to support the lady volunteers we ship in. In time, we should be able to draft in more maintenance men, which would free up your musicians. The colonel has said he's agreeable to that.'

Isaac thought it over, but not for long. 'Will he let *me* transfer, sir?' he asked.

'Already sorted,' came the response. 'He says with your voice, you're wasted in a maintenance unit.'

'Then I'd like to give it a try, sir,' said Spencer. 'But just one thing. Will us coloured boys be allowed into da entertainment?'

'The USO is probably the least segregated part of the entire United States military,' said Holdsworth with a grin. 'But I'll tell you in the strictest confidence that your CO said he'd only allow the formation of a USO unit on his airbase provided that all personnel, and he emphasised the *all*, had full and equal access.'

'Sir, that settles it,' said Spencer.

'Welcome aboard,' came the response. 'Didn't tell you before, but there's an icing on the cake. Your new position carries the rank of sergeant. Only acting to start with, but we'll sort the paperwork tomorrow. We'll have a small celebration when you put up those stripes.' He stood and extended his hand. 'Proud to have you with us, son,' he said, by way of informal dismissal.

Spencer left the office feeling ten feet tall.

* * * *

His sergeant fixed it so Spencer could drive himself to his appointment in Peterborough, at the bank recommended by Flossie's uncle, Bill Harding, who knew the manager quite well as they held the account for The King's Head. At first, Flossie had wanted to accompany him. She worried that the manager might be prejudiced because of Spencer's colour. She feared he might not even be allowed an account, never mind a loan. But he argued that he wanted to do this himself.

'Got to be able to operate on my own if ah's gonna be a black businessman in this country,' he insisted.

'Appointment with Mr Melgrove,' he said to the lady behind the counter. He was shown into an office along a corridor leading from the counter area. A tall, surprisingly young-looking man stood to greet him. Anthony Melgrove, Spencer noticed immediately, had only one arm. His right sleeve was pinned neatly up above his elbow. Which was a shame, thought Spencer, because Melgrove was a good-looking young man with what he thought of as an honest, open face. Straight black hair was Brylcreemed down in a short back and sides. He extended a left hand, which Spencer shook awkwardly with his right.

'Sarn't Almeter, won't you please sit down,' he invited courteously. 'Norway,' he added by way of explanation, looking down at the empty sleeve. 'So I got my old job back. The bank was glad to have me, with so many volunteering or being called up. Lucky, in a way, I got an early promotion, and at least I'll survive the war. Not all our staff will be coming back.'

Melgrove was impressed by the huge black man in front of him in the immaculately pressed uniform. He knew quite a lot about Spencer Almeter – there had been a long phone conversation with Flossie's uncle a few days previous. But he did not let on.

After they had finished that conversation Bill, a wily former company sergeant major, had one more call to make. He wanted to help Spencer. He liked the young black American who appeared to have won the heart of his niece, and he admired the way he stood up for her against the unwelcome attentions of that white airman.

'So, Sarn't Almeter,' said the bank manager, 'I understand you have a business proposition to discuss?' Spencer realised from the clipped pronunciation of his rank he was almost certainly speaking to a former officer. He had rehearsed his case with Flossie. Suddenly, now, it was not so easy.

'I'm engaged to a local lady,' he began, forcing confidence into his voice. 'After the war, we plan to marry and settle in Swanton. In the village,' he added somewhat superfluously, trying hard to speak proper English. Melgrove left him to continue, although he already knew what was coming.

'There's a garage,' he went on, 'and da elderly owner wants to retire. I been workin' with the base maintenance unit…'

He went on to describe his history and the plans he and Flossie had for the future. 'She's been through the books,' he went on, 'and provided a summary of the present financial situation. It's all here,' he said, handing over a sheet of paper.

'As you can see,' he pointed out, 'provided my Flossie keeps da accounts up to date, meanin' she sends out all the bills on time and chases up on payment, then da business can afford to employ Mr Laxham part-time and service the loan. But neither me nor Flossie will be taking anything by way of wages.

'As it stands right now, the way it's operating, as a business da garage isn't really worth anything,' he concluded, 'but I want to buy da freehold. It's a potential gold mine, aftah da war. Fuel sales on a main road, a dealership when civilian motorin' comes back, which it will. You best see how it's taken off back home, in da States. Got to happen here.' In his enthusiasm, despite best intentions, his speech had lapsed.

'And you need finance,' said Melgrove thoughtfully. His time in the British Army had taught him to judge the man, not his background, the colour of his skin or the way he spoke.

'Some, Mr Melgrove, sir,' Spencer responded, 'but not too much. I gots savings, seventy-five pounds sterling, in a Post Office account. Ah only needs the other seventy-five. And me an Flossie, we got security. We own a house in the village. We is prepared to put that up…'

Melgrove was more than half persuaded. If Almeter had been a Brit., he wouldn't have hesitated. But to a foreigner, a black American serviceman… it was unprecedented. Despite what Bill Harding had said, the temptation to go back home to the States after the war might prove too strong…

There was a knock on the door. It opened a fraction.

'So sorry, old chap,' said a voice from somewhere behind him, vaguely familiar to Spencer, although he couldn't immediately think why. 'Didn't know you were busy. The gels out front were all occupied. I'll wait.' The door closed.

Then it opened again. 'Spencer, my dear chap, how the devil are you?' he boomed. Colonel Edwin Houghton strode into the room as fast as his two legs and silver-topped cane would let him. 'It's been a while.' He looked at Spencer's arm. 'And you've been promoted, old chap. Hearty congratulations. Jolly well deserved, and all that.'

'Colonel, you two know each other?' said Melgrove, rising to his feet and quite taken aback.

'Oh yes, we dined together not too long ago. Must do it again,' he said to Spencer. 'Tonio's all right? I'll ask the memsahib to get in touch with that lovely young lady of yours.'

He turned back to the bank manager. 'Wanted a word about the golf club account, but that can wait. Sorry to have interrupted.

'Look after him, young Melgrove,' he demanded, turning to leave. 'I've served alongside these fellows. Splendid chaps,' he echoed over his shoulder, heading for the door and closing it with something of a bang behind him.

The colonel's personal investment account made him the bank's wealthiest individual customer. The golf club's business made an important contribution, too. And there had been the phone call from Bill Harding. Melgrove addressed Spencer, his mind made up.

'The bank will accommodate you,' he said quietly. 'You will also need further funds, if you are to expand as you have indicated, after the war. So I will make sure that we earmark an additional facility, should you need to draw down on it. I believe we shall embark upon a relationship that will prove beneficial to us all.'

Strange, he reflected afterwards, *that the old colonel should pop in like that. It had never happened before. He always made an appointment...*

Chapter 40

Werner and Irmgard had been listening to the news on the BBC General Forces Programme, which was also broadcast on the shortwave frequencies of the Overseas Service. The raid on Munich had been covered earlier in the week, but by Thursday, the twenty-seventh of April, it was no longer an item. He switched off the wireless.

'I really would like to go back into the city, try to find out what has happened to my friends,' said Irmgard. 'Obviously, I can't go in your *Kübelwagen*. Anna says the bus and tram services aren't up and running again yet, but there's no reason I can't ride a bike. At least then I would be able to get around.'

'Where would you stay?' asked Werner. 'All right, you have papers, and you are perfectly innocent, as far as the police are concerned, but your flat's now just a pile of rubble. And you can't ride there and back in one day. It's too far.'

'Ursula's building is still standing,' she countered. 'I'm sure she would put me up for the night. I'd like to go tomorrow.'

Reluctantly, Werner agreed.

'I'll finish off supper,' Irmgard volunteered. Werner had shot a hare. It had been hung, then jointed and marinated in a bottle of his father's red wine for the last twenty-four hours. Initially browned in some of their precious butter, it was being slow-casseroled with stock and root vegetables. After two hours, the aroma was beyond temptation. Whilst she was setting the kitchen table, he went to fetch another bottle of wine. Joe had been invited over for supper with his father, so they were on their own.

'Time for another glass, then we eat,' Irmgard announced, replacing the lid on a huge cast iron dish. Werner had noticed that when in Munich, she had worn typical baggy student clothes, but those he had brought from her parents' home were somewhat more fashionable. Tonight, she was wearing a beautifully tailored pair of slacks and a slightly transparent blouse that made no secret of her *Büstenhalter* beneath.

And although there was an age difference of more than ten years, Werner found her both amusing and extremely good company. He was, he realised, growing very accustomed to their existence together, even after only a few days in the cottage. Perhaps being attracted to her might be more accurate. For the first time in many months, he realised he had not thought of Anneliese every day.

She caught him looking, and her eyes held his for a few seconds before she glanced down to pick up her glass.

'You told me you were Erich Hahn,' she said slowly. 'But I now know that you are Werner Scholtz...'

'And a German, with a father in this country, but working for the British,' he finished for her. 'Don't tell Ursula, not even your parents,' he ordered succinctly.

Irmgard nodded her agreement. She was quiet for a moment, then, 'Do you like me, Werner Scholz?' she asked simply.

He was taken aback. Eventually, he said, 'I have really enjoyed our time together. I hope you have, too.'

'I have,' she said quietly. 'And now, I think supper is ready.'

The hare was superb, although Werner's mind was anywhere but on his meal.

'I'm not really happy about you going on your own tomorrow,' he told her.

'I've taken bigger risks before now,' she responded. 'But here's what I plan to do. Instead of going directly into the city, I'm going to pedal home. I want to see my parents anyway, and we'll agree that I went there the day of the bombing, instead of coming here with you. And I have been living there ever since. That way, if I'm questioned, I have genuine papers, my parents will back up my story, and I have a cast iron alibi for where I have been over the past few days. No need for me ever to mention Buchbach,' she added, 'and no way anyone can prove anything different. I'll go on to Munich on Saturday, stay overnight with Ursula, and I'll be back Sunday.

'Now,' she said firmly, suggesting that she would brook no argument, 'I'll wash, you dry, then we'll have another glass of wine.'

* * * *

Wilhelm Schneider had obviously been detailed to look after him, as he was greeted at the door and taken directly from the entrance hall to meet the commandant.

'Ludvig Volkmar,' he said, offering his full name and extending a hand. 'Delighted to meet you again, General Scholtz, and thank you once more for your understanding. I am so sorry we had to move you from your fine home.'

'I am perfectly all right in the lodge, Commandant,' he replied. 'I'm an old soldier. I can make myself comfortable anywhere. This place was far too big for me anyway, and I thoroughly approve of it being turned into a facility for our wounded.'

'Ludwig, please,' offered Volkmar.

'Gustav,' the general responded.

After a few more pleasantries, he moved on to allow the commandant to greet other guests, not least the local mayor – the *Bürgermeister* had just arrived with his wife. Schneider introduced him to some of the other officers and civilian doctors. The General quite enjoyed the informal celebration, not least because the *Wehrmacht* medical corps obviously had access to food and drink no longer available to the civilian population. But he did not enjoy the company of the *Oberartz* quite so much. It was obvious from a number of unpleasantly jocular remarks, and the occasional laughter with his brother officers, that Wilhelm Schneider was also a supporter of the Nazi Party. After an hour of chatting with a few of his more like-minded civilian hosts, the general felt it was time to leave. He expressed a wish to thank Commandant Ludwig, and the *Oberartz* dutifully led the way.

'Before you go, Gustav,' he said, 'I have a request to make.'

The general raised his eyebrows.

'As you suggested, we stored all the furniture we do not need in your west wing. Which, in fact, was most of it. The pictures were all wrapped and placed there, too.'

'Yes, thank you,' the general replied. 'I gather it was all done most carefully.'

'Would you mind if we were to replace some of the pictures?' the commandant asked. 'Not the family ones, of course, but a few of the landscapes would brighten our officers' main rest room, and I would really appreciate it if I might be allowed to choose one for my office.'

The general thought for a moment. 'I have already taken those of most value for the lodge,' he said. 'If you would like to take some of the others, please help yourself. For the wards, too, if you wish. I hope they will brighten them up for your patients.'

'That is most generous of you, Gustav,' the commandant replied. 'I will have Wilhelm attend to it personally. He also acts as my assistant, in addition to his medical duties, so you can be sure we will continue to take every care. I'm most grateful, and thank you again for coming this evening.'

At the door, the general also thanked Schneider for his courtesy in looking after him and took his leave.

It was not until the following morning that the *Oberartz* entered the drawing room of the west wing, where he knew the pictures had been stored. There was also some furniture: a sideboard, a few tables with chairs upended on top of them, and a chest of drawers below a glass-fronted display cabinet that had once contained a superb collection of *Meissen* and *Fürstenberg porzellan*. The valuable figurines had been wrapped and packed away.

Beneath the cabinet were two half draws atop three that were full-width. He opened the left-hand one to find jigsaw puzzles and a stamp album – presumably to amuse children on a rainy day. Idly, he opened the other drawer and took out an old photograph album. Underneath each photo, on the black pages, someone had annotated a caption in white ink.

He saw "*Gustav, Johanna and Werner, June 1916*" in neat handwriting, the proud parents seated behind a little boy standing to attention in his sailor suit. There were more photographs as he turned the pages, the general in uniform during the years of The Great War, then garden pictures from sunny days in the nineteen twenties. He thought he saw a developing similarity, but it was the final page that confirmed his suspicion. Underneath the formal indoor photograph of a uniformed officer, it said simply: "*Hauptsturmführer* Werner Scholtz, Berlin, 1939". Now he thought about it, the likeness between Werner and his father was all too obvious. The former *Hauptsturmführer* would have been promoted by now, but why had he passed himself off as *Major* Schumann? It didn't make sense.

On the other hand, he had certainly admired the other family friend, that Irmgard woman. She was no Aryan, that was for sure. But she was an alluring little baggage. If Schumann, or Scholz – whatever the *major's* name – was truly by now back at the front, there would be no harm in asking the old general how he might contact her. He had not, however, been slow to pick up the unsubtle response to some of the conversation at the reception. The former General Scholz was no friend of the Party. Perhaps he would pay him a visit this evening, ask about the photograph, try to find out the lay of the land.

* * * *

Werner was relieved when he heard the tinkle of a bicycle bell. He moved quickly to the door, which he had left open to a warm afternoon, to greet Irmgard as she stepped through the frame and leant her bike against the front of the cottage.

'Thank heaven you're back safe,' he said, impulsively giving her a hug, which she returned.

'Come inside and pour me a long cold drink,' she told him. 'I'm so sore. I'm never going to bicycle that far again.'

'Well,' she began in response to his question and setting down her glass, 'at least there's *some* good news.

'As you know, your apartment and mine are gone. You said that Ursula's was still standing, but they were digging people out of the rubble where the boys lived. When I got to Ursula's place yesterday afternoon, all three of them were there.

'It seems Ursula had invited Horst and Gerhard round for supper on the night of the raid. Apparently, it developed into quite a late drinking session, and they were all still there when the second bombing wave arrived. It was too dangerous to walk back to their own lodgings, so the boys bedded down at her place. All three of them survived,' she finished triumphantly.

'That's great news,' he told her, reaching across the table to place his hand over hers. Werner glanced at this watch. 'We're due at the lodge for supper,' he said. 'Time for you to freshen up. I'll go and collect young Roots.'

Joe was in the barn, which was pleasantly warm from a wood stove taken from another cottage. He had also salvaged several items of furniture. Apart from having to share it with a collection of weaponry and vehicles, he had converted the old building into a very comfortable billet.

'You go ahead,' he responded to Werner's reminder. 'I've only just finished working on the last of the window repairs. Give me time to wash and brush up, and I'll be along in a half-hour or so.'

The general was in the kitchen when Werner and Irmgard arrived. Two bottles of red, opened to breath, stood on the table. Dusk was falling. The lights were on, the curtains undrawn, a window half open.

'We might as well sit down in here and wait for Joe,' he told them, pouring drinks. 'Anna's done something with that brace of rabbits you gave me the other day.' Already, there was a tempting smell from a pot on the range.

Night had fallen when Schneider approached the lodge. The front was in darkness, but there was a loom of light from behind the building. Very faintly, on a gentle breeze, he could hear voices. He wasn't sure... they sounded the same as on his previous visit, but Schumann – or Sholtz – should have returned to Italy days ago. Stepping quietly, he made his way across the front façade and then along a paved path to one side. From a few paces behind on a rear lawn, before it gave way to the forest, he could see the same three individuals seated at a kitchen table, glass in hand. He moved next to the door, alongside the window, to listen.

It wasn't really a track, just a way through the trees where a few branches had been lopped to allow easier access. But Joe could see well enough in the light from a gibbous moon. He paused just short of the edge of the tree line. There was a figure leaning against the wall at the back of the lodge, listening to those clearly visible inside.

He made his way in deep shadow afforded by trees and vegetation till he was able to step silently across the lawn to approach the figure – whose total attention was on the open window – from behind. They were about the same height and build, but Joe had used the base gymnasium almost daily to keep himself in top shape for his role as rear gunner. He slapped an elbow throat lock on the intruder and yanked it tight with his free hand. At the same time, he swung him in a quarter circle till they were facing the door. He used his right elbow to flick up the latch and the man's head to push it open. The intruder was choking for air, so he was in no position to resist when Joe pushed him into the kitchen.

'We have a spy,' he said to a startled company.

Werner was the first to react. 'Let's make him sit,' he said, pulling out a kitchen chair. Between them, they pushed him down, and Joe gradually released the choke hold.

'It's *Leutnant* Schneider from the hospital,' exclaimed the general.

'Whoever he is, he's been listening outside. I don't know how long he's been standing there by the window, but he's probably heard every word you've been saying.'

Schneider was leaning forward, elbows on his knees, still struggling to draw breath and, at the same time, dry-retching. Joe stood in front of him, ready to restrain him again if necessary.

The general quickly walked next door into a laundry room and came back with some strong garden twine, which he handed to Werner. 'Tie his hands behind the chair,' he instructed.

'We were talking about the new cell, I'm afraid,' he went on.

Schneider had almost recovered his breathing. 'Please,' he said, 'I won't say anything.' They all detected a hint of desperation in his voice.

'He's a Nazi,' the general told them. 'I had to listen politely to his remarks last evening when he was talking to like-minded colleagues. Some of them were pretty vile. We would be fools to trust him.'

It was Werner's turn to enter the laundry room, where his father kept a few tools in a drawer, handy for any small job around the house. He reached inside the breast pocket of his shirt.

Back in the kitchen, he stood in front of Schneider. Without warning, he punched him hard in the stomach. The *Leutnant* gasped, his mouth opening automatically. Werner took a pair of long-nosed pliers from behind his back and shoved them, hard, into Schneider's mouth, at the same time squeezing the handles and lifting his head back with his other hand.

Schneider's eyes opened in terror. He tried not to swallow, but the capsule had broken, and cyanide was trickling into his throat. Werner dropped the pliers and clamped a hand over his mouth, then chopped him several times in the throat. Seconds later, the convulsions started, soon so violent that the chair whipped on its legs. It crashed over sideways, and Schneider lay still.

Irmgard gasped, then lowered her face into her hands.

'Had to be done,' said Werner, 'or he would have betrayed us all.'

She looked up. 'What do we do now?' she asked.

'We can't bury him,' said the general flatly. 'They have to discover the body, otherwise, there will be a search all over the estate. They'll find the cottage and the barn.'

'We'll dump him in the bushes not far from the hospital, just off the main drive,' said Werner. 'Someone will notice him soon enough in the morning. Right now, there's a strong smell of almonds, but by tomorrow, there'll be nothing from the cyanide to show in his bloodstream, even if there's an autopsy, which is unlikely. Almost certainly, they'll assume it was a heart attack.'

'You used your own suicide pill?' asked Joe.

'I never intended to take it anyway,' Werner replied. 'So give me a hand, we have to carry him outside. Hands and feet job. He's soiled himself.'

The two of them freed him from the chair and picked up the body.

Half an hour later, they were together again in the kitchen. The general left the second bottle of wine for Irmgard but fetched a bottle of schnapps for the three of them. He set the casserole dish aside from the range. It would be another hour before he replaced it. Waste was unthinkable and unaffordable, and the casserole and bread would absorb the alcohol. But it was almost a silent supper.

Chapter 41

Werner decided that he and Joe should keep a low profile for a while. Joe helped General Gustav with what was left of the farm. This, unfortunately, was not an option for Werner. There was always the risk that someone from the village might recognise him, possibly with disastrous results for them all. At least they were almost self-sufficient for food. And the estate continued to produce meat for the pot, although much of it was provided courtesy of Werner's stolen *MP40* or his father's twelve bore.

There had been no obvious reaction to the death of *Oberartz* Schneider. And no further contact until the commandant, returning to the hospital in his staff car, came across Gustav making his way along the drive towards the lodge. The Mercedes stopped, and he wound down the window.

'Good to see you, Gustav,' he greeted him.

The general returned the courtesy. 'How are things at the hospital?' he asked.

'Pretty much all in order,' came the reply. 'Although I don't know if you have heard the news about Schneider?'

'The young officer who kindly looked after me at your most excellent reception?' observed the general casually.

'Indeed,' responded the commandant. 'Obviously, you aren't aware. Sadly, he suffered a heart attack whilst out walking. His body was returned to the family. I arranged representation for all of us at his funeral.'

'I am sorry to hear that,' said the general, speaking slowly and seriously. 'We did not share a political view, but, nevertheless, it is sad news. And I doubt you can afford to lose a good doctor.'

The commandant noted the general's remarks with equanimity. Wishing Gustav a good afternoon, he wound up the window as his staff car pulled away.

Werner had been right, thought the general. *They had accepted the death as a heart attack.*

* * * *

Irmgard set a bowl of soup before him. He sniffed at it appreciatively. 'Don't expect too much,' she cautioned. 'It's basically a root vegetable pottage. But at least there was some stock from the last pigeons you shot.'

'It's good,' he told her appreciatively. 'You're a clever girl.'

She looked at him. 'Is that all you think of me,' she asked very directly.

'Do you remember when I asked if you liked me?' she went on, 'and you made some bland remark about enjoying our time together?'

'I meant what I said,' he responded, wondering where this was leading.

'And I told you that *I* enjoyed *your* company,' she replied, 'which is also true.'

Irmgard picked up her spoon, and they began to eat. Nothing more was said for a while, but they both sensed an atmosphere. 'More bread?' she asked eventually, extending a wooden platter towards him. He shook his head.

Irmgard refreshed both of their glasses. 'This is ridiculous,' she said suddenly, taking a generous gulp as if for courage. She walked round the table and stood beside him.

'I'm no virgin,' she said, 'and neither are you. And unless I'm very much mistaken, we both want each other. Am I not right?'

He stood, half-turned towards her, and they were embracing, before she drew back her head to kiss him, open-mouthed, on the lips. Eventually, they came apart, panting, and not just for air.

Irmgard unbuttoned her dress. It was a warm evening; beneath it, she wore only her *Büstenhalter* and knickers. She hitched her bottom up onto the table, her toes barely touching the floor, and began to unbuckle his belt. Werner fumbled at his shirt buttons, his mind in turmoil. Irmgard slid forward and stood briefly to push down his trousers and undershorts and then her knickers, from which she removed one foot before flicking them aside with the other.

Back on the table, her hand encircled his erect penis as she guided him towards her. Werner felt her ankles rising on the back of his thighs. Now her arms were under his, her hands gripping the back of his shoulders, then down to his buttocks, pulling him deeper inside. One of his hands was behind her back, the other pushing up her *Büstenhalter* as he covered her erect nipple.

'I hate this war. For God's sake, fuck me,' she whispered.

* * * *

Werner listened at his schedule times, but there were no further messages for him after his report on the Munich raid. The BBC Overseas Service reported the German retreat from Cassino in May and their withdrawal from Rome at the beginning of June. But the greatest news of the year was the D-Day landings on the sixth day of that month.

'At last,' Werner observed to Irmgard, 'Germany is now forced to fight on three fronts. The end of the war can be only a matter of time.'

They had settled into a new and happy relationship. Werner had sourced another single bed from one of the disused cottages, and Joe, who was a good carpenter, turned two singles into a generous double. Tactfully, he refrained from further comment.

Irmgard found Werner rather old-fashioned. At first, he usually opted only for *die Missionarsstellung*, but he responded readily to her enthusiastic and more adventurous lovemaking, not always in the bedroom. It seemed to restore his youth, taking away the difference in their ages. But he confessed, one early July afternoon, as they lay naked on the grass alongside a stream running through the estate, that he was troubled by – and bored with – inactivity.

'It's all right for Joe and father,' he told her. 'They can work on the estate. You can go and help Anna looking after Father and the lodge. But apart from the occasional spot of hunting, I have been cooped up in the cottage for almost two months now. I'm being wasted over here – achieving nothing for the war effort.'

'I don't want you taking any more risks,' she responded, half rolling onto her side so she could put her arm across his chest. 'You keep saying the war will soon be over. Then we can begin a proper life together. Surely, if we are safe here, it's better to be patient?'

'There must be something I can do…' he told her, but then pulled her on top. *At least the dear man has learned something*, she thought as she knelt astride him.

But his mind was made up. On his next schedule, he would ask for specific instructions.

* * * *

'What with D-Day and everything, we have been guilty of rather ignoring Werner,' Sir Manners confessed. 'Now it's looking like Paris will be liberated by the end of August, or next month at the latest.'

'I had a message sent for him to wait out,' Doreen responded, 'but that was a while back. Since then, I have been talking to both the Americans and the RAF, as well as the Army. I asked them how we could best make use of a small asset such as we have, in Bavaria, deep inside enemy lines, whilst our troops are pushing on towards Brussels and Antwerp. They came up with an interesting answer.'

'Which is?' put in Bill Ives.

'Telephones and electricity,' exclaimed Doreen. 'Particularly their 'phone system. Apparently, it has separate lines dedicated solely to the use of the *Wehrmacht*. The Army said that if we could degrade the German ability to communicate internally, it could make a big difference. I'm assured this could seriously jeopardise German efforts at the front line – because Hitler is a control freak, and insists on taking all major decisions in Berlin or Berchtesgaden, that then have to be communicated back to the armies in the field.'

'Both the US Air Army and the RAF told me that these enemy facilities are too small and far too numerous to be vulnerable to air attack,' she went on. 'Apparently, neither of them has the ability for such precision bombing, so they have left them alone and concentrated on major industrial targets, as well as morale-sapping attacks on civilian habitation.'

'Then that's what we'll use him for, at least for the time being,' decided Sir Manners. 'We are already doing the same thing in Western Europe, so Bavaria will help us with our efforts further south. Let's get a message off on his next schedule.'

Werner pointed out that whilst he was keen to try, his small team would need a resupply of arms, ammunition and – particularly – additional explosives. But getting it there was the problem. Once more, to his frustration, he was told to wait out.

Bill Ives undertook to find a solution. He asked around, and it was the Americans who came up with the idea. A couple of days after Werner's schedule, he received a 'phone call from an Air Army staff officer who introduced himself as Colonel Paddy Beavers. 'Boston Irish,' he added by way of explanation. He offered to call on Bill and Doreen.

'We're introducing a new variant of our Mustang fighter,' he began once coffee had been served. 'It's the P-51D. Although what I'm about to tell you isn't an original idea. We are stealing it from your Royal Air Force.

'Not too long after D-Day,' he went on, 'the RAF strapped a barrel of beer under each wing of a Spitfire and delivered them to France. All right, a bit of a stunt, maybe, but it was one hell of a morale booster.

'Now,' he warmed to his theme, 'this latest bird of ours is superior to anything the Krauts can put up in any numbers: it's faster than an FW 190 or the Messerschmitt Bf 109. It has a better ceiling, and with two drop tanks, it has a range of 1600 miles.'

'That's all most impressive,' put in Doreen, 'but how does that help us?'

'You need to drop supplies to your cell in the Munich area,' Paddy responded. 'A conventional drop from a single bomber would be suicide. But if we pack one of the drop tanks with what your man needs, and you would know what that is better than me, we ought to be able to fashion some sort of 'chute to see it safely down. With only one drop tank of fuel, the Mustang should still make it there and back, even if the pilot does risk landing on fumes.' He couldn't help a rather satisfied smile. 'But I'm told we have a volunteer and two others who are willing to fly as wingmen, with two drop tanks of fuel, to see off any enemy fighters. These P-51s pack six 50-cal wing-mounted machine guns. They are blowing the Krauts out of the sky.'

He sat back, evidently well pleased with his presentation.

* * * *

Captain Stuart "Boney" Parte flicked the primer switch up to ON and held it for three seconds. Next, he lifted the cover to the starter switch and raised it whilst he counted six propeller blade passes in front of his cockpit. Still holding the starter switch, he moved the ignition magneto switch to BOTH, and the 12-cylinder Packard Rolls Royce Merlin engine spat exhaust flames as it roared to life. Finally, he moved the mixture control to RUN and let go of the starter switch. A touch on the throttle quadrant settled the engine to thirteen hundred RPM, and he continued with his cockpit checks while it warmed up.

Behind him, Lieutenants Rex Barry and "Blue" Beard also taxied their Mustang P-51Ds around the perimeter track. Once airborne, they formatted alongside, climbing at an optimum one hundred and seventy miles per hour. They would cruise at altitude to save fuel, crossing France at two hundred and seventy-five miles per hour before transgressing into Swiss air space. Finally, they would turn north over Austria before descending to their destination.

There had been light flak along the way, crossing the coast of France, but nothing serious. Outbound, they had not been attacked by enemy fighters. Perhaps they had not been identified as a sufficiently large enough formation, although these days, the

Luftwaffe's ability to interdict bombing raids had been reduced significantly. Boney and his wingmen did not expect such an easy ride on the way home, although they could take comfort from their advantage in both speed and altitude.

* * * *

It was almost two in the morning. Although it was high summer, Werner and Joe were both cold, deep in a forest near Augsburg. They were not far from where Werner had dumped the bodies of the three *SS* soldiers after leaving Ilse's farm. But it was isolated. They would have to light a decent fire to indicate their position. And they had to be far enough away from Buchbach not even to hint at any connection. They were both wearing *SS* uniforms and carrying *MP40*s. The site had been chosen a week ago, a decent-sized clearing along a forestry track a good kilometre from the nearest country road.

Boney continued his shallow dive. Navigation had not been too difficult. The mountainous topography of Switzerland and Bavaria was distinctive under a half moon. Now, he could make out the buildings and shadows of Augsburg under his wingtip – they were on course for the grid reference and dropping through three thousand feet. He preferred to rely on his mark one eyeball rather than the instruments. If they were there, the reception party should be about five miles ahead.

On the ground, Werner heard the faint buzz of aero-engines. Gradually, it grew louder, definitely heading directly towards them. It could only be their drop. He turned to Joe.

'Light the beacon.'

Joe recoiled as the petrol-soaked fire ignited with a "whoompf", damn near singeing off his eyebrows. Werner ran to the *Kübelwagen*, parked to face the right direction a short distance away on the track so that the flames would not subsume its headlights. He flashed a dot-dash-dash twice. A light on an aircraft somewhere just south of their position blinked once. The pilot had found them and had seen his Morse "W" recognition signal. A moment later, there was a huge roar as he pulled on the power and began to climb away. A single white parachute drifted down, more or less in their direction.

Werner and Joe ran through the trees to where they thought it would land, less than fifty yards away. *Luck had nothing to do with it*, thought Joe. *It has been a brilliant piece of flying.* The drop tank, trailing its parachute, crashed through a layer of branches, coming to rest as it snagged, bobbing up and down, almost touching the ground. Werner cut it free with his knife. They lowered it gently.

'Christ,' said Joe, 'it's too big.' The people in England had not known what transport arrangements existed at the other end. And it had never occurred to Werner to tell them. It was a standard-sized tank, pretty much the chord of the wing. With the fabric roof up, no way would it fit into the '*Wagen*. With it down, they might as well wave a sign saying, "We've got a drop tank". And it was not that long before first light. Werner hefted one end. Fortunately, it was not too heavy.

'We have to empty it,' he said, 'put the contents in the back of the vehicle and drive with the hood up.'

'There's every chance someone will have seen the drop,' Joe pointed out. 'We could have company anytime soon.'

'We don't have a choice,' Werner pointed out, bending to pick up the nose cone. 'We carry it to the '*Wagen*, chuck everything into the back, put the hood up and run for home. Fast as we can.' Fortunately, the engineers back in the UK had split the drop tank horizontally, with hinges along one side and clips on the other. All they had to do was flick up a line of small levers to release the top and fold it back.

They worked feverishly. The contents had been well wrapped against the drop, particularly the explosives and detonators, so it was more a question of hasty bundling than careful stowage. But it was an anxious ten minutes before they had everything loaded, weapons jumbled with boxed ammunition and other packages, although they had to put the hood up to hold the final top layer in place. Werner pulled down the 'chute and covered the load in the back, then clipped shut the empty tank and stood upright, pausing to listen, but the forest was quiet.

'We can push earth and branches over it,' he said to Joe. 'Won't take more than a few minutes, then we're out of here.'

Driving without lights, Werner followed the track back to the road. At the junction, he switched off the engine to listen again. Nothing, although they still had to circumnavigate Munich to reach Buchbach. Their luck seemed to be holding, but for how long...?

Chapter 42

'Werner kept his last schedule,' Doreen Jackman reported to Sir Manners in their Baker Street office. 'Apparently, they got back to Buchbach without incident. And best of all,' she added, 'the three American pilots all returned safely, despite the best efforts of the *Luftwaffe* somewhere over France. I 'phoned the base commander to ask after them and to express our thanks, which he promised to pass on. He mentioned, in return, that a pilot with the seemingly piratical name of Lieutenant Bluebeard shot down a 109 in the process. But they appreciated the call.'

The SOE recipient of their conjecture was, at that moment, seated in the lodge with his father, Irmgard and Joe.

'I vote we knock off some sort of telephone facility every two or three weeks,' said Werner. 'In a way, it's like the railways. Blow up a line, and twenty-four hours later it's mended. If we cut telephone wires, they'll soon be up and running again. But an exchange building – that could be out of order for quite some time.

'I'll do a recce this coming week,' he went on, 'but I would love to start with something ambitious, like the main exchange in Munich. At the moment, it's probably lightly guarded, if at all. But once we establish an attack pattern, they are going to have to react. The more important targets will soon be protected. So we take them out first.'

'Why don't you let me do the recce?' asked Irmgard. 'My papers are all in order. Safer that you and Joe swanning around in uniforms with no identity documents. And I can take the bus into the city now they are up and running again. No need to risk being caught with a stolen *Kübelwagen*.'

'She's right,' said the general, who had been quiet up till now. 'Much safer to let Irmgard go take a look.'

Werner didn't like the idea one little bit, but he had to admit Irmgard and his father were right.

Unbeknown to them all, whilst the French 2nd Armoured Division paraded through a liberated Paris, on that same 26th August she caught the bus to Munich. She had to walk the last mile. The target of another American bombing raid on 16th July had been an aero-engine factory, but cloud cover meant that they had to go for their secondary objective – they offloaded instead onto the city centre, reducing what was left of it to rubble and killing nearly fifteen hundred people. A new, temporary bus station had been set up outside the worst of the destruction zone. This time, Ursula's building was no longer standing. She had no idea what had happened to the occupants. She, Horst and Gerhard might be anywhere. Or they might be dead underneath a pile of masonry.

With nowhere to stay for the night, Irmgard had to set about her reconnaissance and catch the last bus back to the manor. The main post office had been destroyed, but she knew that the telephone exchange was not in the city centre. It was a separate building with a counter service area to the front and a much larger room housing telephonists and communications equipment to the rear. An alleyway provided vehicle access to a paved yard behind the building, its double doors standing wide open, presumably to allow post office vans to collect and deliver sacks of mail. The back door into the building was also ajar.

Irmgard made a point of memorising the details and then stepped hesitantly into the yard. A large box thing against a wall was humming quietly. She stopped at the door. Inside, she could see a bank of telephonists working at their station. She took a step forward.

'Can I help you, *Fraulein*?' said a voice. She turned to see a uniformed guard standing behind her, a submachine gun slung across his chest. There was a chair against the wall. Presumably, he had been sitting there, watching, as she entered. He was a good-looking young man, no more than her own age. Almost certainly a conscript, she thought, certainly not a battle-hardened veteran.

'I… I've come from the city,' she stammered, trying deliberately to sound like a confused female. 'I was wondering whether I could get through to the counter section from here?'

'I'm afraid not,' he told her. 'This is the telephone exchange. It's quite separate. And you are..?'

'My name's Renate,' she said evenly, using the first name, that of a neighbour, to come into her head. 'Renate Dorf.'

He eyed the attractive young woman in front of him, with her faintly olive skin, dark hair, green eyes and exotic looks. Not your usual *Bayrisches Mädchen*, no blonde hair or blue eyes, but she was a looker. 'There is a door into the counter section,' he told her, 'not for the general public, but I might be able to unlock it and let you through.'

'And what would you want in return?' she asked, her head slightly to one side, smiling and flirting at the same time.

'I'm off duty at six this evening,' he told her.

'Poor you,' she said. 'You have to hang around here all day?'

'It's an important facility,' he replied. 'Has to be guarded, day and night.' Clearly, he was trying to impress her. 'Someone else will take over from me after my shift when the main post office closes. Perhaps you might like to join me; we could go for a beer?'

She touched his cheek with her fingers. Instantly, he blushed. But she did not want to arrange a meeting and then stand him up. That might look suspicious.

'You're a lovely young man,' she said gently. 'But I'm spoken for. He's a soldier like you. But would you open the door for me anyway?'

She had let him down very gently. His pride was intact. He smiled back and gestured towards the door. Imgard had seen all that she needed. Once through the door, he lifted a counter flap so that she could walk into the main concourse. She thanked him and joined a queue but turned and walked into the street as soon as he had closed the door behind him.

* * * *

'We'll give it a couple of days, then go in,' Werner suggested, 'say Tuesday next week. Maybe fairly early in the morning, when there are fewer people about. I'm thinking some time after nine o'clock.'

'Why not later, after it's closed for the day? Then the post office will be empty,' offered Joe.

'The main gates into the back yard were open when Irmgard was there,' Werner pointed out, 'presumably for mail deliveries. It might be locked at night. And besides, the *Kübelwagen* will be a lot less conspicuous by day.'

'It won't be easy with just two of us,' Joe observed. 'Ideally, we want someone to stay with the vehicle. It would help if we could contact Horst or Gerhard.'

'We can't,' said Irmgard. 'We don't even know if they are still alive. But I can do that,' she added, 'stay with the vehicle, I mean.'

'This isn't a mission for a civilian, least of all for a woman,' Werner said.

She rounded on him. 'Why not?' He could tell from her voice that she was annoyed. 'I managed to kill Franz Klein,' she said vehemently. 'You have taught me to shoot – said yourself that I'm pretty good with a Browning HP. We have *SS* and *Schupo* uniforms. I can cut one of them down, stick my hair under a cap and flatten my tits without a *Büstenhalter*. What's wrong with that? At least you can be sure that the '*Wagen* will still be there when you need it.'

There was an awkward silence for a moment. 'She's right, you know,' said Joe eventually. 'It will take two of us to handle the building if we are to avoid civilian casualties. We have to have someone guarding the vehicle whilst we are inside. It's our only way of being sure we can escape afterwards.'

Reluctantly, again, Werner had to agree.

* * * *

They were there just after the post office opened. The yard was rectangular, the building and outside wall forming the top and bottom, with two longer walls on either side. Werner drove through the open gates and parked, rear bumper against one of the long walls. A uniformed figure appeared in the doorway, submachine gun across his chest, eyeing the *Kübelwagen*, apparently unconcerned by their arrival.

'It's the same lad who was here the other day,' said Irmgard quickly. 'Leave the *Schmeissers* in the '*Wagen*. I can handle this. We can get close without a shot being fired. Come with me.' Werner stood behind her and unfastened the flap on his holster.

He was still looking at them, waiting, when they were almost at the door. 'It's Renate,' she said, smiling. 'You didn't recognise me in uniform, did you?'

He stared for a moment in disbelief. 'What the...?'

Joe grabbed his arms as Werner punched him hard in the stomach, clubbing the back of his head hard with the butt of a Walther as he doubled over. He fell to the floor, out cold.

'We'll drag him back to the vehicle for now,' said Werner, 'Irmgard can cover him whilst we go in.' Joe removed the soldier's weapon, and the two of them pulled him across the yard.

Werner lifted a satchel from the back of the *Kübelwagen*, Joe hefted a can of petrol, and they set off towards the building. Werner placed a lump of plastic on the electricity box and pushed in two pencil fuses, just to be sure. Sometimes, one on its own did not go off. At the outside end, inside the copper tube, was a glass phial of cupric chloride. When the tube was crushed, and the glass broken, acid would eat into a wire holding back a stretched spring. Once released, the collapsed spring would activate a striker, which in turn would set off a percussion cap at the other end, inside the explosive. The pencils came with a delay period from ten minutes to twenty-four hours. Unfortunately, they were not entirely accurate. There was a "plus or minus" factor with the timings.

Inside, there were four telephonists, all middle-aged women, wearing headphones and facing their equipment stations set against a side wall. Two more chairs at the far end, nearest to the public post office next door, were unoccupied. The telephonists had not seen Werner and Joe, who were standing by the door. Joe quickly moved along the row, tapping each woman on the shoulder and pointing towards Werner, who made a sign with his hand that they should remove their headphones.

There was a rest area in the centre of the room with a couple of kitchen tables and chairs. 'Ladies,' said Werner, stepping forward, 'this is an emergency. Please leave your posts and sit down here.'

'What's going on?' asked one of the women, but they were complying with his request, the uniform giving him sufficient authority.

Joe returned to the door, his *MP40* now pointing in their direction but down at the floor, not threatening them directly.

Werner ignored the question. Instead, he moved to the centre of the bank of telephone equipment, removed a large lump of explosive, and inserted two more pencil fuses. Next, he opened the connecting door to the post office. There were only two counter clerks and a couple of customers in the front half of the building.

'There has been a bomb threat to the exchange,' he called out. 'Please vacate the building immediately. For your own safety, please wait on the other side of the road.' They scurried out. He closed the double doors behind them and slid home a bolt.

Back in the exchange, he walked over to the telephonists. 'We are going to blow up the exchange,' he said calmly. More than one hand flew to a mouth to cover a gasp of astonishment. 'In a moment, we are going to release you. Please exit calmly, walk out of the yard through the gates, and if you will take my advice, I would go home for the rest of the day.'

'Off you go, ladies,' he said calmly. 'Don't go near the vehicle in the yard – the driver has orders to open fire.' The four women lost no time in obeying.

As the women were leaving, Joe emptied the contents of his can onto the switchboard equipment. Taking a pair of pliers from his satchel, Werner crimped the copper tubes housing the acid. Both pencils were now live.

With a last glance at the explosive, Werner and Joe left the room. Werner paused only to crimp the pencils on the electricity box before jogging over to join the other two at the *'Wagen*. 'Let's throw him in the back,' he said to Joe, indicating the still unconscious figure on the ground. 'We'll chuck him out in the street, safely beyond the blast area.'

'He could identify us,' Irmgard pointed out.

'So we drag him over there and leave him next to that box?' Werner demanded.

She shook her head.

'Fair enough,' he replied, and together they threw him aboard. 'Can't be much more than five minutes to go,' said Werner, jumping into the driving seat. Tyres screeched as he turned for the entrance. Outside, they stopped a short distance away. The lad was dumped unceremoniously on the pavement, minus his *MP40* and spare magazine. Werner had been concerned that the first explosion might blow the pencils away from the box outside, but seconds later, there were two distinctively loud detonations, the second massively greater than the first. Almost immediately, they could see flames flickering above the wall. The building was well alight.

* * * *

'I think we should lie low for a while,' opined Werner to the other two. They were enjoying a celebratory glass of wine after a successful day. There had been nothing on the news, but the general had tried to phone a Munich number, and the service was clearly out of order.

'I thought we might try Augsburg next,' he went on. 'But they are going to be on the alert after today. Extra guards, at least for a while.'

'Agreed,' said Joe. 'We'll just monitor the progress of the war for now.'

'The trouble is,' put in Irmgard, 'that young soldier we spared will have given them a good description of me, although it's probably not such a problem for you two boys. He only got a brief look before you clubbed him unconscious. But don't forget, my complexion is quite distinctive.'

'Nothing we can do about that,' said Werner, 'but best you stay out of Munich. Not that there's likely to be much left of the university anyway.'

Joe set himself up as their war progress watcher, spending time each evening listening to the BBC. Werner listened to the German news. Like Werner's cottage, Joe's barn did not have mains electricity, but the general had produced another accumulator wireless. Before the war the estate had provided a rectifier, which converted alternating current to direct current, to charge the lead-acid radio batteries for those living in cottages.

'Well, the British have surrendered at Arnhem,' he reported towards the end of September. But this was soon followed by better news: the Germans had surrendered at both Boulogne and Calais.

'Your hair looks different,' Werner observed one morning at breakfast. 'It's lighter – not so black.'

'I have been experimenting,' Irmgard replied, 'boiling up loads of daisies to extract chamomile. My mother taught me. It's an old Romany recipe. We make up a solution. It's a bit of a nuisance, but if you keep applying it, day after day, it eventually lightens the colour. I'm hoping to finish up looking like a honey-dark blonde with a suntan rather than a dark-haired gypsy.'

'Suits you,' Werner replied. 'But to me, you're beautiful either way.' She smiled gratefully at the compliment and went back to peeling her hard-boiled egg.

At the beginning of October, they planned and successfully executed an almost identical attack on the main post office and telephone exchange in Augsburg. In November, British Lancaster bombers, using 5-ton "Tallboy" bombs, managed to sink the Tirpitz, the pride of the German Navy.

In December, Hitler's last throw of the dice with The Battle of the Bulge failed to halt the Allies in their drive towards Germany. On Boxing Day, the *Führer* was informed that they could not split the Allied supply lines: Antwerp could not be retaken.

After a quiet Christmas at the lodge, Irmgard announced that she would visit her parents for New Year. She went alone on the bus rather than risking an excursion with Werner in the *Kübelwagen*. To his surprise, instead of staying overnight, she was back that same afternoon, visibly upset.

'What's happened,' he asked as she slumped at the kitchen table and wiped her eyes.

'It's *Mutti*,' she said, desperately trying to hold back her tears. 'Father's distraught. The bastards have taken her. Someone told them that she's Romany. They are going to put her in Dachau…' Head in hands, she collapsed, weeping.

Chapter 43

They changed into uniforms and loaded weapons. Werner carefully selected all the additional items he thought they might need and placed them in a large leather satchel. It took an hour and a half to reach Irmgard's former home, about ten kilometres east of Augsburg, using back roads as far as possible. She had insisted on going with them.

A two-man surveillance team at the edge of a wood watched through binoculars and reported their arrival.

Her father was seated at the kitchen table, head in hands, clearly still agitated and distressed. 'It was the *Ordnugspolizei*,' he told them, the *Orpo*. 'All the police are under the control of the *SS* these days.'

'Some of them are all right,' put in Irmgard. 'Those who were old-time policemen, but there are some right Nazi bastards amongst the younger lot.'

'I went to their station in Augsburg this morning,' said *Herr* Stein, 'and spoke to the *Rottmeister* on the front desk. He seemed sympathetic, but he could not give me permission to see Madlene. Just told me very quietly that she would be interviewed today and transferred to Dachau tomorrow morning. Then an officer came into the room, so that is all I was able to find out.'

'Once she's inside the camp, we'll never get her out,' said Werner. 'And I don't fancy attacking a police station, not with just the two of us,' he added, indicating Joe as well. 'If we are going to rescue her, it will have to be whilst she is in transit.'

'You would do that for me?' asked *Herr* Stein, astonished.

'There will be consequences,' he replied by way of an answer. 'For a start, you won't be able to return to the farmhouse, at least not until after the war. Pack a small bag, just absolute essentials for you and your wife, plus any personal documents you might need. You'll have to leave the livestock – turn them loose. Irmgard, I suggest you stay here and look after your father. Joe and I will be back later.'

'Where are you going?' she asked.

'There's more than one way out of Augsburg,' he told her. 'But eventually, they will have to take the main road, route eight. After that, there's only one turn-off for the camp. That's where we will hit them. They'll be almost there, home and dry, not expecting trouble. But we need to do a reconnaissance this afternoon and make a few preparations on site. Can't risk leaving it till the last moment, tomorrow morning.'

* * * *

Werner parked about seventy-five metres along the street from the main Augsburg police station, facing away from the entrance, which he could see clearly in his rearview mirror. It was still only seven thirty in the morning, and he had already dropped *Herr* Stein, Joe and Irmgard at the chosen ambush point. He sat there for over an hour, but there were few civilian pedestrians about at this time of day and none who wished to engage in conversation with a uniformed *SS* soldier in a *Kübelwagen*.

He watched as a black Mercedes-Benz 320 staff car pulled up outside the front doors. He was too far away to make out ranks, but two uniformed men on either side of a woman emerged from the building. They half-helped, half-bundled her into the back seat. One of the men carried what looked to be an

MP40 submachine gun, and the other, who sat alongside the woman, wore only a holstered handgun.

SS-Sturmbannführer Karl Abel was nervous. They had failed to capture the agent who landed by parachute near Augsburg last year. Three soldiers and a *Kübelwagen* had disappeared after the operation at that farmhouse, and no bodies had ever been recovered. Two dead police officers and a shot-up vehicle had been found in a wood near Augsburg, and Franz Klein, a student member of the Party, was found with his throat cut in a Munich park.

Not long afterwards, there had been a very successful two-man raid on the railway yard signal box: all the appearances of a small sabotage team operating in the area, and more recently, a *Kübelwagen* was involved when the Munich telephone exchange was destroyed, as well as during the Augsburg raid in October. More to the point, the description given by the guard who survived the Munich attack matched that of Irmgard Stein, who was known to be a former member of the White Rose and apparently a close friend of Klein.

But this Irmgard woman has disappeared, nowhere to be found. The head of the Augsburg SS detachment had come up with the idea. Her mother was thought to be a former Armenian, possibly a Romany. Lift her, give the old man her movement to Dachau details, and as the Stein daughter has almost certainly joined up with the resistance team, use her mother to draw them out.

There had been some debate about how to proceed. A *Kübelwagen*, two uniformed men and the Stein girl had arrived at the farmhouse yesterday afternoon. Abel had wanted to raid the building, but his boss had argued against it.

'We want them all,' he had insisted, 'and we don't know how many others there might be. So we stand a much better chance if we take them out when they try to rescue the girl's mother, which I'm sure they will.' *All very well for you*, thought Karl Abel, *but it's going to be me sitting in the decoy vehicle.*

Just then, another message came through to say that the *Kübelwagen* and two men had driven away. They had not returned by nightfall.

'Proves my point,' said the *SS-Obersturmbannführer*, 'and besides, even if they come back, I don't fancy a night attack. Too much of a chance that one or more of them might slip away in the dark. We'll stick with the original plan.'

Werner put the *Kübelwagen* into gear and pulled away quietly. Even if they noticed the single vehicle and its sole occupant well down the street, it would be a familiar sight – no cause for alarm. As he turned a corner, he saw that the Mercedes, too, had set off. He had to reach their ambush site with time to spare, and the Mercedes was faster than his *Kübelwagen*. But they had no reason to hurry. He coaxed every last ounce of speed from his 985 c.c. air-cooled rear engine. Fortunately, even on the longest straight stretches, the staff car did not reappear in his mirror. He would have his vital few minutes to spare.

But Werner was unaware that the Mercedes had slowed half a kilometre from the police station to allow another *Kübelwagen* to appear behind it, followed immediately by a covered *Wehrmacht* lorry which, on the orders of the *SS-Obersturmbannführer* in the *Kübelwagen*, contained an augmented section of battle-hardened men. All of them were survivors from the Russian front. More than enough experienced firepower to deal with a small resistance team.

He raced past the ambush point, turned right onto forest track – no time to turn the vehicle around – grabbed the satchel by its strap and ran back to where Irmgard, her father and Joe were positioned in the undergrowth, on the same side of the road. Joe had an *MP40* with a good supply of magazines. *Herr* Stein had been given a Walther. He had served in The Great War. It took him only seconds to become familiar with it.

After an anxious ten minutes, they heard the growl of vehicle engines. The Mercedes appeared. But there was also the breathy, higher-pitched, air-aspirated sound of a *Kübelwagen*, not yet in view. And more faintly, he could hear the engine rumble of a heavy lorry.

It was a trap. Someone had anticipated a rescue attempt and played them accordingly. *Gott sei dank* – thank God he had set the explosive in a pothole and covered everything with dirt. It was intended to stop the Mercedes, to be exploded in front of it so that they could extract *Frau* Stein. But now, he desperately needed an instant change of plan.

'Joe, take *Herr* Stein,' he ordered. 'Run up through the wood as far as you can, and when I blow that *Kübelwagen*, stop the Merc: tyres, whatever, then take out *Frau* Stein and run on to our *Kübel*. Irmgard and I will hold off the rest and then join you. Make sure the engine's running for when we get there.'

Joe and *Herr* Stein darted away. Werner watched as the *Kübelwagen* approached his bomb. When he depressed the plunger, the blast lifted the vehicle from the road and deposited it upside down on the far verge. No need to worry about the occupants. He heard shots from over his shoulder; hopefully Joe and *Herr* Stein effecting the rescue.

The *Werhmacht* lorry almost stood on its front bumper, so harshly did the driver bring it to a halt. It must have bought them precious seconds, thought Werner. Without warning, the troops in the back would have been thrown forward in a heap, but now they were debussing from the rear, left and right, either side of the road.

'Wait till I fire,' he said quickly to Irmgard, holding up a hand. Suddenly, he realised that they had company. Joe and *Herr* Stein had rejoined them.

'Saw them leaving the lorry. Too many for just the two of you,' said Joe. '*Herr* Stein told his wife where to find our *Kübel*.'

The troops on the other side of the road were obscured by the lorry, but it would be only seconds before they emerged to engage in a firefight. For now, Werner, lying prone, waited till enough on their side of the road were on the ground and moving forward, then adopted a kneeling position and opened fire. A second later, Irmgard and Joe were also firing. The front two men on their side of the lorry dropped to the ground, as did the first man emerging from behind the other side of the lorry. The rest took cover sideways into the undergrowth.

But they had taken out only three of the opposition. The rest would attack, heavy fire from one group whilst the other advanced, alternate fire and movement.

'*Herr* Stein, take your daughter and run for the *Kübelwagen*,' yelled Werner. 'Stay in the trees, me and Joe will cover you.'

'Irmgard,' her father shouted, 'my place is here. Run and look after your mother.'

Werner took a grenade from the satchel and lobbed it towards where the first group had taken cover, to keep their heads down. Joe took another and threw it at the soldiers emerging from the undergrowth on the other side of the road. Werner noticed that *Herr* Stein, who was now holding Irmgard's *MP40*, slipped in a fresh magazine with practised ease.

'We are still outnumbered; they are too strong for us.' *Herr* Stein struggled to make himself heard above the sound of the grenades and returned fire. 'It's my wife and daughter. I'll buy you time. Go,' he screamed at Werner and Joe, then with amazing courage jumped to his feet and charged towards the enemy, emptying his magazine left and right in the process, until a round burst through the back of his head in a spray of bone fragments, brain tissue and red gore.

But his sacrifice had given them a chance – the enemy had gone to ground under his onslaught. Both men threw another grenade. Werner tossed a smoke canister into the road and tapped Joe on the shoulder. They turned to run back through the wood.

They reached their *Kübel*, its engine ticking over. Irmgard must have started it. She and her mother were in the back. Joe took the front passenger seat. Werner tossed the satchel into his lap and jumped aboard. The lorry could drive past the Mercedes, but the survivors would have to climb into the back again, and it would be slower than the nimble *Kübelwagen*. Nevertheless, they could not turn back. Werner had to hope that the track did not lead deeper into the plantation only to finish up somewhere in a dead end.

'Where's *Vati?*' shouted Irmgard over his shoulder. Werner was concentrating on the forest track, driving as fast as he dared. Joe turned to face her, shaking his head slowly from side to side. Madlene had been watching and listening. Mother and daughter looked at each other, their eyes glistening. Irmgard turned to cling to her mother, and they held each other, silently sharing their grief.

Werner gave a sigh of relief when the track eventually led to a narrow lane. He turned in a direction which he hoped would eventually take them back to route eight. Fortunately, they were able to turn left, in the opposite direction from Augsburg, towards Munich and Buchbach. By now Werner was familiar with the country roads, and a report on the events of the morning would not reach the *Orpo* back in Augsburg for quite some time.

He could not risk the main entrance to the lodge, but by the time he parked in front of the cottage, Irmgard and her mother were more composed and not weeping, although he suspected they were still in shock. Joe drove the *Kübelwagen* back to his barn. Werner had invited him to come back for a drink, but he declined. It was a family matter, and he wanted to respect their privacy. Even so, he poured himself a very stiff three fingers of brandy... and then another.

It was growing dark. Joe lit his kerosene lamp. By now, he had dispensed with a glass, and the bottle was almost empty. He had nothing but respect for what the British OSS-types like Werner were doing in occupied Europe. But it was far worse than searching the sky from his turret at the arse end of a B-17. He took a last pull at the bottle and stumbled off to bed.

Werner, Irmgard and her mother had also taken a stiff drink, but only one, and were now seated at the lodge's kitchen table with the general as Werner recounted the events of the last two days. Madlene's handkerchief dabbed at her eyes as he recalled her husband's determination to save his family. 'He was an officer in The Great War,' she whispered. 'Iron Cross, second class. He would not have acted any other way...'

Irmgard was blowing her nose, her eyes shut tight. Both Werner and his father found themselves blinking rather more frequently than usual.

'You can't stay in the cottage, dear lady,' said the general. 'It's too small and it's very basic. Unless you have anywhere else to go, I would be only too pleased if you would accept a room here at the lodge, at least for tonight. I have guest bedrooms. Werner,' he ordered, not waiting for a reply, 'go and light a fire in the garden room and turn back the covers to warm off the chill.'

Although the three of them had not eaten all day, Madlene was so exhausted she would accept only a drink of water. Irmgard took her arm and helped her mother to bed. 'Thank you, General,' she said, sitting down again to a glass of wine. 'It has been a horrible three days for her. I can only hope that she will feel a little better in the morning.'

Chapter 44

Spencer woke to the joyful sound of children in the playground. The last place he had expected to find himself was in northern France, not far from the German border. His entertainment troop, billeted in a primary school, had put on a show last night. Afterwards, they stayed to have drinks with the G.I.s who flocked around the female singers and dancing girls.

He'd been in France for nine months now, since not long after D-Day. In his last months at Swanton, he'd organised what was now a thriving United Services Organisation club, then set up two more at nearby Norfolk and Suffolk Army Air Force bases, but now the war had shifted to mainland Europe.

As January morphed into February, The Battle of the Bulge had ended with defeat for the German forces, and the news came through in early March that British and American troops had crossed the Rhine. By the end of the month, the Russians were massing their forces 60 kilometres east of Berlin, and further south, they were not far from Vienna. The enemy was in general retreat inside the Fatherland.

Spencer was in his element as a member of the Special Services Division. He oversaw a sizeable group of talented civilian volunteers, musicians, dancers, and even a couple of comedians. He enjoyed conducting his orchestra – if not a "Big Band", certainly not far off – and none of his troop of entertainers appeared to resent a black man ordering their existence. However, it was more an exercise in cajoling and shepherding rather than shouting commands.

Best of all, though, he loved singing, where he found he could more than hold his own with his chorus "professionals". But not even they could compete with the showgirls, whose costumes and bare legs produced deafening hoots, foot stamping and whistles from G.I.s starved of American feminine company for months if not years. Today, or so he'd been told, they would cross into Germany. Tonight, another show for the boys.

He really had to try to send another letter to Flossie. But it wasn't easy... move, a new billet, chow, another concert, a late night, and the same again, day after day. He missed her, and now he was worried. She had written to tell him she was pregnant despite their precautions. He suspected it was the night before he had embarked for France. They had been too impatient. It had to be any day now...

* * * *

One last scream of pain, a final push, and a bloodied and mucus-covered war baby slipped into the world. The midwife cut the cord and passed the newborn to her mother's breast.

'You have a daughter,' was all she said flatly.

Not "congratulations, you have a beautiful baby girl", just a frown at a lightly hued infant. Flossie could see the disapproval on her face. A brown baby, the Americans would call her. Half-caste was the even more unkind British expression. Fortunately, a proud Grandma Harding was there to take charge. If she was sure everything was as it should be, she told the midwife, she was free to assemble her things and take her leave. Although she noticed the wretched woman could not resist a final lift of her nose.

Some time later, Flossie looked down at her tiny infant, now wrapped in a warm blanket and in her arms. Gladys pulled back the edge and smiled fondly at them both.

'Won't be easy, girl,' she said.

Flossie knew what she meant.

'I wish Spencer were here,' said Flossie reflectively.

'He's not,' said Gladys firmly. 'But anyone wants to say anything, make an issue, they'll have me to deal with first.' She patted her daughter-in-law's hand. 'Think she's done feeding. I'll settle her for you so you can get some rest. We'll write to Spencer tomorrow.'

'And bring me the books from the garage,' added Flossie. She had worked right up until the last minute. 'We're not making a fortune, but I have to keep it going – watch over everything – till Spencer gets back.'

Gladys settled the baby in its bassinet. Spencer had left a good sum in dollars with her. "For anything, just in case", he had said. But the business had been able to pay for Flossie's medical care.

*   *   *   *

At the Buchbach estate, since rescuing Madlene Stein, Werner and Joe had cut back considerably on their sabotage activities – partly on account of the atrocious weather but also because the authorities had to be on the alert for a small resistance team. They contented themselves with cycling out to cut telephone wires or to place a small charge against an unmanned electricity substation. All of which helped to irritate the Nazi war machine. Besides, it was obvious from listening to the wireless that they were in the final months of the war.

Having nowhere else to go, Madlene had accepted the general's offer of accommodation, in return for which she helped Anna with the domestic duties of the lodge. But food was becoming a problem. The winter had been the hardest of the century, and although Werner and Joe were occasionally able to take game from the estate, it was no longer plentiful. Otherwise, they lived on a diet of stored potatoes and what root vegetables they could dig from the frozen ground. The saving grace was the woodland, from which they took enough timber to heat one room in the lodge, and Werner and Irmgard's cottage, where Joe usually joined them during the day.

* * * *

The weather was warmer now, although even as March surrendered to April, it was still cold for the time of year. Lieutenant General Alexander McCarrell Patch tapped his map with the tip of a pointer. Facing him were the commanders of the 3rd, 42nd and 45th US Infantry Divisions, together with their senior officers and his own staff.

'We have Nuremberg,' he concluded his briefing, 'so now we take Munich.'

At the Buchbach estate, they could hear the distant rumble of heavy artillery.

'If I were the Americans,' said Werner, 'I would attack Munich from the north as well as from the west. That way, they cut off a retreat towards Berlin. I think that as far as they can, they will try to encircle the city.'

'Which makes Buchbach the meat in the sandwich,' observed Joe laconically. 'We're on wooded higher ground, a natural defensive position. Sooner or later, we'll have the *Wehrmacht*, or what's left of it, fighting on our doorstep.'

'I'll talk to father tonight,' said Werner. 'But my thinking is that we use the lodge cellar as a bunker for the general, plus Anna, Madlene and you, Irmgard. Whether you are found by the *Wehrmacht* or the Americans, you are obviously civilians and no threat to anyone.'

'But what about you two?' put in Irmgard.

'We are young men of military age,' Werner explained. 'Hopefully, we can survive the German retreat and make ourselves known to the Americans. We might have to fight if we are going to hold out until they arrive, but either way, the rest of you are better off without us.'

'I want to stay with you,' said Irmgard vehemently. 'I can fight – you know I can. I was by your side on the road to Dachau.'

He shook his head. 'Take a handgun. Father already has one. I need you two to protect your little group – God knows what the retreating Germans might try to do, but at least you won't be completely defenceless.'

'So where will you and Joe be?' she asked, reluctantly accepting the logic of his argument.

'I think we'll move to the barn,' he replied. 'It's a substantial stone building, much better protection than this flimsy cottage, and we'll just have to wait and see what happens.'

That evening, the general reported that the hospital commandant had visited him.

'Some infantry commander has been to see him,' he told them. 'Suggested they evacuate into the city. Apparently, he had to tell him that too many of his patients couldn't be moved, and the central part was mostly rubble anyway. He actually apologised for the fact that some of his men had been painting big red crosses all over our white walls.'

The fighting sounded nearer that night, with artillery rounds exploding not far from the estate. The next morning, Irmgard moved into the lodge. Werner and Joe decided to do a reconnaissance and see for themselves what was going on. Werner had played in these woods as a boy and hunted and shot over the land ever since he had been old enough to hold a .22 rabbit gun. He knew every last track and trail.

'We'll take the *MP40*s and a couple of grenades each,' he told Joe. 'Just in case.'

It was over half a mile to the edge of the woodland, from where farmland sloped gently down to a wide valley. Way in the distance, to his left, was the main road to Munich. Through the trees, Werner could see vehicles, mostly *Wehrmacht* lorries in twos and threes, well-spaced out, racing towards the city where they would make a stand. Across the other side of the valley, he could make out a line of American infantry supported by M5 Light Tanks. Used principally for scouting, nevertheless, their 37mm main armament and three Browning machine guns would be a formidable component in an assault on the ridge.

Werner and Joe went to ground, crawling forward. To their front, just beyond the edge of the tree line, were two foxholes – little more than hastily dug scrapings. One contained a three-man crew with an 8cm *Granatwerfer 34* standard infantry mortar. It was accurate up to just over a thousand metres, but if three extra powder charges were stuffed between the shell tailfins, it could lob a round as far as 2.4 kilometres. The Americans across the valley were within range.

In the other foxhole was a machine gun nest of two MG-42s, christened the feared and hated "Hitler's Buzz Saw" by G.I.s. With a fire rate of 1550 high velocity belt-fed rounds a minute, twenty-five a second, it could literally cut a man in half.

They had obviously been deployed to halt – or at least delay – the American advance, to buy time for the rest of their unit, probably with orders to shoot and scoot. But whoever had sited the German soldiers was clearly not an experienced infantryman. Most likely, an ageing reservist officer or NCO enlisted in Hitler's last desperate measures to defend the Fatherland. They were an isolated outpost: no defence in depth, no mutual fire support. But that said, they could take lives if, or rather when, the Americans decided to advance across the valley.

Werner's mind was in turmoil: seven men, three to service the mortar, two each to the machine guns. But they were ordinary soldiers, called to duty, not the mindless fanatics of the *Waffen-SS*. Somehow, he was reluctant to shoot his fellow countrymen, conscripts, in the back.

But Joe, a few yards on his right, had also sized up the situation, and they were his fellow Americans on the far side of the valley. A mortar man was making ready to drop a shell down the barrel. Joe opened fire, emptying his magazine into all three of the crew.

Tactically, it was a mistake. He should have taken out the machine guns first. One of the pair reacted instantly to the fire coming from behind their position. Hurling the weapon onto the back of the trench, whilst his number two hastily shifted the ammunition belt, he aimed wildly in the general direction of where he thought the shots had been fired.

A high-pitched cacophony of rounds ripped over their heads. Bullets were flying everywhere, hitting rocks and trees. Had it been a direct hit, Joe's head would have been smashed to pieces. But the ricochet still had velocity. His body jerked, and he lay still.

Werner had no choice. He took careful aim and placed a single bullet into the face of the machine gunner. The second crew seemed to have frozen, watching the outcome of their comrades' actions. Only now were they lifting their weapon. Werner's grenade landed in the foxhole. The skirmish had lasted barely a minute. It was all over.

Werner checked on the soldiers, but there were no survivors. He ran back to where Joe lay unconscious, blood flowing freely from a head wound. Werner was not sure how serious it was. He ripped a makeshift bandage from the sleeve of Joe's shirt. They had to get back to the cottage, which was nearest, but it was a long carry. Fortunately, Joe was fit but not heavily built. Werner pulled him up, hefted him over one shoulder, looped two *MP-40s* over the other and set off at a steady pace. He just hoped he could keep it up for as long as it took.

Werner had to stop four or five times, and it was slow progress. A poor diet had done nothing for his stamina. The Americans would be almost across the valley by now. But eventually, he kicked the door open and staggered into the bedroom. He laid Joe on the bed and set to with the limited first aid kit that had been included in their airdrop. When he took the bandage off, he could see a deep crease in Joe's skull, and when he dabbed the blood away, there seemed to be some surface damage to the bone. All he could do was slosh out the wound with antiseptic and apply a thick pad of folded lint held tightly in place with a clean bandage.

Someone fired a three-round burst outside the cottage.

'You in there,' shouted an American voice. 'Come outside. No weapon. Hands high.' Then in faltering German, '*Aus. Keine Waffe. Hände hoch.*'

Werner moved into the main room and stopped a few inches back from the door, hands in the air, facing an American sergeant pointing an M1 Garand semi-automatic rifle at his stomach. A group of eight or ten men stood either side of him, one with a radio on his back, but not bunched. *Experienced, battle-hardened infantry*, thought Werner.

'I am coming out,' he said in English, 'but there is a badly wounded American in the bedroom.' He walked outside and stopped a yard in front of the sergeant.

'Kowalczyk,' he ordered, 'check it out.'

The soldier was back moments later. 'Another civvy, Sarge. Can't say who or what he is, but he's bleeding bad from the head.'

The sergeant only had to nod at his radio operator, who called instantly for medics.

Kowalczyk and another infantryman returned to finish searching the cottage.

The sergeant ordered one of his men to pat down Werner. 'You, sit, hands behind your head,' he said after the soldier pronounced him clean. Werner complied.

'He is an American airman,' he told the sergeant. 'I have been hiding him. I work for British intelligence.'

Which was when one of the soldiers emerged from the cottage holding up an *SS-Sturmbannführer's* uniform.

'Found this in a suitcase, Sarge.' Werner's heart sank. He had removed it from the manor before it had been handed over to the German hospital team and had kept it only because it might come in handy for some, as yet unplanned operation.

'Looks like it fits that Kraut down there.'

'Is that yours?' barked the sergeant.

'Yes, but...' he began.

'We'll check the other one out when he regains consciousness, if ever he does,' he interrupted. 'As for you, we got a war to fight.' He turned to a corporal. 'Take this Nazi bastard and chuck him in the pen with the others. If he gives you any lip, put a bullet in him.'

Epilogue

'You promised to tell me, Dad,' said a teenage Jimmy James Harding. Flossie looked fondly at her son. She loved that for years now, Jimmy had taken to Spencer as an adoptive father. Her gaze moved to her daughter, who was developing into a precocious but beautiful young girl. She was almost as tall as her elder brother. Mollie G., named for both of her late grandmothers, had Spencer's height. They had just finished Sunday lunch in a detached former rectory on the outskirts of Peterborough.

She stood. 'Come on, Molly G., help me clear away. Your daddy has finally promised to pull up a sandbag and tell James his war stories,' she said, only half joking. Her husband had always been reluctant to talk about the past.

'Eventually, I finished up in France, entertaining the troops as a sergeant in charge of quite a big organisation,' he concluded with a hint of pride. He had carefully eradicated his Negro accent over the years. Now there was just a soft, southern burr.

'Germany surrendered early in May forty-five,' he went on, 'but we stayed there for quite some time, just carrying on as usual. It was important to keep our boys' morale up whilst they waited to be shipped back home. There was a points system for being discharged: how long you had been serving, combat experience, decorations, whether you were married, and so on. We Negroes weren't allowed in combat units back when I signed up, so it was forty-six before I eventually got shipped home and released.'

'And Mummy ran the garage till then,' put in Jimmy.

'She sure did,' Spencer replied. 'Bit of a wing and a prayer exercise, but she took on an apprentice under old Mr Laxham, God rest his bones. Kept everything going till I got back here at the beginning of forty-seven.'

'And you used your Army dollars to build up the business,' chimed in Jimmy, who had heard this part of the story from his mother.

'We also had a friendly bank manager,' Spencer recalled. 'Borrowed to build a showroom, took on agencies, just as private motoring was beginning to boom in those post-war years.'

'And now you drive a Jaguar,' said Jimmy proudly.

'Only at weekends,' responded Spencer. 'I use one of our demonstrators during the week, and I couldn't part your mother from her MG TC, no matter how hard I tried. She would divorce me first.'

'What's this about a divorce?' said Flossie, who had returned with an apple pie, Spencer's favourite. Mollie G. set a jug of cream on the table. Flossie only wished that Mollie G.'s and Jimmy's grandma Gladys was still alive to share their Sunday meal. *Not too much cream, girl*, she admonished herself. Spencer said he liked her the way she was, and they made love often enough, but there was a bit more of her now than there had been back in the austerity days of the nineteen forties.

It had been very hard at first, after the war, when prejudice had been at its highest – the days of "no blacks, no Irish, no dogs" in most lodging house windows. But she and her mother-in-law controlled the business until Fred Laxham finally retired, gradually taking on staff – former servicemen only too grateful to find work – whilst Spencer handled the planning and expansion side.

Gradually, if not actually welcomed, they had been accepted grudgingly into the local community. Now, they had three garages in and around the Peterborough area, each with a white manager who at least pretended to defer to Spencer in exchange for a fair salary. A generous bonus system helped.

Yes, there had been prejudice, sleights and insults, reflected Flossie. *Still were, from time to time.* Spencer had not been invited to become a Rotarian or to join the golf club. But people knew that Mr Almeter had been an American soldier, and that helped balance the equation, at least in part.

Although his main focus was on the business, Spencer still made the occasional guest appearance at The Manor Hotel on Saturday nights. The deal was the usual payment plus a complimentary meal for the two of them. He set the money aside for the future. His accountant had advised him to become a British citizen, and he had it in mind to enter politics, just locally at first. Too soon right now, the country was not quite ready. But he sensed that the atmosphere was beginning to change...

* * * *

Werner met Charles Dieter Kaye-Stevens at Munich airport. His eyes were shining with excitement. It was the first time he had been in an aeroplane, and the second officer had even let him look at the cockpit of the British European Airways Airspeed Ambassador. Now, also for the first time, he was abroad, being driven quite quickly along a country road to somewhere called Buchbach.

'Sir, what sort of car is this?' he asked nervously, for *Herr* Scholz seemed a rather imposing gentleman.

'It's a Mercedes-Benz W187 saloon,' came the reply. 'But you can call me Uncle Werner if you prefer. No need for the "sir". And before you ask, it will do a hundred and forty kilometres an hour. That's nearly ninety in English miles.'

'Grandma Kaye-Stevens told me you were married to my mama before she died in the war,' he said.

His Uncle Werner was quiet for a moment. 'That's right, I was, and for a short time, the three of us were together as a family. But afterwards...' there was a slightly longer pause... 'I could not bring you up. We were fighting a war. Fortunately, Grandma and Grandpa Kaye-Stevens were desperate to look after you, their only grandchild.'

'But you stayed in contact with them,' Charles persisted.

'I did,' Werner agreed. 'They send me a letter every Christmas and your latest photograph. I know your mother would have been very proud of you...' Charles noticed a slight glistening in the corner of Uncle Werner's right eye. He kept silent for as long as he could.

'It's jolly kind of you to invite me for a holiday,' he said eventually, then left it at that. But he whistled with admiration when they drove up to the sweeping curved steps and double front doors of Buchbach Manor.

A very pretty, rather exotic-looking lady rose from a sofa when they entered the drawing room. 'This is my wife,' Werner told him. 'We would both like it if you would call her Aunty Irmgard.'

Tea was a rather grand affair, with what Charles thought were smashing cream cakes. 'Let's take your case up to your room,' said Aunty Irmgard, 'and we'll get you settled in.'

'Grandpa said Uncle Werner would tell me what happened to him when he came back to Germany during the war,' announced Charles, as Irmgard was putting away his things.

'He will, probably in the morning,' she replied. 'But for now, I think he has something to show you before dinner. And I'm sure Grandma Kaye-Stevens will have told you, but we are also going to Starnberg for the weekend – it's on the other side of Munich – to stay with your Grandma and Grandpa Hoffmann. Their names are Helga and Dieter, your middle name. They are dying to see you. But you mustn't be upset if Grandma Hoffmann sheds a few tears.'

Back downstairs, Charles and Werner walked outside to a barn. When he pulled open the doors, Charles gasped at the sight: two motor cars, one a massive Mercedes-Benz roadster, the other a much smaller sports car, resplendent in its shining British Racing Green.

'These two have a history,' Werner announced. 'The big Mercedes is mine. I had it before the war, and it was kept in a lock-up garage I rented in Munich. Nearly all the buildings were damaged by the bombing, and part of the garage roof collapsed when the building next door was flattened. But I was lucky. The car was not badly damaged. As you can see, it has been restored to its former glory.'

'It's beautiful, sir,' gasped Charles, forgetting himself for a moment. After a minute or so, his gaze turned to the other car. 'But that one's British,' he exclaimed. 'It's an MG TA.'

'It belonged to your mother and father,' Werner told him. 'After your mother died, I put it in storage at a very kind gentleman's country house in England. At the time, it would have been too upsetting for Grandpa to have kept it at home. But now, that is in the past. We have been talking. When you are old enough to drive, it will be yours. But for now, you will not be flying home. I have had her thoroughly checked over by a very good mechanic who works for me on the estate. She is in first-class order. At the end of your holiday, we shall take a motoring tour together all the way back to England.'

* * * *

Irmgard had hoped for children, but thus far, they had not been blessed, although it was not for want of trying. Her mother still looked after the old general at the lodge. She strongly suspected that it had not always been an entirely platonic relationship, and now they appeared to be a very contented elderly couple. In view of Werner's war service, the estate had been handed back to the family only a few months after V.E. Day. But the general pronounced himself too old to start over again, so he and Madlene stayed in the lodge whilst Werner and Irmgard nursed the estate back to the profitable agricultural business it had been before the war.

The wings of the manor house, at Werner's invitation, were now administered by the Red Cross and used as convalescent accommodation for former military personnel, many of whom were still damaged from the war. Although apparently this facility would soon no longer be necessary, as civilian hospitals were being rebuilt.

The main house was more than big enough for just the two of them and three staff – *Frau* Braun, the housekeeper, *Frau* Koch, the aptly named cook, and Ada, who did the laundry and housework. At the time, Irmgard had demurred, saying that she was quite capable of looking after the two of them herself. But as Werner had pointed out, after the war, life in Germany was desperately hard, and at first, their wages had been the only income for the three women and their families. Without it, *Frau* Braun had told her, none of their children would have had shoes.

Twice, she had thought she might be with child, but each time it had proved to be a false alarm. But now… everything was looking hopeful, although she was not quite ready to tell her husband. Just another couple of weeks, once Charles' holiday was over, Werner had taken him back to England, and they were together again. If all continued to go well, that would be the right time.

The next morning, after breakfast, Charles reminded Uncle Werner of his promise. 'We'll go for a walk,' he said, and they set off around the estate. Werner told him everything up to the moment of his capture.

'This is where the Americans found me,' he said, pointing to a derelict old cottage. 'Me and a wounded American I had been looking after. We had just knocked out a couple of German trenches, a mortar and machine guns, but Joe caught a round to the head, and he was unconscious.'

'So then what happened,' pressed Charles, clearly fascinated.

'The Americans found an old German uniform in the cottage, one that I had not worn since my time in Paris, spying on the Gestapo for a German anti-Hitler organisation. At first, they refused to believe that I was now working for the British. So I was locked up with the other prisoners of war.'

'And…?' prompted Charles.

'It was a worrying time,' said Werner. 'I had been captured wearing civilian clothes, so the rest of the prisoners assumed that I was a deserter. Some of the officers made remarks about seeing that I faced justice later, but fortunately, I was not recognised as a former *SS-Sturmbannführer*.

'However, Joe survived,' Werner went on. 'After a couple of days, he regained consciousness. Told his story to the Americans, and I was hauled in front of one of their de-Nazification interrogators. After that, a message to London confirmed everything, and I was released. My former masters insisted that I return to London for a debrief, but I was allowed to visit the estate first, where I found that, thankfully, everyone in the cellar at the lodge had survived.'

His mind flashed back to that debrief, during which he learned that Margaret Chapman had died soon after giving birth to a daughter. Sepsis – her body had not responded properly to an infection, he was told. *Sort of poetic justice, really*, he remembered thinking at the time. Apparently the child survived. A year or so after the war he received a Christmas card from Sir Manners. Inside was a cutting from a month-old copy of the *Lynn News and Advertiser*, announcing the forthcoming marriage of a young widow from King's Lynn to one Robert Chapman. Werner never had been back for that glass of plum brandy.

And Charles never forgot that first wonderful holiday in Germany. Irmgard devoted her mornings to teaching him Anneliese's mother tongue. In the afternoons, Uncle Werner taught him to ride, and best of all, how to drive the MG on the private roads of the estate. By the time they made a glorious, hood-down trip home across Europe, Charles had a good – if basic – command of his second language. In later life, he would go to Cambridge and become fluent, eventually following Werner's footsteps into British intelligence.

In time, he took his own fiancée to visit his grandparents and eventually their first great-grandchild. Werner and Irmgard's two children, *Fraulein* Madlene Scholz and her younger brother Gustav, became godparents.

The war was well and truly over.